Praise for

"*Graceland* is a sparkling, warmhearted, witty debut. I so enjoyed joining these three generations of women on their action-packed road trip to Memphis!"

—Liane Moriarty,
#1 *New York Times* bestselling author

"Irresistible, addictive, and utterly entertaining, *Graceland* is bound to win readers' hearts. There are few things more delightful than a mother-daughter-granddaughter trio on a road trip. To Graceland! This story of family secrets, broken promises, and the healing power of love will stay with you long after the final page is turned."

—Susan Wiggs,
New York Times bestselling author

"*Graceland* is an exhilarating, edge-of-your-seat road trip with the most sparklingly offbeat set of female characters I've come across in a long time. The knots in which Hope, Dylan, and Olivia tie themselves by doing the right things for the wrong reasons and the wrong things for the right reasons are equal parts hilarious, nail-biting, and moving. Nancy Crochiere writes with such warmth and wit that I felt I was there alongside the women, cheering them on at every step of their crazy journey. . . . A hugely fun, fresh, and zesty read."

—Sarah Haywood, *New York Times*
bestselling author of *The Cactus*

est hits playing in the background. Crochiere delivers enough humor and surprises to keep the reader eagerly turning pages and enough heart to make this one memorable and satisfying journey."

—Stephen McCauley, author of *My Ex-Life*

"With a charming cast of characters, as well as intrigue, adventure, and touching mother-daughter relationships, *Graceland* sparkles from start to finish."

—Sonya Lalli, author of *A Holly Jolly Diwali*

"I can't help falling in love with this hair-raising road trip to Graceland! I was hooked on page one of this bighearted laugh-out-loud debut. Secrets, unexpected turns, and a mother-daughter-grandmother trio show that sometimes the right way can't be found on any map."

—Rachel Barenbaum, author of *Atomic Anna*

"A fun, warmhearted story with fresh and original passengers, *Graceland* is a new spin on the family road trip, complete with a love-story mystery at its center. I loved it!"

—Laurie Petrou, author of *Stargazer*

"*Graceland* is an utterly enchanting update of the American road story. Combining classic madcap antics with an up-to-the-minute look at family dynamics and forgiveness, the novel is at once funny and probing, personal and political, full of both youthful verve and the wisdom that comes with age. Imagine getting to hear slim Elvis and fat Elvis crooning together in harmony—that's how fun it is to read this book!"

—Michael Lowenthal, author of *Charity Girl*

GRACELAND

GRACELAND

A Novel

NANCY CROCHIERE

AVON

An Imprint of HarperCollins*Publishers*

GRACELAND. Copyright © 2023 by Nancy Crochiere. All rights reserved. Printed in the United States of America. No part of this book may be used or reproduced in any manner whatsoever without written permission except in the case of brief quotations embodied in critical articles and reviews. For information, address HarperCollins Publishers, 195 Broadway, New York, NY 10007.

HarperCollins books may be purchased for educational, business, or sales promotional use. For information, please email the Special Markets Department at SPsales@harpercollins.com.

FIRST EDITION

Designed by Diahann Sturge

VW Beetle illustration © Angie Boutin

Library of Congress Cataloging-in-Publication
Data has been applied for.

ISBN 978-0-06-328843-0

23 24 25 26 27 LBC 5 4 3 2 1

For Paul—my copilot, my compass

*We find after years of struggle that we do
not take a trip; a trip takes us.*
—JOHN STEINBECK

*Truth is like the sun. You can shut it out for
a while, but it ain't goin' away.*
—ELVIS PRESLEY

GRACELAND

Boston, MA

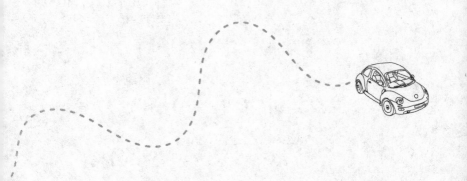

Chapter 1

Hope

Two days before my mother and daughter disappeared, my mother did something entirely out of character. She asked for my help.

She took her time, of course. Say what you want about my mother, the woman won't be rushed. Even after I'd rinsed our lunch plates and tucked the leftover pad thai into her fridge, she refused to explain the message she'd left at my office saying she needed to see me urgently. It wasn't until I'd sunk deep into her overstuffed sofa, and she'd handed me a sloshing cup of tea, that I fully appreciated her genius. My only escape would be to sip my way out.

Finally, though, she seemed to be coming to the point. I could tell because she'd moved to the window.

My mother never plays a scene without using light and shadow to her advantage. If you Google old episodes of *The Light Within*, you'll notice how before delivering a key line, she lifts her chin and cocks her head toward the light. For years, my father and I debated whether her movement was instinctive or if she blocked it out in advance. Either way, whenever Olivia Grant is about to deliver a showstopping line, a window is invariably to her right.

And so, with her signature chin lift and head tilt, my mother shared what was so urgent.

"Before I die," she said, "I want to see Graceland again."

I didn't mean to snort. Never in my forty years had I made fun of my mother's obsession with Elvis—at least not to her face. She'd simply caught me off-balance, and I laughed to cover my panic. Graceland? *Graceland* for God's sake? Just the thought of Memphis made my stomach churn. Leave it to my mother to ask for the one thing I absolutely couldn't do.

"Which part do you find amusing, Hope?" she asked. "Graceland? Or my dying?"

"Mom," I said, determined to steer the conversation away from Memphis, "you're not dying."

She turned and, as if on cue, the green tube connected to her oxygen dispenser caught on the edge of the coffee table, yanking the cannula from her face. I had to give her points for that one. Effective use of props.

"We're *all* dying," she said, repositioning the prongs under each nostril. "I'm just doing it faster than the average seventy-nine-year-old." With the afternoon sun backlighting her profile, my mother was still stunning: snow-white hair pulled back into a chignon, nose long and thin, with a hint of distinctive crookedness. I started to protest, but she waved me off. "No, no, this isn't self-pity. I'm explaining why we need to do this Memphis trip soon. Right away, in fact."

I bent forward and gulped the tea, scalding my mouth. I

needed to end this conversation—quickly, decisively, for all time. My mother didn't realize what she was asking.

"I understand you *want* to see Graceland again, Mom," I said, substituting "want" for "need," the way I did with my daughter, Dylan, when she *needed* Lady Gaga tickets. "I just can't take you anytime soon. Work is out of control." This wasn't the real reason but had the advantage of being true. The entire marketing department at EduLearn was putting in crazy hours. I couldn't afford time off—not after I'd missed a key meeting two weeks ago when Dylan pulled that stunt at school. "Let's plan a trip for later this year," I said, not specifying where. "Maybe in the fall."

My mother clapped a hand to her forehead. "You're missing the point! It's getting harder for me to travel now that I'm tethered to this"—she wagged a finger at the tubing circling her face—"this . . . cannoli."

"Cannula." She knew the word. It was her idea of a joke.

"Whatever." She flung a hand into the air, as if playing to the folks in the mezzanine.

My mother had smoked three packs of Camels a day for most of her life, despite my father's pleas for her to quit. She'd known the risks. And yet when her new specialist at Mass General repeated that she needed the oxygen day and night, even in the shower, I'd watched her close her eyes as if betrayed. *Et tu, nicotine?*

She wandered to her mahogany end table and lifted the photo I knew well: the framed black and white of her with Elvis the night of his 1970 Los Angeles Forum concert. In it, the King's sweaty face is framed by enormous sideburns, and a silk scarf hangs in the V-neck of his jumpsuit. He has one arm around my mother, the young soap star, with her jet-black bouffant. My mother was thirty-three at the time and—as she will be quick to tell you—often mistaken for Sophia Loren. The photo was reprinted in hundreds of newspapers and magazines and appeared in *Life*'s "The Year in Pictures." One columnist even called it the pop-culture image of the decade, pairing the King of Rock 'N' Roll with the Empress of Evil, the nickname given to my mother's villainous character, Andromeda, on *The Light Within*. When I was little, and my mother still lived with my father and me in Memphis, she kept the picture locked in a glass cabinet and let me hold it if I sat quietly on the sofa.

My mother wiped a speck of dust from the glass and replaced the photo on the table. "I need your help with this, Hope." She draped the red scarf Elvis had given her over the top, letting it puddle around the base. I waited. My mother was a master of the dramatic pause. "I've never asked you for much."

Hard to argue with that. For decades, the two of us had lived on different coasts, keeping a continent tucked between us like a pillow between uneasy bed partners. Even this spring, when my mother's health had forced her to move from LA to Boston to be closer to Dylan and me, she'd barely consulted me before hiring a real estate agent, leasing an apartment, and shipping her few belongings. I'd picked up the phone one day astonished to learn she'd arrived.

Since then, I'd stood ready to help. Shopping, errands, doctors' appointments. Whatever she needed. But not this. Not Memphis. My mother had no idea why I'd fled from my hometown almost eighteen years ago, though that wasn't her fault. I'd never told her.

I picked at a loose thread in the sofa cover. My mother was a trained reader of faces, and mine hides nothing. Instead, I pointed to the green tubing that snaked around the floor and connected to her liquid oxygen concentrator, a machine resembling R2-D2. "Mom, how can you even consider flying again? You said it was a nightmare."

"Oh, I refuse to fly." Her tone said I should know better. "Besides, how would we get around Memphis? We'd have to rent a car. Too expensive." My mother could pinch a penny until it squeaked—lucky, given that her last lover had drained her bank account and fled to Argentina. "We'll have to drive," she concluded.

"Mom, you've got to be kidding. That would take, what, two days?"

"Dylan could help."

"Right," I laughed. She couldn't be serious. My daughter drove like she did everything—impulsively, angrily, full throttle. Since getting her license, Dylan had scored two traffic tickets and taken down half our neighbor's fence.

I was done discussing this. Lowering my teacup to the floor, I dug furiously in my purse. "I think that's my phone."

My mother huffed, "This trip is for you, too, Hope. You need to get back to Memphis."

"Sorry, Mom, gotta go," I lied, pretending to read the imaginary text while heaving myself out of the sofa. "My manager called a meeting." Grabbing my bag, I pecked my mother on the cheek and made a beeline for the door.

"We can discuss this more tomorrow," she said.

I halted, my hand on the doorknob. I needed to put this

subject to rest. "No, Mom, we can't. I'm happy to take you shopping, or to the MFA, or a Pops concert, but I simply can't do this Graceland . . . thing."

She was peering out the window again. "You have issues with Memphis."

Her words raised the hair on my scalp, but I kept my voice steady. "I have no idea what you're talking about."

"Really, Hope?" And there it was again. The dramatic pause. Flawless. "I think maybe you do."

OUTSIDE, THE JULY humidity was like breathing water. Another Uber wasn't in my budget, though, so I headed for the nearest T stop. By the time I'd reached Allston Street, sweat dripped down my back, and my pencil skirt clung to my legs. I plunged down the stairs, nearly missing a step as daylight turned to soothing darkness.

The train wasn't crowded, and I collapsed into a seat in a far corner of the car, flipping my phone's camera to selfie mode to use as a mirror. Just as I feared—my cheap mascara was fleeing down both cheeks, making me look like Alice Cooper's less attractive sister. Rummaging through my purse, I unearthed a rubber band and the remains of a granola bar but no tissues, so I spit on a CVS coupon and wiped under my eyes, then yanked my hair back into a ponytail. Not cover-of-*Vogue* material, but good enough for my office.

I ran through the excuses I could offer my new boss for my grossly extended lunch hour and settled on a doctor's appointment. That would work. If anything shut Gary up, it was the fear of too much medical information from a woman. Scrunching down, I rested my head on the hard vinyl seat, hoping the vibration of the train would clear my mind. Instead, I kept replaying my mother's words.

You have issues with Memphis.

Where had that come from? Was it possible she knew something?

I couldn't imagine how. When I'd hightailed it out of Tennessee nearly eighteen years ago, in the late fall of 1998, my mother hadn't questioned my lies about wanting to travel, trying someplace new. My father had died earlier that year, and Mom and I weren't speaking much anyway. I sent her a postcard after I landed in Boston. When I realized I was pregnant, though, I didn't tell her for five months, and I waited until Dylan was six weeks old before sending a newborn photo. Was it possible my distracted and self-absorbed mother had done the math? No, almost certainly not. And even if she had connected my pregnancy with Memphis, she couldn't know more than that. Not the truly shameful part.

Across the subway aisle, a toddler in a Red Sox shirt scrambled onto his mother's lap and kissed her nose. She blew raspberries on his cheek.

I longed to please my mother. Always had. In one of my earliest memories, I'm perhaps three or four, and Mom is bathing me, rubbing a warm, rough washcloth across my belly. I press my nose to the bottle of baby shampoo, breathe in the sweet scent. When I look up, though, she is staring right through me, her eyes dull and sunken. Even at that young age, I knew I didn't make my mother happy.

This past spring, when my mother moved to Boston, I fantasized that the two of us might enjoy a late-in-life bonding, a new détente. We'd share things normal moms and daughters did—confidences, long hugs, favorite Netflix shows. So far, nothing had changed.

The train barreled to a stop and a burly, bearded man plopped down next to the young mother and toddler. The woman took one look at his baseball cap, which loudly proclaimed his pick for president, and scooted herself and child to the other end of the bench. Tensions were running high in that early summer of 2016, made worse by the heat. Both political parties were gearing up for their national conventions. I refused to talk about the election, told people at the office I hated politics. That hadn't always been true. I'd been enamored for a brief time—if not of politics, at least of a politician. Aaron's warm voice, disarming grin, the intense way he held your eyes when he listened. Lately, anytime I turned on the TV, there he was: revving up crowds, providing commentary, dismissing rumors of his own ambition. I kept the TV off.

Since fleeing Memphis as a distraught twenty-two-year-old, I hadn't ventured farther south than Philadelphia. An overreaction? Probably. I'd agreed never to return to Memphis, not to split the country Civil War–fashion, taking the North and ceding Aaron the South. Somehow, though, this felt safer, cleaner. My world and his world, with the Mason-Dixon line between. I planned to keep it that way.

As I CLIMBED the steps from the T station, shading my eyes from the assault of sunlight, I heard quacking. I swiveled toward the Public Garden, but no, the duck noises were coming from my purse. Dylan had changed the alert for my text messages again. A few weeks earlier, she'd switched my ringtone to a car horn, scaring the crap out of me as I'd crossed Beacon Street.

I took refuge under the awning of the Heal Within yoga studio to read her message: "Why won't you take Olivia to Graceland?"

Had my mother even waited until I'd left the building before complaining to my daughter? I dialed Dylan's cell.

"Since when do you call your grandmother Olivia?" I asked.

"She said 'grandma' made her feel like an old fart."

"She is an old fart."

"Well at least *she* doesn't act like one."

A late bloomer in most respects, my daughter hadn't begun snipping at me in earnest until almost a year ago, around her six-teenth birthday. That's when it all started: the military clothes, the neon pink hair, and her kamikaze, take-no-prisoners activism. "Where are you?" I asked. In the background, I could hear loud voices and an odd clanging sound.

"My question first. Why won't you take Olivia to Grace-land? She says it's urgent."

A motorcycle roared behind me, and I leaned my forehead against the yoga studio's window, shoving a finger in my ear. "Trust me, honey, there's nothing urgent in her desire to see Elvis's microwave . . ."

"Hold on," Dylan interrupted. "Someone's beeping in."

"Dylan!"

My forehead still pressed to the glass, I noticed two women behind the desk of the yoga studio staring at me. I stepped back and, for show, tried a deep, cleansing breath, but caught an updraft from the subway and gagged. I hurried off down the sidewalk, phone to my ear.

Why was my mother calling Dylan? For years, she and my daughter had ignored one another. My mother had visited us maybe four times since Dylan was born, and only then if she was traveling to New York for an audition. Dylan had grown up seeing her grandmother on Viagra commercials more often than in person.

After my mother's move to Boston, I'd begged Dylan to spend time with her grandmother. This past weekend, I'd finally wrestled my shame to the ground and bribed her. Dylan had pocketed the twenty, but as soon as we got to my mother's apartment, I wondered what in God's name I'd been thinking. My mother took one look at Dylan's hot-pink hair and quipped, "What's with the clown hair?" Her eyes trained on her grandmother's white updo, Dylan had shot back, "What's with the Q-tip?"

At some point that afternoon, though, the two of them bonded. I'd left them alone while I picked up our Indian takeout, and when I returned, neither of them even looked in my direction. I had the odd sense that the teams had realigned, and I hadn't been picked by either side.

Dylan's voice on my cell brought me back to the present. "Sorry," she said. "Where were we?"

"Can't recall," I lied, pressing the crosswalk button too many times. "I may have dialed you by mistake."

"Oh, yeah, Graceland. Olivia said this was, like, her dying request. She's not dying, is she?"

"Of course not. Your grandmother loves hyperbole."

"That fake lettuce?"

I made a mental note to get my daughter tutoring before the SAT. "Dylan, bottom line, a trip to Memphis isn't possible right now. I can't afford to take time off work."

"That's bullshit, Mom, and you know it."

I stopped abruptly. A cyclist swore and swerved around me. "I beg your pardon?"

"You were just talking about the two of us going to Cape Cod. Remember?"

Crap. She was right. I'd been longing for something Dylan and I could do together and floated the Cape idea. I missed the days when we'd lay our towels side by side at Nauset Beach, dig our toes into the hot sand, and brave the frigid, salty surf. At night, we'd order pizza and share a single fleece throw as we watched *The Princess Bride* for the hundredth time. When recently I'd suggested a week in Provincetown, though, Dylan had scrolled through her phone and said, "Whatever." After checking the price of Airbnb rentals, I'd let it go.

I'd reached my building and was scouring my bag for my security badge. "Memphis is different, Dylan. It's too far."

"What do you have against Memphis, anyway? You lived there half your life, but you won't even talk about it."

I stopped searching. "What?"

"If I ask you anything about Memphis, you make this face, like I asked about your last gynecologist appointment or something."

Did I? This was news to me. Through the phone I again heard yelling, and that same clanging sound. "What's that noise?" I asked, desperate to change the subject. "Why are people shouting?"

The pause was so long, I thought I'd lost her. Finally, Dylan gave a long exhale. "You won't like it."

"I already don't like it."

"We're protesting."

"Dylan, no!" I yanked my hair. It was a bad habit.

"Mom, we have no choice. This bakery in town won't make wedding cakes for gay couples."

She launched into an explanation that I could only half hear over the now-chanting protesters. Dylan and her Gender-Sexuality Alliance group had set up a table in front of the bakery to sell their own, rainbow-colored cupcakes. I had to admit it was creative, and I felt proud of Dylan for fighting for what she believed in. The problem was, she was in such deep shit already.

Last month, my daughter had been so enraged by a lacrosse player who was bullying her friend Emma and Emma's girlfriend on social media, Dylan slashed the tires on the passenger side of his Chevy Malibu. When the kid tried to gun it out of the school parking lot, he'd careened into a construction trailer holding half a million dollars' worth of windows for the school renovation project. Now Dylan had a suspension on her record, not to mention a court date.

When I reminded Dylan of that, she cut me off. "Mom! This protest is nonviolent. We'll be fine."

"Please," I begged, "just don't do anything foolish."

"I can't possibly!" she yelled. "I'm chained to a bike rack."

Inside the building, I slapped my security badge against the sensor and boarded the elevator, punching the seventh-floor button and collapsing against the back wall.

Dylan had always been headstrong, and I'd worried her teenage years would be tough. What I hadn't expected was the anger. Her rage simmered nonstop, just below the surface. She had every right to be furious about the inequities and injustice of the world. What frightened me was how much anger she directed toward me. Nothing I said was right. Sometimes I'd try to talk to her, and she'd turn away. I wanted to ask what the problem was but didn't. I was scared she'd tell me. I was scared it *was* me.

And now, Dylan and my mother had formed this . . . club . . . behind my back. Honestly, I shouldn't have been surprised. The two of them were cut from the same genetic cloth—stubborn, outspoken, dramatic. This past weekend, as I'd returned to my mother's apartment with the takeout, "Blue Suede Shoes" was blasting on the stereo, and Dylan twisted on one heel and then the other. Seated in her wingback chair, my mother pumped both arms in the air.

"What are you doing?" I called out, grinning.

"Trying not to have a stick up my butt," my mother shouted back. That was my daughter's favorite criticism of me. Apparently, they'd been sharing.

When we were getting ready to leave and Dylan used the bathroom, I'd prodded my mother. "You and Dylan seem to have hit it off."

"She has good taste in music. She's coming around to Elvis."

"I'm surprised it took this long to discover your common interests." It was my backhanded way of saying "You've never paid the slightest attention to my daughter." My mother didn't miss the dig.

"I accept your criticism," she said, boxing up the leftover chicken vindaloo. "I'll admit I've been somewhat preoccupied with my career."

"Somewhat?" I fake coughed into my hand.

"Oh, for heaven's sake, Hope." She'd pivoted to face me, her eyes narrowed, a takeout carton in each hand. "Can't people change? Is there no redemption in your worldview?"

Her outburst made me want to suck back my words. "Of course, Mom." I gave her a quick hug, awkwardly working around the cartons. "Of course. I apologize."

Dylan emerged from the bathroom, and my mother hurried over to give her the remaining vegetable curry. I'd stayed in the kitchen, clinking forks and knives into their separate bins, listening to them make plans to see some new documentary.

I'd said nothing at the time, but what I'd longed to ask my mother was this: If you're looking for redemption, Mom, why not start with me?

THE ELEVATOR DOORS opened to EduLearn's glass entrance, and I crept past the gray cubicles of editorial to the marketing department. At one time, sneaking back late from lunch would have sent my colleagues' heads popping over their cubes like the critters in a giant Whac-a-Mole game, but this day, the only sign of life was the clicking of a lone keyboard and the scent of a microwave burrito. Half our department had been let go in April because of slumping sales. College students were no longer buying new textbooks. They rented them or bought them used.

My boss, Gary, a dead ringer for John Goodman before his weight loss, was hired after the layoffs. Gary came from sales and ended his emails with the words "You've gotta believe!" even if the subject was fixing the coffee maker. He adored extroverts, schmoozers, and people who shouted out ideas in meetings, and I was none of these things, so we'd gotten off to a rocky start. The day Dylan was arrested for vandalizing that boy's car, I'd left the office in a panic and missed an important meeting. Gary had, by all accounts, been apoplectic. I hadn't been able to bring myself to explain.

I no longer enjoyed my job but couldn't afford to lose it. I desperately needed to win Gary over. A few days earlier, he'd asked for ideas in combatting the used-book problem and I'd mulled it over, wondering if I could save my skin by taking the lead on this issue. Lunch with my mother had strengthened my resolve. How better to prove—if only to myself—that I was too busy for a goofy road trip?

I planned to march into Gary's office and wow him with my initiative, but I never even made it to my desk. My cell rang. The Stoneham police. I needed to come get my daughter.

ONCE DYLAN AND I were belted into my ancient Corolla, she slunk down in the passenger seat and made a big show of inserting her earbuds. Message received. We weren't going to talk about this.

The cop who'd released Dylan said she'd hurled a projectile at a police officer. Dylan explained the projectile was a cupcake, and it wasn't hurled, but tossed to the officer so he could try one. "Waste of perfectly good Funfetti," she grumbled.

I believed my daughter. Dylan didn't lie. It was a policy she'd adopted around the same time she became an activist and vegan. Like everything Dylan did, though, she took it to extremes. She brooked no exception for "kind" lies. When Emma had asked her opinion of a new haircut, Dylan told her it looked ridiculous, and that was that.

Now, as we drove home, a sliver of sunlight danced over Dylan's fluorescent pink hair, a sharp contrast to her gray hoodie, gray camo T-shirt, and black shorts. Occasionally, she scraped at the floor mat with the badass, shit-kicking boots she'd begged for last Christmas. A phase, I kept repeating to myself about the clothes. Only a phase.

As I pulled into our driveway and turned off the ignition, I considered the paint peeling around the windows of our tiny ranch and wondered if I could do the touch-up myself. I'd almost forgotten Dylan was in the car.

"Know what your problem is?" she said, removing her earbuds, her eyes fixed on the glove compartment.

"I'm sure you're about to tell me."

"You don't want me to take risks."

I hesitated, trying to guess where this was headed. "Not exactly. I'd like it, though, if you stopped to think before you act."

"You want me to be cautious."

"Y . . . e . . . s," I said, cautiously.

"Like you."

Dylan's gaze was direct, taunting.

She unbuckled her seatbelt. "Because what if I'm not like you? What if we're just really different people?"

"I'm sure we are, in many ways."

"No, I mean, what if I'm not like you at all? What if I'm like my father?"

I looked out my window, as if the answer might be found on our neighbor's picket fence.

Dylan threw open her car door and got out before leaning back in. "Guess I'll never know, will I?"

"No," I replied. "You won't."

IT WAS TWO days later when I got the phone call that my mother had gone missing. That Wednesday was a disaster from the get-go. Like the coffee that spilled across my desk while I stuffed Kleenex in its path, bad luck seeped into the cracks of my day and finally poured over the edge.

Since our lunch, my mother had phoned three times to talk about the Graceland trip, as if we were seriously discussing such a thing. I'd begun letting her calls go to voicemail. That morning, though, she tricked me by calling from a number I didn't recognize.

"Quick question," she said after I told her I was busy. "Are you truly, intractably opposed to Memphis?"

"Yes, Mom. Truly, madly, intractably."

She sighed. "As you wish."

I had no time to ponder this. As soon as I'd hung up, the history editor was motioning me into her cubicle. She confided that Gary had called my marketing plan "pedestrian" and been furious when he couldn't find me to talk about it. I frantically revised the document and approached Gary's office several times that afternoon. He was tied up with budget meetings and—from what I could glimpse through the narrow window—in a foul mood.

In between stalking Gary and obsessively revising my marketing plan, I tried to reach Dylan, who wasn't responding to my calls or texts. We'd had a little disagreement the night before on the subject of college (I for, she against). I knew I should give her space, but after hours of silence, I longed for something, even a curt text. Even one asking for money.

By the time I packed up to leave at five thirty, I was wound so tight my neck crackled like a bowl of Rice Krispies. I needed

to unload on someone who understood the cast of characters—
Gary, my mother, and Dylan. I went where I always did in times
of need: to George.

As I PULLED into the parking lot for Robinson Repair, my
cousin George poked his head around the raised hood of a Prius
and waved. At six feet five, George Robinson was a gentle giant
whose curly black hair and cherubic face made him seem a decade younger than his forty-eight years. He wiped his hands on
his coveralls and ambled over, squatting to examine the worn
treads on my Corolla. I rolled down the window.

"Hope, these tires are dangerous. They're balder than Bruce
Willis." Despite his years in Boston, George had never lost his
warm Memphis drawl.

"Two weeks?" I asked, sheepishly. I needed another paycheck.

"I'll do it this weekend. Pay me whenever."

"I don't deserve you, George."

"No." He shook his head, grinning. "No one does, really."

When I'd fled Memphis in the fall of 1998, I'd had no des-
tination in mind, but somehow my car had steered itself to
George. Eight years my senior, George had been my favorite
cousin and an adored babysitter. He'd run the service department in my father's East Memphis Toyota dealership until he
was twenty-five, when my uncle Vern had kicked him out of
the house for reasons no one would explain to me. "Lifestyle
differences" was all my devastated father would say. George
had moved to Boston and started his own auto-repair business.

George had let me crash on his sofa until I could get back on
my feet. After I decided to stay in Boston, he helped me rent a
room near him, in a suburb called Stoneham. ("You don't pro-

nounce the *h*, Hope. It's 'Stow-num.'") Over the years, George had become my closest friend. He doted on Dylan and rolled his eyes at my mother's eccentricities. We shared a love of old, escapist movies like *The Wizard of Oz* and *White Christmas*.

George opened my car door for me. "You look like you need a beverage."

"Or maybe a life overhaul. Do you rewire crazy mothers? Adjust teenagers?"

"You can't afford my rates for those things, darlin'. Let's start with a beer."

THE DIVE IS nobody's first choice of where to eat in Stoneham. Rectangular and gray, it looks like it was picked up by a Kansas tornado and dropped in small-town New England. The picnic-style tables are set with a tiny dish of popcorn, and much of it ends up on the floor, where the staff crunch it into submission rather than sweep it up. It's rarely crowded, though, and they serve a plate of sweet potato fries so good I want to lower my face into them and roll it from side to side.

George and I had our pick of tables on a Wednesday night. We ordered our favorite craft beers. And the fries, of course. Always the fries.

I told George about my mother's Graceland request.

"My goodness," he said, his mouth full of popcorn. "That woman loves Elvis more than Jesus." He reached over to swipe another bowl from a nearby table. "Will you take her?"

"Can't. My job's nutty right now." It wasn't the real reason, but even George didn't know everything about why I'd left Memphis. "What's annoying is she's framed it as some kind of dying request. I feel guilty."

"It's okay to say no, Hope. You're such a people pleaser."

"Yeah, well, pleasing my mother has never been my strong suit." The waitress brought our order and we clinked glasses. The cold beer running down my throat felt heavenly. "She seems to have bonded with her granddaughter, though. She even had Dylan lobbying for her."

"Then you may as well throw in the towel. If Dylan wants it, you know you'll cave."

"That's not fair. I said no to Dylan . . . once."

I reached down to grab my phone, which was buzzing softly in my purse, and scanned the unfamiliar caller ID. I almost didn't answer, then remembered how my mother had called earlier from that odd number.

"So, this is Gus? From Air Systems?" said a confused-sounding young man. "You're the emergency contact for Olivia Grant?"

I pressed a hand to my chest. "Yes, I'm her daughter."

"I haven't been able to deliver her oxygen tanks. We tried three times this afternoon. No one answers the door, and the phone is disconnected."

"Disconnected?"

"Like, those three beeps and a recording?"

I hung up and speed-dialed my mother. I pictured her on the floor, unable to reach her landline. I'd lobbied hard for her to get a cell, but she refused to spend the money. The phone rang once, then the tones. "The number you have dialed is not in service."

Nothing made sense—not the dead phone, not being away from her apartment all day. Her portable oxygen tanks lasted only a few hours. George asked if we should call the police.

I said I'd drive over first and groped for the check. George grasped my trembling hand.

"I'll drive," he said, tossing some bills on the table.

I didn't argue. I was too afraid of what I might find.

I'D NEVER USED my key before, and it wouldn't turn in the lock. I tried twisting it both ways, yanking the doorknob in and out while kicking the door and shouting that we were coming. By the time George managed the correct combination of pull, key twist, and hip check, I was hugging myself to stop shaking.

My mother wasn't there. I chased around her apartment, checking behind her bed and shower curtain, until George called me over. He unpeeled a Post-it from the kitchen counter and handed it to me.

Hope,

Sorry you chose to miss out on the fun. We'll call you when we get to Graceland.

Mom

I slid onto a stool, read it again, and dropped my head into my hands.

"Who's 'we'?" George asked, picking up the note. "Does she have a boyfriend?"

It was a fair question. In the years since my father died, my mother had rarely lacked for male companionship. At one time, she'd kept lovers in both LA and New York so she could flit to auditions on either coast without paying for a hotel. As far as I knew, though, that had all ended with Rafe, the Argentinian who'd taken her money.

"She hasn't mentioned any new love interests."

"I wonder how that would work." He'd opened my mother's refrigerator and scanned the shelves.

"What? Driving?"

"No, sex." He squinted at the expiration date on a tub of yogurt. "All that tubing."

I'd wandered over to my mother's landline and lifted it. "What the hell?" The phone was unplugged, the cord wrapped around the base. I circled the small apartment again, throwing open closets. Her oxygen concentrator was gone, of course. Her rolling suitcase. The red Elvis scarf and photo.

George called after me. "What about that little guy who hangs out in the solarium?"

"Weebles?" Weebles was a little garden gnome of a man, five feet tall with a large belly and baldpate. Someone had named him after those egg-shaped toys I remembered from my youth. "Definitely not Mom's type."

"I wasn't suggesting she was dating him. You said he knows everyone's business. Maybe he spoke with her."

We took the elevator to the first floor, where Weebles was tucked into a striped armchair, jabbering to the woman next to him, whose head drooped forward to her chest.

"Hi, Mr. . . ." I realized I didn't know his real name but barreled on. "I'm not sure if you remember me. I'm Olivia Grant's daughter."

"Yep, your mom introduced us." He tapped a liver spot on his head. "Still got it."

"My mother seems to have taken off . . ."

"Midmorning," he agreed. "I noticed they brought her oxygen concentrator."

"They?"

"She was with the pink girl."

My breathing stopped. "The . . . pink girl?"

"The one with that gorgeous pink hair." He looked confused. "I thought she belonged to you."

Fairfield, CT, to Harrisburg, PA

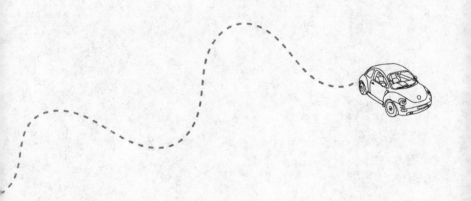

Chapter 2

Dylan

Fuck, it was hot. Gobs of sweat ran down my back. When I cracked open the driver's-side door, a tractor trailer thundered by, inches away. I could have reached out and touched the damn thing. It made the Bug shake like that rickety roller coaster at Canobie Lake Park.

So what was I supposed to do? I was trapped in the breakdown lane. Step out of the car and I'd be roadkill. Stay inside and I'd be boiled like a little pink shrimp.

In the rearview mirror I could see Olivia pace, her head thrown back, hands on her hips. Around the collar of her white blouse, the red Elvis scarf fluttered like an emergency flag. Mom had been right about one thing—my grandmother was a drama queen. She'd barely waited for the Bug to coast to a full stop before throwing open the door, yanking out her oxygen cart, and stomping off down the road. Olivia was pissed, all right. Big time.

"Not my fault," I sang into the mirror. "Not. My. Fault."

Sure, I'd been aware of that clicking noise the Bug made. I'd even asked the girl who'd sold me the car, Bree-Sarah. She insisted it was harmless, a random quirk of old VWs. And if you can't believe Bree-Sarah Navarette-Smith, who can you trust? That girl was in the honor society and student government, both! I don't know much about those clubs, but I'm pretty sure kids get kicked out for lying.

And in the end, what did it matter whose fault it was? We were fucked. Broken down in the middle of East Bum Nowhere. By the time we got the car fixed, Wednesday would be toast, and we hadn't even made it out of Connecticut. Olivia said we had to get to Memphis by Friday if I wanted to meet my father.

That word stopped me. I whispered it out loud. *Father*. I loved the breathiness of it, the way your tongue touched your top teeth and lingered. So much cleaner, less muddy than "mother."

All my friends had fathers, even the ones whose parents were divorced. They coached their kids' soccer teams, taught them to roll gnocchi, and whipped their butts at Catan. Every year on Father's Day, while other families grilled hot dogs and held cornhole tournaments, I stayed home, curled up under my comforter, and read *A Wrinkle in Time,* about a girl whose father is missing.

My parents were never even married. According to Mom, my father had already traipsed off to Alaska to live in a yurt by the time she discovered she was pregnant. They'd broken up and she had no way to contact him. Later, she'd learned through a friend that he'd died.

I believed what Mom told me, that my father was dead, but that didn't stop me from creating a fantasy world where he wasn't. I dreamed he'd knock on our door one day, out of the blue, bringing apologies and gifts. That rumor that he'd died? It had been a mistake, a misunderstanding. No one was to blame.

What an incredible idiot I was. It never occurred to me until recently that my mother wasn't mistaken. My mother was a liar.

In the rearview mirror, I watched Olivia bat away a cloud of road dust, then bend over, hacking.

Shit. Not good. What if Olivia freaked out? What if she called Mom to come pick us up? That couldn't happen. After the lies Mom had told me, I'd die before I got in a car with her. I didn't want to see my mother for a long time.

I slapped the steering wheel with both hands, let fly a string of f-bombs. I wasn't big on apologizing, but I'd suck it up, make nice with my grandmother. We simply had to keep moving. Somehow, we had to get to Memphis.

Checking the side mirror, I waited for a line of cars to whiz by, then launched myself out and ran around the back of the Bug to where Olivia was standing. She didn't turn around. I stood behind her, digging the toe of my camo-print sneaker into the gravel.

"What do we do now?" I asked.

Olivia threw up a hand. "Find us a towing company," she said. "Use the Google."

I didn't even make fun of her for calling it the Google. I figured it wasn't the best time.

It had been only Saturday—just four days earlier—when Olivia had leaned forward in her wingback chair and said, like she was asking about the weather or something, "So tell me what you know about your father."

I nearly spit out my gum. We didn't speak about my father in my house! If Mom had been there, she would've shut that question down in a hot minute. Mom wasn't there, though. Olivia had hustled her out the door to pick up some Indian takeout that she didn't even bother to order until Mom left.

"Why?" My face felt hot. My father was a secret obsession. I didn't discuss him with anyone.

"Just curious what your mother told you about the man," Olivia said.

I studied Olivia, still getting used to the cannula under her nose. I barely knew the woman, hadn't laid eyes on her since I was twelve. The year before, Olivia had threatened to spend Christmas with us but canceled last minute, worried the cold would "wreak havoc with her rosacea." After hanging up the phone, Mom had exhaled loudly. "Of course. Olivia first. Always."

What little I knew about Olivia came from watching clips from her soap opera on YouTube and that Christmas movie where she played the grandma who got run over by a reindeer. Oh, and those horrifying commercials about old men with erectile dysfunction. They were the worst. When my friends learned the lady playing the surprised-but-satisfied wife was my grandmother, they were brutal.

I stood and moved to the window to watch for my mother's car. "I don't know much about my dad," I admitted. "Whenever I ask about him, Mom answers in as few words as possible and rushes off with some lame excuse—she's left the iron on or needs to change the water in the goldfish bowl. So all I have are little scraps of information."

"Such as?"

"They didn't date long. After Mom broke up with him, he

moved to Alaska to protest some pipeline or other. He lived off the grid, in a yurt. No phone, no mailing address."

Olivia peered into the iced-tea glass, brows knit, as if searching for something she'd lost. I had to agree—the story didn't entirely track, especially the breakup part. If Mom had been the one to dump my father, she couldn't have been deeply in love. So why was it so hard to talk about the man? Why all the squirming, the hasty answers?

Olivia sipped her iced tea, offering nothing.

I shrugged. "And then he died."

Olivia coughed. "Did he, now!"

Geez, how could Olivia have missed that fact? Granted, Mom never spoke about the man, but still. "He was part of a protest. Tried to force his way on some Russian whaling ship. Mom didn't tell you?"

"She did not."

Was it possible Olivia had that dementia thing? I chose my words carefully. "Maybe you . . . forgot."

"I do not forget," Olivia snapped. "Your mother is very stingy with information." She put down her glass. "If you're interested, though, perhaps I can find out more about your father."

I fought to keep my voice casual. "That'd be great."

"In exchange, I'd like a favor."

Olivia wanted to visit Elvis's home, Graceland, and thought I could convince Mom to take her. She showed me the famous photo of her and the King and offered to let me hold the red scarf he'd given her. After the concert, she said, the scarf had been dripping with Elvis's sweat, so I gripped it between thumb and forefinger, like it was a dead rodent. Luckily, I couldn't detect any lingering Eau de King.

I told Olivia I'd talk to Mom, but I knew it was useless. No way could I get her to drive to Memphis. Mom hardly ever took time off work, and as far as I could tell, she hated her hometown. But, whatever. I'd do my best. If it meant learning more about my father, even just a photo, I'd try anything.

OVER THE NEXT three days, Olivia called me seven times. For the most part, I didn't answer. I had nothing to report. Mom wouldn't budge.

By the eighth time, late Tuesday, I was in a horrible mood. The Pride bumper stickers I'd ordered had arrived a month late, and the damn things stuck like Gorilla Glue. I was trying to scrape one off Mom's kitchen counter when my cell rang. I kicked the box of stickers across the floor.

Enough. I'd suck it up and give Olivia the bad news.

Olivia, though, seemed unfazed. "No worries," she said. "It was a long shot. We'll simply move to Plan D." She waited, and when I didn't ask, added, "The Dylan Plan."

"Like the name," I said. "No clue what it means."

"We go ourselves. You and I."

"Wait. To Graceland?"

"That's what we're talking about, dear," Olivia said. "Do try to keep up."

I lowered myself onto a counter stool. I'd lost interest in Graceland after Googling it and discovering it didn't have a single roller coaster. But this idea was different. Taking my Bug on the open road? That would be bomb. "Sounds cool. When?"

"We need to leave tomorrow."

"*Tomorrow?*" I checked my phone. Almost five p.m.

"I know, unexpected. Something has come up. I can't explain now. I will once we're underway."

Apparently, Olivia doled out information like other grandmothers did hard candy, breaking it into little bits to make sure you didn't choke. I scrolled through my iPhone calendar to check my waitressing shifts for the weekend. Emma could probably cover them.

"Dylan?"

"Thinking!"

"It's your choice, of course," Olivia said. "Perhaps I've assumed too much."

"Well, a little heads-up wouldn't have hurt."

"Forgive me. I thought you'd *want* to meet your father."

I pulled the phone from my ear and frowned at it. "Olivia," I said, trying again, patiently. "We discussed this. My father is dead."

Olivia let out a long exhale. "I'm sorry to be the one to tell you this, Dylan. Your father is definitely not dead. Perhaps your mother had reasons for lying to you. I don't know . . ."

"So hold on. You think my father is alive? *Seriously?*"

"Yes. And in Memphis, but only for a few days. It's an amazing stroke of luck. The perfect convergence of plans. We need to go right away."

"I'm confused. I thought you wanted to see Graceland."

"Of course we'll go to Graceland! As I said, there are several reasons for the trip."

"But . . ." I waved my hand wildly, trying to get back to the part that interested me. "I don't understand. When did my father get back from Alaska?"

"He was never in Alaska."

I leaned both elbows on the counter. "How—"

Olivia cut me off. "It's a long drive to Tennessee, Dylan, and we'll have an abundance of time to chat. I'll tell you everything I know. But if we're going, I need to pack."

I pressed my fingers into my forehead, struggling to focus. "I don't think Mom knows this. If you're right, and my father is alive, I don't think she knows."

Olivia paused for so long, I wondered if she'd had a stroke. Finally she said, "Dylan, your mother knows everything about your father. What she doesn't want is for you to know."

I fiddled with one of the studs in my right ear, twisting it. At one time, I wouldn't have believed my mom would lie to me, but that had changed a year ago, the morning I'd asked about my father's name. I ran my finger along the line of studs, touching each one in turn. Only the first piercing hurts. You steel yourself for the rest.

"Okay," I whispered. "I'm in."

"Excellent. Meet me here at eight tomorrow morning. And pack light. July in Memphis will be hotter than Hades."

"Wait!" My mind was still reeling. "What am I going to tell Mom? Do you really think she'll let us go?"

"Well," Olivia said in a duh voice, "not if we *ask* her."

WHEN OLIVIA ANSWERED her apartment door the next morning, she was yelling at someone on the phone. She glared at her watch and then at me. Yes, I was like an hour late. Two, at most. As a peace offering, I'd bought Olivia a Dunkin' Donuts coffee in a reusable cup. She accepted it, then marched over to the sink and dumped it out. A little extra if you ask me.

Luckily, Olivia was even angrier with the person on the phone. Her oxygen company hadn't delivered her portable tanks, and she was ripping the guy a new one. She demanded they reroute the tanks to a hotel in Memphis and pushed the disconnect button hard, like the guy could hear that.

"Incompetents!" Olivia railed.

I blinked, suddenly aware of the obvious. "You have an iPhone!"

"I gave those airheads the new number. How many times did they plan to call a dead phone?"

Her old phone was on the counter, the cord wrapped around it. "You disconnected your landline already?"

"I'm only one person, Dylan. Why would I need two phones?"

Olivia's foul mood didn't improve even after I'd hauled all her bags and oxygen gear to the car. We'd barely turned out of the apartment parking lot before she complained, "Good Lord! Does your car always make that clicking noise?"

"Old VWs do that. Bree-Sarah said so."

"Then heaven knows, I'm reassured," Olivia said. "I mean, if *Bree-Sarah* says so."

I wasn't appreciating the sarcasm but kept my mouth shut. I didn't dare piss off Olivia if I wanted to hear about my father. When we stopped at the next light, I put on the Elvis songs I'd downloaded. "That's All Right (Mama)" played first, and the corners of Olivia's mouth curled up a bit. As with a cat, though, you weren't sure that meant she was happy.

Once we were outside Boston, I turned down the music and cleared my throat. "I never asked you about my father because you lived in LA. I didn't think you knew him."

Olivia lifted her travel mug of iced tea. "I didn't. Never met the man."

"So . . . Mom told you about him?"

"Oh good heavens, no. Hope doesn't share anything with me." Olivia shook the cup, rattling the ice cubes. "And certainly not with regard to your father. When she told me she was pregnant, Hope made it clear she wasn't going to say more." She took a sip from the mug. "I didn't press."

"Then . . ." I struggled to find the right question. "How do you know who he is?"

"I added two plus two."

"But which two? You just said you didn't know anything."

Olivia pulled down the sun visor. "I can't tell you everything right now, Dylan. You have to trust me."

A car behind us honked. I'd been drifting across the lane line and jerked the wheel back. Was it possible Olivia knew nothing about my father? Had she tricked me into coming on this trip because she needed a ride to Graceland? Olivia didn't drive, and Mom had often hinted that her main criterion for her LA boyfriends was that they own a car.

I tried a different angle. "Why would Mom tell me my father was dead?"

Olivia freshened her lipstick in the visor mirror. "Clearly she didn't want you trying to find him." She twisted her face side to side, satisfied. "I keep meaning to ask. Did Hope ever tell you his name?"

My mother had, and this was a sore spot, because her story had changed. The original was the one I believed. "I only know his first name. When I was five or six, she told me it was Aaron." I'd had a kindergarten friend named Erin and thought it weird that my father had a girl's name. I glanced sideways at Olivia. "Is that right?"

Olivia dropped the lipstick in her bag and said nothing.

"No offense, but you're not acting any different from Mom. You're not telling me anything."

"What I'm doing is very different, Dylan. First, I'm not lying to you. Second, I'm taking you to meet him. If I can't say more right now, it's for the best."

"But . . ."

"No 'but.' Just twenty hours ahead of us or one going back. You choose."

I closed my mouth. The *click, click, click* sounded louder. I turned up Elvis.

At a rest area, we grabbed lunch, and I offered Olivia iPhone lessons. When I showed her how to dictate text messages, Olivia clapped a hand to her mouth in amazement. After that, we got hysterical with Snapchat filters: my face with a Dalmatian nose, Olivia's with flames coming out of her mouth.

As we drove, I sang along to "Hound Dog," trying out an Elvis impersonation. Olivia laughed so hard, she wiped away tears. Then we sang together, Olivia correcting me on the lyrics, until I knew all the words to "Don't Be Cruel" and "Shake, Rattle, and Roll."

The clicking noise, though, was getting louder, and after Hartford, I felt the car vibrating. Neither of us mentioned it, but I sensed Olivia felt it, too. Then, after a sign for Darien, the car began shaking like Mom's old washing machine. Olivia shouted to take the next exit, but I'd seen a sign for Dunkin' and thought another two miles wouldn't matter.

Okay, so not my best decision.

Chapter 3

Olivia

A dust storm. Now that's what every person suffering from emphysema lives for! I turned away, covering my face with the Elvis scarf as a convoy of eighteen-wheelers thundered past, pelting my legs with tiny stones and leaving my mouth tasting of dirt. I surveyed the heavens for help. Not a single cloud in the sky—not one! Normally, I adore sunshine, but that afternoon, if the dust didn't kill me, sunstroke surely would. How had the girl managed to break down in the only unshaded stretch of road for fifty miles?

Dylan was keeping a safe distance from me, probably afraid I might throttle her. She leaned back against that absurd tin can of a car, poking at her phone, trying to find us a tow company. If she succeeded, it would be a bloody miracle. The first thing she hadn't screwed up all day.

The girl hadn't been my first choice for the trip. It was Hope who needed to return to Memphis, to face her demons there. But, whatever. Dylan could drive—more or less. And once the girl came, Hope would surely follow. With Dylan on board, I could lure Hope back to Memphis.

Unfortunate that everything had to happen so quickly. I'd just learned the day before that the politician was in Memphis for the weekend. With the campaign in full swing, who knew when he'd be back? I couldn't wait another month. I might not be able to climb stairs. No, the timing was critical for both goals—the one for Hope, and also my own plan for Graceland.

The traffic momentarily quiet, I tilted my face to the sun. My Graceland plan was a bold and brilliant scheme if I did say so myself. I'd conceived it several months earlier on that most horrible of days, the Afternoon of the Screaming Boy.

No DENYING IT, my final months in LA were a nightmare. I was dragged to the ER several times, barely able to breathe, once calling an ambulance at two a.m. and then collapsing on my condo's brick walkway. I refused to go on the damned oxygen. Fought the doctors tooth and nail. In the end, though, what choice did I have? My own body had turned traitor.

When that UCLA pulmonologist strapped the infernal tube around my face, I had to tamp down icy stabs of panic. The minute I got home, I phoned my agent. I needed Sylvia to tell me everything would be okay.

"Holy fuck" is what Sylvia said.

Well, that's LA for you. Kick you when you're down. And Sylvia, of all people! I *made* that woman. After I won my second Daytime Emmy, Sylvia hadn't lifted a finger. The offers poured in: commercials, voice-overs, Hallmark Christmas movies.

Once, when I joked about retiring, Sylvia pitched a nutty. "Don't even think about it! You're my gravy train."

And now? When I needed a little boost? Sylvia acted like I had some kind of . . . disease.

My tubing caught on the chair, and I jerked it free. "Sylvia, I'm still the same actor. Surely you can find parts for a 'mature' woman who happens to use oxygen."

I heard the flick of Sylvia's lighter. God, how I could have used a cigarette. Going forward, I couldn't light a candle without risking spontaneous combustion.

"Livvy," Sylvia said after a long exhale. "I don't know, babe." I waited. Sylvia wasn't a woman who lacked for words—though admittedly a fair number were curses. "Do you have to wear that thing all the time? I mean, you know, the part on your face?"

"Only if I want to breathe."

"Shit."

I pictured Sylvia rubbing her eyes, removing the rose-colored Anna-Karin Karlssons that my career had paid for. "Book me a medical show," I said. "What could be more convenient? I come with my own props. Or a crime series, like *Law & Order*. The witness is always an older woman, a shut-in with twenty cats."

"Livvy, you know this business . . ."

"Sylvia, you've said it a hundred times: the TV-viewing population is aging. People want characters who look like them. Think *The Golden Girls*. Think Kirk Douglas, in that movie after his stroke. Think . . ."

"*Harold and Maude*."

"Yes!" At least Sylvia was paying attention, not doing her online shopping. "Sure, it'll be a bit of tokenism at first. The way the Black best friend or gay neighbor was thirty years ago.

But I promise you, Sylvia, it will happen. Oxygen will be the new Black!"

"I just don't want you to get your hopes up, Liv. What are you now, seventy?"

I was nearly seventy-nine, but even my agent didn't know that.

"I mean, it's something to consider. Maybe it's time."

It took three weeks and countless phone messages, but Sylvia booked me a tiny part in a Lifetime movie. The role was Dying Grandmother. All I had to do was lie there and look serene while the family gathered round. An insult for someone of my stature. A cakewalk.

And it would have been, if not for the Screaming Boy.

All the little non-SAG brat had to do was kiss his bedridden grandma on the cheek. Instead, he screamed like I was Freddy Krueger. Perhaps the cannula frightened him. Perhaps his real grandmother was a pervert. Who knew? Regardless, in take after take, he let loose the same bone-chilling shrieks.

I couldn't tolerate screaming children. It stemmed from an incident long ago I didn't like to think about. The boy's shrieks felt like someone was scraping my nerves with a fork. Finally, I couldn't endure it any longer. Throwing off the blankets, I grabbed my portable oxygen tank and told the director I was done.

He had a complete hissy fit, of course. The scene was a one-day shoot. If I left him hanging, my reputation would be toast.

It didn't matter. I had no choice.

BACK AT MY apartment after the Screaming Boy fiasco, the top of my head felt like it was being pried off with a can opener.

I put Elvis on the stereo. The ballads. I didn't bother removing my makeup. After scouring the freezer for an ice pack, I grabbed what I could find—a Lean Cuisine—and pressed it to my hairline. I lay on the sofa, a glass of Scotch at my side.

I understood what this meant. My career was over. The fabulous career that had rescued me—first as a young woman fleeing from her mother, and then, later, as a young mother fleeing from herself. Sylvia was already ignoring my calls. Soon my friends in the business would follow suit. I'd watched it happen countless times—that quiet slide into obscurity. Even been party to it. For years, my former costar Rose had sent me holiday cards with a pathetic scrawled note: "If you hear of any parts . . ." I never replied.

My time had come. Best to admit it. I refused to end up like those crumbling, Botoxed, has-beens who shuffled across the Emmy Awards stage on someone's arm, smacking their lips, mangling their teleprompter lines. That's not how I'd go. I'd lived a great life and owed my fans a great ending. Robin Williams had it right: take your leave while people will still miss you.

It wouldn't be easy. Nothing worth doing was. But I'd go out on my own terms, thank you. Not pushed around the grounds by some aide or hooked up to machines in a hospital. Not like . . . I shuddered, repositioned the Lean Cuisine. No, I wouldn't repeat my father's mistake.

I lay on the sofa a long time, staring at the famous photo of Elvis and me, until a new idea began to take shape. A tad absurd, but also brilliant, if I did say so myself. A plan worthy of my body of work and the reach of my fame.

I would end my life at Graceland. I would die in Elvis's bed. My final act would link me forever with the King. Newspapers around the country—perhaps the world—would reprint the iconic photo of us together. Never would there be another tour of Graceland without whispers of my name.

I glanced at my oxygen tank. The only question was how to pull it all off, given my challenges. I'd need help. And it had to be soon, while I could still navigate a few stairs.

Then the phone rang, and it was Hope.

Later, I couldn't even recall why my daughter had called. I hadn't truly listened to anything she'd said. I was focused on one thing: how to get Hope to take me to Memphis.

It would be an uphill battle, for sure. Hope had a long-standing grudge against her hometown. From what I could piece together, something had happened with that politician, the girl's father. Whether he'd broken Hope's heart, or she'd broken his, it hardly mattered. She needed to move on.

I drained my Scotch and poured myself another. The more I thought about it, the clearer it seemed: Hope needed my help. Hope had always been a hider, but in the years since she left Memphis, she'd drawn inward even further. Hanging onto that damn secret forced her to keep everyone at arm's length. Dylan. Me. Even other men. Hope hadn't managed to hold down a romantic relationship in eighteen years.

Well, I could help her move beyond that. I hadn't been a rock-star mother, but it's never too late to make amends. This trip to Memphis would be my gift to Hope.

And if, in the process, I got what I myself wanted—well, where was the harm in that?

THE GIRL JOGGED back toward me, her tank top soaked with sweat, her pink hair ablaze in the afternoon sun. That hair! At first I'd found it an eyesore, but I was getting used to it. Pink was Elvis's favorite color, after all.

The towing company she had on the line could help us, but not for an hour.

Should've known better. Never send an extra to do SAG work. I held out my hand and she passed me the cell.

"Yes, this is Olivia Grant, grandmother of this stranded and traumatized child. And your name is? Ron? As in Reagan?" Pause. "Oh yes, a hero of mine, too." I jerked a finger toward my mouth and Dylan snorted. "Ron, I'm wondering if you recognized my name, Olivia Grant? No? Well if you can't get a truck here in under fifteen minutes, the headline in tomorrow's newspaper will read: 'Legendary soap star dies as towing company ignores her desperate pleas.' It's ninety-eight degrees out here, Ron. I'm elderly, I'm on oxygen, and I have ten thousand followers on Facebook. Send a truck *now*." I squinted at the screen, poked the red button, and handed the phone back to Dylan.

"Does that work?" Dylan asked.

I shrugged. "Runs about sixty/forty. We'll see."

The tow truck arrived fifteen minutes later, driven by a pimply teenager who clearly had no idea what he was doing. As he struggled to hook up the car, a police cruiser glided into the breakdown lane.

"Shit!" Dylan yanked on my sleeve. "Do you think Mom put out an Amber Alert?"

"It's two thirty, Dylan. Your mother hasn't figured out whether she can sneak out for lunch yet, never mind what you're up to."

I was right, of course. The cop offered us a ride to the repair place, where we waited until the Bug arrived. By the time the grease-covered mechanic informed us we needed a new drive shaft, it was four thirty and the shop closed in half an hour. He could get to it tomorrow afternoon.

"We need it done now!" Dylan shouted, slapping her hands on the counter.

I gripped Dylan's arm and guided her to the door. Closed it after her. Then I did what Elvis had taught me to do. I took care of business.

When I emerged from the office with news the car would be ready by eight a.m., Dylan's mouth hung open.

"There are three ways to get what you want, Dylan. Charm. Threats. Cash. Always use them in that order."

Still, the cost of greasing that man's filthy palm hadn't been insubstantial. I refused Dylan's plea for a hotel with a hot tub and "one of those minibars." No, I'd been considering our options since we'd broken down. I had old show-business friends in Fairfield, a city we'd passed not twenty minutes earlier. I'd even considered meeting Rose and Rudy for lunch if we hadn't gotten such a late start. Rose and I had a complicated relationship, and I'd thought, more than once, how it might be nice to mend that fence on the way to Graceland.

Rudy answered my call and—just as I'd hoped—insisted on putting us up. He was out doing errands and could get us in a flash.

"Great," Dylan moaned as she maneuvered my oxygen concentrator out of the Bug. "Tell me again who these people are?" Subtext: Are they at least famous?

Rose, I explained, had been the original star of *The Light Within*. She'd played the blond, kindhearted Krista, while I, an unknown, had been cast as her scheming, dark-haired cousin. "The show really took off when they introduced Andromeda," I said. "Nothing like an evil character to boost ratings." I tossed the Elvis scarf over my hair, fastened it under my chin. "In the early seventies, I left the show to marry your grandfather, and without my character, the ratings tanked. *Light Within* was canceled. A decade later, though, they resurrected it, and this time, I got top billing." I paused, thinking of the girl's tendency to blurt. "But I wouldn't mention any of this in front of Rose."

"How come?"

An ancient station wagon pulled into the lot, and I lowered my sunglasses to wave. By the time *Light Within* was revived, I explained, Rose had become quite heavy, and the producers hired someone else to play Krista. "So there are a couple things Rose has never quite forgiven me for. One of them was leaving the show."

"And the other?"

I kept my gaze on the thin, gray-haired man who emerged from the car and ambled toward us. "Rose was the one who got us backstage to meet Elvis," I whispered. "And Elvis picked me."

Chapter 4

Hope

George and I left Weebles in the solarium and returned to my mother's apartment, where I paced from the kitchen to the living room and back. I paused at the window where my mother had stood two days earlier, insisting she needed to see Graceland again. The sun had set and all I could see in the glass was my reflection. I yanked the blinds closed.

George poked around again in the refrigerator, peering into a Thai takeout container that smelled strongly of garlic. That Monday lunch with my mother seemed a lifetime ago.

My calls to Dylan went to voicemail. My daughter never listened to phone messages and hated when I left them. I left two anyway. Finally, I gave in and texted her, convinced they couldn't still be driving. My mother would need to stop and switch to the oxygen concentrator so she wouldn't run out of portable tanks. My message to Dylan was short and to the point: "Please call ASAP."

"What if they're already in trouble?" I moaned to George. I

pictured my mother alone on some deserted road while Dylan trudged for miles to get help. "That car's a piece of crap."

Dylan had bought the bubblegum-pink 1998 VW Beetle three weeks earlier, from a senior at school, spending her entire waitressing savings, $750. The Bug was a steal, she insisted. Completely updated! Bree-Sarah had added cupholders *and* a USB port! All it needed was brakes.

"It doesn't have *brakes*?" I'd shouted, waving both arms. "What else is missing? Tires?"

"Just the extra one."

I'd called Bree-Sarah's mother to explain that a sixteen-year-old couldn't legally buy a car and demand Dylan's money back. She said I needed to talk to her husband and "good luck with that." In the end, I'd grudgingly let Dylan keep the Bug. George fixed the brakes at a massive family discount and in-sisted we bring it back for a thorough once-over when he was less busy. I should have made Dylan do that. I hadn't. I couldn't afford more repairs.

"I was an idiot to let her keep that car."

George studied his work boots. You can tell a lot about what George thinks by how thoroughly he examines his boots.

I wandered into my mother's bedroom and noticed a handful of pages in the recycle bin beside her desk. Everything was ma-genta. Her printer must have run out of black ink. I snatched them and flipped through the streaked pages. On top were MapQuest directions to Memphis. What knocked the air out of me, though, were the pages beneath it: an article from the Memphis newspaper, *The Commercial Appeal*. Right there, in the pink headline, his name. Aaron Breckenridge. Speaking this weekend in Memphis.

I lowered myself slowly into the chair.

How long had she known?

And more importantly, what had she told Dylan?

I gathered all the sheets, folded them in quarters, and shoved them into my pocket. It didn't matter. My path was clear.

George was still in the kitchen, his hand in a box of crackers. "Really hungry," he said.

"I'm going after them."

He choked a little. "Say that again?"

I framed it as a safety issue. "I can't let them do this. My daughter can barely drive, my mother can barely breathe."

"How are you gonna stop them, Hope? Drive twice as fast? Catch them on the highway?"

"Maybe," I said, though even I knew crazy when I heard it.

"Sweetie . . ." He circled the counter and rested a hand on my shoulder. "Weebles said they left midmorning. They could've stopped in Manhattan for a six-course dinner at the Plaza and still have an unbeatable head start. Why not fly? Meet them in Memphis."

I pretended to consider this idea. How could I explain to George that I had to find them *before* Memphis? That years ago, I'd signed an agreement saying, among other things, I would never set foot in Memphis again. "If something happens to them along the way, if they break down or my mother needs help, I could get to them faster."

George was squinting past me. "Hand me your phone." He punched in my passcode while muttering, "You need to stop using Dylan's birthday for everything." He swiped through several screens. "Remember when Dylan lost her phone at the Red Sox game, and afterward, I set up that phone-tracking app for you?"

"Vaguely?" My phone was a graveyard of apps I'd down-loaded with the best intentions.

"Well, if we know where her phone is . . ."

I closed my eyes, prayed. *Please God, let this work.*

"Same password for iCloud?" I hung my head. He typed it in, waited, then frowned. "Really?" he asked the phone, then showed it to me. "It says they're in Fairfield, Connecticut. That's only a couple hours from here."

I stared at the phone. "*Fairfield?* What did they do? Walk?"

"I'm zooming in." He flicked the screen. "They're definitely off the highway."

"My mother has friends in Fairfield, but she hasn't seen them in years." Was she so cheap she wouldn't spring for a hotel? Did she plan to crash with friends all the way to Tennessee?

"Well, assuming this is right, I take back what I said about flying. If we act fast, maybe we can catch them."

"We?"

He shrugged. "You can't do this alone, Hope. If you have to chase them all the way to Memphis, that's a lot of driving. Plus, your car is a sack of shit."

"I can't ask you to come." But my protest sounded weak, even to me.

"Come on, we're talking about Dylan," he said. George treated Dylan like she was his daughter. He'd coached her T-ball team and taken her to father-daughter dances. "Besides," George added, "it's been ages since I've been back to Memphis." I must have made a face, because he quickly added, "If we even have to go that far."

I gave him a hug. "If you're sure. I mean, as long as you're willing to drive as far as . . . necessary."

"Absolutely." But from the look in his eye, I could tell there was more. "You don't mind if it's Jordan who drives, right?

"Of course not," I said. Almost immediately, though, I wondered if that was true.

I'D MET JORDAN almost eighteen years earlier, after crashing on George's sofa for a few weeks. Still struggling to put my life back together, I'd moved out of his place, begun renting a room from one of his customers, and purchased my first cell. Its buzzing woke me from a deep sleep.

George's voice sounded scratchy and oddly strained. "Hope, I'm in kind of a tough spot and wonder if you could do me a favor."

He'd been driving back from Boston and was pulled over for a missing license plate light. He'd had more than one drink, and the cop cited him for DUI. Could I come pick him up at the Stoneham police station?

On the drive over, I tried to make sense of his final comment: "I don't want to alarm you, but you may not recognize me." Had someone at the bar roughed him up? Had the police?

Once I'd identified myself at the station, I sat on a wooden bench and checked my phone. In my peripheral vision, I noticed a tall blond woman in a black skirt and mauve pumps come through the inner door. A hooker, I assumed, and poked at my messages, not wanting to stare. The woman walked over and stood directly in front of me until I looked up.

"I hope this isn't going to damage our friendship," she said with a soft, southern accent. Under a heavy layer of foundation and lipstick, the woman had George's face.

I took a minute to process this new information. Aware that

whatever I said would set a tone for our future relationship, I chose my words carefully.

"Only if you ask to borrow my sweaters."

I KNEW NOTHING about gender performance or fluidity back then, but on that drive home, Jordan referred to herself as a cross-dresser.

"Don't people these days prefer 'transgender'?"

"Cross-dressing is different from being trans. If I were trans, I'd actually be a woman, born in a man's body." Instead, she explained, the feminine side of her simply demanded an outlet. "Cross-dressing makes me feel whole."

Given the auto-repair business, Jordan said she was content to be George during the week and Jordan on weekends. People could refer to her according to how she presented—George or Jordan—and use "he" or "she" pronouns, respectively.

That was when I learned, too, about the reasons George had left Memphis. My uncle Vern, who'd started his only son tinkering with cars at six years old, had heard rumors about George's cross-dressing. They'd argued, and Uncle Vern ended up in the hospital with angina.

"It was actually my mom who suggested I put some distance between myself and Memphis for a bit," Jordan said. "I picked the Boston area because I knew a drag queen who'd moved there. And yes, Hope, that's a different identity, too."

OVER THE YEARS, because of our work-week schedules, I ended up spending most of my free time with Jordan. We went on walks, took in movies, and worked through the *New York Times* crossword puzzle together. Now, though, as I tried to imagine traveling through the Deep South with six-foot-five Jordan in her poufy wig, heavy makeup, and Italian pumps, my stomach tightened. Even in supposedly liberal Boston, a cross-dressing person brought out the nasty in some people.

"I'm hoping we find Mom and Dylan in Fairfield," I said as I wiped cracker crumbs from my mother's counter. "But if we have to chase them all the way to Tennessee, do you think folks will be okay with Jordan?"

"I'm a southerner, Hope. These are my people."

I raised an eyebrow.

"Yeah, some of them just don't know it yet." He grinned. "Not to worry, I'll be careful."

I wanted to hit the road as soon as possible, but George convinced me we should go home and get a few hours' sleep. He was right. It made no sense to arrive in Fairfield after midnight, when everyone would be asleep. He'd pick me up at four a.m.

We headed home. As we turned out of my mother's parking lot, George was still shaking his head. "I don't get why your mom would do this. What's her deal with Graceland, anyway? How many times does she need to see it?"

"She probably wants to commune with the King's spirit one last time," I said. "Who knows? The woman is a complete cipher. I've never been able to crack her code."

George patted my knee. "In fairness, sweetie, she didn't give you much chance."

He was right. My mother had abandoned my father and me when I was six, jetting off to resume her role in the rebooted *Light Within*, which had moved its filming from New York to LA in the late sixties. My father had always insisted the word "abandoned" was too harsh since Mom returned to Memphis most weekends and holidays, but it felt right to me. For the first year, whenever she packed to leave, I hid under the kitchen table and sobbed. The image of my mother with suitcase in hand weighed on me throughout my childhood, like a heavy wool coat reshaping its wire hanger.

"Your dad was such a sweetheart," George continued. "I was surprised he and your mom stayed married."

"Me, too, but he adored Mom. Tolerated her eccentricities."

"I remember how I'd show up at your house around supper time, and your dad would fix me a Swanson frozen dinner and I'd join the two of you watching *Odd Couple* reruns. He was such a sweet man."

"He was. He didn't deserve to be abandoned like that."

"You didn't deserve it either, Hope."

"Sure." I picked up my phone, checked again for messages. I wasn't going to argue with George, but I knew better. Deserve my mother's abandonment? Far worse than that. I'd caused it.

AFTER GEORGE DROPPED me at home, I wandered through the dark, silent house, searching for God knew what. A note, perhaps? Something that said my daughter had thought about me, had cared that I might worry? I found nothing. No scrawled envelope on the kitchen counter, no memo pad next to my computer, no Post-it stuck to the bathroom mirror.

Dylan and I had argued the night before. No worse than any of our fights, and I'd been more upset than she was. Or so I'd thought.

I'd come home from work to find her in my bedroom, rifling through laundry baskets of unfolded clothes, flinging T-shirts and shorts around the room.

"That's one way to get the laundry out of those baskets." I joked, jimmying off a pump. "I can show you other methods, whereby the clothes are arranged thematically, in piles." When she didn't respond, I added, "You'll need those skills at college."

She didn't lift her head. "Not doing college."

I stood lopsided on the one pump. Dylan had hinted at this before. Never a strong student, her grades over the past year had gone from mediocre to terrible, but she still had senior year to change that. "Dylan, college is important. You don't want to wait tables for the rest of your life."

She held up a camo T-shirt, tossed it in a pile. "I'm going to be an activist."

I kicked off the other shoe, sending it flying. It hit my dresser. "That's not a job."

"Okay, an activist *filmmaker*."

"Then you're better off waiting tables." I wasn't being fair but couldn't stop myself. "You'll make more money."

"That's what's important to you? Money?" Her voice was cold.

"I know what it's like to struggle, Dylan. It's no fun. You need a career, a job that's secure."

"Like yours?" She jerked a finger toward her open mouth.

"Is my job that bad?"

"You can't be serious. Working in little cattle stalls? Sucking up to your boss? Chanting, 'You gotta believe'?" Dylan gathered the pile of clothes she'd been collecting and headed toward the door. "You make fun of Olivia, but at least she's an actress, not a fake." She slammed the door behind her.

I lay down on my bed and closed my eyes. Dylan didn't mean it. She was trying to hurt me. Succeeding, in fact, but that was okay, because, honestly, she was right about my job. Gary and his slogans had sucked all the joy out of it. In recent months, I'd fantasized about finding a new job, doing marketing for a nonprofit like Heifer International or an AIDS foundation. I longed to be part of a team, working toward something I believed in. I'd felt that way once before, when I'd worked for Aaron back in Memphis. Unfortunately, after fifteen years at EduLearn, I worried that my skills wouldn't transfer, or I'd have to take a pay cut. Mostly, though, I worried about my resume. That, too, contained a lie.

I SAT AT my computer desk and opened Outlook. I'd email Gary, let him know I wouldn't be in the office tomorrow. He wouldn't like me disappearing again with little warning, but what choice did I have? Assuming we caught my mother and Dylan in Fairfield, I could work all weekend.

An email popped up from the iTunes account Dylan and I shared, confirming the charge to my Visa for downloading two dozen Elvis songs. Dylan must have chosen some music for the road. I scrolled through the list, pausing briefly at the first song: "That's All Right (Mama)." Somehow I couldn't read it as reassurance.

In the two hours since I'd found the newspaper article about Aaron in my mother's trash, I'd calmed down a little. My mother might have printed that piece for any number of reasons. Over the next week, both presidential nominees would announce their choice for running mate, and Aaron was strongly favored for the Democratic VP spot. Given that I'd briefly worked for Aaron—which, apparently my mother remembered, though I'd never been sure—that would explain her interest.

I leaned back in the office chair, hands clasped behind my

head, and considered the worst possibility. Even if my mother suspected I'd been involved with Aaron and guessed he was Dylan's father, she wouldn't share her suspicions with my daughter. Not without telling me. This was my mother, for heaven's sake. The woman wasn't evil. She wasn't . . . Andromeda.

It was past eleven and I needed to shower and pack. Instead, I sat looking at my desktop. The background photo was Dylan and me at Nauset Beach, our hair blowing wildly, our arms wrapped around one another. Had that been two summers ago? Three? So much had changed.

I'd sworn I'd be a better mother to Dylan than mine had been to me. Was I? I felt ashamed to admit it, but when Dylan had turned down my offer of a Cape Cod vacation, I'd almost been relieved. Much as I longed to spend time with her, an entire week alone together made me nervous. In a tiny Airbnb, there'd be so little space, so much time for quibbling and probing. Dylan's oblique reference to her father a few days earlier had twisted my stomach like a dishrag. Thank God that for most of her life, Dylan hadn't been all that interested in the man. She'd asked only a handful of questions and seemed satisfied with my answers.

At midnight, when I crawled into bed, I checked my text messages. No response from Dylan. Not then, and not when I woke every half hour until 3:30 a.m.

Chapter 5

Dylan

I've always wondered if Olivia would have chosen to stay at Rose and Rudy's if she'd known about the ferret castle.

Even from the outside, you could tell their house was a mess. The wraparound wooden porch was sinking in one spot, and the screen door had this huge, gaping hole. Rudy held Olivia's arm as they climbed slowly up the steps. I followed, carrying her oxygen tank in its little cart. Despite his ridiculous man bun, Rudy seemed okay. Olivia said he'd danced in Broadway shows like *Hair* and *Grease,* but he was most famous for dancing on sofas in Furniture King commercials.

Rudy held open the screen door and hollered for Rose. A heavyset woman tottered down the hallway. Rose had huge doe eyes, like a Disney princess's, and her white hair was cut chin-length with bangs. "Livvy!" she called out. "So good to see you!" Her voice was all gravelly, like she used to smoke, too. She hugged Olivia then pulled back, gesturing to the tubing around Olivia's face. "What's all this?"

"Air," said Olivia with an exaggerated sigh. "Turns out we need it. Who knew?"

Rose pouted her bottom lip in sympathy, but her expression seemed a little smug. *I may have put on a few pounds*, it said, *but at least I'm breathing on my own.*

Rudy showed Olivia to the guest room and me to a small study with a pullout sofa "courtesy of Furniture King." The room smelled like cat pee, and in one corner, cardboard boxes and tubes were taped together, like kids had made a fort. When something furry slipped past one of the cut-out windows and slid down a tube, I shrieked.

"We'll put the ferrets in the basement," Rudy said, shaking the structure until another one emerged and ran across my feet. Rudy herded it from the room.

I kept my eye on the boxes, not sure if there were more furry things inside. When Rose returned carrying sheets and a pillow, she insisted I go look at the far wall, covered with publicity shots from *The Light Within*.

"That's me," she said, indicating a busty blonde, seated beside a guy in a tux. "And that's your grandma," she nodded toward the dark-haired woman with heavy mascara resting a hand seductively on the man's shoulder. "From Season Two. That's when Andromeda started getting all that attention."

I'd watched some clips of the soap on YouTube. The worst part was the tacky opening music and baritone narrator. "Even when darkness surrounds us, we still have *The Light Within*." Yeesh.

Rose pointed to another photo. "And this was from Season Four, when Andromeda plotted to steal Krista's husband."

"Did she succeed?"

"Oh, you know soaps. They go back and forth for an entire season. But no, in the end, the bad girl never wins." She patted me on the shoulder. "Not in that world."

RUDY GRILLED SALMON for dinner. Rose lowered herself into a dining room chair, complaining about the heat and her swollen ankles. She opened a bottle of wine and offered glasses to everyone, including me. Olivia raised her eyebrows but didn't stop me from taking it.

The ferrets ran in and out and slithered between everyone's legs. They made my skin crawl. Rose scooped one onto her lap and talked to it like it was a baby. An entire wall was devoted to photos of the ferrets dressed in ski sweaters, cowboy hats, T-shirts, French berets.

Rose kept sneaking glances at Olivia's oxygen concentrator, tucked into a corner beside her chair. When Olivia reached down to adjust the tubing, Rose peppered her with questions. How many hours a day did she need it? ("All of them.") "What would happen if our power went out?" ("I'd switch to the portables.") "What if you run out of portables? ("You don't want to know.") To each answer, Rose nodded earnestly.

"So why Graceland, Liv?" Rudy asked as he set mismatched plates on the table. "Didn't you get enough of it when you lived in Memphis?"

"I took Hope to Graceland when it first opened and never went back. It was too sad, so soon after we'd lost him."

Rose muttered, "So soon after *you* lost him."

There was an awkward silence, so I jumped in. "Olivia's going to meet with the curator."

Olivia met my eye, and her brows lifted almost imperceptibly. A warning?

"Are you?" Rose asked. "Whatever for?"

"Ann and I are just catching up," Olivia explained. "Her mother was a friend in Memphis." Olivia turned to face Rudy. "Did you know that Dylan is quite the budding activist? She helped form her school's Gender-Sexuality Alliance."

Rose looked annoyed at the abrupt shift in topic. Rudy turned to me. "So nice that kids are coming out early these days. Good for you, Dylan."

"Actually, I'm not gay," I explained. A ferret leaped onto my lap, and I shoved it off. "I think I might be pansexual, but I'm still exploring." "

"*Pan*sexual?" Rose chuckled. "You're attracted to cookware?"

"Rose!" Rudy snapped. "Don't be rude. That's the new term for bisexual, isn't it, Dylan?"

"No," I said, a bit snippier than I intended, but Jesus, old people thought they knew everything. "It means I'm attracted to people regardless of their sex or gender identity."

Rudy said he'd been involved with Broadway Cares/Equity Fights AIDS and asked a lot of questions about my GSA protests. "What you're doing is important work," he said. "I hope you continue it in college."

"I'm not sure college makes sense for me." I felt pleased with that mature turn of phrase. "I might be an activist filmmaker. Like Michael Moore."

Rudy flicked his eyes to Olivia, who'd taken that moment to help herself to more asparagus. "Well," he said, "you'll figure out what's best for you. I wish I'd finished college. Dancing on sofas was hard at sixty."

"If we'd both stayed in LA—" said Rose.

"But we didn't, Rose," he interrupted, though not unkindly. Still, Rose turned her head with a sniff. "And so now, I'm seventy-eight and work the grill at a breakfast joint to pay the electric bill."

"Enough about you, Rudy," Rose said, pouring herself more wine. This was her fourth glass, by my count. "Teenagers don't want to hear about old people. Let's talk about when we were young and beautiful." She turned to me. "Did your grandmother tell you how she and I met Elvis?"

Given Olivia's earlier warning, I hesitated. "A little."

"Okay, but has she told you the *whole* story?" She drew out the word "whole" like it was borderline dirty.

"Rose?" Rudy smiled nervously, his eyes on Olivia. "I think Olivia should decide what stories to tell Dylan."

"Oh, not *that*!" Rose said. She was clearly drunk. "Not to worry, Liv, I don't intend to spec-u-late." She made it three separate words.

I didn't know where to look. A ferret circled my feet and I nudged it away.

Olivia reached for the wine and poured herself a tiny bit, replacing the bottle on the side away from Rose.

"I'm sure Dylan would enjoy hearing how we met Elvis." Olivia turned to me. "I only got the opportunity because of Rose. She was a close friend of our soap's producer."

Rose leaned across the table toward me and whispered: "She means I was fucking him."

Taken by surprise, I laughed out loud.

"Rose!" Rudy almost shouted. "That's not appropriate."

Rose sat back, proud of herself. "Dylan is almost seventeen. She knows what it means."

"That's not the point . . ."

"Do tell the rest, Rose," Olivia interrupted. "You're a much better storyteller than I." Olivia winked at me, discrediting anything Rose said.

Rose eyed Olivia, then the wine bottle, now out of her reach. "Oh, there's not much to tell." She slumped back in her chair, defeated. "As I said, I was *dating*"—here she turned toward Rudy to see if the word met his approval—"this producer, and he was a cousin of someone in Elvis's entourage. Red? Sonny? I can't recall. Anyway, he was able to get us backstage after the show." She drained what was left in her glass and plunked it down in front of Rudy, as if he might redeem himself by getting her more. Rudy motioned for me to pass the bottle. "I was quite the looker in those days," Rose continued. "I was hoping Elvis would invite me back to the suite." She watched Rudy pour the rest of the wine into his own glass and sighed. "Elvis did that with pretty girls, you know. Asked them to hang out with his entourage at the hotel where they'd party till dawn."

"Long story short, Rose didn't get what she wanted," Rudy said.

"No, I didn't. Elvis chatted with Livvy and me about the show, and our studio photographer took some pictures. We got barely five minutes before some goon hustled us out so Elvis could change. I was hopping mad. Then, as we're leaving the building, the goon chases us down and asks Livvy . . ." Here she stopped and glared at Olivia, who was studying the ceiling. "He asks *Olivia* if she would like to go to a private party with Elvis."

Olivia chuckled. "Rose actually said to the man, 'Are you sure he didn't mean me?'"

Rose sniffed. "Well, not for nothing, but I was the star. Liv's character was supposed to appear in one season. They kept making her part bigger and bigger."

"I think Elvis actually preferred brunettes," Olivia said. "He dated blondes, but remember, he married a brunette."

"True," Rose said. She seemed relieved to have an explanation and turned back to me. "Beyond that, I know no more. Your grandmother ditched me for her night with Elvis. And she would never tell me—"

Olivia interrupted: "Rose didn't speak to me for weeks."

"I didn't." She snickered. "I was so mad. And right about the time we started talking again, Livvy up and elopes with Harold and moves to Memphis."

"Wow." I'd never heard the story in order before. "Why Memphis?"

"That's where your grandfather lived, dear," said Olivia. "Once he finished his studies at UCLA, his parents needed him home to run the business."

Rose had stolen Rudy's wineglass. "But wouldn't you know it?" she said between sips. "Without that bitch Andromeda, our ratings tanked, and *Light Within* was canceled. My life was ruined. All because your grandmother eloped."

"Now hold on, Rose." Rudy was smiling. "Ruined? If that hadn't happened, you wouldn't have moved back to New York and married me."

"Like I said," she muttered.

Olivia stood and began jimmying her oxygen machine out of

the corner. "Well, it's been lovely, but Dylan and I should get some sleep. Thank you both for a wonderful dinner."

Rose paid no attention. She was speaking to me. "I always wondered if your grandfather would have moved Olivia to Memphis if he'd known about Livvy and the King."

Olivia smiled as she met Rose's eyes. Her tone was matter of fact. "I had no secrets from Harold."

"Really?" Rose smirked. "None?"

Olivia lifted her chin and focused her gaze on the window behind Rose, in that funny way my mother always made fun of. "Not a one," she said.

She swiveled her oxygen concentrator around and headed down the hallway, pulling the machine behind her. "Come along, Dylan. Time for bed."

I followed, nearly tripping over a darting ferret. Behind us, dishes clattered into the sink.

Once Olivia and I were inside the guest room, I closed the door behind us. "What did Rose mean about you and Elvis?"

"Oh, Rose." My grandmother let out a puff of air. "She likes a good story. If she doesn't have one, she'll make one up. You get to bed, Dylan. We have a long drive tomorrow."

I CHECKED UNDER the sofa bed for free-range ferrets. It seemed clear. My phone showed eleven missed calls, seven texts, and four voicemails from my mother. Most said "call me" in different yet increasingly annoying ways.

Olivia's door was still open a crack. I knocked softly and slipped in. Olivia was sitting on the bed, reading a paperback. I thrust the phone at her face. "The gig is up."

"Jig," Olivia corrected. "The *jig* is up." Olivia scanned the messages and handed back the phone. "Goodness. Your mother does have some obsessive-compulsive tendencies, doesn't she?" She shook her head tight and fast, like she was being electrocuted.

"What should I say?"

Olivia lifted her book, *Me Before You*. "Say whatever you want. Hope was bound to notice you were missing at some point."

"I wish she'd mind her own business."

Olivia flipped a page. "Perhaps that's what she's doing, dear. Finally."

Back in my room, I flopped on the squeaky sofa bed. I wanted to call my mother and scream at her, but I knew what would bother her more: silence. How perfect was that? Silence was what my mom had been offering for years.

As far back as I could recall, I'd tied myself in knots to avoid hurting my mother. Anytime I'd ask a question about my father, Mom's eyes would go dull, and her mouth would stiffen. She'd answer in a few words and find any excuse to rush away. I got it. Thinking about my dad was painful. So every time I asked about him, I swore I'd never do it again—never make Mom that sad. Sometimes I'd go a year or more, until I couldn't help it, and some question would burst out of me like an alien exploding from my guts. I'd listen to Mom's brief, pained answer, and be right back where I started. The guilt. The vows to try harder.

From what little Mom said about my dad's protests, I decided he'd been a man of deep conviction. Someone brave and bold, who'd risked his life—even died—in pursuit of his beliefs.

It was all a pack of lies, of course, but I didn't know that. So when Emma and I held our first GSA rally, and I started screaming at this bunch of homophobic bigots, it felt like someone had pulled back a curtain. I understood. I was like my dad. All the things my mother blamed me for—my impulsiveness, my arguing, my risk-taking—I got from my father. Mom wanted me to be cautious, obedient, people-pleasing, like her. Well, fuck that.

I'd heard about this Ancestry.com organization that could help you learn about your family tree, but I wasn't eighteen, so I couldn't do the DNA test. Still, I could search for my father in the company's database. I signed up on the website for a free trial and immediately hit a roadblock. I remembered my father's first name, not his last. Had Mom even told me? This was seriously messed up. My dad was half my identity, and I didn't know his full name.

After a sleepless night, I dragged myself out of bed early and got dressed. In the kitchen, I poured myself some cereal and sat at the counter, kitty-corner from Mom. She was scowling at the cable bill.

When I asked about my father's last name, some muesli tumbled off Mom's spoon. She wiped her mouth with the back of her hand. She was still looking at the bill, but—I could tell—no longer seeing it.

"Smith," she'd said. "James Smith."

I nodded, placed my half-eaten cereal in the sink, and went upstairs to dress for school. In the year since, though, I'd never told anyone that name, not even Olivia. I knew with absolute certainty that my mother had been lying. And it devastated me.

A few days later, on my sixteenth birthday, I dyed my hair.

Not a few streaks of color, but full-on, searing-hot pink. I got turned away from the tattoo parlor for being underage, but went to the mall and had them pierce more holes in my ears.

Before, I had known only half myself. Now I was becoming whole. I was embracing my flip side, the part of me I'd inherited from my father—the bolder, braver, Dylan. The Badass Dylan.

Chapter 6

Hope

The sun hadn't risen when I heard the crunch of Jordan's tires turning into my driveway. Four a.m. Bless her. Grabbing the two travel mugs I'd filled with coffee, I hustled outside with the overnight bag I'd packed. I prayed we wouldn't need it.

Even in the predawn gloom it was hard to miss Jordan's bright orange-and-scarlet dress as she leaped down from her Robinson Repair pickup. She beamed when I complimented her outfit, fanning the skirt to show off the poppies. Given how I was dressed, the two of us seemed like more of an odd couple than usual. Exhausted from lack of sleep, I'd thrown on ripped jeans and an Old Navy T-shirt and had pulled back my hair, still damp from my late-night shower, into a messy ponytail. Jordan, in contrast, looked camera-ready with a heavy application of foundation, eyeliner, mascara, and lipstick. Her wig was a dark blond and flipped back on both sides, Farrah Fawcett-style.

Jordan one-armed my suitcase into the back as I hopped into the cab. The seatbelt stuck and I yanked at it furiously. "Calm down, sweetie," Jordan said as she settled herself in the driver's seat. "We got this." I let the belt retract, took a deep breath, and pulled it out smoothly. Jordan head-bobbed a *told you so* as she threw the truck into reverse.

"Any word from our fugitives?" she asked.

"None." I was optimistic, though. The address I'd dug up online for Rudy Rosenbaum matched where the tracking app placed Dylan's iPhone. If we could surprise them there, I could take my mother aside, talk some sense into her. Right now, she didn't understand the danger.

As we drove, I kept the phone in my lap and lifted it constantly to peek at the blank screen. I knew it wasn't rational. The phone would quack if I had a message, and the odds of Dylan texting me at this hour were nonexistent. Still, every so often, I checked the Find My iPhone app to confirm the red dot was still in Fairfield.

Jordan tuned the radio to a seventies and eighties station and sang along. She had a lovely tenor voice and an odd passion for some of the sappiest pop music of our youth: the Captain & Tennille, Barry Manilow, Starship. I tried not to say anything, but when she began singing harmony to "Muskrat Love," I cringed.

"Don't be a snob," Jordan said.

"That song will be stuck in my head for days."

"Then choose something you like better. Sing along. It'll take your mind off things."

I gave her a sidelong glance. "You know I don't do that." I didn't sing in front of anyone. In fact, I had a horror of any type of public performance—singing, karaoke, line dancing, even reading aloud to school children. I hated having people's eyes on me.

Jordan sipped her coffee and shook her head. "How are you Olivia Grant's daughter?"

"No idea," I admitted. "God knows, my mother tried to change me. She gave up on singing but signed me up for every kind of dance class imaginable—ballet, tap, jazz. I hated them all. Even today, I break out in hives at the sight of a disco ball."

"No offense, Hope, but talk about casting pearls before swine. I'd have killed for tap lessons."

"You would have been great at it, too. It was torture for me, having the teacher and other kids watching." I fiddled with a rip in my jeans. "Before every lesson, I'd hide in the bathroom cabinet, under the sink."

"That's so odd. Olivia must have realized how much you hated it."

"She truly believed she was helping me. She's told me as much."

Jordan replaced her coffee in the cupholder. "Yeah, my father thought he was helping me by kicking me out of the house when he discovered my cross-dressing. He figured if I had to choose between that and my family, I'd choose family. He didn't understand that what he was asking me to give up was me." She adjusted her mirror and changed lanes. "Same with you, Hope. You're not an extrovert, but your mom was determined to make you one."

"Do you remember when I was six, and Mom tried to make me sing 'Happy Birthday' to my father in front of a room full of party guests? She lifted me up on that chair, and I was so terrified, I peed all over it."

"Clearly Olivia didn't get you."

"No. I wasn't her favorite daughter."

Jordan eyed me sideways. "Don't be silly. You're her only daughter."

"Not true," I said. "You know that."

"Yes," Jordan admitted. "I do."

JORDAN WAS OLD enough to remember my sister, Beth. I wasn't.

When I was eight, I discovered the box of photos high on a shelf in my father's closet. Pictures of an elfin toddler, a dark-haired beauty with dazzling blue eyes and long lashes. The photos puzzled me. Who was this girl who'd celebrated a birthday at my dining room table, pirouetted around my living room, wrapped her arms around my beaming mother?

When my father found me on his bedroom floor surrounded by the pictures, he sat next to me and sifted through several, smiling. "This is your sister, Beth," he'd explained. "She died before you were born." He lifted a photo of Beth in a lion costume, roaring at the camera, and handed it to me. Beth was a character, he'd said. A nonstop chatterer. A girl who loved ballet and show tunes. At three, she climbed onto the piano bench at my parents' dinner party to sing "Over the Rainbow."

My father didn't have to tell me I was nothing like Beth. I knew. I was shy and slow to make friends. I adored jigsaw puzzles, pored over books, organized my stuffed animals by natural habitat: jungle, desert, ocean. My hair was straight and the color of Idaho potatoes.

After Beth died, my father said, they'd decided to have another child, right away. I was born less than a year later. When I was older, in college, my father had elaborated on their determination to conceive—how my mother had timed her ovulation, summoned him from work in the middle of the day. In sharing this, my father's heart was in the right place. To him, it proved I was a wanted child. Instead, what I heard was: you were a replacement child.

They named me Hope Elizabeth. What I heard was: they were hoping for Beth.

WE STOPPED AT a rest plaza near Sturbridge to change drivers. I told Jordan I needed to get away from my phone, but really, I was dying to go faster. As I backed out of the parking spot, I handed Jordan my phone, still open to the texts I'd sent Dylan last night. Jordan, nothing if not nosy, scrolled through them. I let her, hoping she wouldn't notice when I picked up speed.

"I hate to nitpick, sweetie, but it's possible sending twenty texts was overkill," she said. "And good grief, were you actually starting a new one just now?"

I checked the side mirror and moved into the fast lane. "Do you think I should send it? We need them to stay put."

"Well, the quickest way to get them back on the road is to send this."

"Okay, erase it, please."

"Done," Jordan said. And then, "Oops."

The text Jordan accidentally sent was gibberish, the letters *hqpun* with a tented accent over the *u*. She had no idea how she'd done it, and I didn't expect Dylan would respond. We'd barely driven a mile, though, before my phone quacked.

"It's Dylan!" Jordan called out. "Do you want me to read it?"

"Yes!" I twisted in my seat, searching for an opening to change lanes. If my daughter was communicating again, I needed to reply.

Jordan typed in my password and scanned the message. "Oh dear."

"What?"

"It's in all caps."

"Read it!"

"It says, 'STOP TEXTING ME IT'S FIVE THIRTY A.M.'"

"Hit reply! Tell her I need to talk to her. I'll pull over."

Jordan glanced nervously at the three lanes of traffic I was crossing, but typed the message, making clicking sounds with her fake nails. A few seconds later, I heard the *bloop* that meant Dylan had responded. Jordan read aloud, "'What part of "stop texting me" don't you understand?'" Jordan shook her head. "I have to say, Hope, I saw that one coming. . . . Oh, wait, here's something more." She squinted.

"What?" I careened into the breakdown lane and hit the brakes hard.

"It says, 'Oh, and by the way, thanks for lying to me all my life.'"

Shit.

I threw the truck into park, snatched the phone from Jordan, and pressed the speed dial for Dylan. It went to voicemail. I texted madly, "Dylan, please pick up. I need to speak to you." I watched, waiting for the message to say "delivered." Cars roared by. Five minutes passed. Why wasn't the message delivered?

"She turned off her phone," Jordan said quietly.

One of my legs was shaking and I pressed on it to make it stop. *She knew. Dylan knew about Aaron.* My mother had stuck her nose into something that was none of her business, and now my daughter understood. I'd been lying to her for years.

WITHOUT A WORD, I unbuckled my seatbelt, slid out of the cab. Jordan didn't ask, just hopped down and circled around the truck. She took my place at the wheel, readjusted the seat, and signaled to merge back onto the highway.

For several minutes, we drove in silence, my thoughts tumbling over one another. I stared at the back window of a passing Volvo decorated with stick figures: father, mother, boy, girl, dog. No doubt the family inside was playing I Spy and snacking on grapes and cashews with healthy fats. I hated them.

"Hope," Jordan asked finally, "what was Dylan talking about?"

I fiddled with the seatbelt strap. "Who knows?" I said. "It's Dylan. What's she ever talking about?"

"Something, usually, is my impression." Jordan frowned at the road ahead.

"Then you tell me!" I snapped, my tone surprising us both. The truth was, Dylan often shared things with Jordan she hadn't told me. Jordan would mention a test Dylan had bombed or a boy she'd kissed, then see from my surprise I knew nothing about it. Jordan always felt horrible. So did I.

"Don't get mad, Hope," she said. She reached into the snack bag between us and took out an apple, then held it against the steering wheel without taking a bite. "Honestly, it's not that hard to figure out. You claim I'm your best friend, but in all these years, there's one thing you won't talk about. What happened to you in Memphis. You cried on my sofa for two weeks after I took you in." She flicked me a look. "That's right. I heard you at night. And then suddenly you're pregnant and won't discuss the father. I decided long ago it wasn't my business, but now I'm gonna ask you, straight-out. Hope, were you assaulted?"

My head jerked back, shocked. "No! Oh God. That isn't it at all."

"Are you sure?" Jordan's tone was gentle. "Because that shit is hard to talk about."

"It is, and no, please don't think that. It's nothing that awful." I paused, taking in everything Jordan had said. She wasn't just my cousin, she was my closest friend, and she was right— I'd told her nothing about my issues with Memphis. I'd abided by the nondisclosure agreement for over seventeen years, too afraid to do otherwise. Now, my world was collapsing, and Jordan had dropped everything and was driving me halfway across the country. The least I could do was tell her the truth.

Or, you know, most of it.

"I'm worried you're going to judge me," I said, sipping my coffee. I'd told Jordan I needed more caffeine before starting my story, so we'd zipped through a McDonald's drive-through in Rockville, Connecticut.

"Seriously?" Jordan said. "You're afraid the person sitting next to you, whose penis is tucked into her brand-new pair of Spanx, is going to judge you?"

"Thank you for that visual, but yes. It's a long and complicated story. The short version is, I fell for a guy who wasn't who I thought he was."

Jordan made a sound like a game-show buzzer. "Sorry, the judges need more information. And it has to be consistent. Not like the two different stories I've gotten before."

"What?" Admittedly, Jordan and George sometimes acted like such different people—Jordan ebullient and opinionated, George more serene and nonjudgmental—I'd occasionally found myself repeating something to Jordan that I'd already told George. But I'd told no one about Dylan's father. "That can't be right."

"Well, one version came from Dylan. She told me her father had lived in a yurt in Alaska and died in a whaling protest."

"Oh, right." I sipped my coffee. "Yeah, that . . . wasn't true."

"It did seem a little convenient. And I can imagine how furious she is if she's discovered it's a lie."

"My mother figured it out. I don't know how." Reflexively, I picked up my phone to check for messages. "What was the version I told you? And why don't I remember?"

"You were drunk. Remember maybe ten years back, when you broke up with that electrician guy? Or was it the firefighter? Which was the one I really liked?"

As far as I knew, Jordan had liked most of the men I'd dated over the years. She couldn't understand why I kept breaking off relationships before they got serious. I had trouble explaining it myself. "Skip past that part," I suggested.

"You invited me over. We put Dylan to bed, and you started making gin and tonics. I stuck with beer."

"Ohhh, this is sounding familiar. Was I really hungover the next day?"

"Horribly. I brought Dylan to the zoo. Anyway, that night

you got hammered and were railing about men being assholes, so I took advantage of the situation and asked about Dylan's father. And you said, drunkenly, 'Do you know him?'"

I rubbed my eyebrows. "So from that you deduced he wasn't dead. Anything else?"

"You said he'd been an ill-advised one-night stand and you hadn't kept his phone number. Not your exact words, but the gist."

I reviewed each of those points. "To be honest, nothing you said isn't true. Just . . . simplified. It *was* a one-night stand. And it *was* ill-advised. And I *didn't* keep his phone number, though I'm pretty sure I could find it if I wanted to." I paused here. This was new territory for me, but if my secret was safe with anyone, it was Jordan. "He's . . . a politician," I said. "So, you know . . . a website, and all that."

"A politician? In Memphis?"

"Well, DC. But he lives in Memphis. At least, his wife and kids are there."

"You're gonna have to help me here. A Memphis politician who works in Washington, DC? You mean, he's in Congress?"

"Yeah, something like that."

"What is *like* Congress?"

"You know. The Senate."

Jordan gave me a long look. Longer than I was comfortable with, given she was driving. "Let me get this straight. Dylan's father is a United States senator? You *slept* with a senator?"

"He wasn't a senator back then. He was just getting started in politics."

Jordan was frowning. "He's not that guy—what's his name? They're talking about him as a possible vice president pick. Breckenridge? Andrew Breckenridge?"

"Aaron," I said, brushing a crumb from my lap. "Aaron Brecken-ridge."

"Noooo." Jordan drew out the word. "You're screwing with me. The guy who's all about character?"

"Yeah, well, meet the skeleton in his closet."

She turned again to study my face, as if waiting for me to break out laughing. "Jesus, Hope, I'm impressed!"

"It's not something I'm proud of."

"Tell me what happened. No, wait. You said he was married."

"Engaged, back then. Bad enough." Traffic was slowing ahead, taillights popping on and off like warning signs. *Danger, Hope Robinson.* I couldn't focus. "Can we continue this later?" I asked Jordan. "My mind is in too many places. I need to figure out what I'm going to say to my mother when we find her. Not to mention my daughter."

"Of course, sweetie. And don't ever worry about sharing this stuff. I'd never judge you."

I nodded, grateful. Though I suspected she would if she knew everything.

THE ACCIDENT SOMEWHERE ahead of us, right before Hartford, was bad. All three lanes of traffic were stopped dead and a medical helicopter hovered, then landed. Dylan and my mother couldn't be involved—the iPhone still placed them in Fairfield—but that didn't stop my stomach from churning.

Storm clouds had rolled in ahead, dark and threatening. We opened the windows while we still could, listening to the scream of emergency vehicles and the whir of traffic helicopters. Eventually a local radio station reported the breaking story: a six-car pileup with serious injuries. So we sat. The smell of

exhaust made my throbbing headache worse. I dumped everything out of my purse, searching for Advil, but no luck. Dylan
must have swiped it.

Jordan drummed her fingers on the wheel and kept sneaking
looks at me. I'd asked for a break in talking about Aaron, but
when it came to gossip, Jordan was the least patient person on
earth. I leaned an elbow on the window well and dropped my
head into my hand. "Go ahead," I said, finally. "Ask."

"This Breckenridge guy? He knows about Dylan, right?"

I could see the rain starting in front of us, connecting sky
and highway. "He found out I was pregnant." The image in my
mind, though, wasn't of Aaron. It was of a strange little man in
a seersucker suit, sitting on a park bench.

"You didn't answer the question. He knows he has a
daughter?"

"Yes," I said. Big drops of rain plopped, one by one, onto the
windshield. "He didn't want anything to do with her."

Jordan turned on the wipers. Her jaw was set tight. "Asshole.
That's why you didn't want Dylan to know."

I dug my fingers into the tight place between my neck and
shoulder. That was one reason.

"It's okay, sweetie. We all love people we wish we hadn't. No
regrets. You got Dylan."

Twenty minutes passed before the car in front of us moved,
an hour as we crept toward an exit. We no longer had much
chance of catching my mother and Dylan in Fairfield. I tor-
tured myself with what-ifs. What if I'd checked on my mother
earlier yesterday? What if we'd started driving last night? What
if . . . I'd never lied to my daughter?

I pulled out my phone. I knew it might backfire, but I had no choice. I sent Dylan a text message. "On the way to Fairfield. Please stay put. I need to talk to you. It's urgent."

I hit send and the message said "delivered." Ten minutes later, when I checked her location on the Find My iPhone app, the red dot was gone.

Chapter 7

Olivia

Alone on Rose and Rudy's back patio, I sank into a lawn chair, threw back my head, and opened myself like a morning glory to the light. Why shouldn't I enjoy a little early-morning sunshine? Skin cancer wouldn't be what got me.

I've always been drawn to light, rarely bothered by heat. Even on the soundstage of *The Light Within*, under spotlights that made other actors fan themselves with scripts, I didn't perspire. Once, in our early days, Rose brushed against my cool arm and proclaimed, "My God, Livvy, you're a reptile. No warmth, whatsoever!"

Was it a joke or a diss? Hard to tell with Rose. Ours had been such an odd friendship. One part affection to two parts rivalry.

Wind chimes tinkled on the porch, but the house itself was quiet. No one stirring this early. Oh well. I'd hoped for a chance to talk privately with Rose—make peace with her on our way to Graceland. Seemed the right thing to do.

I wouldn't apologize for ruining her life, of course. Not my fault the soap failed after I left. Blame the writers. The new villain meant to replace Andromeda was a churlish buffoon with no cunning, no sex appeal. That's what killed *Light Within*.

In fact, if Rose was honest with herself for ten seconds, she'd recall that she was secretly thrilled when I announced I was leaving the show. When I told her, in her dressing room, a flicker of delight passed over her face before she caught it, and turned it into feigned sadness. Rose was a good actress.

I'm not claiming I never did Rose wrong. I did. It was Rose who'd obtained the backstage passes to meet the King. At the time, she was by far the bigger star. But Rose was lazy, not given to hustle like I was. Hustle had gotten me where I was. I couldn't turn it off.

And so, on the night of the LA Forum concert, when the photographer took a photo of the three of us together—Rose, Elvis, and me—I slipped him a note. Elvis stood between us with a hand over both of our shoulders, and I placed my hand over his, sliding the scrap of paper under his fingers. The King didn't react, didn't flinch. Women slipped him notes all the time. He palmed the note and squeezed my shoulder once to let me know he had it.

As I say, I knew how to hustle. I'd done my research. I'd asked around, talked to people in the industry. I knew where Elvis's heart lay.

My note said: I'm Olivia Grant, your new Ann-Margret.

I'D BEEN HOPING to make amends to Rose during our visit. Tell her that story. Privately. It would please her to know there'd been a reason why Elvis had chosen me. How, once again, I'd played the villain.

But in the end, Rose was still Rose. Never could hold her drink. Even if I'd told her, she wouldn't have remembered it in the morning.

My husband, Harold, used to say that everything happens for a reason. "Bullshit," I'd reply. I had no patience with such nonsense. It wasn't fate that had brought me to Rose's doorstep—it was my will and the damn broken drive shaft. And if God or fate or Tinker Bell or whoever-the-hell-you-believe-in had wanted me to make amends with Rose, they would have stopped her from getting tanked. I was done trying.

No, if there was any lesson in seeing my old costar, it was to remind me of the sad place she'd ended up. Like so many of our friends, Rose had been a white-hot star, gracing the cover of *Soap Opera Digest*, cohosting *The Mike Douglas Show*, swimming in Rock Hudson's pool. One by one those actors had disappeared, sinking silently under the winter ice of oblivion. No one had even seen them struggle.

That wouldn't be me.

A LIGHT CAME on in the kitchen and a flash of pink skirted by the window. Dylan. Surprising to see her up at this hour, but Dylan was nothing if not surprising.

Turned out the girl was decent company. So different from Hope! You could talk to Dylan. She didn't keep her thoughts under lock and key. If you made it past the prelude of teenage angst and unfiltered nonsense, Dylan hit every note in the adolescent aria: exhilaration, despair, longing, fury, confusion, self-doubt. The raw emotion took my breath away.

Oh, Dylan's high spirits would need to be kept in check,

for sure. The child had no self-control. She was a blender with the top off. I'd have to be careful how much I shared with her, especially on the father issue. The last thing I needed was her posting something on Facebook or Twitter.

Dylan threw open the sliding glass door and marched toward me, clearly out of sorts. Her hair was tussled, as if she hadn't bothered consulting a mirror, and her black T-shirt proclaimed, "It's Science, Bitch." She thrust her phone under my nose, demanding, "How'd this happen?"

I guided the girl's hand to where I could read the message. From Hope. She was on her way here, to Fairfield. I released the phone back to Dylan. "No idea."

"How does she know where we are? Did Rose call her?"

"Unlikely." I heaved myself out of the chair. "Given Rose's condition at dinner, I'm not sure she'd have remembered her own name, never mind Hope's." I headed into the house, calling over my shoulder, "Perhaps your mother keeps a tracking device on you."

I was joshing of course, but when I turned back, Dylan glared at her phone. The girl let out a string of curses and followed me inside, poking and swiping, and grumbling about some phone-tracking app, as if I were listening. "It's off," she said. "Now what do we do?"

"Do?" My suitcase was packed and on the bed. I zipped it closed. "Have breakfast, I suppose. Then Rudy will drive us . . ."

"No!" she interrupted. "We have to leave now. We can't let Mom find us here."

"Honestly, Dylan, your mother would have made everything easier if she'd agreed to drive us in the first place."

The girl banged her hand against the door. That got my attention. "You don't understand! Mom will make me go home. She doesn't want me to know about my father."

Were those tears in the girl's eyes? I was speechless. I hadn't realized how much this trip meant to her. The whole let's-find-your-dad angle had been an afterthought, a means to an end.

"She'll talk you out of going," Dylan said.

I had to laugh at that. As if Hope could talk me out of anything, never mind this trip. Still, I moved to the window and craned my neck to check the driveway. The girl had a point: Hope could be unusually stubborn about certain things, and God knows, Memphis was one of them. No, the way to get Hope to Memphis was to stay just out of her reach and lure her there, mile by mile. Hope was the proverbial frog who wouldn't jump out of the pot as long as I raised the temperature a smidgen at a time.

Not that it would kill Hope to return to Memphis. Well, as far as I knew.

I drew the curtains. "Show me the Googley maps again."

Google offered two different routes to Memphis. Both went through Pennsylvania, but the faster route dipped south to Maryland and Virginia, while the other swung west across the state before dropping down through Ohio and Kentucky.

I pointed to the latter. "We'll go this way."

Dylan pushed aside my finger. "No, we don't want to do that. See? It adds forty minutes," she said. "That would be crazy."

I grinned. "Exactly."

FOR A MAN who'd once danced to "Aquarius," Rudy dawdled and dragged his feet beyond belief. I wanted to poke him as he brewed coffee, scribbled a note for the sleeping Rose, and hunted for his car keys. All the while, Dylan eyed the door nervously. She seemed convinced that any second, Hope might pop her head through the hole in the screen, like Jack Nicholson in *The Shining*.

In the car, Rudy gave me the third degree about Graceland. What was the draw? Why now? Well, none of his damned business! I offered perfunctory responses and listened to his completely erroneous account of Elvis's final hours until he accidentally reminded me of something. No one was allowed upstairs at Graceland, where the King's bedroom was. "Only the family," he insisted. "They've left everything exactly as it was when he died. I thought you'd know that, Livvy. You, of all people."

How embarrassing. I'd only been to Graceland that one time and I'd forgotten. Since then, I must have watched a dozen Elvis biopics and could picture every inch of the upstairs. Those TV images had taken the place of memory.

Rudy shot a backward glance at Dylan before adding, with a grin, "Unless you remember his bedroom because the King himself showed you."

"That's what Rose thinks, clearly," I said. "But no, I never laid eyes on Elvis during my years in Memphis." I fiddled with the knot on the red scarf, wrapped twice around my neck and tied sideways. "It's disappointing, though, about his bedroom. I did so want to visit the place he was last."

Rudy smirked. "I believe that was on the commode."

I struggled to tamp down my annoyance. Fine. Before he died, Elvis had gotten up to use the toilet and hadn't made it back. So what? That bathroom was en suite, technically part of the bedroom. I'd see about this arcane rule that barred visitors from that special place. Perhaps the general public wasn't allowed, but surely exceptions were made.

At the repair place, the girl kicked into high gear. While the mechanic charged my card, Dylan dragged my oxygen concentrator around the back of the Bug. When Rudy tried to help by bringing over my extra tanks, Dylan raced around the car and pried them from his hands. She patted Rudy's back and pointed him in my direction. Rudy raised both hands in surrender and ambled back.

A quick hug should have been the end of it. Instead, Rudy took me by both arms and apologized for Rose's behavior.

"Rose has suffered a lot of disappointment," he said. The Bug's horn beeped, and I waved at Dylan. "It's hard to be a star one day and a nobody the next."

"Never occurred to me," I deadpanned. Another, longer beep from Dylan. I raised a finger. One minute.

Rudy, though, didn't take the hint. He launched into a story about some fan who'd asked for Rose's autograph, then realized she wasn't Debbie Reynolds and tore it up, right in Rose's face.

Enough. I had to put an end to this. I promised to call Rose, even though I had no intention of doing so. Quite frankly, what had happened to Rose was my worst nightmare, and I couldn't get away fast enough. I was still detangling myself from Rudy's grip when Dylan laid on the horn and threw the car into reverse.

I heard the crunch immediately. Everyone did.

Chapter 8

Hope

Rose and Rudy frowned at me through the screen door. They had no idea who I was. I'd met them once when I was twelve, on a rare family trip to New York, but back then I'd had wire-framed glasses, braces, and legs like a newborn giraffe. My story about a last-minute decision to follow and surprise my mother and daughter probably sounded as loony to them as it did to me.

Rose said they'd left an hour ago. She cradled something in her arms that looked like a weasel wearing a sunbonnet.

"Car's all fixed," Rudy added. "Brand new drive shaft." He must have seen me blanch. "They didn't tell you it broke?"

"We haven't been in touch in the last . . . day or so." *Holy shit, a drive shaft?* That sounded important.

"Too bad about your mom's oxygen machine, though."

"Sorry?"

Rudy explained how Dylan had backed over my mother's oxygen concentrator. I put a hand to the door frame to steady myself. Without the concentrator, could my mother even make it to Memphis? She often seemed way too dismissive of her need for oxygen. Like she could go cold turkey anytime she put her mind to it.

"They were gonna have a new machine sent to their next stop," Rudy said.

"*Where?* Did they say?"

Rudy squinted into the distance. I wanted to reach through the screen and shake the man. He looked to Rose, who shrugged. "Can't recall that they did. You might want to phone them. If it won't ruin the surprise."

As I climbed back into the truck, the Rosenbaums ventured onto the porch, still cradling the furry rodent. Rudy shaded his eyes, studying the pickup, no doubt curious why my daughter's car was a piece of crap while I rode in a truck with "Robinson Repair" decals on the doors. Fair question.

When I told Jordan about the drive shaft, she lowered her forehead to the steering wheel.

"Hope, I'm so sorry. I told Dylan to bring it back to the shop."

"It was my fault. I was waiting until I could pay you." Stupid, stupid, Hope. How had I let money take center stage in the worst decisions of my life?

I pulled out my phone and typed: "Dylan, that car is a menace. Tell me where you are *now*. We'll meet and make a new plan." I hit send, reread the message, and added: "Your grandmother's health is in danger. Call me."

I dropped my head back and closed my eyes. "Ferret," I whispered. "That's what it was."

"Onward?" Jordan asked quietly. "To Memphis?" When I nodded, she tapped at her GPS. "Which way?"

Shit.

I sat upright and examined the two routes Jordan showed me. Of course there were options—why hadn't I thought of that? I chose the shorter, praying it mapped the same way from the repair place.

Jordan backed down the driveway and turned on the radio. As she followed the directions to the highway, she hummed along with the piña colada song. I hugged my arms across my chest and tried to calm the cyclone stirring in my gut.

I was headed to Graceland.

I'D BEEN TO Graceland once, when I was six.

My mother took me when the mansion opened to the public, in 1982. I have a vague memory of the Jungle Room, with its green shag carpet on the floor and ceiling. What fixed the visit in my mind, though, was what happened after. On the drive home, my mother made me promise not to tell my father where we'd been.

"Why?"

"Your father's not a fan of Elvis."

This rang true. My mother only played Elvis records when my dad was at work. I agreed not to tell. I liked sharing a secret with my mother. Having recently peed on her chair in front of party guests, I wanted desperately to please her.

Unfortunately, my dance school was having a recital that night, and even though I'd sworn I'd perform, as the day wore on, I dreaded the sea of eyes, the flashing cameras, the teacher hissing at me. After my mother dragged me, shrieking, from the closet where I'd been hiding, my father intervened, squatting down to my level and encouraging me to take deep breaths.

He smoothed back my hair and asked me what was wrong. "I can't go," I cried. "I'm too tired!"

"Too tired to dance?" he teased. "That's silly."

"I am!" I insisted. "Mom made me walk all over Elvis's house and I feel sick."

There was silence, then, except for my sniffling. My father's eyes were on my face, but his mouth grew tight.

My mother said, casually, "We did the Graceland tour. Everyone is talking about it. You can't live in Memphis and not go."

My father rose without looking at either of us. He grabbed his wallet and keys and left the house. I heard his car turn over in the driveway.

My mother sat down in her chair, lit a cigarette. "Well, now you've done it," she said. "I'll have to call us a cab."

"Daddy says we shouldn't lie," I said, ignoring that I'd just lied about being tired.

My mother blew a smoke ring and sighed. "Sometimes a lie is a kindness, Hope. It can protect someone's feelings."

I performed in the recital that night, in my little French can-can outfit with the jaunty beret. My mother was right—apart from the flashing cameras, it wasn't that bad. I missed only one sashay, when I noticed the empty seat beside my mother. My father stood in the back of the room.

In my memory, it was the very next day that my mother received the phone call asking her to return to LA, to star in the resurrected *Light Within,* but that timing seems unlikely. It's equally unlikely that she hung up the phone and immediately rushed upstairs to pack. And yet, that's how it plays out in my mind.

What I remember clearly is sitting on the floor, under the

kitchen table, sobbing, while my mother waited outside for the taxi that would take her to the airport.

"This is a great thing for your mom," my father said, crawling under the table to sit with me. "Acting makes her happy."

But even at six, I knew what lay behind his words. That I didn't.

I scanned the road constantly for Dylan's Volkswagen, certain its Pepto-Bismol color would stand out against the gray, overcast day. Given Jordan's slavish devotion to speed limits, any chance of catching up to them was slim. Still, I couldn't stop searching. Around Parsippany-Troy Hills, New Jersey, I glimpsed something pink on the horizon and pitched forward in my seat. It turned out to be a tattered billboard of a couple frolicking in a Poconos hot tub. Part of the heart-shaped tub had torn off and was flapping below the sign.

What was I going to say to my daughter when—if—I caught up with her? She was already furious at how I'd lied to her. My one consolation was that she didn't know about my agreement with Aaron. By signing that, I hadn't just promised to lie to Dylan for her entire life, I'd done something much more shameful. I'd taken money for it. Dylan would never forgive me. So if somehow she made her way to Aaron and found out . . . I couldn't bear to think about it.

Reminders of the coming election were everywhere: on the bumper stickers of passing cars, the competing lawn signs at every exit. For the first time in history, a woman was about to become a presidential nominee, and in the next few days, she was expected to announce her VP pick. Some commentators named Aaron the favorite, others leaned toward the labor secretary or the guy in Virginia. I didn't know what to hope for.

Aaron had broken my heart, chosen someone else over me, then paid me to keep silent about his daughter. I had every reason to hate the man, but my feelings about him had always been a confused jumble of regret and longing, anger and hurt, admiration and disdain. Aaron had made me promise never to return to Memphis, and if somehow he learned I was there, it would spell disaster. It would mean I'd broken our contract, and I'd have to pay back money I no longer had. And yet, in utter defiance of logic, I actively indulged in a fantasy of bumping into him, perhaps as he jogged along the river path. He'd tell me he regretted the agreement and would ask to see a photo of our daughter. He couldn't acknowledge her right now, but he'd stare at the picture and grasp my hand for a long second before parting.

Jordan had tuned the radio to a twenty-four-hour ABBA-thon, and I jumped as she began belting out the chorus of "Dancing Queen." After the second time the station played "Mamma Mia," though, I begged for something new. Jordan told me to open the glove compartment. An Elvis CD in a cracked jewel case dropped onto my lap.

"Excuse me?" I eyed her sideways.

She grinned. "All great road trips need a soundtrack."

"No thanks." I tossed the CD back into the glove compartment. I knew my aversion to Elvis was irrational and directly related to how much my mother loved him, but I wasn't in the mood.

When my phone rang, I grabbed for it, praying it was my daughter. I was disappointed to see Gary's number, though not surprised. In the email I'd sent him, I'd said to call if he needed anything.

"Is this the Great Vanishing Hope?" Gary asked, a clear edge in his voice. "One minute she's here—"

"It's a family emergency, Gary," I jumped in. "Unexpected. I'm trying to deal with it quickly."

"Hope, I'm not going to mince words. This disappearing act—"

"I've been meaning to talk to you," I interrupted again. "You asked for ideas to combat the used-book problem and I want to volunteer."

There was a long pause. "Say that again?"

I explained how I wanted to help him out on this issue. I could suggest some ideas, write up a proposal. Exactly *what* I'd propose was a problem for another day.

Gary's silence may have been surprise, or possibly surprise mixed with horror, but after some throat-clearing, he warmed to the idea. Yes, now that I mentioned it, he'd love something to present to the Editorial Board. They were meeting on Monday. Was that possible?

I swallowed hard and choked out, "Sure!" I'd brought my laptop. Once we stopped for the night, I could put in some time.

"That's what I like to hear!"

"Okay, great—" I tried to end the call, but Gary wasn't finished.

"Hope?"

"Yes . . . Gary?"

"What is it you have to do?"

I looked skyward for help. "Write the proposal?"

"No! You've gotta . . ."

"Oh!" I cringed. "Believe."

"That's it, Hope! That's how you get to be a star."

"Yessiree," I said, chuckling in a way that made me hate myself. Perhaps I'd inherited more of my mother's acting skills than I'd realized.

I SHOT JORDAN a puzzled look as she steered the pickup into a deserted pull-off somewhere in the middle of God-Knows-Where, Pennsylvania.

"Bio break," she explained. "Too much coffee."

There were no porta-potties in sight, only a drooping plastic fence separating pavement from woods with two no-trespassing signs. I couldn't tell if the place had once been a weigh station or was private property. "You don't want to wait for a rest area?"

She rolled down the windows and turned off the ignition. "No, this is easier."

I understood. At rest stops, Jordan often got in trouble no matter which bathroom she used.

As Jordan stepped over the downed fence and entered the woods, I cringed for her beige espadrilles. Jordan spent a lot of time at Nordstrom Rack clearance sales, searching for size 14 shoes that weren't hideous. It took a while for her to disappear from sight, as her dress, with its explosion of scarlet and orange poppies, wasn't exactly designed for camouflage. Not unless one were hiding in a Marimekko outlet.

I thought again about the rural areas we'd be driving through. With the frame of an NFL linebacker, Jordan didn't pass easily as a woman. Even in supposedly liberal Massachusetts, people stared. Once they got it, most folks shifted their gaze, but not everyone. Jordan herself was admirably patient. "I'm tall. Their brains need a little processing time." As grateful as I was for Jordan's company on the trip, I worried folks in backwoods Virginia might need more than a little processing time. Then I chastised myself. *Don't make assumptions. Don't be a snooty northerner.*

A cool breeze blew through the truck's open windows, raising the hair on my arms. I scrolled through my phone, ignoring the gravelly crunch of a car pulling into the drive behind me. I had a text message from the sandy-haired firefighter I'd dated last fall. Could we have coffee sometime? He'd enjoyed our time together, still didn't understand why I'd broken things off. I closed my messages without responding. How could I explain what I didn't understand myself?

I was checking my work email when a hand slapped the driver's-side door. My shriek reminded me of the sound Dylan's guinea pigs made when I used to clip their nails.

"Sorry to frighten you, ma'am." The state trooper looked the part, right down to the aviator sunglasses and Dudley Do-Right hat. I kept my hand on my heart. He pointed to the empty driver's seat.

"Oh. My friend took a stroll in the woods to, uh . . ." I couldn't hit on the appropriate word for this context. "Urinate," I finished, not quite satisfied with the choice.

"Didn't see the signs, I guess." It was sarcasm. He flicked his head toward the woods. "We see a lot of drug activity in the woods here. You don't have to walk far to step on a needle."

"Oh, we didn't know. We're not from around here."

"It's also got a reputation as a hookup spot. For men."

"Huh," I said. "Wouldn't have guessed that, either."

The officer squinted at something over the hood of the truck: Jordan's orange shape emerging from between two oak trees. The trooper clearly struggled to reconcile the skirt with the six-five frame.

"Your driver?"

I nodded.

"License and registration please."

"NATURE CALL" WAS how Jordan explained her trip into the woods. I filed that phrase for future use and passed Jordan her wallet and registration. The trouble would start now.

"And you'd be George Robinson?" The trooper shifted his eyes between the picture and her face.

"Yes," Jordan replied.

"And where are you headed, Mr. . . . ." He caught himself, stopped, and didn't try to correct it.

Jordan said, "Memphis."

"Love Memphis," the cop said. "I'm a huge Elvis fan."

"Me, too!" I called out, opening the glove box to hand him the Elvis CD with the cracked jewel case, as if this corroborated my story.

"Love the King!" he said. "Been to Graceland twice."

"Oh, yeah," I agreed. "Can't get enough of that . . . Jungle Room."

He examined both sides of the CD, no doubt wondering why it had been stepped on more than once. "What's your favorite Elvis song?"

My mind went blank. "Ohhh, that's tough," I said, squeezing my eyes tight, as if struggling to choose just one. Finally, a title popped into my head. "Jailhouse Rock!"

"Huh." The trooper looked surprised. "I like 'Unchained Melody' myself." He handed Jordan back her license and registration. "You'd think it'd be vice versa."

Jordan nodded. "Funny world we live in."

THE TROOPER LET us off with a warning about trespassing and suggested we use a Dunkin' restroom in the future, as they were cleanest. After a five-minute discourse on who wrote the best Elvis tell-all, he made me type the author of a two-volume Elvis biography into my phone.

"Why in God's name did I claim to be an Elvis fan?" I said as I deleted it.

Jordan merged back onto the highway. "No clue. Puzzles me when you do things like that."

Her tone was light, but I bristled. "Like *what*?"

"We've discussed this before, Hope," she said. "You have a tendency to—how shall I put this—make shit up."

Jordan had mentioned that before, and I'd brushed it off. Now I was annoyed. "For instance?"

"I don't know." She tapped her thumbs on the steering wheel. "If someone gives you a purple scarf, you'll say 'I love it! It'll look perfect with my new sweater,' when I know you hate purple and don't have a new sweater."

I blew out a puff of air. "Everyone does that."

"Do they? Do you really like my outfit today, or were you just being nice?"

"I love it!" I insisted. What I thought was: *Shit. She's right. I do that.*

"I'm not criticizing, Hope, just observing. Not ten minutes ago, you were hating on Elvis. Next thing I know, you whip out his CD and claim to be his biggest fan. It's like a reflex with you. Like throwing people off track is what's important."

I changed the subject, pointing to a sign for Philadelphia and asking Jordan if she'd ever been there. No point continuing that conversation; I wasn't going to make Jordan understand. That's what lies do. They protect us and those we love. My mother had taught me that.

Chapter 9

Dylan

I wondered if Olivia might be having an aneurysm. Her eyes were closed, and she held her phone in one hand while pinching the bridge of her nose with the other. She'd been arguing with her oxygen company forever.

Seriously. For. Ever.

"Wait, wait, wait," Olivia shouted, making me leap about a foot in the air and grip the steering wheel harder. "You're charging me *what* for delivery to Roanoke?" She threw back her head and muttered, "Will no one rid me of these scam artists?"

I was glad Olivia didn't yell at me for driving over her oxygen machine, but she hadn't been real chatty since then, either. We'd had to remap our route. Without her oxygen concentrator, we couldn't risk taking the slower route through Pennsylvania, even if it might lose Mom. Olivia plotted how far we could drive with the tanks she had left, added some wiggle room, and confirmed our room at the Hampton Inn in Roanoke, Virginia. I looked at her calculations and grumbled a bit, convinced we could make it farther.

Thank God Olivia didn't listen to me.

As soon as Olivia hung up, she speed-dialed her fan-club president, Frances, who did all her social media. Olivia said there used to be an Elvis-themed diner outside Pittsburgh. Could Frances Google it and post a photo? Mention Andromeda might visit?

I shook my head and whispered, "We're not going by Pittsburgh anymore. We're going the other way."

Olivia asked Frances to hold and lowered the phone to her chest. "Yes, but your mother doesn't know that."

I had to laugh. "Olivia, you're kind of diabolical."

"Well, you don't play an evil character for almost forty-five years without some of it rubbing off."

After Olivia finished with Frances, she dropped her phone into her bag, leaned back, and closed her eyes. Olivia had been more tired on this trip than I'd expected. I'd been saving a bunch of questions for when she was in a better mood—like once we'd gone a few miles without breaking something—but now my grandmother looked like she could nod off, and I needed to talk. The endless trees, highway, and gray sky were starting to hypnotize me. I had no idea driving cross-country would be so boring.

"Olivia." I poked her arm. "Can I ask you a question about my father?"

Olivia clapped a hand to her forehead. "Dylan, we've been over this."

"No, listen," I cut in. "I'm not asking who he is. I'm just wondering . . . do you think he knows about me? I mean, that I exist?"

Olivia exhaled loudly. Her head was thrown back, like she

was searching the car ceiling for an answer. "Honestly, I have no idea. If he does know and he's never acted on it . . ."

"Then he's a douchebag."

"That *is* a possibility," she acknowledged.

"But if he doesn't know—I mean, if Mom never told him . . ." I waited to see if Olivia would finish the sentence. When she didn't, I did. "Then Mom's kind of the douchebag."

Olivia leaned forward and checked the gauge on her portable tank. "Don't be too hard on your mother, Dylan."

"Why not? She's a liar."

"Hope has a long history of getting in her own way." Olivia lifted her seatbelt to brush something off her shirt. "People like that, sometimes they just need a little push."

AFTER I TURNED off the ignition at the 7–11 in Allentown, Pennsylvania, Olivia was still asleep, so I poked her shoulder until she opened her eyes, sputtering and complaining. Well, too bad. If she didn't want us to drive off the road into a ditch, she needed to stay awake and talk. Olivia asked for a hot tea. When she noticed my hand out, waiting for money, she grumbled some more, but gave it to me. You just can't please some people.

Once we were back on the highway, I realized there was one way to keep Olivia talking to me. "What's so great about Graceland?" I asked. "I mean, it's just a house, right?"

"Yes, a house." Olivia sighed, tossing her phone at her purse. "And not an especially big one, by today's standards."

"So . . ."

"Good grief, Dylan, give me a minute! I'm thinking how to explain." Olivia churned the tea bag up and down through the hole in the lid. "How about this. Have you ever felt like someone saved your life? Metaphorically, I mean. Gave you the strength to keep going in hard times."

I considered the people who'd been there for me in a pinch. George, maybe, after I was arrested for slashing that asshole's tires. Mom had gone apeshit, but George had rubbed my head and whispered that next time I wanted to trash a car, he'd show me better ways.

Olivia, though, didn't wait for me to answer. "Elvis had his first hit when I was seventeen, and I fell hard for him. Those ice-blue eyes. Sometimes they were twinkly and sometimes haunted, but they were like a window into his soul. I could tell he struggled, like me." Olivia sipped her tea and made an ugly face. The apple-cinnamon organic must have been a bad choice. "I bought Elvis's records with my allowance. I had to sneak them into the house and play them on an old record player in the basement when my mother wasn't home."

"Why?"

"Mother thought Elvis was the devil, the way he gyrated his hips. This was the 1950s, remember. My mother was a religious nut, but she wasn't alone in her opinion. Not in Hackensack, New Jersey. Plenty of preachers gave sermons on the immoral way Elvis moved his body. Frank Sinatra called him a sex maniac."

I almost choked on that one. Had my grandmother seen Miley Cyrus? Nicki Minaj?

"I read all his fan magazines, too, and learned that Elvis had bought a mansion, with tall white columns and a sparkling blue pool. To me, Graceland seemed like heaven. I planned to marry Elvis someday and live in that mansion. That dream kept me going when living with my mother was hell.

"When I was nineteen, just after the release of 'All Shook Up,' I came home from the secretarial school I was attending and saw a fire burning in the backyard. My mother was throwing my magazines and records in it. I caught her arm midair and begged her to stop. She pushed me to the ground. Said she was doing it for my own good, and I'd thank her someday."

"Jesus."

"Yes, I believe she mentioned him, too." Olivia sipped her tea and grimaced again. "I barely spoke to my mother after that. The following year, I took a secretarial job in New York and started auditioning. At twenty-five, they cast me on *Light Within*."

I had to admit, Olivia's mom sounded worse than mine. "What did she say about your date with Elvis?"

"Mother was gone by then."

"Sorry. When did she die?"

"Oh, she didn't die. Well, she did eventually, of course, but starting in my early twenties, she was in and out of institutions. They'd have some name for it these days. Borderline personality disorder, or similar. Back then, people just said she was crazy."

"You had a kind of messed-up childhood." Mom had never told me any of this.

"It was a long time ago. My father did what he could. He was my rock." Olivia dropped the apple-cinnamon tea in the cupholder, done trying. "In my experience, mother-daughter relationships are always a bit fraught," she said. "A girl needs a father."

AROUND HARRISBURG, OLIVIA suggested we grab Panera sandwiches and top up the caffeine. I don't know how they brew their iced coffee in Pennsylvania, but man, did it improve my mood. While I fiddled with the Elvis playlist, Olivia switched her portable oxygen tank, then studied her watch.

"Everything okay?"

She said it was, so I pulled out of the rest stop and turned up the volume on the King. I had to give the guy credit—his stuff was catchy. I learned the words to "All Shook Up" and "Memphis, Tennessee." Olivia said that when Elvis first started performing, he was just a nervous kid who couldn't control his knees, but the girls shrieked and clapped, so he kept doing it. Olivia and I sang along and jiggled our legs and laughed until I almost peed myself.

After we'd driven for an hour, Olivia leaned back against the headrest and closed her eyes. I switched off the music and kicked up my speed. Around Boston, 80 miles per hour is nothing. Cars zip by you on both sides.

When blue lights flashed in the rearview mirror, I lifted my foot off the gas and moved right, hoping he'd pass. The cop moved right, too. My pulse fluttered, but the cop didn't put on his siren. Maybe he was getting off at the exit. I returned to the middle lane. He followed, turning on his siren and jamming his cruiser up my car's butt.

"Jerk!" I signaled to pull over.

Olivia woke up and looked back over her shoulder. "Were you speeding?"

"A little."

"Good."

Olivia never said what I expected. After I turned off the car, though, I got what she was thinking. "Shit. Do you think Mom reported us?"

"Unlikely," she said. "You were speeding. Apologize and take the ticket. We don't have time to spare."

The cop sat in his cruiser, doing God knew what. Olivia opened the glove compartment. Out tumbled a tire gauge, a metallic blanket, a tube of wet wipes—every safety device Mom had shoved in there. "Where's the registration?"

The cop knocked on the window. I rolled it down. From TV, I knew just what to say. "Can I help you, officer?"

"You can help me," he shouted, in a major rush of bad breath, "and yourself in the future, by pulling over when an officer has his lights flashing." Spit flew out of his mouth and landed on my hand.

"Jesus!" I wiped his gross spit on the car seat. "You don't need to be a dick about it."

Hard to say who yelled first: my grandmother, shouting, "Dylan!" or the cop, screaming, "Out of the car!" It was pretty much a tie.

Roanoke, VA

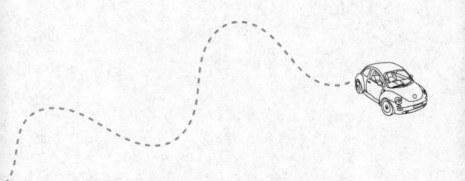

Chapter 10

Hope

As we drove through the green hills of the Shenandoah Valley, Jordan sang along to the Elvis CD, and I felt cracks developing in my aversion to Elvis. His soulful rendition of "Can't Help Falling in Love" got to me. I'd heard the song before, hundreds of times, but context changes everything. Now it collided with memories of Aaron.

I'd fallen so hard for him. In all the years since, I hadn't experienced those feelings with anyone else. It made no sense—I knew how the Aaron story ended, and it wasn't good. He hadn't been the person I'd imagined he was. Yet thoughts of him still crept in when I watched an old Cary Grant movie or indulged myself in a romantic novel. I've learned that you can love somebody truly, deeply, regardless of whether he deserves it.

As I quietly searched my bag for a tissue, my phone quacked, and my heart leaped from my chest. I snatched my phone from the console and stabbed frantically at my messages.

"What is it?" Jordan asked.

"Damn. CVS. I can get forty percent off one item."

"Honey, next time we stop, let me show you how to turn that shit off."

With my phone in hand, though, I did another check of email and social media. Dylan rarely used Facebook anymore. "It's been taken over by people *your* age," she complained. She preferred Instagram, though even there, she rarely posted.

My mother, in contrast, had thousands of Facebook followers, not to mention a deranged sycophant who ran her fan page. Olivia Grant's posts fell into three categories: Elvis news (amazingly, the man still generated it, decades after his death), soap opera gossip, and photos of kittens, because apparently kitten posts got the most likes. Mom also had a Twitter account, @WhatWouldAndromedaDo? Her followers tweeted their problems and Andromeda solved them. Trouble with an unruly teenager? Military school. Neighbors with a barking dog? Poison its kibble. Cheating husband? Rub his boxers in poison ivy.

I read a few of her old posts to Jordan. "They're meant to be funny, but still. The idea of my mother giving advice is scary."

Jordan was munching on roasted almonds. After a few minutes, she said, "Know what I find odd?" I waited as she finished chewing. "You're a good judge of character."

"You find that odd," I said. "Thank you."

"Hear me out. Remember when your colleagues at Edu-Learn were so excited about the new boss? The minute you met Gary, you knew he was a tool."

"Please let's not talk about Gary."

"Okay, okay. So think about the men you've dated over the years. The electrician . . . was that one Jim? Or was Jim the banker?"

"Both were Jim." I didn't want to talk about old boyfriends, either. Jordan claimed I went through men so quickly that she didn't bother to learn their names, only their professions: electrician, firefighter, merchant marine. "Get them together in a room, and they could sing 'YMCA,'" she'd once joked. I wasn't in the mood for that.

"My point," Jordan persisted, "is they were all decent, well-meaning types. The kind of guy who returns his shopping cart to the corral." She tapped her thumbs on the steering wheel. "So how did you not see that this Breckenridge guy was trouble?"

It was a question I'd often asked myself. "No idea. I worked closely with him for five months. I thought I knew him."

Jordan crunched her almonds. "I'm just surprised he turned out to be such a jerk."

"Me too."

UNFORTUNATELY, NOT TALKING about Gary didn't make him disappear. Our earlier phone call had excited his interest.

"Hope," he bellowed when I grudgingly picked up his next call. "Do you have a minute?" He didn't wait for an answer. "I've come up with an idea."

"For . . . ?"

"The used-book problem! I don't mean to steal your thunder. I'm just an innovator by nature."

I squeezed my eyes tight. "Great. Fire away."

"Coupons!"

"Sorry. What?"

"Sprinkled throughout the books. Students will tear out the coupons and voila! No resale."

"That's certainly . . . creative." I crossed my eyes comically at Jordan, who stifled a laugh. "I worry instructors won't like it much."

"They'll warm to it. They like free stuff, too. I'm giving this idea to you at no charge, Hope. You figure out how to execute. Send me a proposal tomorrow."

"I'll try, Gary. I'm on my way to Memphis."

"Memphis?" I couldn't blame him for his confusion. I never spoke of my hometown and didn't sound like a southerner. "You'll be back tomorrow, though."

Did he not understand where Memphis was? "I'll be gone the rest of the week." My email to him had mentioned only Thursday, but I was slowly adjusting to a new reality.

"Hope, the board meeting is Monday."

"I'll work this weekend," I added quickly. "You can call me anytime."

"I will. Remember, I took a chance on you." Gary loved nothing better than a good underdog story—an employee pulling something out of his or her butt to win the day. He believed his management style inspired this. "I know you won't let me down."

I hung up, thinking, *If I don't, Gary, you'll be the only one.*

WE'D PASSED SIGNS for Lexington, Virginia, when Jordan switched the radio to an NPR station covering the upcoming national conventions. "Noooo," I moaned. "Find another station. Whatever you want! Ricky Martin, Wham!, the Partridge Family. . . ."

Jordan clicked the radio off. "At least now I understand why you hate politicians," she said. "Though I do need to point out,

Hope, that it's a privilege to be able to ignore politics. Not all of us can afford to—"

"I know," I cut in. "Dylan lectures me all the time on my white, heterosexual, cisgender privilege. And it's not that I don't care or want to support the right causes—it's just easier not to hear Aaron's voice or see him on TV."

Jordan threw me a look. "It does beg the question: How in the world did you get involved with that man in the first place?"

I took off my sunglasses and wiped them on my T-shirt. This part of the story was innocent enough. "By accident. I needed a job."

"Wait—you were on his staff? How did I not know about this?"

"I wasn't paid at first, just a volunteer. It was soon after . . ." The words stuck in my throat, and I felt foolish. How many years had it been?

"After your dad died?"

I nodded. My father and George had remained close, even when George's relationship with his own father was strained and he'd moved to Boston. Dad and George exchanged letters, photos, Christmas gifts. When my father passed away during my last semester of college, George had returned to Memphis for the funeral. He'd seen firsthand what a wreck I was. For weeks, I could barely drag myself out of bed. I cut classes, skipped exams, didn't turn in papers. What George didn't know—what no one knew—was that I'd never graduated from the University of Memphis.

"I had a horrible time finding a job" was all I said. "I was so desperate, I applied at Kroger, and even they rejected me."

"Seriously? You'd have bagged groceries?"

"I needed to pay rent."

Jordan frowned. "Hope, I'm sorry. Your mother may be tight with a penny, but she wouldn't have let you starve."

"I refused to take money from my mother. We weren't on good terms back then."

Jordan nodded. "Oh, right. I forgot. You blamed her for what happened to your father."

"Well, not blamed her exactly . . ." I stopped to consider. "No, you're right, I blamed her." I lifted my phone for a quick check. "Let's not go there. I'm mad enough at her right now."

"Okay, but you still didn't explain how you ended up in politics."

"Oh, right. I started as a volunteer on Aaron's campaign . . ." I trailed off, still looking at my phone. Something new on my mother's Facebook page had caught my eye. "Shit."

"What?"

The photo she'd posted was of an Elvis-themed diner in western Pennsylvania—a place advertising Heartbreak Hamburgers and Hound Dogs. The caption said "Andromeda" might stop there. I switched to Google Maps and reviewed the options from Fairfield to Memphis. "I can't believe it," I shouted. "They took the longer route? Why?" I tugged at my hair. Had she done it on purpose? To lose me?

Jordan said nothing. I knew she wouldn't want to change course to follow them. I did and said so.

"Hope, that's crazy talk. Even if we made up the time we've lost and drove the exact same roads, the odds of catching sight of them are one in a million."

Jordan was right, but I couldn't let go. If there was any chance of stopping them before Memphis, I needed to try. "What are our options?"

"There are no options! You're just going to have to meet up with them in Memphis."

"I can't!" I was slapping my sunglasses against my leg in a way that probably wasn't good for them.

Jordan glared. "Don't be ridiculous."

"I can't go to Memphis!" I repeated. "I . . . signed an agreement."

She squinted so hard her eyes were slits. "I'm sorry. What?"

"I signed an agreement with Aaron. I promised to never return to Memphis."

"You're kidding, right?" She kept jerking her head to look at me. "A contract that says you can't go back to your hometown? Hope, that's not a thing."

"It's complicated. It's a long story."

"Well then," she said, signaling and swerving into the exit lane, "I need to hear it. We'll get dinner, and you'll start from the beginning and tell me everything. I mean it, Hope. Everything."

Chapter 11

Olivia

The girl was right: that cop was a dick. Still, I planned to have a stern talk with Dylan about the difference between being right and being stupid.

By the time I pried myself out of that clown car, the officer had cuffed Dylan and dragged her to his cruiser.

"Officer," I cried, all weak and warbly. Andromeda had used that shaky voice in Season 37, when the Libyan pirate tied her to the captain's chair before she broke free and clocked him with a whale bone. Yes, *The Light Within* had jumped the shark that season.

"Ma'am," yelled the cop. He had one hand on Dylan's head, ready to shove her inside his car. "I told you to stay put."

"I need . . . help." I dropped to my knees. My slacks would be filthy.

"She's out of oxygen!" Dylan shouted. I gave the girl credit. She was quick on the uptake.

A door slammed. No doubt Dylan was in the squad car now.

What was taking the man so bloody long? If I hadn't been faking, I'd have been dead.

As I clung to the open door, something under the passenger seat caught my eye. A jumble of papers. I slid them out. Several homework assignments, tests marked with a C or D, and—hallelujah—the registration. I placed it on the seat as footsteps approached.

Lights, camera . . .

I could have played the scene in my sleep. The coughing, the sucking for air. In Season 12, Andromeda had been trapped in a smoky elevator in a burning skyscraper, and in Season 23 (or was it 24?) she'd caught double pneumonia after her mobster boyfriend capsized his cigar boat in a frigid lake.

"Ma'am, do you need an ambulance?" The cop still sounded angry, like I was doing this for my amusement. Well, I was . . . but he didn't know that.

"My tank." I coughed. With a shaky hand, I pointed to the back seat.

The officer peered into the car suspiciously. Pushing the front seat forward, he lowered my portable tank to the ground, so I could switch the tubing. The old tank hadn't run out, but, again, the cop wouldn't know that.

"Thank you." I sucked in air with grateful gasps. "That's why . . . my granddaughter . . . was speeding. Had to . . . switch tanks."

The man responded, as expected, with a lot of blathering, his tone registering somewhere between grumble and shout. The girl shouldn't have done this, that, and the other thing. I made a big show of agreeing. Eventually, he got to the part I'd been waiting for. He'd let the girl off with a warning, this time, but she needed to obey speed limits and show proper respect. In other words, he didn't want to deal further with my medical issues.

After the officer helped me to my feet and returned to his car, I arranged myself in the Bug and waited. No doubt Dylan, when she returned, would be fuming. Or traumatized. Or both. That was okay. I'd happy her up.

I'd decided to give the girl a gift.

DINERS ARE MEANT to be fast, but nobody had told the staff at this one. The lone waitress was regaling truckers in the back with some long-winded story.

Dylan and I slid into the red Naugahyde booth. Keeping one eye on the blathering waitress, I removed the file folder from my bag and placed it on the table, keeping one hand on it, as if training a dog. Dylan needed to demonstrate patience and control. The girl started to reach out, then caught herself. That was okay. Self-control was a muscle. It could be strengthened.

The waitress was jabbering before she even arrived at our booth. When she came up for air, she leaned in to stare at me. "Your eyes are amazing. Are you . . . "

"Yes, I am," I said. "And I'll have iced tea, thank you."

"You didn't let me finish."

"You were going to ask if I was Andromeda."

She looked puzzled. "No, I wanted to know if you're wearing tinted contacts."

"In that case, the answer is no, and I'd still like the iced tea."

The waitress stepped back. "Hold on! Were you in—what was that soap?"

I forced a tight-lipped smile, nodded, and handed back the menu.

"I'm sorry," she gushed. "I didn't recognize you because of the . . ." She gestured across her face to indicate the cannula.

I'd had it. "Yes, and I didn't recognize you as a waitress because you're not actually waiting on anyone. Could you try to be more convincing in that role?"

The woman jerked her head back, as if slapped. She took Dylan's drink order and turned on her heel.

I tapped a finger on the folder. "Here's why I've been secretive about your father's identity, Dylan. I'm only making a guess. If I'm right, he's a public figure, a person of some importance. You cannot share this information with anyone." I slid out a copy of the Memphis *Commercial Appeal* article and pushed it toward Dylan. The headline read: "Breckenridge to Head Fundraiser. Senator a Likely VP Pick."

I'd seen the article last Sunday—a piece of luck, for sure. It reported that Memphis's favorite son, Senator Aaron Breckenridge, would headline two local events in the coming week: a fundraiser for city- and state-wide candidates Friday evening, and a speech at the University of Memphis on Saturday. Then all the stuff about him being a possible choice for vice president, a decision that could be announced any day.

I waited patiently as Dylan scanned the article, her brows knit. You couldn't predict Dylan. Sometimes quick, sometimes dreadfully slow. I pointed to his name: Aaron.

"No, I get it. But are you showing me this just because the guy's name is Aaron, and he's from Memphis?"

I closed my eyes and mentally counted to three. "I'm showing you this because your mother worked on his campaign for state legislature."

"Are you sure? Mom hates politics."

"Yes, I'm sure. That part isn't in question."

"Mom never mentioned it."

"Well, how surprising!"

Dylan bit off whatever she was about to say as the waitress returned. The woman placed our drinks on the table and took our order making no eye contact.

I inhaled deeply and adjusted my tone. "Your mom worked for this Breckenridge fellow after college. Hope didn't call me often in those days, but when she did, she sounded quite taken with him. I can't recall the specifics. To be honest, it wasn't so much what she said as how she said it. Your mother doesn't hide her feelings well."

"That doesn't prove . . ."

"What would you like, Dylan? TMZ footage? I told you it's an educated guess."

"And that's all it's based on?"

"That, and the fact that your mother quit her job with Breckenridge and left Memphis exactly eight months before you were born."

Dylan raised her eyebrows. Finally, the girl was interested.

"After she left the campaign, Hope phoned me from a friend's place in Nashville and insisted I play dumb if anyone wanted to locate her. I asked what any parent would: 'How much did you embezzle?' Got a rare laugh at that one." I closed the folder, jimmying it back in my bag. "All she'd say was that she'd had a falling out of sorts. Didn't want to talk about it."

"Well, that sounds like Mom. The not talking about it part."

"Yes, and here's the kicker. Shortly after Hope called, my agent received a phone message from Mr. Breckenridge asking to speak with me. He wanted to know how to get in touch with your mother. She'd left no phone number or forwarding address."

"Did you give it to him?"

"No. I respected your mother's wishes. I mean, who knew? Perhaps she *had* embezzled!" Dylan's jaw dropped. "I'm joking, Dylan."

"So you never talked to him? Breckenridge?"

"No. Sylvia played me his message, and I had her call back saying we had no information."

Dylan sipped her water. "The timing fits. And his name. But how can we know for sure if he's my father?"

"A reasonable question," I said. "I propose the most direct method."

"Which is?"

"You ask him."

Dylan collapsed back against the padded booth. "You want me to walk up to a US senator and ask if he's my father?"

"Not exactly. We'll work out the details later. But politicians are slippery, so it has to be done in person. We want to catch him off-balance."

Dylan fought to suppress a smile, but I could imagine the neurons firing, lighting her up from inside. Her father wasn't just alive. He was *somebody*.

The waitress brought our lunch and Dylan picked quietly

at her salad for a while before asking, "So why are we driving all the way to Memphis? We could have ambushed this guy in DC."

I offered my best pouty face. "Then I wouldn't have been able to visit Graceland."

The girl's laugh was full-throated. She was turning out to be a decent companion. For the briefest of seconds, I wondered if I could explain my plan for Graceland in a way Dylan could understand. Not yet. Maybe later.

I PULLED MY oxygen cart from under the diner's awning, lifting my face to the warm afternoon sun as Dylan retrieved the car. I could just devour bright, warm days like this. No telling how many more I'd have. I closed my eyes, tested my resolve. Yes, I could still carry out my plan for Graceland. Olivia Grant was no sentimentalist. I'd do what was best, even if in rare moments like this it made me a teeny bit sad.

As I settled myself in the Bug, Dylan flicked her head toward our waitress, smoking around the side of the diner. "I can't believe that woman recognized you. How long has that soap been off the air? Ten years?"

It's possible I clicked my seatbelt with more force than necessary. "Four. But it aired for nearly forty-five. So, really? Not so surprising." Pulling down the visor, I rubbed lipstick off my front teeth. "I'll have you know, Dylan, that at one time, everyone knew my face. I could barely eat in a restaurant. So many fans would stop by my table, my dinner would get stone cold."

"Wow. That sounds horrible."

I ceased rubbing, considered this odd comment. *Had* it been horrible? Annoying, perhaps. Especially those nights when I'd stayed home because it wasn't worth the trouble to go out. "It was also quite flattering, of course," I hurried to explain. "I couldn't shop for groceries without seeing my face on one tabloid or another."

"You and Mom are so different. She hates having her picture taken. She said just knowing her photo would be on a magazine cover would make her sick to her stomach."

"Well, lucky for Hope she's in no danger of that happening."

"So, how are we going to approach my father?" Dylan asked, in an apparent non sequitur that made my head spin. "He's kind of famous, right? We can't walk up to him on the street."

"No, of course not. Let me handle that. You concentrate on getting us there on time."

That seemed to satisfy Dylan, who shifted into the fast lane and sang along to "Heartbreak Hotel." A few dark clouds had rolled in and a smattering of raindrops hit the windshield. Dylan flipped on the wipers. I checked the gauge on my oxygen tank. I'd feel better once we got to the hotel, where the new tanks and concentrator would be waiting. And though it felt a tad obsessive, I twisted around to check the gauge on the tank behind Dylan's seat—the one the cop had helped me change. My memory was that it was half full.

Only it wasn't. My heart hammered as I checked the meter again. In the commotion with the cop, I must not have closed it all the way.

It wouldn't be enough.

Chapter 12

Hope

I pushed the combination plate closer to Jordan, who wasn't pulling her weight with the nachos. The Roanoke Mexican restaurant was quiet at this early dinner hour, the smell of chili powder and cumin wafting from the kitchen. Over the sound system, Waylon Jennings lamented his "Burning Memories." Jordan nudged the chips back toward me and leaned forward, her elbows on the table. No one was leaving until I coughed up the story I'd promised.

I started at the beginning.

AFTER MY FINAL, horrible semester at college, I'd been a mess, unable to find work. A local bakery had advertised for counter help, and when I headed in to apply, I ran into a former sorority sister gripping a large coffee in each hand. Veronica could talk a blue streak, and I pitied her coworkers if she planned to drink both. She'd graduated two years earlier, so she knew nothing about my father's death and its aftermath. When I told her about my frustrating job search, she said she was helping a guy running for Congress from Tennessee's 9th district and insisted volunteer work would beef up my resume. Before I could protest that I knew nothing about politics, she was leading me to campaign headquarters to give it a try.

As I trailed Veronica up the stairs to the third-floor walk-up, I was surprised by the graffiti, broken railings, and battered floorboards. At school, Veronica had bragged constantly about her brushes with the rich and famous, and I was certain she'd befriended me because of my mother, Memphis's Soap Queen. When she opened the door to the office, I couldn't picture Veronica working there. The place had once been an apartment, with kitchen cabinets painted an electric blue. Folding tables were piled high with computer printouts and a jumble of phones. Behind a Formica counter serving as a desk stood a sturdily built woman with a short blond afro. She was on the phone, breaking someone's balls over missing lawn signs.

Veronica waited for the drill sergeant to finish. "Our candidate, Aaron, is the underdog," Veronica whispered. "The incumbent is a jerk, but it'll take a minor miracle to unseat him."

"And Aaron is . . . a Republican?"

She looked at me aghast. "No, a Democrat. Aren't you?"

"Kind of apolitical. Will that be a problem?"

She shrugged. "Probably not. We're desperate. Just don't advertise it."

The sturdy woman hung up and sauntered over, sizing me up. "Who've we got here?"

Veronica said, "Shelley, this is Hope. She needs some office experience. Her resume is a disaster."

I shot Veronica a horrified look and thrust out my hand. "I'm a good writer."

Shelley squeezed it so tight I winced. "How are you at licking stamps?"

"Fabulous."

"I like your friend," she said to Veronica, then turned back to me. "When can you start?"

I glanced at my watch for no reason. "Now?"

"I take that back," Shelley said. "I adore your friend."

I stayed all day: stamping envelopes, folding fliers, proofing a mailing piece. The mindless work was soothing ointment for a soul scraped raw. I looked forward to meeting our candidate, this guy I was blindly helping. Veronica was reassuring. "You're going to just love Aaron."

I paused my narration, staring at the guacamole on my chip.

"And so you did," Jordan said.

"And so I did." I set down the chip. "Damn those Jedi mind tricks."

"I'm sorry, sweetie," she said. "Sorry you got hurt."

"No one to blame but me. I walked into it."

"Stop being so hard on yourself, Hope. You couldn't have known."

No, I explained to Jordan, there was definitely a moment on that first day, before I met Aaron, when I should have walked. Because Veronica, for all her nonstop chatter, had managed to bury the lede. As we descended the crooked stairs at the end of the day, I asked how she became involved in the campaign. She gave me a puzzled look, then mentioned a name I'd hoped never to hear again.

"Carly, of course. Didn't I say that? Aaron is engaged to Carly Boyd!"

"Great!" I beamed. But all I could think was *Shit, shit, shit.*

"So who is this Carly ho?" Jordan asked.

I struggled with how to describe Carly Boyd. She'd been a sorority sister at the U of M—my year, not Veronica's. Strawberry-blond and stunning, Carly was outgoing, hysterically funny, and hated me for no reason I could figure out. As best I could explain it to Jordan, Carly was a carnivore, and I was a leaf-eater. She saw me as prey.

Carly had an infectious laugh and was a wicked mimic. Her friends stayed close out of fear she'd turn on them. I knew Carly had money, though not the extent of it. The Aston Martin she drove should have been a clue. She'd lost her mother to cancer when she was only five—a pain I could empathize with, even though I'd lost my mother somewhat differently. Rumor was her father gave her anything she wanted except the time of day.

In fairness, Carly had a generous, giving side. She volunteered with disabled students at a local high school. Ever since she was sixteen, she'd taken two of those teens to the prom, helping the girl choose a beaded gown, the boy rent a tux, and the couple pose together for photos against glittery streamers. Her picture appeared in the paper with the new couple each spring.

I never should have joined that sorority. Veronica had talked me into pledging, certain the girls would be as enamored of my Soap Queen mother as she was. The pledges were invited to a huge party, and I decided that for once, I'd be the life of it. I drank and was loud, throwing my arms around my new friends to sing "American Pie," falling and laughing during the Electric Slide. The sorority sisters loved *that* Hope; unfortunately, she wasn't the same Hope who moved in sophomore year and reverted to her bookworm, quiet self. After leaving the dining room one night, I heard one girl whisper, "Wasn't she the one who was so much fun at the party?"

In the spring of that year, I came out of my room late one night and heard some girls laughing in the kitchen. As I descended the stairs, I realized they were poking fun at my Eeyore pajamas. The pj's were a gift from my father that apparently nobody but me found cute. "I feel so out of it," Carly was saying. "No one told me that Eeyore is the new Pooh!" She made another crack about my baggy sweatpants and Gap sweatshirts. Everyone laughed. I slunk back to my room.

That might have been the extent of it if I hadn't started dating one of Carly's old boyfriends in the fall of my senior year. I had no inkling it might be a problem until a sorority sister hinted, "I'd be careful about that if I were you." Another asked if I'd gotten Carly's "permission." I thought she was joking. Carly had been the one to dump him, after all.

One night I came home from the library and found Carly and a handful of her friends in the living room, leaning over a coffee table, listening to something on a tape recorder, and howling with laughter. Halloween was the next week, and the recording sounded frightening: whispers, moans, and screams like a woman being stabbed repeatedly. Finally, I understood: the recording was of a couple having sex. One of the girls looked up and noticed me. She whispered to the others. Carly looked away. The post-coital giggling and conversation continued. I realized the couple on the tape was Ben and me.

Someone apparently had placed a tape recorder under my bed, and though no one would identify the person responsible, I thought I knew. An anonymous Good Samaritan left the cassette on my desk, and I destroyed it, but the damage was done. The story had gotten around the school. I quit the sorority and searched for a room off campus. I could have moved home with my father—in retrospect, I'd have given anything if I had—but at the time, it seemed childish. I rented a room from a hair stylist named Ashlee who had three rotating boyfriends and asked if that would be a problem. I said nothing was a problem. I believed that. Until three months later, when my father died.

AFTER LEARNING WHO Aaron was engaged to, I probably shouldn't have returned to his office. I almost didn't. But I woke the next morning depressed about my job prospects and frustrated from having to tiptoe around one of Ashlee's boyfriends snoring on the sofa. I'd keep my promise to Shelley and work one more day. I liked Shelley. She'd gushed over a press release I'd rewritten and shared photos of her little boy, Owen, and her partner, Sandy. "Shelley and Sandy," she'd joked. "Why we don't live in Aruba is beyond me."

Aaron, on the other hand, I was prepared to dislike. What kind of person would marry Carly Boyd? I worried Carly might drop by and asked Shelley that morning about Carly's involvement with the campaign. She said Carly had never set foot in "this pit," and wanted nothing to do with politics. That said, Carly's father was Aaron's biggest backer, a real player in the party and the person who'd recruited Aaron to run. "Richest man in Tennessee," Shelley whispered. "You didn't hear that from me."

Shelley and I were alone in the office late that afternoon when I finally met Aaron. He barreled in and waved distractedly in my direction while calling out to Shelley that he'd located the missing lawn signs. His opponent's volunteers had been caught stealing them, he said, pounding the counter with glee. I didn't think Aaron was as good looking as Veronica had implied, but with his lanky frame and wavy dark hair the word "wholesome" came to mind. He reminded me of Tom Hanks in *Splash*. My father and I had loved that movie.

"Have you met our new volunteer?" Shelley asked as Aaron headed for the inner office.

He pivoted to look at me, then Shelley, then back at me. "You're not Kendall?"

I'd met Kendall earlier that morning. I wasn't thrilled to be mistaken for her.

Aaron rushed over, holding out his hand. "I'm so sorry. I thought we'd met. I'm Aaron."

"Hope," I said, shaking his hand.

"Perfect!" He grinned. "You don't happen to have a sister named Prayer, do you?"

I shook my head. "I once had a friend named Destiny, but she moved."

"No worries," he laughed. "Hope is just what we need."

I STOPPED THE story there, as Jordan and I needed to get back on the road. While Jordan signaled the waiter for our check, I had to smile at the irony.

As it turned out, I was the last thing Aaron Breckenridge needed.

Chapter 13

Dylan

Just as we passed a "Roanoke, 1 mile" sign, Olivia gasped and pitched forward in her seat.

"What's wrong?" I yelled. "Are you okay?"

Olivia waved at me to keep driving, so I did, but she kept taking in sharp little breaths followed by endless exhales. Like she had bad air in her lungs and couldn't get it out.

By the time I saw the sign for the Hampton Inn, I'd nearly missed the turn, and the Bug jumped the curb. At the hotel entrance, I drove onto the sidewalk and leaped from the car.

"Wait here," I shouted.

Stupid thing to say.

I sprinted to the check-in desk, pushing aside an elderly couple in matching golf outfits.

"I need help!" A young, bearded man was on the phone and held up one finger. "It's an *emergency*!" I shouted. "You have a package for Olivia Grant. Oxygen tanks. She can't breathe."

The man put down the phone. "Should I call an ambulance?"

"Just get the package! Now!"

He ran an eye over the reception area and checked under the counter before running his fingers across a keyboard. "I have a reservation for Olivia Grant. Nothing about a delivery."

"She had them sent here. Where are your packages delivered?"

"Right there." He pointed to a small FedEx box in the corner, clearly not big enough, and returned to the computer. "There's no note with the reservation." His head shifted between me and the screen like a Boomerang video. "I don't know what to tell you."

"*Shit!*" I slapped a hand on the counter and raced back outside, throwing open Olivia's door. Olivia was pulsing up and down in a horrible way. Her lips were blue.

"They don't have the tanks."

She closed her eyes and heaved forward in a hideous gasp for air.

"The hospital's five minutes away," shouted a voice behind us. The clerk had followed me. "Quicker than an ambulance." He pointed down the street. "Turn right, then go straight for about a mile, then left. You'll see it."

I jumped into the driver's seat and bounced the Bug off the curb. At the corner, the car in front of us stopped for a yellow light, and I laid on the horn. Snatching Olivia's phone from the console, I yelled, "I'm calling your oxygen company." I took Olivia's thumb and held it against the home screen to open it. I found Air Systems in Olivia's recent calls and pushed redial just as the light changed. "We are experiencing unusual call volume," the recording said. I pressed zero, and it went to voicemail. As we careened around the corner, I waited for the beep and screamed: "You idiot, douchebag, incompetent assholes. Can't you do a single fucking thing right?"

Rocking forward in her struggle for air, Olivia gave me a thumbs-up.

I THOUGHT OLIVIA would be fine once she was hooked up to oxygen. Even in the ER, though, her breathing was ragged, like she'd just run a 10K. Three doctors examined her. No one seemed real keen on talking to me, but from what I overheard, they were worried Olivia's "air hunger" episode had created other issues with her heart. An orderly wheeled Olivia out for tests.

When they returned, Olivia waved me close and whispered, "Take some money from my bag and get something to eat." Her voice was still raspy. "Circle back in half an hour. I'll see how fast I can get out of here."

"What about the tests? What if the doctors want you to stay?"

"Grifters, all of them," Olivia huffed. "They need to fill beds. If they can't find something wrong, they make it up."

I plucked a twenty from Olivia's purse and wandered the halls, pretending to study the black-and-white photos of old Roanoke while I tried to piece things together. How could Olivia leave the hospital? She needed her oxygen tanks. And now that it was after business hours, the freaking Airhead company wouldn't call back—especially since I'd been so busy cursing them out that I hadn't left a name and number.

Other questions worried me even more. What should I do if Olivia insisted she was fine, and the doctors said she wasn't? Mom claimed Olivia inhabited her own reality. Was that true? What if—here was a truly scary thought—*I* was actually the more responsible party on this trip?

Eventually I found the hospital cafeteria and bought a Greek salad, no feta. I snagged a table in the back next to a bulletin board full of boring shit about patients' rights. Searching through my bag, I picked out a pink-and-blue bumper sticker that said, "Trans Rights Are Human Rights," pulled off the backing, and stuck it across the bottom of the bulletin board. When I turned around, a young woman in scrubs was eating pizza at the next table and watching me. Shit. Was I in trouble? The woman smiled and lifted her chin in approval.

I grinned back. Before I became an activist, I'd been a nobody. Then I'd slashed that jizzbag's tires at school, and kids clapped me on the back, said I was ballsy. I felt like a woman of action, someone my father would've been proud of. Now I was going to meet him. I imagined his strong grip as we shook hands, the way his forehead would crease as we discussed important issues. I had lots of ideas, and as a senator—hell, maybe vice president—my father had the power to make those things happen. Most importantly, though, he'd love my spirit. Appreciate me for who I was, not the boring person Mom wanted me to be.

I picked up my phone, ready to give that oxygen company another piece of my mind—plus, a callback number—but my phone was already vibrating. The manager at the Hampton Inn had our packages. They'd been sent to the other Hampton Inn, out by the airport, by mistake. Did I want to come get them? Well, hell yeah!

When I got there, the hotel manager was so apologetic, she paid for our room and upgraded us to one with a balcony. Olivia was going to lose her mind. I drove back to the hospital blasting "That's All Right (Mama)" at full volume and brought a fresh oxygen tank to the ER in Olivia' cart. I'd help her get dressed and we'd leave. Maybe check out the minibar.

But the ER room where Olivia had been was empty. I asked at the desk for Olivia Grant, and the guy typed in her name, then excused himself. A woman accompanied him back and hovered behind him, scanning the screen. She moved around the counter to speak to me.

"I'm sorry, honey. There was a problem with your grand-mother."

Chapter 14

Hope

From the outside, the Tater Tot Motel and Grille in rural Virginia made me worry we'd been wrong to pass up the Super 8 twenty minutes earlier. Although the billboard-sized sign looked freshly painted and proudly offered free ice, the tater tots logo resembled nothing so much as a pile of dog droppings.

The office smelled like ketchup, apparently from the dark red scented candle on the counter. An old man hobbled in from a back room. A few tufts of white hair sprouted from the top of his head and his eyebrows turned up at the end like a Klingon's.

Before I could open my mouth, he said: "Only got one room left and it's got two twins." He gestured vaguely at our truck. "Feel free to push 'em together, if you and the mister prefer."

I glanced back at the truck, wondering how Jordan would feel about sharing a room with me, and also what the motel owner would say if he saw my mister. Right on cue, the truck door opened, and Jordan emerged, her arms clasped behind her, stretching forward and back. "Let me check with my friend," I said.

I told Jordan I was fine to keep driving, but she yawned. "I'm okay sharing a room if you are, Hope. It's after nine and I'm pooped. I could sleep on a sidewalk." We'd lost almost an hour when, twenty minutes outside Roanoke, I realized I'd left my wallet in the restaurant. We'd had no choice but to retrace our steps.

Back inside, I handed the man my credit card and waited for him to say he'd been wrong, that room was taken. He didn't. As he ran my card, though, he watched out the window as Jordan did tai chi. With a sly grin, he handed me the receipt to sign.

"Your friend—she wouldn't happen to be a performer, would she?"

I almost said no, she was an auto mechanic—maybe like the one who fixes your car, because, really, do you know what your mechanic wears on weekends? But I was tired. My tight-lipped smile was a nonanswer.

"I know'd it," he said with pride. "I seen a great show over in Louisville with a big gal like that."

I had no idea what kind of show he'd seen and wasn't going to ask. I slid my receipt from the counter and left.

THE PANELED ROOM was unremarkable if you didn't count the bright orange bedspreads and Mr. Potato Head wall clock. Exhausted from worry and lack of sleep, I longed to pull the blanket over my head and melt into oblivion. Unfortunately, I needed to get started on that presentation for Gary. As Jordan unloaded her toiletries, I tossed my laptop into my bag and slung it over my shoulder.

"I'm going to check out the Tater Tot Grille. See if they serve anything that isn't alliterative."

"Oh, don't be so damn picky, Hope," Jordan called after me. "Just go with the tuna tartare."

Outside, the sun had set behind the huge motel sign, and a pink haze rested on the distant hills. Procrastinating, I unlatched the gate on the chain-link fence to take a closer look at the pool and sat on the end of a chaise lounge. Discarded towels were draped over plastic chairs and a solitary pool noodle floated in the deep end. The water, illuminated by pool lights, was turquoise yet oddly opaque. A few years back, when a Boston woman had lain dead in the deep end of a public swimming pool for two days before anyone noticed, I'd wondered how that was possible. Now I knew.

After that tragedy, the media had been full of articles about drowning, reminding people that a swimmer's distress is harder to recognize than one would think. A drowning person doesn't shout or flail their arms. Instinct takes over, prioritizing breathing so the person can't call for help, and forcing their arms to the side to keep their head above water.

This wasn't news to me. Years earlier, in the wake of my father's death, I hadn't thrashed about or called for help, but quietly slipped under. It was Aaron who'd thrown me a rope. Working for him had given me purpose, a reason to get out of bed each day. Something—someone—I believed in.

By MIDSUMMER, MY responsibilities on Aaron's campaign had snowballed. It had nothing to do with skill—I was simply putting in more time than anyone else. I drafted personal letters to supporters and likely voters. I clipped newspaper articles about high-school scholars and athletes, laminated them, and mailed them to parents with our congratulations. Impressed by my initiative, Shelley gave me a key to the office and had me supervise the phone volunteers while she canvassed with Aaron. Veronica made a snide remark about my promotion, but she put in half the time I did and gossiped more than worked.

I returned to the office in the evenings, eager to hear Shelley's and Aaron's canvassing stories. We pulled beers from the minifridge and opened bags of Tostitos. The energy of the campaign lifted me up, and I offered my own ideas. What about meet-the-candidate backyard barbecues? Wasn't a new park being dedicated in East Memphis? Should we go to that? What could we do to make a splash at the Fall Festival? Shelley and Aaron praised and encouraged my suggestions. Walking home after our meetings, I wanted to skip down the sidewalk.

Through Aaron, for the first time, I became interested in political issues. Aaron believed deeply in bipartisanship and thought people of integrity from both parties should work hard to compromise and find common ground. He worried that the politics of hate was taking us down a bad road and recalled the unlikely friendships of Tip O'Neill and Ronald Reagan, or Ted Kennedy and Orrin Hatch. Coming from a family of hunters, he supported people's right to own handguns and rifles, but was determined to get automatic weapons off the street. And probably because of his graduate degree in geology, Aaron was already, in 1998, concerned about global warming, and promoting sources of clean energy. In his carefully researched positions, I found something I could believe in.

My feelings about the man himself were more complicated. Aaron was good with people—funny, charismatic, charming—but he also knew it. He was a little too sure of himself for my taste. I watched him lose his temper more than once over the tactics of his opponent, and although Shelley stopped him from doing anything rash, her furrowed expression told me she worried. Sadly, none of that got in the way of the little crush on him I was nursing. Aaron was a good listener and I delighted in making him laugh. He always asked what I was reading, or what movies I'd seen, and begged for stories about my crazy roommate and her rotating boyfriends. Once, as I pointed to a problem in the database and he leaned in, putting his hand over mine to control the mouse, sweat broke out along my hairline.

Still, I told myself my little crush on Aaron was harmless. The man was engaged, after all. To a woman who hated me.

One Friday, Shelley and Aaron took the night off, and I was alone in the office, updating the database and feeling a little blue. I wandered into the tiny inner room and opened Aaron's desk drawers. Bins of pens, Post-its, and paper clips were meticulously organized. Below them was a drawer with a boxed dressed shirt and three rolled ties. On a bookshelf I found a boombox and small stack of CDs. Two were Bob Dylan albums. My father had loved Dylan, and I'd grown up with his music.

I shouldn't have brought the CDs and boombox back to where I was working. When Dylan began singing "Time Passes Slowly," one of my dad's favorite songs, my eyes filled, and I lowered my head onto my folded arms.

The CD had been finished for several minutes when I heard a key turn in the lock. I was upright and blowing my nose when Aaron appeared. He started to say something, then stopped.

"It's not the work," I said quickly, wiping under my eyes.

"Good," he said. "Because if my campaign has this effect on people, I may need to rethink things."

"It was the song." I stopped, afraid my voice would break.

He squinted, confused.

"Sorry." I lifted the boombox from the floor to the table. "I borrowed your Bob Dylan CD."

"Dylan did this to you?"

His face was so serious, I couldn't help smiling. "My father was a huge fan. He died earlier this year and I've had some trouble getting past it." I pressed my mouth tight to regain control. "Probably more than is healthy." I made it through the sentence, barely.

"Losing a parent is hard." I'd heard Aaron mention his dad in speeches but had no idea if his parents were still alive. "Maybe you could use a break," he said. "Why don't we go get coffee next door? We can talk about Dylan." He added hastily, "Or not, if that makes it worse."

"You must have tons to do."

"Not till eight thirty. I'm taking my fiancée to a movie. She won't mind if we have coffee first."

I was pretty sure she would, but I grabbed my sweater and followed.

Turns out it's hard to have coffee with a guy running for Congress. Two firefighters, a young couple, and an elderly woman using a walker stopped by our little table to shake his hand. I nearly spat my coffee when the woman asked if I was Aaron's fiancée. He joked I was a campaign volunteer who only got paid in caffeine. After she left, he said, "We're not going to be able to talk here. Let's take the coffee back to the office."

Outside, though, the sweet smell of barbecue filled the air and a gentle breeze cut through the day's humidity. I didn't want to return to the office. I suggested we walk a couple blocks to a small park overlooking the Mississippi.

I often brought my lunch to this park, with its gorgeous oak trees and benches tucked randomly into curves of the paths. Scattered throughout were some historical markers, cannons, a large statue. We found an empty bench and sipped our coffee. Aaron asked about my father.

How could I describe my dad? A man who read me the entire Lord of the Rings series, beat me at Scrabble, and helped me with thousand-piece jigsaw puzzles. After my mother returned to her soap opera, my dad and I ate dinner most nights on TV trays, watching *The Light Within*, which our housekeeper videotaped daily, and then some seventies rerun, like *The Odd Couple* or *M*A*S*H*. The sound of my father's nasal, honking laugh made everything funnier.

Aaron said his dad was an ex-Marine who later trained as a Presbyterian minister and died in a hunting accident when Aaron was thirteen. His father had been soft-spoken but firm and highly principled—a role model to his son, whom he took on long hikes and camping trips. "I still talk to him, ask his advice on things. Do you think that's crazy?"

"Depends," I said. "Does he respond?"

He grinned. "You sound like my fiancée. She's a skeptic, too." A breeze on the back of my neck made me shiver. Had Aaron mentioned my name to Carly? I knew I had to say something soon before it was too late.

"The day my father died, he sent me a sign." He tilted his head to watch my reaction, then continued. "The afternoon of his hunting accident, I went completely numb. I didn't know what to do. I wandered deep into the forest behind our house, and standing there, right in the middle of the path, was this amazing buck with, I swear, antlers this big." Aaron held out both arms. I widened my eyes, impressed. "The sun was shining through the leaves, and the buck's head and neck were shimmering. I stood there and it looked right at me. I knew it was my father telling me that he was okay."

"Amazing." Although I didn't believe in signs, it was clear Aaron did, and I respected that. "I wonder what sign my father would have sent me, since we didn't hike." I laughed. "Maybe an *Odd Couple* rerun."

Aaron shrugged. "Or a Bob Dylan song."

That sent a shiver up my spine. I picked off a leaf that had blown onto my skirt. "My father's favorite song was 'Time Passes Slowly,' about the unhurried pace of life in the mountains. It reminded him of his childhood around Gatlinburg. Do you know it?"

"Well, that *was* my CD," he said, rolling his eyes. "I won't sing it for you, though. For that, you should be thankful."

"I'm not sure it's Dylan's singing that makes the song."

"Hey, hey, hey," he warned. "Watch that."

"Oh, I love Dylan's lyrics. Very poetic. My father wanted to name me after him, but my mother didn't like Dylan for a girl."

"I love the name Dylan, girl or boy," Aaron said, sipping his coffee. "And that song is one of my favorites, too. There's a line at the end, something about staring straight ahead and trying hard to stay on the right path. Sounds like something my father would say. Keep moving toward what's right." He wiped a drip off the side of his cup. "It can be hard to do in politics. More complicated than it seems."

"Hard to do in life," I agreed. "More complicated than it seems."

We were both silent. I thought about the disagreement Aaron had with Shelley two nights earlier. Someone had given Aaron dirt on his opponent, a man whose business dealings were underhanded and arguably illegal. Aaron wanted to make the information public, even though leaking it might compromise our source. He argued that the incumbent was scum, with ties to every unsavory element in Memphis. Taking him down was for the greater good—the end would justify the means. Shelley disagreed, insisting they keep their campaign positive and above reproach. "We won't sell our souls," she said. Aaron deferred to her, but I had the sense that he wasn't happy. The next day, when I mentioned the argument, Shelley shook her head. "Aaron is more ambitious than he seems," she said. "We need to watch that."

Aaron tipped his head back for the last swig of coffee, then crumpled the cup. "I'd better go. I'm meeting Carly in fifteen minutes. Can I walk you back to the office?"

It was now or never. I had to come clean. I screwed up my face, as if having trouble with my memory. "Did I mention that Carly and I were in the same sorority at the U?"

"Really? You know Carly? No, you never told me that."

"I doubt she'd remember me." I was downplaying it, hoping he might not say anything to Carly. "I was the quiet type."

"Yeah." He laughed. "Carly's definitely not the quiet type."

As we walked back toward the office, silently, enjoying the beautiful evening, I made excuses for why Aaron had fallen for Carly. She blinded people with her charm and drew them closer to her with confidences and quick-witted barbs. Aaron was thirty-two, a decade older than me, but he'd done his graduate work in geology in the Yukon and served five years in the Marines. I wondered if he might be a little naive about women. He shrugged off Carly's shopping sprees and lack of interest in his campaign as if most women were like that. Something very old school there.

I asked what movie he and Carly were going to see.

"No idea." He grinned. "She'll tell me when I get there."

THE SOUND OF giggles woke me from that memory. The moon had risen above the Tater Tot Motel and in the dusky light, a young couple unlatched the pool gate. The man carried a bottle of wine and plastic cups; the bikini-clad woman held towels. They were headed for the hot tub, and the woman shrieked when I moved from the shadows. I assured them I was leaving and scooted out the gate.

A phone was ringing nonstop in the dark motel office and reminded me I should check my own landline at home. Almost no one used that number, including me, and it took three tries to access my voicemail. When I finally succeeded, though, I had a message. A woman named Brenda from someplace in Roanoke, Virginia. Her soft voice was hard to hear, and my first thought was Crap, what else did we leave at that Mexican place? But no. Something about my mother.

Shit, shit, shit.

I raced back to the room and dumped out my purse on the bed to find a pen. I managed to play the message again without deleting it and took down the number.

Jordan emerged brushing her teeth. I was surprised she was still awake. "Wha'a matter, sweetie?" she asked as my shaky fingers hit the wrong button and I swore. "Wha' wrong?"

"Some hospital in Roanoke has my mother. Shit! I hate these menus." Finally, a human being picked up. When I repeated the message I'd received, he put me on hold and then transferred me. Jordan spit out the toothpaste and brought me a glass of water. "I can't believe this." I moaned. "We were just in Roanoke! I thought my mother and Dylan went the other way."

After two more transfers, a woman with a heavy Scandinavian accent answered. "I'm so sorry you've been passed around," she said. "Unfortunately, the situation has changed."

"Changed how?"

"We've lost your mother."

Chapter 15

Dylan

I was gasping by the time I skidded around the corner into the hospital room where the nurse said they'd put Olivia. I nearly collided with a technician wheeling out some monitor. "Be careful!" the woman snapped.

Olivia was propped up in bed. Her eyelids fluttered, as if she could barely hold them open. "They drugged me." Her words slurred together, like she was drunk.

"They said you had a panic attack."

She lifted a hand in a half-hearted *whatever!* It flopped back down. "Told them I couldn't stay. Wouldn't take no for an answer." She reached for her phone on the side table and knocked it off. "Hampton Inn called."

"I know! I have your oxygen tanks and the new concentrator." I picked up her phone and sat in the chair beside her. "What happened? Why did you freak out?"

"Can't stay in hospitals."

"Your insurance won't pay for it?"

"Not that." Olivia shook her head wearily. "Long story." She closed her eyes again, and I assumed that was the end of it until I heard her murmur, "Last time I woke up in a hospital, my daughter was dead."

OLIVIA MADE A popping sound when she slept, like spaghetti sauce starting to boil. I slunk down farther in the chair. At first, Olivia's words had scared the living crap out of me. What did she mean, her daughter was dead? What a creepy-ass thing to say. Then I realized it was the drugs talking. The doctors must have given her some good shit. As soon as Olivia dropped that bombshell, she'd conked out, and I'd checked my phone. Nothing was wrong with my mother. In fact, Mom was texting me nonstop. Verifiably not dead.

I wanted to get to the hotel, but when I jiggled Olivia's arm and said her name, her eyes opened to little slits, then closed again.

"The sedative should wear off soon. They didn't give her much." The shadowy figure in the doorway stepped inside. It was the same nurse I'd seen in the cafeteria. "When your grandmother panicked, she tried to rip out her IV. The orderlies had to tackle her."

"Can't we do something to wake her up? We need to get going."

"I don't think so, but the doctor will come through soon. You're welcome to wait."

Like I had a choice.

I slumped back in the chair and picked up my phone. For the first time all day, I had time to kill, so I Googled Aaron Breckenridge. Since the diner, I'd managed only a quick glance at his photo. He had wavy dark hair like me—well, when mine wasn't pink—and a single dimple. Now I went to his Senate website and pored over his bio. The man was an ex-Marine who'd done geology graduate work in the Yukon, which wasn't exactly living in a yurt, but closer than I'd expected. In terms of his politics, though, I found little about the issues that interested me, like #MeToo or LGBTQ rights. On Twitter, Breckenridge posted stuff about tax breaks for small business owners and improving veterans' hospitals. Blah, blah, blah, shoot me now.

Switching to Google Images, I discovered a photo of him and his wife. So he *was* married. His wife was pretty good-looking for someone my mother's age. I clicked on a photo of Breckenridge with a boy at a Little League tournament. The caption said the kid's name was A.J. Aaron junior, no doubt. Ick. A different shot showed him with two boys. The other one was probably Chase, or Blaine, or, God help me, Zander. But no, when I clicked on the photo, it said his younger son's name was Dylan.

I WAITED AN hour while Olivia slept. When I couldn't stand it any longer, I tried gently shaking her arm and whispering her name. I nearly lost my shit when suddenly, with a loud scraping of metal rings, the curtain was yanked aside by a hugely pregnant doctor. The woman started talking to Olivia before she was fully awake, pumping a pedal to raise the top of the bed. She introduced herself as Dr. Chu and ordered me to leave. Olivia, her voice still hoarse, insisted I stay.

Being that pregnant must be a bitch because Dr. Chu was cranky as hell. The woman's navel looked like a cork about to pop through her tight scrubs As she checked Olivia's heartbeat, sliding the stethoscope down the back and front of her gown, I explained that we had Olivia's oxygen tanks now, so we should be all set. Doctor Downer didn't even respond.

"Your blood work showed dehydration," she told Olivia. "Probably from when you were breathing so hard, though maybe just from traveling. Did you bring water in the car?"

"I certainly can do that going forward." Olivia's voice was steadier now, and her tone was polite. "Air and water are two things I should be able to control."

"And yet," the doctor said crisply, "here you are." Perched on a stool, her belly pressed against a portable desk, Dr. Chu typed into her laptop. "I want you to stay the night, so I can keep an eye on you."

I started to interrupt, and Olivia shook her head quickly. "I can't do that," Olivia said. "We're on a schedule."

"You can change your schedule. Your EKG was abnormal when you came in. I'm going to order more blood work so we can rule out an MI."

"MI?" Olivia huffed. "I already have COPD. Aren't those enough letters?"

"Funny," the doctor said, though she didn't smile. "Myocardial infarction. Your low oxygen might have caused a heart incident. I need to make sure before I let you go—especially since, apparently, I'm releasing you into the care of a teenager."

I noticed a slight pause before Olivia replied, "Of course," in a voice that was hard to decipher. Annoyed? Resigned?

The doctor was reading something on her laptop. "When you were incapacitated, we phoned your emergency contact. Hope Robinson?" Olivia wouldn't meet my panicked stare. "I'd feel better releasing you to her care. Let's see what tomorrow brings."

As soon as the doctor left, I let loose the string of f-bombs I'd been holding in.

"Dylan, calm down. We're going to be fine." Olivia shot a glance over her shoulder. "I've busted out of tougher joints than this."

Chapter 16

Hope

"You *lost* her?" I yelled into the phone. "What does that mean? My mother . . . died?"

"No, no!" the hospital administrator replied. "Sorry! I mean, literally, lost her. We can't find her."

I lowered myself onto the bed. Jordan had spit out her toothpaste and stood behind me, her hand on my back. "I don't understand," I said.

"Her granddaughter wheeled her to the cafeteria, and they must have left the hospital together. Security is checking the video. We believe your mother left willingly, though, of course, we can't be sure."

Of course she did. Massaging one temple, I tried to refocus. "Why was she in the hospital?"

The woman read through the doctor's notes. Apparently, my mother's portable oxygen supply had run out, and they'd resolved that issue, but wanted to keep her for observation. Unfortunately, the doctor treating her had gone into labor two hours earlier. Maybe one of the ER doctors could call me? The woman didn't sound terribly confident.

I squeezed my eyes shut and said that wouldn't be necessary. "I think I have a pretty clear picture."

The woman heard this as criticism. "Well," she scolded, "your mother should not have taken off like that. There are procedures. She could have signed herself out against physician's orders."

Just what I needed—to be yelled at for my mother's misbehavior. I hung up.

JORDAN WENT TO bed, but I was too rattled to sleep and headed off again to the Tater Tot Grille. I nabbed a booth in the back and asked for coffee. And then, screw it, a side of tater tots.

Roanoke? *Roanoke?* We'd had *dinner* there. How the hell could my mother be in Virginia, when according to her Facebook post, she'd stopped at some Elvis-themed diner near Pittsburgh? I opened Facebook and reread her post. It was vaguer than I'd remembered, saying only that Olivia Grant *might* drop by. I Googled the diner. The photo she'd posted was a screenshot from their website. I slammed the laptop shut. My mother was deliberately throwing me off their trail.

I ran through our options, but nothing had changed. They'd probably left Roanoke already. All Jordan and I could do was stay the course and try to beat them to Memphis. I had to keep them from going anywhere near Aaron.

The tater tots arrived, hot, golden, salty, and crisp. I inhaled them, then opened my notes on Gary's project. "Coupons" was all I'd written. Ugh. How could I make coupons in a textbook less tacky? Perhaps something from Staples or OfficeMax, to help students buy school supplies? Special offers from Dell and Apple? Maybe we could work with Barnes & Noble, to get discounts at their campus bookstores. I listed a few more ideas, suggested how we might partner with those organizations, drafted an email to Gary, and hit send. I prayed it would be enough to appease him. Show him I was on the job.

I ordered one more cup of decaf and gave myself permission to type Aaron's name into my browser. It had been several months since I'd done this, and not surprisingly, the search linked me to a dozen op-eds on possible vice presidential candidates. Aaron was the most moderate choice, which could be a plus or minus. Several commentators claimed his popularity was all about character. Aaron was principled, for sure, but Shelley had often reined him in—fought his impulse to go after his opponent with guns blazing, using every tool at his disposal. She'd argued against leaking that dirt even as he argued the end result would justify the means. No denying Aaron was ambitious. I'd learned that the hard way.

I clicked on a few more links. A *New York Times* op-ed said Aaron's record was "so clean it squeaks." An NPR interview hit on the same point, with the interviewer asking, "Are there no skeletons in your closet, Senator? None?"

"My life is an open book," Aaron had replied.

I closed the laptop with more of a snap than I'd intended.

If that's so, Aaron, it's only because you've ripped out some pages.

I slept terribly and hauled myself out of bed just before seven, throwing on cutoffs and a clean T-shirt. My stomach sloshed around like a washing machine. If lack of sleep and nonstop worry weren't the culprits, the four cups of coffee—two regular, two decaf—I'd downed at the Tater Tot had pushed it over the edge. And yet, somehow, my solution was more coffee.

I was determined to leave the motel as quickly as possible, and had my bag packed, but was torn about waking Jordan. The shadow of a wig on top of the dresser encouraged me to give her space. Hand on the doorknob, I called out: "I'm getting some coffee at that convenience store down the road. Can I bring you anything?" Subtext: we'd be eating on the fly again.

I expected a groggy reply, but Jordan was awake. "Big and black, please. And the largest muffin they have."

"Will do. I'd like to get on the road as soon as possible."

"Roger that. Ready in a flash."

I appreciated her enthusiasm, even if I didn't quite believe the time estimate. She'd told me once how long it took her to shower, shave everything, fix her hair, and apply makeup. I was prepared to be grateful if she was ready in under an hour.

The Food 'N Fuel convenience store offered pump-your-own coffee and a unique assortment of muffins including pistachio and apple chai. The girl behind the counter had hair streaked with periwinkle blue and a lower lip pierced by an arsenal of metal. Two studs hanging from her nose looked to me like dripping snot. I trained my eyes on the muffins.

"Any you'd recommend?"

She cupped a hand to her mouth, as if someone in the empty store might hear us. "Stick with the blueberry."

"Okay, two blueberries," I whispered back. I added, "I like your hair," even though I didn't, at least no more than I liked Dylan's. This was exactly what Jordan accused me of—saying stuff to please people. But I'd felt the need to say something, and her hair was more attractive than the artillery.

Outside the store, I rested the coffees and muffins on a picnic table. Jordan wouldn't be ready yet, so I took a seat, punched open my coffee lid, and sipped. No aroma. It tasted like coffee-flavored water. I considered asking for my money back but decided not to. The girl had reminded me of Dylan.

I stared down the road at a line of billboards promoting a law firm, two local candidates, and a new breast cancer facility. I paused on the last one. It made me think again of Shelley. Had she been one of the lucky ones?

AARON'S CAMPAIGN HAD taken a sucker punch to the gut in late August when Shelley was diagnosed with a malignant breast tumor and needed a radical mastectomy. She told us this early one morning as she and Aaron were leaving to canvass for the day. Even Veronica was too shocked for words, and Aaron hugged Shelley and told her to go home, take some time off. Wiping at an eye, she insisted that was the last thing she needed. She grabbed her bag of brochures, headed for the door, and called back to Aaron, "Get a move on, lard ass."

Shelley interviewed three candidates to replace her, but none were even remotely a good fit. Aaron decided we would make do until Shelley recovered and split her job between Veronica and me. I was shocked when Aaron added us to the payroll. I asked Shelley how this would work with our stretched-to-the-limit budget, and she assured me it would be fine, though she didn't elaborate.

Veronica's nonstop talking made her a nightmare at door-to-door canvassing, so Aaron and I took to the streets together, every day from ten to four. We chatted up old men in bed-room slippers, women in gardening gloves, and beer-bellied guys pushing lawn mowers. Most folks were cordial, though a few griped about roads or taxes or too much government. One geezer who interrupted Aaron every time he started to speak said, "Well, I still ain't voting for you, but I'll shake your hand." Another woman screamed at him and threatened to write a letter to the newspaper. After she slammed the door in our faces, Aaron deadpanned, "That went well."

I wasn't the relaxed schmoozer Aaron and Shelley were, so I took notes while Aaron did the talking. At the end of the day, Shelley would call me from her hospital bed or living-room recliner to go over the numbers. The work was both exhausting and oddly exhilarating.

The fact that my feelings for Aaron were straying danger-ously toward the romantic was neither here nor there. He was engaged. I tried not to twist everything he said about Carly into a fantasy that he was growing frustrated with her and checked my elation when I learned that he and Carly didn't live together. Apparently, Carly had a part-time job coaching gymnastics an hour from Downtown Memphis and preferred to hang by her dad's pool while Aaron worked day and night on the campaign. "Plus," he added, "she thinks my apartment is a dump."

As Aaron drove us to canvass in Millington one morning, he said, "Oh, by the way, Carly does remember you."

My heart sank. "She didn't like me much," I blurted.

He puckered his mouth into a that's-absurd face. "You're imagining things. Carly can come off as judgmental some-times. I don't think she means to. It all depends on her mood. She and I have definitely disagreed on people."

I felt certain I was one of them.

I gripped the armrest and asked if Carly minded that he drove around all day with another woman.

Aaron fiddled with the radio, trying to get a weather forecast. "I don't think so. She never minded that Shelley came everywhere with me."

Shelley was pushing fifty and in a committed relationship with another woman. I didn't think the situation was comparable. Part of me was devastated that he did.

The other part of me heard, with interest, that he hadn't specifically told her.

Not long after that conversation, Aaron took off a Sunday afternoon to spend with Carly. "So she doesn't dump me." The next day, he looked like shit. When he couldn't focus on my copy for a mailing piece, he apologized. "Carly and I had a little blowup last night. Still trying to find my equilibrium."

"I'm sorry," I said, though I wasn't.

"The campaign hasn't been easy for her. She hardly sees me."

"Should we . . . get her involved?" I asked, planning to kill myself if he said yes.

"Oh, God, no." He laughed. "She'd be a horrible distraction. She demands my full attention."

I WAS STILL clutching my coffee on the picnic table—though not drinking it—when a shuffling behind me made me sit up straight. The blue-haired girl from the convenience store was striding toward me, a large cup in each hand.

"I'm so happy I caught you," she said. "That coffee was horrible. I made you two new ones."

I thanked her, and she trotted back to the Food 'N Fuel. I stood and headed back toward the motel. Even from a distance, I could make out a tall figure in a mint-green skirt hoisting our suitcases into the truck. I checked my watch. I'd been gone less than twenty minutes.

"Bless you, Jordan," I whispered.

THE BLUEBERRIES THEMSELVES were fresh and tart, but the muffin crumbled into a million pieces. We were headed toward Knoxville, driving through some gorgeous green hills and valleys. I must have passed through here when I'd left Memphis almost eighteen years earlier, but I had almost no memory of that trip. A flat tire somewhere in Maryland. A new box of tissues purchased at each stop.

As we passed another hospital sign, Jordan asked, "Do you think your mom's really okay?" For all her joking about Diva Olivia, Jordan was fond of my mother. In May, they'd had a ball watching the Daytime Emmys together. They'd rated all the gowns on a scale of exquisite to wouldn't-wear-it-on-a-bet.

Jordan's question was fair. When I'd checked my landline messages again, I'd discovered an earlier message from the hospital saying my mother had suffered a panic attack, asking me to call. "No idea if she's okay."

My answer must have sounded short, because she added, "I realize you're pretty upset with Olivia right now."

I sighed. "That's how Mom and I work. We take turns upsetting each other." I crumpled my muffin paper. "Or maybe 'disappointing' is a better word."

"Hope . . ."

"What? It's true."

Jordan sighed. "I'm sorry that having Olivia as a mother made you feel somehow not worthy."

I let out a long exhale. "It's not that I feel unworthy, exactly. Just not . . . enough." When I glanced over, Jordan was frowning. "That's the best I can explain it. I've never felt that I was enough for her." I hadn't been enough for Aaron, either.

Jordan reached over and patted my hand. "You're plenty for me, Hope."

"Thanks." I mustered a weak smile.

Probably sorry she'd taken the conversation down this road, Jordan switched on the radio. As we listened to Hall and Oates beg Sara to smile, I thought about something I'd overheard when I was maybe seven or eight. My dad and I had picked up my mother at the airport, late. I'd been dozing on and off in the back seat until I heard my mother, all excited, say she'd shown my photo to an agent who thought I could be the next Punky Brewster.

My father shot a look to the back seat to confirm I was sleeping. "Livvy, that's nuts. Hope can't even bear to sit for school photos. I had them retaken twice, and she still has this pained look on her face, like she desperately needs to pee."

"She'll learn."

"No, she won't." His voice was warm but firm. "You have to let Hope be Hope. Otherwise, we shouldn't have had her."

My beloved father would have been devastated to know that whenever I replayed that conversation in my mind, it was in his voice that I heard, "We shouldn't have had her."

Chapter 17

Olivia

What a world! Who thought I'd see the day I'd be delighted to wake up in a Hampton Inn?

Hoisting myself out of bed with an unbecoming grunt, I steadied my feet on the dizzying striped carpet and scanned the queen bed next to me for signs of life. Dylan had to be somewhere under the mountain of blankets and comforter. God help us if the girl had stayed up all night watching an *Erin Brockovich* marathon.

I detached my cannula from the oxygen concentrator and hooked it to one of the new portables, still chuckling over the bossy, prego-saurus doctor who'd wanted to impound me in that hospital. I'd shown her. After she'd waddled off, I asked permission for Dylan to take me to the cafeteria in a wheelchair. Once there, I'd changed into my own clothes in the restroom, and Dylan and I had strolled out the front door.

Well . . . Dylan had strolled. I shuffled. The whole hospital experience had knocked the wind out of me. I could admit to that.

Hospitals gave me the heebie-jeebies. Nursing homes, too. I refused to pass from this life into the next smelling of disinfectant and pee, my last act on earth drinking apple juice through a straw. That was how people ended in such places—not with a bang, but with a diaper.

I'd seen that kind of death before. My beloved father had wasted away from Lou Gehrig's disease, and I had no intention of following in his footsteps. I'd direct my own final act, thank you very much. That hospital experience had taught me a valuable lesson. I'd been too cavalier about my oxygen. I wouldn't repeat that mistake.

Once I'd showered and dressed, I turned my attention to Dylan. We needed to get moving. I grabbed what felt like a leg under the comforter and shook it. The girl sputtered, then threw off the covers and glared at me. I began folding my clothes and noticed her watching me as I stowed my pill bottles. When I reached down to hoist my suitcase onto the bed, Dylan leaped up, shouting she'd get it.

"For heaven's sake, Dylan! I'm not an invalid."

Dylan stepped back. "Sorry! You seemed a little shaky last night."

"Shaking with relief! I'm just delighted to be free of that place."

Dylan moved to the window and twisted open the blinds. "You sure said some crazy shit after they drugged you."

I stiffened. Had I let slip something about Graceland? "For example?"

"You said last time you were in a hospital, your daughter died."

Ah. That was a different issue altogether. Was it possible

Dylan knew nothing about Beth? Of course it was. Hope was good at secrets, even those not her own.

Well, if I was going to chastise Hope for hiding things, I needed to be more forthcoming myself. I'd enlighten the girl. Do some sharing, as the touchy-feely types like to say.

I'd practiced talking about Beth. Over the years, through trial and error, I'd learned to keep my hands occupied. People were more comfortable if we didn't make eye contact. So as I told Dylan about my first child, I fiddled with the clothes in my bag, refolding things several times that had been folded adequately to begin with. I spoke about the small girl who'd been Hope's sister, and about the accident. How my four-year-old had been in the back seat when a truck had T-boned our car. How I'd woken in the hospital to learn my daughter was gone. "Ever since," I concluded, "I've suffered from a bit of PTSD about hospital stays."

When I looked up, Dylan was sitting on her bed, a hand over her mouth. "I had no idea about any of this," she said. "I'm so sorry. How bad were you hurt in the crash?"

"Pretty badly." I tucked my meds into a corner of the suitcase. "This was before airbags, remember. I was in a coma for nineteen hours. Broke my arm, two ribs."

"Your husband, too?" The girl had never met her grandfather. She slid off the bed and reached under it for her duffel.

"Harold wasn't with us. I was bringing Beth to preschool."

"Wait." Dylan jerked upright. "You know how to drive?"

"Technically."

"But Mom said you never learned."

"Hope has never seen me drive. I haven't since the accident."

Dylan flung her duffel onto the bed with some force. I

understood. Here was yet another untrue thing Hope had told her.

I hadn't meant to fuel that flame. "You need to cut your mother some slack on this one," I said. "The accident was a painful subject in our family. I never spoke to Hope about it. Not once."

The truth was, I had no memory of the accident. A blessing, surely, though I'd always wondered if my horror of screaming children was a remnant of that terrible day, some repressed memory of the moment before impact. I shivered. The air-conditioning.

"Well, thank you for telling me," Dylan grumbled. "At least someone isn't keeping secrets."

I leaned over my suitcase to pull the zipper around. In all honesty, I'd liked talking about Beth, saying her name. Now that we were headed back to Memphis, it felt right to remember my daughter.

As I straightened, Dylan was suddenly beside me. I started to protest that I didn't need help, when the girl lurched forward and hugged me. A long embrace. Tight. It took my breath away.

THE BUFFET BREAKFAST offered chafing dishes of rubbery scrambled eggs, undercooked sausage, and biscuits and gravy. Free, though—there was that. And fast. I made myself tea and snagged a table at the far end of the room while Dylan loaded a bowl with granola and a mountain of fruit.

I couldn't stop thinking about that hug. I hoped the girl wasn't getting attached. Something I hadn't considered, though God knows why not. People adored me, often regardless of how I treated them. It was a gift. I'd pay better attention going forward. Hard as it might be, I'd have to make myself less lovable.

I felt bad, too, that Dylan believed I wasn't keeping secrets. The fact was, I had a big one I couldn't share with her. No telling how Dylan might react to my plan for Graceland. She'd done well enough with the news about her father. I might tell her eventually, just not yet. I needed to get my own house in order.

While Dylan helped herself to toast, I unzipped the little compartment inside my handbag and pulled out the bottle of pills. I opened it and counted them, then replaced the lid, locking it with a twist. The recent experience with air hunger had unnerved me. Suffocation and panic were not what I wanted to feel as I took leave of this world. Counting the pills was reassuring. I had more than enough to transport me to la-la land, to avoid any discomfort. Enough, even, to do the job, though removing my cannula at the last moment would seal the deal.

Dylan dropped her heaping plate on the table. "Mom won't stop texting me. I'm thinking of blocking her."

"Don't. We need to keep tabs on her. What was this morning's missive?"

"Same old crap. I'm endangering your health. Please meet up with her somewhere. Yada yada yada." Dylan shoved a spoonful of granola into her mouth and didn't stop talking, a habit I needed to speak to her about. "What's wrong with Mom, anyway? Why doesn't she want me to meet my father?"

I sipped my tea. "Not sure. Perhaps the man doesn't know about you, or perhaps she's trying to protect his career, but she's making too much of this. We're going to approach him quietly, in private, not schedule an interview with Fox News. Whatever happened between Hope and that man, she needs to acknowledge it, get over it, and move on." I reached over and snatched a piece of toast from Dylan's plate. We had to get going.

"I've been wondering," Dylan said. "When did you figure out Aaron Breckenridge was my father? When he called you all those years ago, looking for Mom?"

"Of course not. I didn't even know your mother was pregnant then. No, it was not that long ago, actually. The last time I visited Boston. Three years ago? Four?"

"Five. I was eleven."

"Whatever. I'd turned on the TV and there he was on *Meet the Press* or one of those political shows. I said to Hope, 'Isn't that the man you worked for?' Do you know what she said?" I leaned forward, opened my eyes wide for effect. "'No!'"

Dylan's fork halted midair. "It *was* him she worked for, right? You're sure?"

"Of course I'm sure! The question was rhetorical, for God's sake. Did Hope think I was stupid?"

"Phew." Dylan opened a small tub of maple syrup and poured it on her granola.

"Even if I hadn't known better, your mother wouldn't have fooled me. Hope is a horrible actress. When she lies, her voice goes up an entire octave."

Dylan nearly choked with laughter. "And she talks way too fast."

"Exactly. Like Kristen Chenoweth on crack. You should have seen the way she lunged in front of me to switch off that TV! That's when I put things together. Later that morning, I asked you to remind me of your birthday and sure enough, when I counted back nine months, Hope had been in Memphis, working on his campaign."

I steeled myself for Dylan's next question. Why hadn't I told her any of this before? If I'd known who her father was years ago, why wait till now? And really, what could I say? It had never occurred to me. Dylan had been a child, not a real person. I'd filed away the information until I had a use for it.

Dylan's mind was elsewhere, though. She rotated the cube of cantaloupe on her fork, examining it from all angles. "You didn't remember it, though."

"What?" The girl could be confounding.

"My birthday. You've never remembered it. No card, nothing."

True. Over the years, I'd chosen to ignore birthdays, especially my own. "When is it again?"

"Next week. July twenty-first. Maybe this year, we can celebrate together. Get a cake."

"Yes." The toast had lost it appeal. I put it down, half-eaten. "That would be fun." I pointed to Dylan's plate. "Two more bites and we need to leave."

Dylan scowled, but I dropped my napkin on the table and stood, pleased. Already I was making myself less lovable.

In a vehicle the size of a postage stamp, pretending to sleep was a practical matter. I could take only so much of Dylan's blathering about #MeToo or banning six-packs to save turtles. I needed time to think, to plan.

I was also spending an inordinate amount of time arguing with Harold.

I bickered with my husband silently, of course. Only idiots speak out loud to the dead, as if they can't hear you otherwise.

When I pictured Harold up there in the ether, he was wearing his favorite argyle sweater, relaxing in his favorite armchair, his reading glasses still a tad crooked on his nose. (In heaven, they'd managed to fix the bald spot on the crown of his head, though. That was nice of them.)

On most issues, Harold was easygoing. About Hope, though, the man could be downright opinionated. Harold didn't agree with my plan to force Hope back to Memphis. I knew he wouldn't. Over the years, whenever I'd given Hope a little push for her own good, Harold had fought me tooth and nail.

"Liv," Harold said this time, "you've got to let Hope handle her problems in her own way."

"Handle? Hope can't even see that she *has* a problem."

I couldn't fault Harold for being blind to Hope's issues. I hadn't recognized them myself until earlier that spring. Alone at home, tethered to the bloody oxygen tank, I actually listened to what my daughter said on the phone. (Funny when you thought about it. The oxygen was meant to help my breathing, but it'd done amazing things for my hearing.)

And that was the trick, wasn't it? You have to listen closely to Hope because she rarely shares what matters most. Back then, when I asked what was new, she'd insist breezily that everything was fine. "Oh, Dylan and I are great! Nothing to report!"

Once I was paying attention, though, I called out Hope on her faux-breezy bullshit. It took time, of course, but over the course of a few weeks, Hope gradually offered more. Turned out, she was going through a tough patch with the teenager. Dylan had become a stranger, grunting at her mother, not meeting her eyes, dressing like Bradley Cooper in *American Sniper*. Hope was terrified she was losing her daughter.

I knew how Harold would react to this news. "Dylan needs a father."

That was Harold's answer for everything, and maybe it would help, but I didn't see any prospects on the horizon. Hope went through men like chewing gum.

Then, suddenly, that Breckenridge man was all over the news, and I'd all but kicked myself at my own stupidity. That secret I'd figured out years ago. Was *that* where Hope's issues had started? With that man? That one big secret, and the boatload of lies needed to cover it up?

"Don't you see, Harold?" I persisted. "Dylan was getting older, asking questions. To keep everything hidden, Hope was pushing her away."

I knew Harold would understand, eventually. A problem like Hope's had to be confronted head-on, and this trip to Memphis was the way to do it. The experience would be painful, for sure, but there was no getting around it. Hope needed to rip off the Band-Aid, give her wound some air, some sunlight. What we keep hidden doesn't heal. It festers.

Knoxville, TN, to Nashville, TN

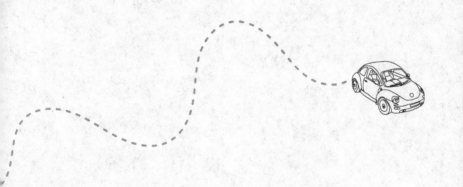

Chapter 18

Hope

"This is it!" Jordan sang out. I had to grip the armrest as she veered hard into the parking lot of the Lookie Here Bar & Grill.

"You can't be serious," I said. The sign featured a giant illuminated winking eye.

"Hope, you have no sense of adventure."

Jordan loved nothing better than a good dive and had been craving barbecue since we left New England. Something about these run-down joints said home to her. Something about them said *Deliverance* to me.

We entered through the saloon-style doors and grabbed a booth. A sheet of white paper was spread over the red-checkered tablecloth. This was gonna be messy. Jordan ran her hand across the table lovingly. "My daddy used to take us to a great barbecue place over the bridge in Arkansas," she said. "I was eating their pulled pork and white bread before I was weaned."

I pictured a chubby baby George and his four older sisters, their faces covered in barbecue sauce. "Sounds blissful."

"It was." Jordan's smile was thoughtful. "I miss those times with my dad."

George and his father had reconciled, if imperfectly, before Uncle Vern died. Vern had told his son, "I don't care what you do as long as I don't have to see it."

"It wasn't ideal, but I understand how much it took for my father to meet me there," George had told me, philosophically. "Thank goodness love wins in the end."

A server arrived with large, dripping glasses of ice water. While Jordan quizzed her about specials, I glanced at my phone. Nothing new. As I waited for Jordan to finish, I noticed a tattooed guy at the bar to our left squinting at her. The man caught my eye before slowly twisting back.

A PILE OF crumpled, orange-stained napkins surrounded our plates by the time I thought about the squinty-eyed man again. He'd been joined by two companions and flicked his head in our direction while they craned their necks to see. My last bite of coleslaw tasted sour.

I'd been with Jordan before when someone had lobbed a slur in her direction. Earlier this spring, with my car in the shop for a new transmission, Jordan had driven Dylan and me to Stop & Shop for groceries. We were carrying our bags from the store when, across from us, three middle-aged women in church clothes stuffed themselves into a Ford Focus. As they backed out, the woman in the back, whose fake eyelashes would have put Tammy Faye Bakker to shame, rolled down the window and called to Jordan, "I hope you know you're going to hell."

Dylan charged at the car. "You'll get there first, you ugly, bigoted bitch," she screamed before the car peeled away.

Jordan shook her head and grinned. "Now, Dylan. That's not very Christian of you."

As they stowed the groceries, Jordan and Dylan laughed about the lady's terrified face and how she'd probably peed her Depends. I hung back, stunned, wishing I'd had the presence of mind to do what Dylan had.

Now, as I shifted in my seat at Lookie Here to keep an eye on the men, I knew we should hightail it out of there. I beckoned our server to ask for the check.

As the waitress started to leave, Jordan touched her sleeve. "Quick question? I need to use the powder room, and don't want to cause a ruckus. Which room would you prefer I use: the one that I'm dressed for, or the one I have the plumbing for?"

My stomach twisted. The restrooms were down a hallway behind the bar.

Our server frowned like she didn't understand, then took in a quick breath and mouthed, "Oh!" Given Jordan's size and heavy makeup, most people understood she was cross-dressing, but apparently our waitress had seen only a very tall woman.

"Gosh," she said, smiling and shaking her head in a pleasant way that instantly doubled her tip. "I don't know. Let me ask my manager."

"Hold on," I interrupted, fumbling with my wallet. I was covering our meals, gas, and hotels for the trip, though Jordan had tried a couple times to snatch the check out of my hand. "Let me give you my credit card, because we need to run." After the waitress left, I whispered, "Those guys at the bar have been giving us the stink eye."

Jordan glanced over. The men were watching TV. Shit. Had I been imagining things? "I'll pee quickly, and we'll zip," she said.

The waitress returned with the credit card receipts. "On the restrooms?" She leaned toward Jordan, sharing a secret. "Here's what the manager suggests. I'm gonna check and be sure that no one is in the ladies'? And then, if you wouldn't mind," she said turning to me, "while she's in there, why don't you wait outside and tell people it's occupied? Is that good? That way, we won't surprise anyone or ruffle any feathers."

I could have kissed the girl. Even when people meant well, they sometimes screwed up Jordan's pronouns. I exhaled deeply and thanked her.

As soon as the waitress gave the all-clear signal, we picked up our stuff and headed to the narrow corridor with "Ladies" and "Gents" signs sticking out of the wall. The hallway was only steps from the end of the bar. Once Jordan had gone inside, I rested my back against the wall, pretending to be absorbed with my phone. In my peripheral vision, though, I could see the three men whispering and jerking their heads in my direction. A drop of sweat ran down the side of my face.

The guy next to Squinty, with a shaved head and bushy walrus mustache, slid off his stool and moved toward me. His buddy, a skinny fellow whose jeans hung off his hips, followed. If things got ugly, I decided to take the skinny one and let Jordan handle the Walrus. Behind them, though, was Squinty, with a giant eye tattooed on his neck. Who'd handle him?

"Howdy," I said, then wanted to slap myself. *Howdy?*

The Walrus jerked his chin toward the restroom. "Your friend ain't no lady."

"Don't see many folks like that around here," added Skinny. "He got a problem?"

My heart was thumping so hard I was sure they could hear it, but something in Skinny's "folks like that" comment called to mind the Tater Tot motel owner. The one who'd been excited to see a "performer" like Jordan.

"As a matter of fact"—I smiled, forcing myself to switch pronouns—"he does." I stepped in closer to them, which seemed to catch them off balance. "He wasn't supposed to leave the movie set dressed like this," I whispered. "Ron Howard is going to kill us! But we were just dying for some good barbecue, you know? The caterer on set is horrible."

Skinny backed up to look me over. "You're in a movie?"

"Well, *I'm* not. I'm . . . a makeup artist." I flushed as I realized I wasn't wearing a speck of makeup. "But my friend . . . well, if people realize who she—I mean he—is, we're gonna be in huge trouble. Someone takes photo, it goes viral, and suddenly our secret filming location isn't secret."

"What secret location?" asked Skinny, his eyes wide. "Around here?"

Sweat slithered down my back. I didn't even know what town we were in. The Walrus gave Skinny a look like he couldn't believe what an idiot this guy was. "If she says it's secret, do you really think she's going to tell you?"

"Dang. You can't say?"

"No." I resumed breathing. "So please don't create a scene, okay? We're already late getting back to the set, and you know what a bitch Angelina Jolie can be."

"Angelina *Jolie* is in the movie?" Skinny did a little jig.

I slapped both hands over my mouth. "I didn't say that. You did not hear that from me."

The Walrus gestured at the restroom door. "Who is he?"

I locked my lips with an invisible key.

At the bar, Squinty slid off his stool and sauntered over. Skinny pulled him aside and whispered.

As if on cue, Jordan opened the ladies' room door. She took in the whispering duo and turned to me, trying to decode the situation. I gripped her arm and gestured to the men to let us pass. Nobody was more surprised than I when they did.

I turned back to them. "Remember, not a word." Their eyes were fixed on Jordan's face.

Jordan waited until we were in the parking lot before she said, "Hope, what the . . . " I pointed vigorously at the truck doors, and she clicked the remote to unlock them. Before we could get in, though, the three guys pushed through the restaurant's doors and barreled toward us, Skinny waved a knife.

Or not a knife. An iPhone.

"Just one photo," Skinny called out. "We won't show it to anyone."

I feigned impatience and took the phone, telling Jordan to go pose with the nice men. Jordan shot me an appalled look. "Quick!" I repeated through gritted teeth.

Jordan was a head taller than all three, and Squinty yanked Skinny out of the way to stand next to her. Jordan cautiously lifted her arms around the shoulders of the two closest men and gave a lopsided smile.

"There." I thrust the phone back at Skinny. "I took a bunch in case someone was blinking." The Walrus tried to hand another phone to me. I waved him off. "You'll have to share. And please keep your promise. If those photos get around, my ass will be in a sling."

Jordan and I climbed into the truck as the three men huddled to check the photos. "Go!" I whispered. "But don't gun it. I don't want to seem scared." I was, though, and my heart raced as I glanced in the side mirror and saw the Walrus striding toward us. Jordan reversed out of the space, but the Walrus knocked at my window. I rolled it down a crack.

"Vince Vaughn, right? He's just got to be Vince Vaughn!"

I shrugged and gave my best *sorry!* smile. As we pulled away, I told Jordan, "Don't stop moving."

Behind us, I heard Skinny yell, "We love you, Vince!"

As we drove down the dusty frontage road, I stayed turned in my seat, watching for anyone following us. I gave Jordan a running commentary on everything she'd missed. It wasn't until we merged onto the highway, and I faced forward again, that I noticed the stiff way Jordan was holding her jaw. She was angry.

"What?" I asked.

"*What?*" Her tone was incredulous. "Hope, what the hell were you doing back there?"

"Saving you from getting the shit kicked out of you?"

Her laugh had an edge. "Seriously? You thought those people were dangerous?"

I huffed but said nothing. I *had* thought that.

"Those guys were weenies. Maybe they wanted to bully someone, push them around a bit. But they weren't interested in a fight."

I fiddled with the broken edge on my phone case. "You don't know that."

"Trust me, I've gotten the shit kicked out of me enough to tell the difference."

"Fine. We perceived the situation differently. No big deal."

"No big deal to you. Very big deal to me. How are people like that ever going to understand people like me if you go pretending I'm not real?"

I squirmed in my seat. "Those guys weren't going to understand you no matter what either of us said."

"Maybe not, but it sure would have felt good to try. Even if I had to get punched a few times, I would have been proud to tell them who I really am, knowing that my friend Hope was standing with me." Clouds had drifted in to cover the sun and Jordan pulled off her sunglasses and dropped them on the console between us. "Lie about yourself if you want, Hope. But going forward, please don't lie for me."

We didn't speak for a long time. I stared at nothing—trees, highway, horizon. Jordan was right, of course. I could see that now. Instead of standing up for her, as Dylan had done in the supermarket parking lot, I'd pretended she didn't exist.

I leaned my head against the window. What was wrong with me? How long had I been "making shit up," as Jordan had put it? Had I always?

Maybe. Even Aaron had called me out on it once. I closed my eyes and remembered that night. It was the same evening, toward the end of the campaign, when my world tilted on its axis.

ONE THURSDAY NIGHT in late October, Aaron and I were working alone, shoving cold pizza into our mouths with one hand while going over spreadsheets. Around seven thirty, he glanced at his watch and rose from the table, saying he was meeting an old Marine buddy for a beer. He'd been moody over the past week, even a bit sullen, so I was glad he was taking a break. I stayed in the office to revise a mailing piece. Veronica stuck her head in and rummaged around but seemed tired and didn't say much. She took some paperwork home.

It was after nine p.m. when Aaron reappeared and dropped into the chair across the table. I guessed he'd had more than one beer.

"Shelley called," I told him. "She's planning to be back Saturday and cover the festival with you." When I looked up, his head was on the table. "You okay?"

"Fine. It was good to talk with my buddy."

"I hope you discussed something besides the campaign," I said as I closed the program.

He lifted his head, studying me. "Dave was helping me with some personal issues."

"Oh." Unsure if I should ask more, I said, "Well, that's what buddies are for."

"Buddies tell you the truth."

Yep, definitely more than one beer. Maybe three or four.

"Are you my buddy?" he asked.

I didn't know if I should be flattered or devastated by Aaron considering me a buddy, but I nodded cautiously. "Of course."

"Then why haven't you told me the truth?"

Adrenaline rushed through my body. I had no idea where this was going. "About?"

He picked up a pen and twirled it. "About Carly."

My throat tightened. Shit. I shook my head, feigning confusion.

"You knew her better than you let on."

I struggled to keep my tone neutral. "I knew her, Aaron, but not well. I wasn't somebody Carly had much interest in."

"Explain," he said. "And stop using that kind of language."

"I don't understand . . ."

"Somebody she didn't have much interest in." There was a mocking tone in his voice I didn't like. "Tell me the truth, Hope, or you're not doing me any favors."

"Fine," I said, exasperated. "Your fiancée hated me. She was an incredible jerk to me."

"Thank you!" He tossed the pen and let it drop. "Now you're being honest."

Immediately, though, I regretted it. "Look, I really didn't know Carly."

"No, no, no. Stop changing your answer. This is helping. I mean, it's not fun, but . . . helpful."

I couldn't stop. "Most people at school thought Carly was hilarious. It's just—she could be hard on people. You said so yourself. Can you please not repeat that to her? She hates me enough as it is. I'm going to lose my job over this."

"You're not losing your job. Don't be stupid."

"You wait."

"Anyway, what you say is true. Carly is funny. And smart. There are dozens of things I adore about her. But lately I've been noticing that she and I have real differences in the way we deal with people."

"For instance?"

"You said it. She can be pretty rough on people. The other night, she referred to some woman as a slut." I tried to catch Aaron's eye, convinced that woman was me, but he was talking to the table. "To be honest, it's been eating at me for a while. That's why I wanted to talk to Dave."

I couldn't stop myself. "What did Dave say?"

He blew out some air and gazed up at the ceiling. "'Cut and run. She's not the one for you.'"

"Yikes." I hadn't expected that.

Aaron hadn't either, apparently. "I know. Hard to think about. My father taught me to honor my commitments. It's never led me wrong."

I struggled to keep my words neutral. "Yes, that's a tough one."

"Tough isn't the issue. The question is, what's right? Is it right to keep a promise, even if I'm worried it might be a mistake? Maybe I'm not trying hard enough. Relationships take work." His eyes met mine, held them. I could feel the heat rising in my face.

"Aaron, I don't know what to say."

"No advice?"

"I can't offer an opinion on this. I'm too . . ." I stopped, having no idea where I was going.

"Close?"

I opened my mouth, but no words came out. My ears were on fire.

"Because that's the other part of the equation. That's where it gets complicated." He stood, taking his jacket from the back of the chair. "If Carly is the woman I truly want to marry . . ." He paused, one hand still on the chair. "Then why do I want to spend every waking moment with someone else?" He shook his head as he put on his jacket. "Don't answer that. It's better if you don't." He moved toward the door.

"Did you drive?" I whispered hoarsely. His apartment was a few blocks from the office. Usually he walked.

"No." He was holding the door open. "But just so we're clear? I'm not as drunk as you think I am." Without a glance in my direction, he closed the door behind him.

THE NEXT DAY we'd canvassed as usual, taking notes on the people we met, rating their likeliness to vote for Aaron, and discussing the Fall Festival. We didn't mention our conversation from the night before, but if eye circles were any indication, neither of us had slept well. We'd taken my car, and when we quit around six p.m., I drove to Aaron's apartment and parallel parked. He sat there as if struggling to remember how a car door worked.

"I'm going to talk to Carly tonight," he said, finally. "I need to be honest with her. About my doubts."

"I hope that goes okay," I said. I couldn't imagine how it would. "Her father's put so much money into your campaign."

"Thank you, Hope," he said crisply, his eyes downcast. "I hadn't considered that."

"Sorry, that was stupid." Everything told me to shut up, but I plowed ahead. "Would it be better to wait until after the election?"

"Dump her once I've gotten what I want? Assuming I win, of course, which isn't looking likely." He linked his hands behind his head and squeezed. "Forgive me. I'm on edge." His voice was thin and raspy. "I'm hoping Carly's father backed me because I was a good candidate, not because I was dating his daughter."

I went back to the office. I was still there, around eight p.m., when the phone rang. Veronica answered and launched into a long story about the afternoon's phone-banking. Aaron must have interrupted her because she handed me the phone looking hurt. He asked if I could meet him in twenty minutes at the park, by our tree. I agreed, trying not to sound giddy in front of Veronica. I'd been struggling all day to keep my expectations low. Carly represented everything I longed to be—gorgeous, outgoing, the life of any party. How could I possibly win against her?

When I packed up to leave, though, Veronica said she'd walk with me. After we'd gone a block together, I stopped, smacked my forehead in mock frustration, and said I'd forgotten something at the office. Her eyes fell to the ground. Given Veronica's tendency to talk nonstop, she probably sensed when someone was ditching her.

By the time I circled the block and made it to the park, I was out of breath. Aaron was there, illuminated by the path lights. He guided me into the shadows under the tree, leaves crunching beneath our feet. I thought his hand lingered on my back a moment longer than necessary.

Carly had taken the news surprisingly well, he said. She'd teared up and suggested Aaron take some time to think about it. They'd made a date to talk on Sunday.

"And you?" I was scared to ask. "How do you feel?"

"It was hard. Maybe even harder because she took it so well. Carly is a wonderful person, and it's not that I don't love her. I'm just not sure we're a good fit. It kills me to break a promise, but I can't move forward with these doubts." He took both my hands in his and heat flashed through my body. "I might feel differently if it weren't for you, Hope. I get up each day excited to be with you. Given that, it doesn't feel right being engaged to someone else."

The wind had picked up off the river and he brushed my hair from my face. I could have died, right there, and been happy. He'd chosen me. He could have had Carly, the most jaw-dropping and room-silencing person I'd ever met, and he'd picked me. Hope Robinson.

We talked for a while about what came next. We agreed, more than once, to wait before exploring any kind of relationship. Finish the campaign. Let Aaron free himself from obligations. And then, I reached behind his neck and was kissing him, thinking all the while that it was a mistake, but the greatest, most wonderful mistake I'd ever make.

Instead of a key, Aaron's apartment had a keypad where you punch in a code. The lock clicked and he pushed open the door, holding it for me, then closed it behind me. He didn't turn on a light, but the shades were open, and the city lights illuminated the room as he brushed back my hair, gripping it without letting go. He leaned in and pressed his lips softly against mine, and gently moved forward until his body melted into mine and his mouth was moving all over my mouth, and I drew him in closer. I was sinking into something way too deep and didn't care.

WHEN I WOKE, Aaron was sitting in an upholstered chair, his head bowed. He wore boxers and a T-shirt and rested his elbows on his knees.

"You're thinking this was a mistake, aren't you?"

"No." He raised his head. "No, not for a second. I do need

to put my house in order, though. I need to officially break off my engagement."

"Maybe you should wait."

"Excuse me?"

"I know, I know." I waved off his puzzled expression. "I did a lot of thinking after you were asleep. Amazing what occurs to you between one and two a.m. There are only ten days before the election. I'm worried breaking your engagement will suck attention from your message."

"Really?" he murmured. He was staring at the floor again. "It's only an engagement. Why would anyone care?"

"You know what Shelley says. You can't predict what voters will latch onto. The race is a nail-biter. The last thing you need is to look flighty or commitment-phobic." I rose from the bed, wrapping the sheet around me.

He half smiled, his mind clearly elsewhere.

I took a few steps toward him. "And here's what else. With Shelley returning, I'll step back and be less visible."

"I don't like you less visible," he said, picking at the sheet.

"Aaron, if word gets out that your engagement is on the rocks, people are going to look for anything salacious, especially another woman."

"Okay, okay," he said. "So we won't do *this* anymore." He grabbed both my arms. "But I need you, Hope." He kissed me. "Being with you keeps me centered. You make me laugh."

"Shelley is worth three of me. What you need is to stay focused, finish the campaign. After that, we won't need to hide." He started to argue, and I took his face in my hands.

"Aaron, even before I fell for you, I believed in you. I refuse to be the person who gets in your way."

He started to say something, and I kissed him to shut him up. I didn't know it would be the last time.

JORDAN HADN'T SAID a word since our disagreement after the barbecue joint. I offered her some trail mix, and she said no. I asked if she wanted me to put on the Elvis CD, and she bobbed her head once. Clearly, she wasn't over my blunder.

I apologized. Told her I wanted to do better. "I respond well to a little kick now and then."

She gave me a half smile and one of those puffs through the nose that's not really a laugh. I thought I'd really blown it. Then Jordan started to talk. What she said wasn't new, but I heard it in a new way. How hard it is for cross-dressers to feel accepted when for years, they've been the punch line of jokes. How hidden they can feel, how different, even within the LGBTQ community. Why so many remain closeted to their families— the pain they experience, knowing they're not being loved for who they are.

As a teenager, George had come out to his mom long before his father learned about his cross-dressing. George begged his mother to please see him as Jordan. Aunt Joan had finally agreed and stood in the doorway to her bedroom, staring at Jordan in her thrift-store dress, pearls, high heels. She'd slowly walked over and held Jordan's face in both her hands. She'd said, "Not the blue eye shadow, sweetheart. Not with your complexion. Try brown."

Jordan grinned. She loved that story. "I know it was hard for my mom. This was Tennessee, in the eighties. It meant the world to me that she saw me. But that's as far as she took it. She couldn't tell my father. She couldn't be a true ally."

Jordan glanced at me. "I know you love me, Hope, and I understand if you can't be an ally, but you have to understand that it hurts."

I told Jordan that I wanted to be an ally, that I would try harder. I said, "If it's any consolation, when I thought there might be a fight back at the restaurant, I was planning to take the skinny one."

She turned her head to regard me for a moment. "The fella with the bad leg?"

"Yeah."

Her nods were slow, deliberate. "Well, that was real brave of you, Hope. Damn brave."

I reached my hand across the seat, and she put hers in mine and squeezed. I promised myself that going forward, I would be the friend, cousin, and ally Jordan deserved. Speak only the truth.

Just as soon as this mess was over.

Chapter 19

Dylan

Was there a difference between acting and lying? I wasn't sure, but I was laughing my ass off at Olivia. She was on the phone, bullshitting someone in Aaron Breckenridge's office with a dead-on southern accent. Who would have guessed Olivia had grown up in Hackensack? I hadn't known myself until we'd passed through New Jersey, and she'd riffed on *The Real Housewives*.

Olivia was pretending to be a faculty adviser for the University of Memphis newspaper. "You may recall," she was telling Breckenridge's office manager, "how the *Daily Helmsman* did a lovely piece on the senator a couple years ago? Oh, you *do* recall?" Olivia turned to me with comical wide eyes. "Wonderful! We have a young reporter keen to interview him before his speech Saturday." There was a long pause. Olivia scowled. "She needs only fifteen minutes. I'm sure you can squeeze her in." Pause. "Tons of young voters on campus, you know."

Olivia made a hand puppet to show the woman was blathering on. "Tomorrow, five p.m.? Perfect. The reporter's name?

Dylan . . . Grant. You'll love her. She's a real peach." Olivia hung up and tucked away her phone.

Pinpricks of excitement danced down my spine. "What will I say? I mean, how do you ask someone if he's your father?"

"I might not start with that question out of the gate," Olivia said. "Warm him up. Say you're interested in his Memphis roots, his first campaign for Congress. Then ask if he remembers a volunteer named Hope Robinson."

"What if he says no?"

"Then he's lying, and you'll want nothing to do with him. I don't think that will happen, though."

I didn't either. "Do you think he really cared for Mom? I mean, they didn't just . . . hook up?" I wasn't sure Olivia would understand that phrase, but she seemed to.

"I'm a pretty good reader of voices," Olivia said. "And trust me—the man who left me that phone message almost eighteen years ago? He wanted to find your mother. Badly."

OLIVIA LIFTED A spoonful of her chicken noodle soup and let it dribble back into the cardboard bowl. She was pissed that I'd insisted on Subway for lunch. Well, excuse me! I thought we were in a hurry.

I'd nearly finished my Veggie Delite sub when an ancient woman in a wheelchair burst through the door, pushed by a round-faced priest. The old woman had huge eyes and a pencil-thin body, like a gecko's. She stared at Olivia, then whispered to the priest, who bent to listen.

The priest pushed the wheelchair close to our table. "Sorry to bother you," he said to Olivia. "By any chance, were you on TV?" When Olivia nodded, the man clapped his hands together.

"You were right, Mom," he shouted into the gecko's ear. "That's Andromeda!" He turned back to Olivia and me. "My mother watched *The Light Within* every day at three o'clock."

The old woman raised a knobby finger that shook as it hovered. "Very bad woman!"

"No, Mom! That was her *character*." The man giggled, his cheeks rosy. "She's a little confused."

"Very bad!" spat the woman.

I flashed Olivia a look that said, *Time to get out of here*, and crumpled my sandwich paper.

"I'm so sorry," the priest stage-whispered to Olivia. "It's a tribute to your acting. She believes you really are Andromeda."

"No worries." Olivia smiled as she stood to collect her trash. "At times, I was confused myself."

The priest pushed the chair toward the counter, but the gecko twisted to keep a wary eye on Olivia, who stuck out her tongue and wiggled it devilishly. The woman clutched at the priest's jacket.

I held the door for Olivia. Once we were outside, I laughed. "You shouldn't be so mean to your fans."

"They expect it," she said. "They love Andromeda because she was evil, not in spite of it."

I wanted to ask Olivia more about that once we got going. When I climbed into the Bug, though, she was reading something on her phone and grimacing, like she was in pain.

Olivia said, "Not possible. She can't do this to me."

Chapter 20

Olivia

The selfish, irresponsible woman! How dare Ann Abernathy cancel on me! Although not surprising when you consider that family. The father was a vodka-swilling lech; the mother, a tennis-skirted, bleached blonde with a precancerous tan. The Abernathys always had more money than class.

My hand shook as I hit redial and got Ann's assistant, a young woman with one of those annoying baby voices. She sounded twelve.

I laid into the babysitter. "Does Ann Abernathy care nothing about her commitments? If she wants to skip town, she can leave after she fulfills her obligation to me. Why does it have to be Sunday?"

"Her father died."

"He'll still be dead on Monday!"

No response to that, only a keyboard clicking. Finally the child reported that Ann wasn't in, and unfortunately, her schedule before Sunday was fully booked.

"Will Ann be at her office on Saturday?"

"Yes, but . . ."

I hung up. I'd go to Graceland early Saturday and talk to Ann. The only way to get things done was in person. That's how I'd handle Ann Abernathy, and that's how Dylan would confront Aaron Breckenridge. The personal approach had become something of a lost art. A shame, really. It got results.

I'LL ADMIT I was cranky after that phone call. I'd grown tired of listening to Dylan complain about her mother, how Hope didn't understand her adventurous nature, didn't want her to be an activist. Not true, I protested. Hope simply didn't want her to be a *stupid* activist. That got her bent all out of shape.

"Why do you keep defending her?"

"Dylan, your mother isn't perfect. That said, you're not the first person whose parent didn't support her life choices."

"Oh, because your crazy mother didn't want you marrying Elvis? Like that was going to happen."

"Mother also wasn't keen on my becoming an actress. She said it was a harlot's profession."

"What's that?"

I searched for the politically correct term. "Sex worker."

Dylan raised her eyebrows. "Harsh. Did your dad think that, too?"

"No. Dad tried to broker the peace between us. It didn't work. In the end, my acting drove Mother over the edge."

While I rummaged in my bag for hand lotion, I told Dylan about my starring role as Amanda in my secretarial school's production of *The Glass Menagerie*. How my mother had railed, for weeks, because the play was written by "an immoral homosexual." Mother had lost her grip at that point. She'd shower daily for over an hour to "cleanse" herself. Twice she'd walked out our front door with no clothes on.

"My father went to see the play alone. During my solilo-quy in scene one, when Amanda prattles on about her gentle-man callers, I saw this ghostly figure enter the theater from the back. My mother's hair was dripping wet, and she was holding a shower brush out in front of her. The white bathrobe didn't do a good job of concealing that she was naked underneath. On the plus side, she'd remembered the bathrobe."

Dylan's mouth hung open. "What did you do?"

"What I had to—I stayed in character. My father and another man leaped up and dragged my mother from the theater. I just stood there, staring into the near distance, until everything died down. Then I finished my speech. Got a standing ovation."

Dylan had forgotten her earlier annoyance with me. "You deserved it. That must have been hard."

I squeezed the hand lotion on my fingers and rubbed it in. "It was a lesson. I learned staying in character could get me through the tough times."

The girl squinted at the road ahead. "I didn't know what you meant, earlier, when you said sometimes you believed you were Andromeda. Maybe I get it now. You had to stay in character."

I considered. "Sure," I said agreeably. "Close enough."

In truth, that wasn't it at all, but how could I possibly explain in a way the girl could understand? Stay in character, yes, that got you through. But at what cost?

Dylan wouldn't know about the physicality of acting. One couldn't slip into an evil woman's skin every day for decades, as I had, without it having an effect. The emotion might be faked, but what it did to your body, your mind, was real. The character takes up residence inside you. After a time, you lose sight of where you end, and the character begins.

When Harold was alive, and I'd slip into Andromeda behavior, he'd call me on it. Tell me to snap out of it. After Harold was gone, I had no one. Then *Light Within* was canceled, and it had taken me years to separate from my dark side. To figure out what I'd lost. And more importantly, what might remain.

Chapter 21

Hope

After the experience with Squinty and the Rednecks, I wanted to make amends to Jordan. So as we drove from Cookeville to Nashville, I shared more of my Aaron story. I left out only the most shameful part—what happened later, after my move to Boston.

THE DAY AFTER I slept with Aaron was the start of the Fall Festival. It was to be Shelley's first day back, and she would accompany Aaron, working the crowd as needed. I'd planned a day full of the errands I desperately needed to do, like laundry and grocery shopping.

That morning was sunny with a soft breeze that smelled of burning leaves. I stopped by the office to drop off some envelopes I'd stuffed. Veronica had on headphones and didn't look up, so I left the materials and made a quick exit. I grabbed coffee at the shop next door and strolled to the park, sitting on the bench near the gorgeous shingle oak where I'd kissed Aaron. I'd brought a paperback and opened it without reading.

My mind was full of Aaron—his mouth on my mouth, the way he'd run his thumb along my cheek and neck, then let his hand wander down my back. After we'd made love, we'd raided his freezer and eaten bowls of Ben and Jerry's before starting in again.

A shadow fell across my lap. When I looked up, my face went numb.

Even crying, Carly was stunning. Her long, wet lashes clumped together, making her eyes look greener than I'd remembered. She wore a sundress and cardigan while I had on a stained sweatshirt and baggy sweatpants. She was Marcia Brady to my Jan. No—not even Jan. Peter.

"I'll keep this short," she said. "Aaron didn't mention names, but I know it's you. He talks about you in such glowing terms."

I didn't speak. I had no script for this situation.

"I'm not going to pretend we're friends," she continued. "You blame me for what happened at school, even though I wasn't responsible. Some of those girls would do anything to please me."

That put me back on firmer ground. "And did it, Carly?" I coughed, finding my voice. "Did it please you?"

"Let's just say I've learned a lot about karma over the past two months as I watched Aaron drift away." She pulled a tissue from her pocket and dabbed at her eyes, somehow without smudging her mascara. She sat on the bench beside me. Shit.

I shifted instinctively and tried to cover it by dropping my paperback into my bag. "What is it you want from me?"

"I'd like you to do the right thing and give Aaron and me a chance to work it out. Stay out of our way for a couple weeks. Take a . . . vacation or something."

"I can't do that. We're in the last days of the campaign."

Carly brushed at a spot on her Coach handbag. "Why am I not surprised?" she said quietly, then turned to face me. "Then consider what's best for Aaron. My father is furious. If Aaron breaks our engagement, Daddy will crush him. You know how close this race is. If my father trashes Aaron in the press, he'll lose. Not only that, he'll demand Aaron return the twenty thousand dollars."

"He can't take back a campaign contribution," I said. Was that even true? I didn't know.

"It wasn't a contribution. It was a personal loan to pay you and Veronica."

I closed my eyes. *Oh my God, Aaron. How could you be so stupid?*

"So," she said, "since you've always had trouble doing what's right—"

I interrupted. "Why do you keep saying that?"

"Come on, Hope. Let's be honest. Cheating isn't new to you."

Was she talking about her old boyfriend I'd dated? I frowned in confusion, lifting my palms, the picture of someone falsely accused—until instantly, I understood. I lowered my hands.

During my final, horrible, semester at the University of Memphis, I'd tried at the last minute to save myself. Even though I'd attended few classes, hadn't studied for tests, and submitted laughably stream-of-consciousness papers, I was still passing most of my classes with a D, and in one case, a C-minus. The exception was Communications Ethics, a course I needed for my major. The instructor was new and kind. In recent weeks, I'd confided in him about my depression after my father's death and showed some effort by turning in a couple assignments. The problem was the twenty-five-page research paper that composed half our grade. I simply couldn't pull it off.

My friend Josephine had taken the course the previous year, with a different instructor. I asked if I could borrow her paper and alter it slightly. I convinced myself that it wasn't truly plagiarism and was harmless. A victimless crime.

What I didn't know was that Josephine's instructor had saved several model papers for his successor, and Josephine's was one of them. My professor called me into his office two days before graduation. Josephine was there, sobbing. "Tell him I didn't know about this!" she cried.

Of course I took full blame. It wasn't Josephine's fault. And so, I was expelled from the University of Memphis.

Carly's smile grew wider. "That's right. I've been doing a little detective work. I always wondered why you didn't walk at graduation."

The corner of my mouth was twitching, like it had when I was a child, sitting for school photos. I pressed my lips together to make it stop. I needed to talk to Aaron, to tell him. But what if this changed things? What if this stupid, horrible mistake turned his stomach, as it was doing to mine just then? He and I had barely started anything. He might decide it was best to walk away.

Carly continued. "You're familiar with daytime TV, Hope. So let's make a deal. You disappear, and I won't tell Aaron about what an unbelievable slimeball you are."

"Disappear? What does that mean? For how long?"

She shrugged. "A couple weeks. Doesn't matter where, just no contact with Aaron."

"That's impossible. I need to tell Aaron something. I can make up an excuse."

She was shaking her head. "No seeing him, no calling him. Starting now."

"You know, Carly, this isn't just your decision. Aaron gets a say . . ."

"Hope, you may be a colossal fuckup, but you're not stupid. We both know Aaron. When he wants something, he's blind to the pitfalls. You may be who he wants in the moment, but he'll wise up when he considers the optics. You're not who he needs. You don't have the skill set. You'll drag him down."

I closed my eyes. I felt like Carly had sliced me open and I was bleeding out. I wanted desperately to protest. The problem was, I knew in my heart she was right. I was a fuckup. I was not what Aaron Breckenridge needed.

"How do I know I can trust you?" I whispered. "I could return in two weeks, and you might still tell him."

"Unlike you, Hope, I'm honest. I'm tough, but I'm real. I'm one hundred percent me." She stood up and looked out toward the river. "You're not real, Hope. I don't know what the fuck you are."

I helped her out. "A disappointment."

I LEFT A note in the office for Aaron, Shelley, and Veronica. I had to leave town for a family emergency and wouldn't be in touch until after the election. I didn't say where I was going. I apologized, said I was resigning from the rest of the campaign, and would root for them from afar. Then I went to Aaron's apartment and used his keypad to open the door. He'd apologized the night before for his password, CARLY. The note I left him was in a sealed envelope and didn't mention her. I couldn't risk Carly going back on our deal. Instead, I repeated the lie about the family emergency, and insisted the timing was fortunate—he could focus on the campaign without me as a distraction. I told him how much I'd enjoyed our night together and cared about him. I implored him to focus on what was important. Win the election so he could be who he was meant to be.

I didn't own a cell phone back then. Aaron did, but I'd uphold my end of the bargain and not call. In my heart, I didn't believe Aaron would go back to Carly, though that didn't mean he'd choose me. Not if he understood the baggage I came with.

Josephine had been begging me to visit her in Nashville. She was thrilled when I asked to stay with her for a couple weeks. I threw what I needed into two duffel bags and left before Aaron and Shelley were done at the Fall Festival.

In my rush to leave, I left my toiletry bag on the sink at Ashlee's apartment. The bag had my birth control pills. It was Saturday night when I discovered it was missing, and Ashlee's boyfriend Lamar, who worked for FedEx, promised to overnight it to me. By Tuesday morning, though, the package still hadn't arrived, so I went to Planned Parenthood. They gave me new pills, told me to take two, and said I'd probably be fine.

I tried to enjoy my time with Josephine, appreciate the Nashville sights she took me to, but my mind was two hundred miles away. Should I call Aaron? At least twice, I repacked my duffels, then convinced myself to wait, to be patient. All would be well.

Three days before the election, the Memphis paper broke a damning story about Aaron's opponent. An anonymous source accused the guy of accepting illegal campaign contributions and conducting shady business deals. I couldn't believe Aaron was involved in the leak—Shelley wouldn't have allowed it—but Josephine just shook her head. "That's politics," she said. "It's a dirty business."

Aaron won the election by three hundred votes. I was packing to return to Memphis the next day, when Josephine handed me a letter that had appeared in her mailbox. It was addressed to me but bore no return address. Inside was a newspaper clipping with an engagement photo of Aaron and Carly, listing a wedding date in two weeks. I called the church to confirm, then the venue, a private club. They'd all been booked in the last week.

So Carly had told him. And he'd chosen her—the one who would help him succeed, not the one who would drag him down.

I had no idea who'd sent me that clipping or how they'd found me. It didn't matter. I drove back to Memphis and dragged everything out of my room that could fit in my Corolla. I owned no furniture except my father's old comfy chair, and I sobbed as I dragged it out to the street. I taped a note to it that said, "Free to a good home."

When I left that afternoon, I couldn't see out of the back of my car. I drove north with no clue where I was heading.

WHEN I TOLD the story to Jordan, I didn't mention being expelled, and she didn't notice anything missing. She directed her fury at Carly.

"Well, that explains it," Jordan said. "Breckenridge married that woman for her money. Who cares if she's evil, as long as she's rich?"

I wasn't going to argue with Jordan, though my take was different. Carly had convinced Aaron that she was an asset, and I was a liability. He'd wanted to win that election—to have a career in politics—more than he wanted me. Shelley had said that Aaron was more ambitious than he seemed. She'd been a good judge of character.

We were approaching Nashville, and a billboard showed the iconic image of young Elvis strolling down the driveway outside his mansion and read "Graceland, 4 Hours." The temperature outside had hit ninety and Jordan fiddled with the air-conditioning. "At least Breckenridge had the sense to divorce her."

I was checking my messages and put down my phone. "I'm sorry. What?"

Jordan turned, her eyebrows raised almost to her hairline. "You didn't know they're divorced?"

"How would I know that? It's not like he sends me Christmas cards."

"Normal people Google their exes."

I had, of course, done exactly that at the Tater Tot the previous night, though nothing I'd read had mentioned that detail. Now I searched on my phone. The dates given for Aaron's marriage on Wikipedia showed he and Carly had divorced late last year. I was still processing this information when Jordan said, "You never told me how Breckenridge found out you were pregnant."

"Oh," I said, pretending to search for something in my purse to buy myself time. "A mutual friend." I found a pack of gum and offered a piece to Jordan, who frowned and declined. We'd reached the part of the story I wasn't going to share, not even with Jordan.

"So . . . Aaron got in touch with you? "

"His representative did," I said, stuffing the gum in my mouth.

Sensing from my staccato answers that I wasn't going to talk about it, Jordan whispered an almost inaudible "okay, then." She clicked on the radio, and I fiddled with the gum wrapper, reorganized my purse, stared out the window. I wished I could crawl into the glove compartment and disappear.

I'd always had a talent for making myself invisible. Only once had it failed me.

Seventeen years ago, hugely pregnant, I sat on a park bench in Stoneham. I kept my eye on a six-year-old girl who shrieked and chased other kids around a climbing structure. Eight months earlier, I'd made a deal with the girl's mother to babysit her daughter after school and on breaks if I could live rent-free in the extra bedroom in her house. The mother's name was Tiffany. Another hair stylist. Go figure.

I smiled at the thin man who sat down next to me on the park bench. He was oddly dressed in a blue seersucker suit and straw fedora. With his slight build and huge glasses, he reminded me of the actor Wally Cox. He opened a box of Thin Mint Girl Scout Cookies and held out the open sleeve. I wasn't in the habit of taking food from strangers, but he tore open the wrapper right in front of me, and I was so hungry.

The baby inside me shifted and I felt something—a foot? An elbow?—protruding below my ribs. I should have eaten more than the single slice of bread and peanut butter I'd shoved in my mouth at lunchtime, but I hated to take Tiffany's food. She was a struggling single mom, too.

"When's your baby due?" The man had a southern accent. I'd become used to such questions from strangers.

"Four weeks." I smiled. "Too soon." I wasn't joking. I had no idea how I'd pay for the hospital. Little money, no insurance. I'd been to the obstetrician three times. During the last visit, the nurse had lectured me for canceling appointments.

"Planning to stay here?" the man asked.

"Sorry?" My eyes were searching for my little charge, Miriam. She was on the swings.

"I was asking if you intend to live here. In this area."

"I . . . guess so."

The man folded over the cookies' plastic sleeve and closed the box. "Let me be more direct, Ms. Robinson. Do you plan to make Boston your home or return to Memphis?"

Cold pinpricks raced down my spine. My head said run, but I could barely waddle and couldn't leave without Miriam. I scanned the park. The picnic area was full of young mothers who would rush to my aid if I screamed. The danger wasn't physical. I simply didn't know what it was.

I used my iciest voice. "How do you know me?"

"I've been looking for you for quite a while, Ms. Robinson. May I call you Hope?"

"No."

"Very well. No need for animus. I'm here to offer you help." He reached inside his suit jacket and handed me a business card. Marlin A. Fish, Private Detective.

"Your parents were funny people," I said, instantly regretting my cruelty.

He sighed. "They were anglers all right."

I checked on Miriam again. "I need to get a child home soon. What is it that you want, Mr. Fish?"

"You usually stay longer. Tiffany works late on Tuesdays."

I pushed myself off the bench and turned to face him. "So let's review what we've established: you're a creep who's been stalking me and my friend. What else do I need to know before calling the police?"

"Ms. Robinson, please sit. Again, I'm here to help. I think my offer will interest you. It comes from someone who wishes the best for you and your child. My client was . . . concerned . . . to learn of your current situation."

Aaron. In spite of everything I'd told myself about him over the last eight months, I felt a surge of elation. Aaron had been looking for me. I swallowed my pride and choked out: "Aaron sent you?" I hadn't tried to contact Aaron to tell him about the pregnancy. Even if I could have faced that humiliation, I wanted to keep the baby and feared he wouldn't. Better he didn't know.

He sighed. "I'm sorry, Ms. Robinson. As a private detective, I'm not at liberty to divulge my client's identity."

What was this game? I clutched my tote bag.

"And in this case, protecting the name is not simply policy, it's also the point. The reason I was hired."

"I'm sorry. To protect . . ."

"The father's name."

I sat then, slowly, lowering myself onto the bench with one hand pressed against my belly. Had I understood that correctly? The man was here to keep Aaron's name from being sullied—by me, by my baby? Not possible. Not Aaron. Yes, the man had hurt me. He'd chosen someone else over me. But this was a whole new level of ugly.

"I don't believe you," I said. "I don't believe your goofy business card or—"

He interrupted. "I can't give you a name, Ms. Robinson, but let me offer some details that might help: the evening of October twenty-third, 1998. A park, overlooking the Mississippi. Two people in the shadow of a shingle oak tree. Need I go on? Or does that assure you we have the correct parties?"

Of course it did. Only Aaron could have described that scene, would have mentioned our shingle oak tree. It felt like a sucker punch to the gut.

Fish continued. "My client is prepared to offer you a deal—a significant sum of money if you sign an agreement to never reveal the identity of your child's father and never return to Memphis."

"I'm not planning on doing either of those things," I said. "I don't need his money."

The man chuckled. "Ms. Robinson, with all due respect, you do. Or if not, your child does. My client is prepared to offer you an initial payment of a hundred thousand dollars, with follow-up payments of ten thousand a year until the child reaches maturity. The initial sum should be enough to pay your medical bills and provide for a maternity leave until you can get settled and find work. The rest? Well, consider it . . . child support."

I lowered myself back to the bench. I couldn't believe the amount, but then, $100,000 would be nothing to Aaron now that he was married to Carly. He could afford that kind of insurance.

Fish continued speaking and I caught random phrases. ". . . generous offer . . . enough to get you past this unfortunate accident . . . well, if it was an accident . . ."

I stood again, leaned down, and put my face close to his. *"How dare you?"*

"Ms. Robinson, forgive me. That was uncalled for." He rose and removed his hat, brushing off a dead leaf that had lodged in the brim. "Please take some time to consider this offer. It will be the only one you receive." He raised a hand. "No, don't answer now. I'll meet you here tomorrow. Let me know then." He replaced his hat, tipped his head, then ambled toward the parking lot with a bowlegged gait.

Once Marlin Fish was out of sight, I glanced over at Miriam, happily digging by the pond, then I sat and crumpled forward, my face hidden in my hands so the mothers in the picnic area wouldn't see my tears.

That night, I lifted Tiffany's cordless phone from its stand and replaced it several times. I hadn't spoken to my mother in months, not since I'd told her about the pregnancy. She'd offered to help, and I'd said no. Since my father's death, I'd been barely able to listen to my mother's voice. I hated the thought of taking money from her, but the encounter with Marlin Fish had been a wake-up call. My situation was desperate.

When I finally dialed my mother, though, a man answered.

"I'm trying to reach Olivia Grant," I said, confused.

"This is Remy." The man had a French accent. "Olivia is out right now. May I help you?"

"I'm Olivia's daughter?"

"Ah, you are Hope!"

"Yes, Hope. And I'm sorry, Remy . . . who, exactly, are *you*?"

He laughed. "Why, the love of your mother's life, of course!"

I hung up, appalled. That was how long it had taken my mother to replace my father? I wanted nothing to do with her.

The next day in the park, I accepted Marlin A. Fish's offer. I felt ashamed, but the money would provide security for my baby. It would pay for the hospital, an apartment, and a little time before starting a job search. It would be Aaron's only contribution to our child's life. On that, at least, we seemed to agree.

I signed the single sheet of paper that Fish had handed me: for a one-time payment of $100,000, with annual payments of $10,000 a year over eighteen years, I agreed to never reveal my baby's father to anyone, and never return to Memphis. The last part wasn't a sacrifice. For me, Memphis was an endless museum of hurt.

Fish wrote the check as I sat there. I realized he'd probably expected me to negotiate. No matter. It was more than enough.

The detective rose and again tipped his hat. "You've made a good choice, Ms. Robinson," he said. "You did the right thing."

AFTER SHAKING OFF that unpleasant memory, I felt grumpy. I asked Jordan to please stop humming "Walking in Memphis." It was making me crazy. She switched the radio back on, and we listened to Elvis croon the opening of "Kentucky Rain." Jordan shot me a helpless look. The number of Elvis songs had doubled since Knoxville.

"Leave it," I said. Elvis's achy, soulful rendition suited my mood. Damn him.

As we left Nashville, signs warned of construction ahead.

All lanes merged into one and we crept along, bumper to bumper. I clutched at my hair in frustration. Aaron's fundraiser that night was being held at the ritzy Peabody Hotel, diagonally across the street from the Doubletree, where I'd booked rooms for Jordan and me. I'd hoped to arrive an hour before the event started and wait outside the ballroom, watching for my mother and Dylan. I doubted they'd attend—the tickets were outrageous—but my mother was nothing if not unpredictable.

Earlier, Jordan had begged to come people watch with me. I explained that as much as I loved her company, I needed to be invisible, and she was not helpful in that respect.

"I do turn heads in my lavender dress," she'd acknowledged.

We made it through the construction in twenty grueling minutes. For some reason, though, traffic still crawled. A breeze carried the smell of something burning.

"Look." Jordan pointed to a plume of smoke that blackened the road ahead. "There's the slowdown." She glanced over at me. "Honey, if you keep yanking on your hair like that, you'll go bald."

I released the fistful I'd been holding in a death grip. "I won't make it to the fundraiser now. Not before it starts."

"Maybe you could sneak in late, once the lights are down."

It wasn't a bad idea. I certainly didn't want to pay the $250 per plate ticket, and this would give me more time to get ready. "I might even have time to shower and wash my hair," I said.

"Yes, you want to look your best."

"That isn't it," I snapped. "It just needs it."

"Right," Jordan said. "That's what I meant."

We crept slowly past the long line of flashing fire trucks and police vehicles until, finally, we saw the smoldering remains of a Ford Taurus. I let out a breath I hadn't been aware I was holding. It wasn't a VW.

"We should be good now," Jordan said as the traffic thinned, and she picked up speed. "Clear sailing."

"Thank God," I said. Finally my luck was changing.

Memphis, TN

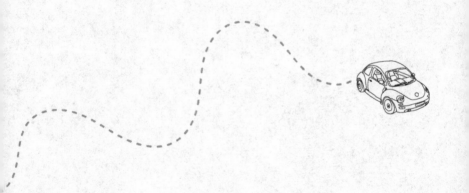

Chapter 22

Olivia

Impossible. The child had never heard of the Peabody ducks? I was dumbstruck. Had Hope been raising her daughter under a rock?

The girl didn't even notice the ducks at first, she was so busy gaping at the Peabody's two-story lobby, marble staircase, and wood-and-stained-glass ceilings. When I directed Dylan's attention to the five mallards swimming in the grand fountain, she seemed perplexed. I explained that these ducks lived in a special duck palace—that's right, a palace—on the hotel roof. A uniformed Duckmaster—yes, that was his title—brought them down each morning on the elevator. He guided them as they waddled along a red carpet and hopped into the fountain. There they swam until the Duckmaster marched them back to the elevator at five p.m.

"You're shitting me," Dylan said.

"I never shit anybody," I said. "The tourists love it."

To be honest, I'd forgotten how lovely the Peabody was. Harold and I had known the family who renovated the hotel in the early eighties. Thank goodness I asked at the front desk for their son Jon-David because I wouldn't have recognized the stout, bearded man who waddled toward us, as if in kinship with his ducks. He kissed me above the cannula on both cheeks.

"I'm delighted you called ahead, Olivia! I've put you and your granddaughter in a Celebrity Suite. On me."

"Oh, Jon-David, I never expected that. I can't let you." In fact, I had, and could.

"I do have a favor to ask." He lowered his head and regarded me coyly.

"Listening."

"My daughter-in-law produces one of the Memphis morning shows. She'd love to have you as a guest."

I sighed. "J.D., look at me. I'm a mess. I have to wear this cannelloni." I screwed up my face in comical frustration. "Nobody wants to see me like this."

"Olivia, stop. You look stunning, as always," he said. "Come now, what will it take?"

"Well . . . perhaps there's one small thing."

What I asked wasn't much. I wanted the hotel to keep news of my stay quiet, perhaps use a pseudonym at the front desk. I hated to sound paranoid. Toward the end of my time in Memphis, I'd experienced a problem with a stalker: a very tall blond woman. As unlikely as it seemed, I could have sworn I'd seen that woman earlier that day.

I wasn't making that up. Well, not all of it. As Dylan and I'd driven into town, Dylan had noticed an unusually tall woman on the block ahead and slammed on the brakes. From the back, the woman had looked exactly like Jordan. Was Hope already here, in Memphis? Had she brought Jordan? And who else?

An entire SWAT team? Out of an abundance of caution, I'd directed Dylan around the block, and we approached the Peabody from the other direction.

Now, as the bellhop loaded our bags onto a cart, Jon-David assured me I'd have privacy. I was to alert him immediately if the tall woman appeared at the hotel. Downtown had become safer since I'd lived here, but one couldn't be too careful.

THE TEAL WALLS of our Celebrity Suite were hung with landscapes in gilded frames, and arrangements of lilies and hydrangeas graced every nook. Lovely! The girl's jaw dropped as she explored the kitchenette, bedroom, and formal dining room. In the parlor, she flopped backward onto the sofa, picked up the TV remote, and clicked excitedly.

"Olivia, you won't believe this!" she called after me. "Netflix *and* Hulu!"

"Oh, brave new world that has such streaming options," I murmured.

Much as I enjoyed Dylan's enthusiasm, I was tired. I rolled my oxygen cart to the bedroom and opened the blinds. I had to lean forward on the sill to catch my breath. The emphysema was getting worse. No denying it.

Below my window, out on B.B. King Boulevard, young people chattered and laughed. I moved closer, brushing back the curtain. Such a gift to be young! How many times had I strolled down that sidewalk in the dusty light of summer, a warm breeze on my face, Harold on my arm? Did these millennials appreciate what they'd been given? I hadn't. Over the years, I'd imagined myself into dozens of characters, acted out a hundred adventures, but I'd never imagined myself old.

Still, I was handling the descent with dignity if I did say so myself. And I had my plan for Graceland in place. I'd never deluded myself it would be easy. What I knew in my bones was this: the danger was in waiting.

My beloved father had done that. Waited too long.

It was during my third year on the rebooted *Light Within* that I'd moved my father to LA, to be closer to me. Bedridden, he was sinking deeper into ALS. I hired caretakers and visited him daily unless our shooting schedule went to hell, which it often did.

One day, I raced over at lunch and found him crying. He'd sent his caregiver away. He pointed to his lower nightstand drawer, indicating I should open it. Inside was a pistol.

"Can't . . . lift," he said. His words, by then, were a soupy burble.

"I don't understand, Dad." I did, but I couldn't accept.

"Prop . . . it . . . up."

"I can't."

I sat on my father's bed and covered his hand with my own. Sobbing, he finally made me understand. He'd come up with this plan a year earlier but had procrastinated. Kept putting it off. He'd waited too long.

I believed in my father's right to die—to choose his own time—but I couldn't help him. I'd go to jail. My beautiful career . . . ruined.

I put the gun in my purse and called his backup caretaker. I had to return to the set.

In the end, it took my father two years to die, paralyzed, unable to see, hear, or communicate, though his brain functioned like a normal person's.

When guilt ate at me, I buried it deep in my character—Andromeda, who was fearless. Andromeda, who didn't give a shit.

The lesson, though, was seared into my brain like a cattle brand.

When I saw my time coming, I'd make a plan. And stick to it.

I SPLURGED THAT night and took Dylan to a four-star restaurant inside the Peabody. Jon-David secured us a table in a dark, quiet corner. The prices were scandalous. Still, they guaranteed we wouldn't run into Hope.

My filet mignon was pink and tender, but I managed only a few bites before pushing it aside. In contrast, the odd tower of kale-and-beet shavings the chef concocted for Dylan was a huge hit. After dinner, the girl ordered sorbet and I sipped my tea. I was feeling fondly toward Dylan and worried for her. The girl was going to be blindsided by my Graceland plan. I wanted to prepare her somehow. I approached the topic obliquely.

"I know you're excited to meet your father tomorrow, Dylan," I began. "Mine had a profound impact on me." I told the girl a bit more about Dad, how he'd shielded me from my crazy mother, smuggled Elvis magazines and records into the house, helped me hide them in a locked trunk. I described his struggle with ALS, sparing the girl the worst details, but explained how, before he'd procrastinated, he'd planned to take his life.

"Hold on." Dylan squeezed her eyes shut, perhaps battling a brain freeze from the sorbet. "Your father planned to commit suicide? And you thought that was a good idea?"

"People have the right to choose their own end, Dylan."

"My friend Emma volunteers on a suicide hotline. Sometimes people think they want to die, but they just need therapy or drugs."

"You're talking about young people. Healthy people. I'm talking about someone with a disease."

"Mental illness is a disease."

The girl had clearly been brainwashed by her friend. "I'm not going to argue with you, Dylan, but I, for one, plan to choose my time. I refuse to spend my final days on earth slowly suffocating."

"But how do you know when that will be?" she persisted. "I mean, what if the doctors can do some procedure or give you some new meds, and you're fine for another five years."

"I'm sure that's what my father thought and that's why he waited too long. You simply have to pick a time and stick to it."

Luckily, the server arrived just then with our check, providing an easy out from the conversation. I could see now that the girl was too young. She hadn't seen enough of the world's cruelty. I'd done what I could to prepare her. One day, Dylan might think back on our conversation and understand.

THE GIRL INSISTED on getting a souvenir for Emma—a rubber duck or some other nonsense—in the shop that sold Peabody duck paraphernalia. I waited outside, thank you.

As I leaned against the wall in front of the duck store, a crowd of people in black tie and cocktail dresses approached the elevator. I turned to see others ascending the marble staircase and peering over the mezzanine balcony. Tuxes. Gowns. Everywhere.

Oh dear Lord. Breckenridge's fundraiser.

How had I forgotten the event was at the Peabody? Dylan couldn't know. That would be a disaster. She'd want to go, and for the love of God, $250 a person? If the child wanted to hear her father speak, she could do it Saturday evening, at the university, for free.

I scanned the lobby. Unlikely the man himself would parade through, but who knew? And what if Dylan saw him? The girl was nothing if not unpredictable. We needed to leave.

As I swiveled my oxygen cart to enter the store, I felt a tap on my shoulder. A woman's voice. "Excuse me?" I pivoted back, surveyed the tapper. The woman's red dress didn't drape flatteringly, but her shoes were pricey. Her enraptured, awestruck look, though, was classic. My fans did pick their moments.

"Aren't you Olivia Grant?"

"Yes." No point in lying. I was too well-known in Memphis.

"Back in town for a visit? With family?"

How nosy! I gave a pursed-lip half smile and cut to the chase. "I'm afraid I don't have any paper." The woman looked puzzled. "For an autograph?"

"Oh!" she said, as if that hadn't been her goal from the start. She hesitated, then reached into her bag and pulled out a folded program and handed it to me with a pen.

Dylan was in a checkout line behind a dozen people, so I took pity on the poorly dressed woman. On top of everything else, she had the largest nostrils I'd ever seen that weren't on a horse. "To whom should I autograph this?"

"Oh!" she said. "To Veronica."

Chapter 23

Hope

As we drove into Memphis, I stared out the window, gripping the armrest. The river, the Pyramid, the graceful curves of the New Bridge. Everything was at once achingly familiar and oddly unreal. Home. Not home. Mine. Not mine.

Once Jordan exited the highway, I rolled down the window, trying to take it all in. Even a fleeting glance down familiar streets showed me a different Memphis. Instead of boarded-up store fronts, restaurants offered outdoor-seating where couples sipped wine and poked at arugula. The change from eighteen years ago wasn't seamless—on some corners, homeless people still slept in doorways—but overall, it was remarkable. As we waited for the light, a convertible beside us shared Al Green's "For the Good Times."

It had taken a few phone calls to learn the schedule for that night's fundraiser. Aaron wouldn't arrive until after the dinner, thank God, when he'd take the stage with a handful of candidates for local and state office and give the keynote address.

My goal was to figure out if Dylan and my mother were at

the event. If they weren't, fabulous. I'd sneak out as quickly as possible. If they were . . . that was trickier. I had to prevent them from getting anywhere near Aaron.

This was all hypothetical, of course. Who knew if my mother and daughter had even arrived in Memphis yet? Or what they had planned. After mulling for two days over what I'd say when I finally confronted them, I'd concluded my best defense was a strong offense. A new lie. I wasn't sure who Dylan's father was. I'd been dating more than one man at the time. Three, in fact. I felt a bit sheepish about the number before realizing this detail formed the plot of *Mamma Mia!*, and no one had called Meryl Streep's character skanky. In any case, the story could work.

I checked into my room while Jordan parked. I showered in five minutes, blow-dried my hair in two, and threw on the simple black dress I'd packed, a no-iron shift I'd worn to everything from cocktail parties to funerals. It was perfect for a dimly lit fundraiser where I needed to be invisible. I'd forgotten to pack any nice jewelry, so I texted Jordan to ask if I might borrow her pearls.

"Only if you take the earrings, too," she wrote back. "I'm not going to have you pair my pearls with that dangly Jody Coyote stuff you wear."

The woman I'd spoken to said over three hundred people were attending—a reassuring number. Obviously, I couldn't let Aaron see me, but I wasn't worried. Based on my limited experience with such events, the lights would be low, and afterward, Aaron would have people pressing in from all sides, wanting a word. His staff would make him scarce as quickly as possible.

I dreaded hearing Aaron speak, even from a distance. At the Tater Tot, when I'd clicked on a YouTube video of him touring a VA hospital, I'd turned it off at the sound of his warm chuckle. What would it feel like, being in the same room with him? What emotion would win out? The anger? The hurt? The regret? The longing?

Jordan met me at the elevator, and I lifted my hair so she could fasten the necklace. She pressed the earrings into my palm, hugged me for luck, then zipped back to her room. She was having dinner with one of her sisters, then would wander the touristy areas, keeping an eye out for our fugitives. I used the hallway mirror to put on the earrings, pinched my cheeks for color, and reminded myself that the point was not to look attractive, but invisible. No problem. That was my superpower.

THE NOTES FROM the piano ragtime progression faded as I climbed the stairs to the Peabody's mezzanine and strode down a long hallway. A folding table blocked access to the Grand Ballroom. With the dinner over, I hoped to talk my way in for a reduced donation. After that, I'd have to play it by ear. I prayed the room had a dark corner where I could sit and scan for Dylan's pink hair or my mother's white updo.

A young woman wearing a hijab typed on a laptop, while an older woman with spiky silver hair shuffled through papers. I waited for the young woman to look up. Instead the silver-haired woman did. Her head jerked back.

"Hope?"

My stomach dropped straight through to the lobby. "Shelley!" I forced some enthusiasm. "Hi!" I'd been so focused on avoiding Aaron, I hadn't considered running into someone else I knew.

She detoured around the table to give me a hug. "Wow." She

was clearly struggling with what to say. And why wouldn't she? I'd worked closely with her for five months and then disappeared. "You look great. What's it been? Twenty years?"

"Just about." To buy myself time to think, I said, "Your son must be grown now." It worked. She pulled a phone out of her jacket pocket to show me Owen's new baby. No doubt Shelley, too, felt relieved to have something to talk about. Eventually, though, common courtesy dictated she ask me something.

"And how about you? What have you been up to?" Shelley was a master of small talk and wouldn't acknowledge the elephant in the room: *What the hell happened?*

"I work for a small publishing company, in marketing."

"That's great. Where?"

"Oh . . . Seattle." I hated lying to Shelley, but I couldn't have her search for me online or try to friend me on Facebook. A burst of laughter and applause inside the ballroom provided the perfect segue. "To be honest, I'm only in town for a few days and heard about this fundraiser. If I make a small donation, would you let me slip in and listen to the speakers?"

She waved a hand. "Screw the donation. You put in your time. You can have my seat." To my protest, she replied, "No worries. My candidate has already spoken." Shelley nodded toward the woman with the laptop. "I need to help this young lady close up shop. I'll stick my head in later for Aaron's speech." She motioned for me to follow her to the double doors and leaned her head in close to hear the murmur of the speaker. "Hold on while this guy finishes, then I'll sneak you around back."

That sounded perfect. "You don't work with Aaron anymore?" I was praying I'd heard that right. I didn't want her mentioning she'd seen me.

"No, I stay local. Aaron needs the big guns. Now Veronica—you remember her, right? She still works in Aaron's Memphis office. She's here."

Veronica, I thought. *Shit.* I didn't want to run into her, either.

Shelley cracked open the door and listened, raising a finger. I felt a rush of warmth for her. She'd been a good friend to me all those years ago and I hadn't thanked her or even said goodbye.

"Shelley," I whispered, "I'm sorry about the way I left. It was a personal issue . . ."

"Hope," she said, closing the door and resting a hand on my shoulder. "No worries, compadre." Her direct eye contact told me she had a pretty good idea what the issue had been. Shelley had always been a talented reader of people. No doubt I'd done a terrible job hiding my feelings for Aaron.

The audience applauded, and Shelley motioned to follow her inside. I took a deep breath and focused on my task—scouting for my mother and daughter. The ballroom was dimly lit and packed with round tables of eight people. I kept my head down as Shelley led me behind the last row. Out of the corner of my eye, I saw men in black tie and women in tight gowns, but no one with pink hair.

Instead of staying in the back where staff and volunteers usually sit, Shelley turned and proceeded along the left wall toward the front. I stopped, shaking my head no, but she waved me forward. People at nearby tables turned. Eyes lowered, I slunk down the aisle.

Thankfully, Shelley's chair was in the farthest corner of the room, so close to the stage it couldn't be seen by the person at the podium without some serious *Exorcist*-style head spinning. As I sat, Shelley patted my back and waved before hurrying off.

Eventually, I found the courage to raise my eyes to the stage. If Aaron was there, he was seated on the other side of the podium. I exhaled.

The throaty woman speaking had rehearsed some great one-liners, and the audience howled with laughter. I pasted on a smile and followed their cues while scouring the ballroom for my daughter or mother. From my corner I had a decent vantage point, and after a few minutes of craning my neck to see around my tablemates, I concluded my fugitives weren't there. When I sat back in my chair, the unshaven young man on my right smiled quizzically and imitated my head tilts. I rubbed my shoulder and whispered, "Stiff neck."

"And now, here he is," drawled Representative Throaty, "our own native son, a champion for the state of Tennessee, and one of our country's great beacons for the future, Aaron Breckenridge!" The room rose to applaud. I stood, backing deeper into the dark corner, and pulled at my dress, which clung to my damp skin. I made a final sweep of the room.

As the crowd sat, I scooted my chair back to where I could see only part of Aaron's profile. Occasionally, when it felt safe, I leaned forward to sneak a glance. I'd seen recent photos of Aaron, of course, and caught glimpses of him on TV. His face wasn't as narrow as it had been, as one might expect from a man no longer thirty-two, and he'd grayed at the temples. On the plus side, he'd clearly hired someone to do his tailoring. For once his suit fit.

Aaron had been dealt a tough hand following the throaty comic—he wasn't as entertaining. He seemed sincere, though, and far more polished than the man I remembered. He spoke without notes, his gaze lingering on different tables. Even in the far corner, I feared Aaron might look my way, and I kept bending down, pretending to adjust the heel strap on my shoe. The unshaven man next to me turned.

"Need something?" he whispered.

For you to mind your business, I thought. But I smiled and mouthed no. I tipped my chair back against the stage and closed my eyes, as if reflecting deeply on Aaron's points about health care and immigration. His pleasant, modulated voice transported me back to that tiny campaign office over the sporting goods store, where after long days canvassing, we'd chatted about John Grisham novels and climate change, job creation and Bob Dylan's *MTV Unplugged*, whether Walmart would save Memphis or kill it. He'd listened to me, and I'd felt seen.

The creak of a door opening in the back of the ballroom forced open my eyes. Someone sneaking in late. My mother? Dylan? No, even in silhouette, the well-heeled woman was taller than Dylan, younger than my mother. At the podium, Aaron spoke about the issues facing Tennessee and the country at large: the need to stimulate growth, add jobs, repair infrastructure, and provide health care for all its citizens. He ended with climate change. The need to address it immediately. "This should be a bipartisan effort. Few issues are as pressing. We have to invest in sustainable energy and cut back on carbon emissions, or our children and grandchildren will have no earth to inherit."

At the words "our children," a shiver ran down my back. I'd been carried along by his voice, lulled into remembering the man I'd fallen for. But Aaron wasn't that person. Whatever he said, however he presented on the outside, he had an unattractive, ambitious side. He hadn't just rejected me, he'd rejected his child. He'd lured me into an agreement

I regretted. He'd hired that creepy little man on the park bench. *You've made a good choice, Ms. Robinson.*

Aaron was wrapping up, encouraging the crowd to support the candidates onstage with him. He ended with one of those political lines cravenly designed to catapult people from their chairs: "May God bless the state of Tennessee and the United States of America."

The audience did as scripted and leaped to their feet. I followed suit. In the back, someone gave a loud, fingers-in-your-teeth whistle. Shelley. I could make her out, standing by the woman who'd slipped in late. That woman raised a phone to her ear and opened the ballroom door. The light from the corridor illuminated her. Veronica.

Shit. Had she seen me? Had Shelley told her I was there?

I stood too long wondering. The candidates had come forward in a line to wave to the crowd. Now only a few yards away, Aaron turned in our direction, applauding the volunteers at our table and—I realized later—probably looking for Shelley. His gaze passed over me briefly, then returned and held mine for a couple beats.

Shit. Shit. Shit.

Time to go. I reached down to snatch my bag from under the table, and when it resisted, I yanked.

The unshaven man yelped and gave a surprised hop. "Hold on!" he called out, reaching down to disentangle his leg from my purse strap. He brushed off the bag, but instead of giving it to me, he clasped the hand I'd held out and shook it. "I'm Tim, nice to meet you."

"Hope." I glanced right to see if I could exit the side doors. Two men blocked the nearest.

Tim gripped my hand, leaning in to be heard over the hub-bub. "You work with Shelley?"

"Not anymore." I twisted away. "Sorry, I need to run. Nice to meet you."

Tim didn't answer. He pointed behind me, his eyebrows raised. I pivoted.

"Hope," Aaron said. "What a surprise. Do you have a minute?"

SHIT, SHIT, SHIT.

Without a glance at the people pressing in around us, Aaron took my elbow and guided me toward the side exit, ignoring calls of "Senator, Senator." The two men guarding the door opened it and blocked for us. Out in the hallway, hotel staff rushed by in both directions. We climbed a few stairs to another hall. The pounding in my ears drowned out everything else.

Aaron opened a door labeled "Dressing Room" and led me in. The small space was empty except for a wool dress and fox-fur shawl hanging on a clothes rack. Not his, I assumed, though I'd learned you never know. He turned and spoke to someone outside the door.

I could think of no explanation for my being there. Seventeen years ago, I'd taken Aaron's money and promised never to return to Memphis. Yet here I was, not just in Memphis, but sitting front row at one of his events. Not simply in violation of our deal but flaunting it.

My breath caught. *Oh my God.* Aaron thought I was there to extort him! At this critical juncture in his career, I'd resurfaced to demand more money. Brilliant. For a confused second, even I was impressed by my cunning. No wonder Aaron had to get me alone. He needed to contain the damage.

Aaron closed the door, opened his mouth to say something, then scratched his head, looking at the ceiling for help.

From habit, my hand flew to my hair, yanking it back from my forehead. "This is not how it looks."

He frowned. "How does it look?"

Someone knocked on the door. Aaron cracked it open, and a voice whispered to him.

"Five minutes," he said. More muttering from without. "No, I'm too tired. We'll deal with it tomorrow." Aaron closed the door, and someone knocked again. He raised both hands as if to say *Welcome to my life*. "Is this okay?" he asked. "You're not trying to catch a movie or something?"

I shook my head a fraction of an inch. My mouth may have been open.

Leaning in through the barely open door, a balding man with tiny, red ears murmured something to Aaron, who raised an index finger and opened the door wider. "This probably looks bad," he told the man, "my ducking into a closet with a woman. Hope is an old friend. A volunteer on my first campaign, in fact. Oh, wait." He stepped back, revealing behind the bald man someone in a red dress and Prada pumps. "Hope, you remember Veronica, don't you?"

The woman bent sideways to see around the man, like a Von Trapp child popping out to say, "Cuckoo." Veronica was more matronly than the college graduate I recalled. She wore reading glasses low on her nose.

"Great to see you again, Hope." She didn't seem surprised, though, so Shelley had spilled the beans. It no longer mattered.

I responded in kind, but she was back listening to Aaron and the bald man. To give them space, I turned and focused on the only thing in the room, the hanging fox fur. Real, it turned out. The poor creature's tail was shoved in its mouth. I empathized.

Aaron closed the door and turned back to me, exhaling loudly. "Let's start over. It's good to see you, Hope."

His tone was confusing. I knew this conversation would eventually turn ugly. In movies, the most spine-chilling villains speak soothingly at first.

"I get it," he said to my silence. "You must hate me."

I had no idea how to respond. I hated him. I loved him. I regretted him. I'd do it all again. Pick a card.

"It's fine," he said. "I don't expect you to forgive me, but God, Hope, I would have liked the chance to talk to you after that night. I turned around and you'd . . ." He made a sweeping hand motion.

"Disappeared," I whispered hoarsely.

"Yes! And not just a little." An edge had crept into his voice. "You vanished like a pro."

I didn't know what he was implying. I remembered Detective Fish hinting that my pregnancy hadn't been an accident. "You make it sound like I was the one who did something wrong."

"No," he said. "Only that . . . I wish I'd had a chance to explain."

Now I was pissed off. "You knew where I lived."

His mouth opened and closed. "I don't know what you mean. Your roommate—that hair stylist—said you'd gone to stay with a friend and then vanished."

"You talked to Ashlee?"

"*And* all three of her boyfriends! I tried everything . . ." Another knock at the door. "Jesus!" He ran a hand through his hair.

"Clearly we need more than five minutes." He cracked the door and barked, "What?" Then: "Crap." A pause. "No, no. Fine. Give me thirty seconds." He turned back to me. "I'm sorry. The governor wants to talk to me. You know how it goes."

"Of course," I said. "He hates it when I duck his calls."

His grin was tight-lipped. "I'd really like to talk to you, Hope." He glanced at his watch. "Can you meet me somewhere in an hour? Are you staying locally? Christ, do you still live in Memphis? Maybe all these years you've been hiding in plain sight."

I squinted at him. Was he gaslighting me? His stooge had been mailing me a check since 1999. "I can meet," I said.

"Great. My condo complex has some social rooms. It's probably the only place I can be right now without paparazzi. I'll get you the address. Meet me there around ten?" He pulled a phone from his jacket pocket. "What's your number?"

I wasn't sure I wanted Aaron to have my number, but couldn't think of an excuse, so I gave it to him. He punched it in and sent the call, and I answered so it would save to his phone.

"Fabulous." With his hand on the door, he stopped. "Needless to say, a lot of people would like my phone number, so please keep it to yourself."

"Of course." Keeping things to myself was just one of the many services I offered.

"Text me if anything comes up. I do want to talk to you, Hope. It would mean a lot to me."

"Sure," I said, struggling to make sense of what had just happened.

As Aaron opened the door, his phone beeped and he glanced at it, smiled. "My son, A.J. He likes to check in after big events." His eyes met mine. "Do you have kids, Hope?"

My frown and slow headshake weren't meant as a lie, or even an answer, but rather an expression of utter bewilderment. *How can you say that?* I opened my mouth to ask, but the bald man grabbed Aaron by the shoulder, pulling him from the room while handing him a different phone. Aaron raised it to his ear. "How are you, Governor?" He waved at me and cocked his head in apology before striding away.

That was when I finally understood. He didn't know.

I SLAMMED THROUGH the hotel doors and took off down the street. I didn't think about where I was heading, didn't know I could walk that fast in heels. My thoughts sprayed out in all directions, like Coke from a dropped can.

I speed-dialed Jordan. Words tumbled out in an incoherent jumble.

"Hope, calm down," she said. "You're not making any sense. You saw Aaron?"

"Yes." I was panting. "Well, he saw me. It was an accident. He put me in a closet."

"What?"

"Not a closet. You know, one of those little rooms with clothes . . ."

"Sweetie, have you been drinking?"

"Jordan." I gasped for breath. "He doesn't know about Dylan. At first, I thought he was just fucking with me, but I could tell by his face."

From her silence, I thought I'd dropped the connection. "Hope," Jordan said slowly, "you told me Aaron *did* know. You said he wanted nothing to do with her."

Of course I'd told Jordan that. I'd believed that. "Hold on. I'm . . . crossing an intersection." I wasn't, but I needed time to think. How could I explain that Aaron didn't know without telling Jordan about the creepy little man on the park bench? How I'd been bought. How I'd willingly taken the money he offered and promised to lie to everyone for the rest of my life. The most shameful of my secrets. "Actually, you know what?" I said. "You're right. I just figured it out. It was a misunderstanding."

"Sweetie," Jordan said. "You sound muddled. Come back to the hotel. We'll get you some coffee. And maybe a blood-alcohol test."

"No, no, I'm good. I'll explain later." I insisted she tell me about her evening.

I tried to focus on Jordan's play-by-play—she'd had dinner with her sister, Angie, who'd had a nose job that didn't go well—but my mind was elsewhere. How could Aaron not know about Dylan? If he hadn't made that agreement with me, who had? Who knew about the park, the tree, our kiss? Had Aaron told Carly those intimate details? That alone felt like a betrayal.

Jordan planned to walk around Beale Street looking for Dylan and my mother. As she ran through the places she'd check, I realized where my feet had taken me: the park where Aaron and I had first kissed. Our park. The sun had set, and the place seemed smaller than I remembered. I stood in the center and rotated, slowly, full circle. Two teenagers canoodled on a park bench, a pregnant woman pushed a double stroller, and an old man lumbered up the walk with a stiff knee.

Jordan was silent. I realized she was waiting for a response to some question I hadn't heard. "Hope, are you sure you're okay? Should I come meet you?"

"No, I'm going to wander around a bit. Don't wait up."

"If you're sure."

"I am, thanks," I said, as a shiver ran up my neck. The old man approaching me didn't have a stiff knee. He was bowlegged.

I lowered my phone as the man stopped and tipped his hat.

"Ms. Robinson," said Marlin Fish. "It's been some time."

Chapter 24

Dylan

I wanted to punch a hole in the window of the duck store when I realized how Olivia had tricked me.

I was in the Peabody lobby, face pressed to the glass of the dark and shuttered store. A few hours earlier, I'd been waiting in line to pay for Emma's duck socks with only four people ahead of me, when Olivia had burst into the store and insisted we needed to go *right then* to see that Memphis Pyramid. Like the monument was going away or something.

There's no arguing with Olivia when she sets her mind on something. Plus, I was using her Amex to buy Emma's gift. So I drove her to the freaking Pyramid. We rode the elevator to the twenty-eighth floor and stood on the observation deck for an eternity, looking out at the river and that double-humped bridge decked out in red lights. The view was nice, but enough already! Then Olivia decided she wanted to see her old house again, so I took her to East Memphis, where we drove by her husband's old car dealership, a park, a cemetery, and—I kid you not—their favorite grocery store. I wanted to rip my face off.

Finally, we returned to the hotel, and while Olivia showered, I slipped back downstairs to find the store closed. A spray-tanned woman in a sparkly dress stopped to peer in the window beside me. She whispered to her husband, "I didn't think Breckenridge's speech was all that special, did you?" My scalp went all tingly.

The guy yawned. "He's watching every word these days. He wants that VP spot." He put a hand the woman's shoulder and steered her toward the lounge. "Come on, let's have that martini."

I spun around. More tuxes and gowns were squeezing into the lounge. Had Breckenridge's speech been here tonight? The Peabody? Jesus . . . had Olivia known?

Of course she had.

It all made sense. That's why Olivia had dragged me from the Peabody and kept me away all evening. So I wouldn't realize my father was there, in the same building.

I took the elevator upstairs and slammed the door to our suite. Olivia, in a Peabody robe, emerged from the bathroom.

"You knew it!" I shouted. "You knew he was here!"

"Of course I did."

Olivia had a knack for throwing me off my game. "Why?" I sputtered.

"You need to trust me, Dylan," she said, moving back into the bathroom, but leaving the door open. "We follow the plan."

"It's just . . ." I crossed my arms and leaned against the door frame. "Sometimes I don't know whose side you're on."

"Side?"

"You keep making excuses for my mother, a pathological

liar, and you don't even tell me my father's in our hotel. Seems like we're not on the same team anymore."

"Oh, for goodness' sake, Dylan." Olivia squeezed toothpaste from the travel-sized tube of Crest onto her toothbrush. "Stop trying to divide everything into sides and teams, or good and bad. Only the most ignorant people see the world that way." She fluttered a hand to shoo me out of the bathroom doorway. "Do you know what the word 'nuance' means?"

I scowled.

"Look it up!" she demanded and shut the door.

I WASN'T IN the mood for word games. My father was in town, and he might be out there, somewhere, having a late dinner or shaking hands on that famous Beale Street. I waited until it was quiet, then gently opened Olivia's door and heard her soft breathing. I slipped out of the suite.

Outside, even at nine thirty p.m., the humidity smacked me in the face. A bass guitar thundered from a few blocks away, so I headed in that direction.

Beale Street, with its bright lights and flashing signs, smelled of tacos, beer, and cigarettes. The touristy shops were closed, but the bars were alive with clinking glasses and rowdy laughter. How stupid to think I might run into Breckenridge here. Even if he were inside one of the nicer restaurants, I wouldn't know. I hated to admit it, but Olivia was right. I needed to follow the plan.

A block past the hubbub, in a small park, was a statue of Elvis rocking out on his guitar. I took a photo for Olivia that didn't come out well even with the flash, then sat on the cement steps at its base. After a few minutes, I stretched out and lay on my back. I needed to think things through.

Tomorrow I'd meet my father. He'd believe I was a reporter for that newspaper. Shit, what was the name? *The Daily Helmet*? *Hemsworth*? Never mind, I wouldn't say it. In fact, once I was alone with Breckenridge, did I need to pretend? I'd just get to the point. Did he remember a woman named Hope Robinson? As long as he said yes, the rest would be easy. I pictured the scene. Breckenridge, who'd been studying my face, struggling to figure out who I reminded him of, would frown in confusion, disbelief, then—gradually—understanding. The corners of his mouth would curl up in a smile. Maybe his eyes would fill with tears. Awkward, but I could handle it.

I had another fantasy that I knew was stupid, but whatever, it made me happy. Maybe if I went to his speech Saturday night, Breckenridge would call me up onstage. Introduce me to the audience. Man, the rush of that moment. People would see us together and think, of course, that fits. Bold politician, activist daughter. Nut doesn't fall far from the tree, or whatever that expression was.

There was another possibility, of course. One I hadn't thought about much. What if Breckenridge *did* know about me? What if Mom had told him to stay away, and he had? Or perhaps there'd been some misunderstanding between them. Maybe he'd wanted to be in my life, but Mom had made it too hard. I wouldn't judge the man until I heard him out.

"Miss, you can't sleep there."

I jumped up. A police officer stood on the sidewalk.

I almost cursed her out since she'd nearly given me a heart attack. Instead I muttered "Fine" and headed back down the street. A little self-control, I was learning, could save you some trouble.

I wandered back down Beale. The band I'd heard earlier, playing in a space between two buildings, was taking a break, and I wound my way into the crowd of folks sitting at picnic tables, waiting for the next set. I sat on a bench beside two young women holding hands, one with a nose ring and the other with a baseball cap and tattoo sleeve. The nose-ring girl smiled, so I smiled back.

A folded newspaper lay on the table. The nose-ring girl said it wasn't theirs, so I opened it. Sure enough. Front page. A story about Breckenridge that focused on the Peabody fundraiser and his speech at the university tomorrow.

The nose-ring girl was reading over my shoulder. Rude, but I let it go. I said, "I guess this Breckenridge guy might get to be vice president."

"Yeah." She grimaced. "Not a fan."

The girl may as well have hit me. I blinked. "Really? Why not?"

"Do you know how long it took him to come out in favor of equal marriage? Even Hillary beat him."

I felt sick. *No. Not possible.*

Her baseball-capped friend shook her head. "This is Tennessee. He can't seem too liberal, or he won't get reelected."

Nose-ring pointed a thumb at her friend. "She was raised Republican, so she cuts him slack. I don't. He's a weenie."

The band was picking up their instruments again and I mumbled something about the time and stood. I asked the nose-ring girl, "Do you happen to know Breckenridge's position on trans rights?"

She didn't take her eyes from the stage, just repeated, "Weenie."

THE IMPORTANT THING was not to overreact, I told myself, kicking sideways at a low cement wall. You can't trust random people sitting on the street. Even ones with cool body art.

It had grown darker. I'd never walked alone in a city at night, but the moon was out and the streetlights kept it from being creepy. As I approached the Peabody, I slowed as a tall figure strode toward me. She wore a lavender dress and was whistling "Pretty Woman."

Jordan.

I considered running, but what could Jordan do—hold me down until Mom came? Besides, Jordan and I had always been buds. Sometimes I shared stuff with Jordan that never got back to my mother. I knew because Mom would have flipped out.

Jordan stopped short, surprised. "Hey there, young lady." Her smile was friendly, nonthreatening.

I kept my distance. "You're a long way from Stoneham."

"I'm here with your mom."

"No duh."

"You need to talk to her, sweetheart."

"Why? She lies to me."

Jordan sighed. "Well, I'm not going to get into it with you, Dylan, but people bend the truth for a lot of reasons, and not all of them are bad. Maybe she felt she had to."

"Why?"

"*Why, why, why?* Jeepers, how old are you? Two?" Jordan was trying to make me laugh.

I wasn't having it. "Guess I don't understand liars."

Jordan stepped aside to let a group of teenagers pass. One stared at Jordan, and I glowered back until he looked away. "Look, you've learned stuff about your father recently. Am I right?"

"How long have you known?"

Jordan huffed out a laugh. "Not as long as you, trust me. And I get that you're eager to know more, but you need to slow down and think. Your mother loves you. She would never do anything to hurt you. If she kept certain things secret, maybe, just maybe, she had a good reason."

I kicked a stone down the sidewalk. "What is it you know?"

"Sweetheart, you need to talk to your mom, not me."

"She doesn't want me to meet my father. Why does she get to choose? She's not always right, you know."

"That's true, but she does always have your best interest at heart."

"Not seeing it."

"Dylan, stop." Jordan sounded angry and a passing couple twisted to watch. Jordan motioned us closer to the building and lowered her voice. "Consider for a minute. The man is a public figure, at a key point in his career. Any questionable behavior from his past—it's not something he'd want to come out right now."

I glanced back toward Beale. "You know what's funny?" I tapped my fist against the hotel. "In health class, they teach kids to take responsibility for their actions. But apparently if you're a white, cisgender male politician, you don't have to."

Jordan held up both hands. "Preaching to the choir here, Dylan. All I'm saying is that the timing, perhaps, isn't ideal."

"Yeah. Wow. Maybe he should have thought of that." I

skirted around Jordan, moving toward the Peabody door. "Well, thank you for this chat. Any chance you can avoid telling Mom you saw me?"

"I'm not going to lie to her."

"I hope she gives you the same consideration." Did Jordan raise her eyebrows at that?

"Just speak with your mother, Dylan. That's all I'm asking. It's not hard."

I burst out laughing. "Not hard? Talking to her about my father? Where've you been?"

Jordan stepped forward, like she had good news to share. "Things have changed. Your mom understands she needs to be more . . . forthcoming. In the last few days, she's really opened up."

"That so? What did she say?"

I could tell from the droop in Jordan's smile she wished she could take it back.

"Spill the beans," Dylan said. "I'd rather hear it from you."

"Dylan."

"Huh. Bad news, then."

"No . . ."

"Let me guess. It was a one-night stand, and she never told Breckenridge she was pregnant?" Jordan had pursed her lips, and I couldn't tell if that meant it wasn't true, or she simply wouldn't say. "Worse?" Here I let loose with a new possibility, one I hadn't fully considered before. "Maybe he *does* know about me and doesn't want anything to do with me. Maybe he *told her* to say he was dead. Is that it?"

Jordan looked at her shoes. My stomach dropped. Mom always joked that when Jordan didn't want to tell you something to your face, she stared at her shoes.

Shit. That *was* it.

"Dylan . . ."

"No, it's okay," I whispered, opening the hotel door. "Good talk."

I'd stepped inside before I realized what I'd done. Now Jordan knew where Olivia and I were staying.

Fuck it. Nothing mattered.

I dropped my head against the back wall of the elevator. Clearly, without realizing it, I'd carried this ugly scenario about my father inside me all this time. And fuck, I wished it didn't make so much sense. What if, all along, Mom had been protecting me from the ugly truth that my father was a jerk and didn't want me? Or worse, protecting Aaron Breckenridge from having a little stain on his flawless character.

What kind of a hypocrite must Breckenridge be? Hiding the truth because it was inconvenient? Rejecting your own child? Well, I had a history of dealing with jerks like him, and I had the ammunition.

I'd blow the asshole up.

Chapter 25

Hope

The handkerchief in Fish's suit pocket was folded into a triangle, as it had been the first time I'd met the detective, all those years ago. That same straw hat. His face was more deeply creased, and his pants hung a little too loosely. How had this little man intimidated me back then? Now outrage trumped my fear.

"My goodness," I said. "It doesn't take Carly long to release her winged monkeys, does it?" It was only a guess, but it was all I had.

"We live in a world with eyes, Ms. Robinson. I assume everything I do is watched. I recommend others do the same."

"You lied to me, Mr. Fish. You led me to believe Aaron had sent you."

"I told you my client's identity was a private matter."

"A park by the river, you said. A shingle oak tree."

"I did say those words. It's interesting to think about what constitutes a lie. Do you ever think about that?"

I wasn't about to be insulted by this shit weasel. "You tricked me. I thought Aaron knew about his child. I thought . . ." My voice quavered and I fought to steady it. "I thought he didn't want her." Despite my efforts, tears spilled over. Fish reached into his breast pocket and offered his handkerchief, but I waved it away and rummaged in my purse. "I don't know how people do jobs like yours." I found a balled-up tissue. "How do you sleep at night?"

He took off his hat, rubbed a spot on his head. "Like most folks, rather poorly. I do what I'm paid to do, Ms. Robinson, regardless of whether I think it's right, wrong, or somewhere between. In truth, I find most things are in the middle."

I blew my nose and said, "You can twist anything so it seems like it's the middle."

"Sounds like you've had experience with that."

He didn't seem to be smirking, only mulling, but I lashed out. "You know what? I haven't always chosen well. I've made mistakes. But that doesn't mean there wasn't a right or wrong—it means I fell short." Snot was dripping from my nose, and he again offered his handkerchief. This time, I had to accept. I wiped and blew. "If everyone throws their arms up and says there's no right or wrong, then we've lost our compass. We're on a road to nowhere." I wiped under both eyes and handed him back the soggy handkerchief.

Fish slid it into a pocket, which made me feel worse. "You're surely right about that, Ms. Robinson. You're a thoughtful person and I regret having to bother you again." He put his hat back on his head. "Nevertheless, here we are. I'm retired now," he continued. "I only came here tonight as a favor to a client who paid me well over the years."

"Carly." I wiped my nose with the back of my hand this time. "I should have guessed."

"Well, as you say, perhaps I stacked the deck. Regardless, you're in violation of the agreement you signed."

"Look, Mr. Fish, I can't afford to break that agreement. I don't have the money to pay her back." My phone quacked and I lifted it from my bag to glance at the home screen. A text from a Memphis number I didn't recognize.

"Then why are you *here*, Ms. Robinson? You do understand, don't you, that you're risking everything by being in Memphis?"

I sniffled again. "I don't *want* to be here. My mother and daughter took off without telling me . . ." As soon as the words left my mouth, I realized my mistake.

"Why are your mother and daughter in Memphis?"

"My mother is an Elvis freak," I said, hastily. "She's ill and wanted to see Graceland one last time. I wouldn't take her, so my daughter did."

"Is that so? Well, I certainly hope that's the case. I spoke to my client tonight about cutting you some slack. After all, Memphis is your hometown, and you've stayed away for almost eighteen years. But I'm not sure I can help you if you've violated both parts of the agreement. If other family members know . . ."

"I haven't told my mother or daughter anything about Dylan's father," I said, truthfully. Which wasn't to say they didn't know.

"And the reason you were at Senator Breckenridge's event tonight?"

Fish knew that, too? Damn. "Stupid curiosity," I said. "I shouldn't have gone." Did he know Aaron had seen me? Spoken to me?

"Very well, Ms. Robinson. As I said, my job is to make sure we're on the same page. The agreement is specific. At a minimum, it prohibits you from revealing the identity of your child's father. To anyone. I'm afraid I need to emphasize this point. An-y-one."

"I get it," I said, brushing away a fallen leaf with my shoe. "Not even the father."

"No one. And may I suggest it would be in everyone's best interest if you left Memphis in the next twenty-four hours?"

"I'll try. I can't promise."

"I like you, Ms. Robinson. So please try. Try really hard."

I HURRIED AWAY from my meeting with Fish, back toward the Doubletree, not stopping until a passing trolley on North Main Street forced me to catch my breath. I stepped into a doorway, checking my phone. It was getting low on battery. The text message alert I'd heard earlier was for a link to Aaron's condo complex with "as promised" typed below it. No time for chatty messages in his world. I saved his number in my contacts simply as Aaron.

Tilting my head against the cool brick of the dark doorway, I closed my eyes. Aaron didn't know about Dylan. He'd never known. I wasn't sure how Carly had managed that, but regardless, I had a decision to make. Should I tell him?

I didn't take long to decide. The answer was no. Neither of us could afford the fallout. Fish would try to recover the $260,000 I'd been paid over the years—money that had gone toward my maternity bills, a down payment on our house, childcare, Dylan's braces. Money I didn't have. I'd probably lose our house, and how would that help my daughter? And for Aaron, could the timing be worse? According to the political commentators, a hangnail could tip the scales on the VP pick. An affair with a staffer and secret child was bad enough. What if they found out about the hush money? No matter what Aaron said, it would look like he and Carly had paid me off.

And finally, there was Dylan. Already she hated me for lying to her. What would happen when she found out I'd done it for money?

I double-checked the condo address Aaron had sent and stepped out of the doorway. I wasn't sure I could look Aaron in the eye, but I needed to hear what he had to say. His tone had been oddly apologetic, not accusatory. Was it possible Carly had kept her promise to me and not told Aaron I'd been expelled from the U of M? If so, why had he chosen Carly? Why hadn't I been enough for him? These were things I both dreaded hearing and ached to know.

Aaron's high-rise condo building was new since my time in Memphis. Gleaming white, with row upon row of balconies, it sat on a bluff facing the Mississippi. Inside, the lounge and an adjoining room were jam-packed with a wedding afterparty. The security guard at the front desk called up to Aaron and handed me the phone. "I didn't realize those rooms were booked," Aaron said. "I hope this doesn't sound like a ploy, but would you be willing to come up?" I said I trusted him.

Aaron's condo had more furniture than his apartment years earlier, but the same look of someone with no time to decorate. I recognized a photo of the Memphis skyline at night and a framed print of hazy peaks in Great Smoky Mountains National Park. Maybe Carly had sent him packing with only the artwork that he'd brought to the marriage. Or maybe he had a nicer place in DC.

Aaron asked me to have a seat in the living room and returned with a bottle of Chardonnay and two glasses. "Wine?"

I nodded. Truthfully, a fifth of vodka sounded good, but I'd stick to one glass of wine. I'd listen to what Aaron had to say and not offer much. Far too easy to slip and mention my daughter.

"Excuse the mess." He lifted a stack of paper from the coffee table and dropped it on one of the chairs. "I'm rarely in Memphis long enough to unpack. So where's home for you, Hope?" he asked, pouring us both some wine.

I hesitated for a second, remembering what I'd told Shelley. "Seattle."

Maybe that lie wasn't necessary. If all went well, I'd leave Memphis soon with my mother and daughter and Aaron Breckenridge would have no reason to seek me out. But I wasn't taking any chances.

"Oh." He seemed surprised. "I thought maybe you'd ended up in LA, with your mom."

"No. In fact, she just moved to be near me. In Seattle," I added, unnecessarily.

"And you like it there?"

"Seattle?" *Jesus, how many times was I going to say that?* I shrugged. "Kinda rainy, but otherwise fine." I wanted off this topic, so I asked about his kids. He pulled out his phone and showed me photos. They were good-looking teenagers, though the younger boy, maybe thirteen, needed a couple years to grow into his nose. Googling Aaron over the years, I'd learned his sons' names, and yet when he said, "And that's Dylan," my heart fluttered uncomfortably in my chest.

"They're good kids," he said. "Dylan's going through a phase right now. The divorce didn't help."

"Divorces generally don't."

"Are you . . . divorced?" he asked, adding quickly: "I don't mean to pry. You're not wearing a ring."

I'd forgotten that men notice that. "No, not divorced. Well, not married, either. Just dating." I paused, realizing that the last date I'd had was over eight months ago. "Actually, not really dating either. I'm sort of . . . between disasters."

He laughed. "That surprises me. I've always pictured you living on a cul-de-sac with an architect, five kids, and a collie."

I was amazed he'd thought about me at all. What I mustered was: "A collie?"

"Maybe it was a golden retriever." He shrugged. "I've never been good with dogs."

Aaron asked what brought me back to Memphis and I said my mother was visiting an old friend. Not entirely untrue if you considered Elvis her friend and a trip to his memorial a visit. I changed the subject to Shelley. How great it had been to see her.

Aaron rubbed a thumb across the stemless wineglass, as if trying to remove a smudge. "She must have been surprised," he said. "Did you say anything about why you'd left?"

"I mumbled something about personal issues."

He wiped again at the smudge. "In the interest of complete transparency . . . she knows."

"What?"

"I went a little nuts after you disappeared. She guessed about us. Or at least, she told me what she suspected, and I didn't deny it."

My turn to wipe at an invisible smudge.

"I looked everywhere for you, Hope," Aaron said, quietly. "You gave me nothing to go on. Not a word to Shelley or Veronica. I finally found a number for your mother."

I shook my head in disbelief. "Wait. You spoke to my mother?"

He squinted a bit, struggling to recall. "I left a message. I think it was her agent who called me back."

This was new information. "What did you say?"

"Nothing personal. I mean, I didn't say, 'I slept with your daughter, and she disappeared.'"

No, but clearly that's what she took from it.

"Anyway, according to the agent, your mother didn't know where you were. Traveling the country, or something."

At least my mother had covered for me. I could see, though, how she'd eventually pieced things together. "Aaron, look, I'm incredibly flattered that you asked around . . ."

"Asked around?" He made a face like I didn't get it. "Hope, I hired a detective."

"A detective?" A chill ran up my spine. "Do you remember his name?"

He looked at me oddly. "Lincoln James. He was a hunting buddy of my dad's. Why?"

"Sorry." I waved a hand. "Doesn't matter." I took a big sip of wine. "I appreciate everything you did to try to find me, Aaron. And truly, I don't blame you for what happened. You had a tough decision to make."

"You don't understand. Please. Let me explain."

Something clawed at my chest that made me fear, oddly, that I might cry. To keep control, I stared at my wineglass. Thinking I was looking for more, Aaron poured me another.

He said, "Let's start with the morning I last saw you."

AFTER OUR NIGHT together, Aaron had asked Carly to meet him at his apartment. It was the morning of the Fall Festival. As soon as Carly walked in the door, he blurted that he needed to end their engagement. Just as she had before, Carly remained calm. She said, "I understand you have cold feet. Lots of guys do." Then she asked if there was someone else. Aaron didn't want to lie, so he'd said, "There may be." Cool as a cucumber, she said, "Well, I'm completely certain I want to marry you. But if you're not sure, then take the time you need."

I held up a hand. "Did you tell her the other woman was me?"

"She didn't ask. She kissed me on the cheek and said I knew where to find her when I'd decided. That was it."

Interesting. The Carly who'd confronted me in the park a few hours later had been a teary, vitriolic mess.

Aaron continued: "I didn't see Carly for a couple days, while I was looking for you. Between that and the campaign, I was a little crazed. I'd left my apartment to meet with that detective when Carly appeared in the parking lot. I'll cut to the chase. She was pregnant."

I frowned at my wineglass. He'd just showed me photos of their sons. The oldest was fifteen—two years younger than Dylan.

Aaron plowed ahead. Carly said she'd have the baby regardless of what he decided. "I didn't know what to say, what to think, which way to turn," he said. Late for his appointment with the detective, he made some excuse and rushed off. As he drove, he asked himself what his father would have done. "He would have told me to do the right thing. Keep my promises, own up to my responsibilities. But another part of me felt it was wrong. You shouldn't marry someone if you're in love with someone else."

I kept my eyes on the table. Was he aware of what he'd just said?

"I was so confused. I was driving along this winding road and it was drizzling and foggy. Out of nowhere, this deer leaped across the road. I slammed on the brakes and turned the wheel hard. I must have come within an inch of hitting its tail and ended up on someone's lawn." He coughed, took a sip of wine. "I turned to see where the deer had gone, but it had vanished. Just, poof." He paused, looking at me, willing me to understand, to interpret it as he had.

"You saw it as a sign from your father," I said.

"How could I not?" Aaron sipped his wine. "I sat there, stunned, asking, *What are you trying to tell me, Dad?* A pickup had stopped behind me, and the driver came over to make sure I was okay. What he said was 'Wow. You stopped just in time.'"

AARON'S PHONE HAD beeped, and he went into the kitchen to make a call. I heard him rattling around in the refrigerator, saying he'd deal with it tomorrow. When he returned with a new bottle of wine, he poured us more and sat back on the sofa, running his fingers through his hair. "I never met with the detective. I drove to Carly's and told her I'd honor my commitment to her and responsibility to our child. She agreed we'd do some counseling." He gave a wry laugh. "Somehow that never happened. She wanted to be married quickly, before the pregnancy showed. All her life, she'd dreamed about her wedding. I thought I could at least give her that. We were married three weeks later."

"And it turned out she wasn't pregnant."

"No, she was. She had a miscarriage. On our honeymoon, in fact."

"I'm sorry," I said, but I must not have sounded sincere, because his expression changed to one of curiosity.

"You don't believe me."

I bit my lip, wondering if I was being catty. "I believe *you*, Aaron. If Carly had a miscarriage, then truly, I'm sorry for the loss. It just seems a little . . ."

"Convenient?" He twirled his wineglass. "I hear you. I had a moment where I wondered. But she was *so* upset afterward." He got up to pour himself some water. "I don't know. Maybe I needed to believe her. To convince myself I'd done the right thing." He took a long drink. "It doesn't matter. I can't regret my marriage to Carly because it gave me two wonderful kids. What ate at me over the years was what happened with you." His phone was ringing, and he glanced at it, pushed a button. "I figured you'd heard about our engagement—that's why you didn't come back. Or maybe you'd decided you were better off without me. Regardless, I regretted not having the chance to see you and explain."

Aaron excused himself again and this time went into his bedroom to return the call. I ran a finger around the rim of my wineglass and thought of the irony. He'd agreed to marry Carly thinking she was pregnant, while at the same time, I really was pregnant, though I didn't know it yet. What he'd said should have made me feel better. After all, I'd assumed his feelings for me hadn't been that strong, that they'd crumbled under Carly's insistence that I was a liability, not good enough for him. When he'd had to choose between me and his future in politics, he'd chosen the latter, and taken as a consolation prize the pretty, charming, and wealthy wife.

Instead, I felt bereft, though whether for the lost opportunity years ago, or the one now, I couldn't be sure. I would have enjoyed staying in touch with Aaron if I could have. Again, I tested the idea of being honest with him. Telling him about Dylan. I'd spoken so self-righteously to Fish. Shouldn't I consider moving toward what I knew was right?

I didn't have a choice. I'd made too many shitty decisions that shaped this one—choices that provided no way out. For now, my parting gift to Aaron Breckenridge would be to leave him in peace.

Aaron and I talked for two more hours. I wasn't sure I could carry on a conversation for that long without mentioning Dylan, but I spoke carefully, considered my words. My stories about Gary and his nutty slogans made Aaron nearly choke on his wine, and he told me crazy, insider tales of the DC scene. I admitted to disliking politics. "I'm not surprised," he said. "I'm sure I did that to you"

Aaron told me about the two-day camping trip he'd squeeze in with his sons that coming week. They'd drive to Gatlinburg, hike in the Smokies, fish in the Little Pigeon River. As he spoke so proudly of his kids, an ache settled in my chest. This is what I'd cost Dylan.

Around midnight, I decided I should go. His condo was only a few blocks from the Doubletree, and I turned down his offer to walk with me. As I opened the door, though, he pushed it closed again.

"Hope," he said. "I just want to say again how sorry I am for everything."

I turned to face him. I hadn't planned it, but I put one hand on the side of his face and kissed him gently. I was saying good-bye, but he grasped the hand and didn't let go. We stood there, silently, and he ran his hand softly down my other cheek, Then he kissed me back, longer. When we separated, I noticed the lines under his eyes.

"Not a good idea?" I said before he could.

"Not in the least." He rolled his eyes. "But when has that ever stopped us?"

I knew it was crazy. I knew it was just one night and I'd never see him again. He believed I lived in Seattle. But when he pressed me up against the door to kiss me passionately, the same way he had eighteen years earlier, I realized that I hadn't felt this way about a man for exactly that long, and I let myself enjoy it. For once, I didn't worry about pleasing anyone but me.

Chapter 26

Olivia

After that first visit to Graceland years ago, I never went back. Yes, it was the King's home, and it held special meaning to me, impossible to express. It was also, though, a mecca for free-range nutters.

I'd always been a *devotee* of the King, not some wackadoo fan. You'd never find me wearing Elvis pajamas, drinking from an Elvis teacup, or owning an Elvis wall clock with wildly swinging legs. No, I appreciated the man in all his complexity. His humble passion for his music. His dazzling, showman's soul. The inevitability of his self-destruction.

And so, when a family of six clambered aboard the shuttle bus at Graceland wearing identical hound-dog T-shirts, I nearly lost my mind.

Dylan was seated next to me, her eyes closed, her head resting against the bus window. I elbowed her gently. "Really?" I whispered. "You're telling me that those toddlers are going to appreciate Priscilla's china?"

Dylan grunted and twisted away. Fine. Probably didn't sleep well after her little escape from our suite the night before.

Oh, I knew the girl had stepped out. She carelessly let the door slam on her exit, and when she returned to the suite, she was swearing a blue streak. I didn't intend to ask her about it and didn't have to. In the morning, a red message light blinked on our suite phone. Jordan. Begging me to please stay put. Hope needed to speak to me.

So the girl had taken an extracurricular stroll and bumped into Jordan. Well, good to know. Thank you, Jordan, for that heads-up. I'd wanted to get to Graceland early—to beat the crowds and confront Ann Abernathy before she'd had her coffee. Now, all the more reason to decamp immediately.

Once I'd shaken Dylan awake, her mood was as black as the T-shirt and shorts she threw on. She didn't utter a word during our stop for breakfast, and at Graceland, she disappeared into the restroom during my loud negotiations with their ticket sellers. After we arrived at the mansion, though, she gave me nonstop lip. What was so special about Elvis's cupboards? she grumbled as she carried my oxygen cart up the steps. Why would she want to see his toilet? She'd rather stick sharp things in her eye. That kind of talk.

Inside the foyer, it became unbearable.

"This is it?" she asked, surveying Elvis's living room with its grand piano and stained-glass peacocks. "I've seen bigger homes on *House Hunters*."

I ignored her. I'd worn sunglasses and a scarf to conceal my identity and was examining the roped-off staircase to the second floor, where Elvis's bedroom was, when a young man materialized out of nowhere.

"Please don't touch, ma'am," he said. His blue polo shirt had a Graceland logo.

I removed the hand I'd rested on the rope and muttered to no one in particular, "This place is crawling with docents."

Clearly, the girl didn't know what a docent was. She jumped back and scanned the floor.

By the time we reached the Jungle Room, I'd had it with Dylan's attitude. She took one look at the green-shag carpet on the ceiling—which Elvis had installed on purpose so he could record there—and fake vomited. I lost my temper.

"For heaven's sake, Dylan! If you visited Mahatma Gandhi's house you wouldn't make fun of the straw mats or rice bowls. That's not what the experience is about."

Dylan scowled and went quiet. Probably trying to figure out if Mahatma Gandhi was the same Gandhi she knew about.

Finally, we entered a room filled with glass cases that displayed the King's bejeweled outfits, his records, and video clips of his movies and TV appearances. In the third case, I saw it instantly. The *Life* magazine cover with the photo of Elvis and me after the LA Forum concert. I leaned in closer, pressing my fingers to the glass.

Another blue-shirted docent stepped out of the shadows. "Please don't touch the glass, ma'am."

I was amazed to hear Dylan leap to my defense. "That's *her* in that photo with Elvis," she snapped.

The woman peered into the case, then at me. I removed my scarf as if in a movie reveal.

"Oh my goodness!" The woman almost tripped backward. "You're Andromeda! I was such a fan of your show!"

I dipped my head graciously.

"Our new curator added that photo. She couldn't believe it wasn't in the exhibit before."

"The picture did get some play in its day," I allowed. "Speaking of Ann, can you tell me where I might find her? The person at the ticketing area said she was here, at the mansion."

"I saw her, not that long ago." The woman unhooked a walkie-talkie from her belt and stepped outside, returning after a few minutes. "If you wait outside by the pool, Ann will be over in a bit."

I TOLD DYLAN I needed to speak to Ann Abernathy alone. The girl threw up her arms and stomped over to the Meditation Garden. After she lowered herself onto the concrete steps that formed a graceful semicircle around the burial plots for Elvis and his family, I thought she might reflect on the lovely inscriptions, or even—harkening back to our conversation the night before—on life and death itself. Instead, she keeled over backward and covered her face with her hoodie.

I seated myself on a stone bench facing a large white statue of Jesus flanked by two praying angels, with a cross behind him and "Presley" etched into the base. Jesus had both arms raised to the side, palms up. Oddly, the pose reminded me of an actor taking the stage on *The Tonight Show*, flapping his arms skyward and prompting the audience to cheer.

Oh, how my mother would have hated that comparison.

Then again, Mother would have liked nothing about my being here.

WITH MY EARLY *Light Within* earnings, I was able to place my mother in one of the better mental asylums. And yes, back then, that's what they were called. I didn't visit often. The asylum was in New Jersey, and I was in LA, and even this top-of-the-line institution smelled of Lysol and pee. Plus, my presence agitated my mother, who still had an unfortunate tendency to call me a whore.

The last time I visited was just before I eloped with Harold. My mother looked ancient, drugged. She stared at a crucifix on the wall.

"Here's your daughter, Mrs. Grant," gushed the aide. By that time, Andromeda had become a household name. "We see her on TV, don't we? You must be so proud."

My mother refused to speak. After the aide left, I prattled on about the weather, the news, and all sorts of nonsense, then told her I planned to marry Harold and move to Memphis. There was a long silence. When my mother finally spoke, it startled me.

"Jesus Christ is famous," she said.

"That's true, Mom. About as famous as you get."

"He will be remembered forever." She turned to me. "Elvis Presley will be forgotten tomorrow. *You* will be forgotten tomorrow." She closed her eyes and tilted her head back in a way that made me think she was fainting, then lurched forward to spit at me.

"Okay, Mom." I rose, wiping at the saliva on my blouse. "We'll see about that."

WHEN ANN ABERNATHY appeared by the pool, I hardly recognized her as the cute little girl who'd played with Hope. She'd grown into a praying mantis of a woman, with large, wide-set eyes and a triangular face. Nowhere near as attractive as Hope, who inherited my lovely oval face and sparkling blue irises.

After the required pleasantries—my condolences on her father and requests to remember me to her mother—our business was transacted in under a minute. Ann had made room in her schedule to see me later that day. In truth, it was the least she could do, but I expressed my thanks.

When, for the second time that day, I shook Dylan awake, I said we could be on our way. I was coming back to see Ann at four.

"But I have that interview with Aaron Breckenridge at five. And we're going to his speech tonight."

"I can't come to the interview, Dylan. The man would recognize me." She clearly hadn't considered this and nodded slowly. "And in terms of the speech tonight, you'll be better on your own, not dragging an old lady."

Dylan remained silent as we made our way back to the shuttle bus. I expect she felt a little abandoned. In truth, this was not how I'd planned things, but there was nothing I could do, or wanted to do. To be honest, in many respects, the timing was perfect.

Chapter 27

Hope

In the condo elevator, Aaron kissed me and held our foreheads together. He was tied up in meetings all day at the Sheraton but hoped we could get together after his speech tonight. He'd be in touch, maybe late afternoon.

"Seems unfair that your Washington and my Washington aren't closer," he whispered.

I thought it was some joke about politics before I realized: *Seattle, stupid.* How badly I wished geography were the biggest problem separating us. "We really screwed this up, didn't we?" I said as the doors opened.

Aaron's phone buzzed. His taxi was waiting. He hugged me quickly and left, his phone pressed to his ear. We'd agreed I'd sit in the lobby for a minute and let him exit the building alone. Neither of us wanted a photo of us leaving his condo together, looking scruffy and sleep-deprived.

I collapsed into a wingback chair and checked my phone. I'd run out of battery sometime that night and commandeered Aaron's charger in the morning. Just before boarding the elevator, I noticed I had messages from Jordan, and opened them now. She'd found Dylan. I called her, ecstatic.

"Where the heck are you?" she shouted. "When you didn't respond to my texts, I started banging on your door at seven a.m."

"I went for an early walk," I said. "My phone died. I should have left you a note." I couldn't tell if any of that made sense. After all, I was talking on my phone.

Luckily, Jordan was too preoccupied with her news. "They're staying at the Peabody. I saw Dylan go in there."

I dropped my head into my hands. Another bad call. I'd told Jordan not to bother checking the Peabody because my mother was too cheap to stay there.

Jordan was at the hotel already, searching the parking garage for Dylan's car. Could I come right over?

I started to say yes, then realized I was still wearing the dress I'd worn to the fundraiser. Why hadn't I just admitted to Jordan that I'd spent the night with Aaron? Here she'd been out late finding Dylan, and what had I been doing? Having a good time. "Actually, I wandered farther than I meant to," I said. "I'll be there as soon as I can."

"Okay," she said, perhaps a bit puzzled. "Text me when you get here."

I took off for the Doubletree as quickly as my idiotic heels would allow.

WITH NO TIME to shower, I rolled on enough deodorant to choke a horse and threw on a clean skirt and blouse. I wanted to look nice in case I saw Aaron again. Not that it mattered, of course.

Jordan was seated in the Peabody lounge, her eyes closed and her head thrown back over the top of the sofa. Not a good look for someone doing surveillance—or trying to downplay an Adam's apple for that matter. I collapsed next to her. Without raising her head, she said, "They left." After checking the parking garage, she'd spotted the Bug at a light two blocks down.

We thought they might be headed to Graceland. It was, after all, my mother's excuse for coming, though it might well have been only that. At least I knew they weren't seeing Aaron, since he was in meetings all day. Would they go to his speech tonight? Try to talk to him afterward? Getting face time with Aaron couldn't be easy, but I was never sure what connections my mother had, especially in Memphis.

Jordan sat up straight. "Say, what in the world were you telling me on the phone last night? You saw Aaron? Spoke to him?"

"Just briefly, in his dressing room. It was fine, actually. All good."

"*Good?*" Jordan's eyes were huge, struggling to reconcile this with what I'd told her about Aaron. "He didn't mind you were in Memphis?"

"No, no, he's over that."

"You said something about Dylan, too. That Aaron didn't know—"

"That she's here," I interjected. "Aaron doesn't know she's in town. And we need to keep it that way."

"You're right." Jordan recounted her sidewalk meeting with Dylan. "I may have left her with some less-than-positive feelings about her father, but it's for the best. Maybe she'll think twice about wanting to meet him."

I prayed Jordan was right. I knew Dylan, though. When she set her mind on something, she didn't let go.

Jordan and I settled on a plan. There was no point trying to follow my mother and daughter to Graceland, even if we knew for sure that's where they were headed. Aaron had told me the Elvis attractions had expanded to both sides of the street, and the mansion could be accessed only by shuttle bus. I planned to hang out at the Peabody and catch our fugitives when they returned. Jordan, who was eager to visit some of her old Memphis haunts, promised to check in periodically.

I POSTED UP by the Peabody elevators, snagging a waitress for some coffee. The lounge didn't serve food, only little silver trays of nuts, and after I finished mine, I pinched the remnants off a deserted table nearby. I tried to do research for my EduLearn proposal on my phone but found I couldn't work and still watch the elevators. I crossed fingers that the memo I'd sent to Gary from the Tater Tot was enough to satisfy him until Monday.

Around ten, the Peabody grew crowded as people arrived for the duck parade. I cursed the hotel guests who blocked my view of the elevators. Random tourists plopped down beside me, and a few tried to strike up a conversation. I told them I had impetigo and they might want to sit elsewhere. For the most part, they did.

Around one p.m., I ordered a Memphis Blues Martini to keep me going. I was beginning to wonder if my mother and daughter planned to return at all. At some point, I'd have to shift my surveillance to outside the auditorium where Aaron would speak. That would be their last chance to catch him in person. After that, he was going camping with his sons.

I'd just drained my second martini and was fantasizing about jamming something in the player piano when I heard the familiar squeak of my mother's oxygen cart and saw her pulling it toward the lobby. I bolted from my chair, steadying myself after the drinks, then skirted a table and two armchairs, nearly knocking over one of the waitstaff. The commotion caught my mother's attention. She hesitated, then moved toward me with a big smile.

"Hope! So glad you decided to join us."

"Mother," I said through gritted teeth. "How dare you?"

She took me by both shoulders and embraced me, then circled to my side, as if to take a seat and chat. "Dylan and I are having a marvelous time. I don't know why you haven't been back to Memphis in so long." My mother cocked her head. "Then again, maybe I do." She held one arm oddly behind her back, as if brushing something away. I glanced behind her to see Dylan halt midstep, her eyes flitting from her grandmother to me. She spun around and dashed for the exit.

"Dylan!" I shouted, loud enough to turn heads. I zigzagged around my mother's cart and sidestepped a chair when something behind me crashed. Several people gasped and one called out, "Oh my God." I pivoted and couldn't find my mother. Only when I followed people's eyes did I see her ankles sticking out from behind the sofa.

Racing back, I pushed aside bystanders and dropped to my knees. I righted her oxygen cart and straightened the cannula, worried it might have cut off her air. Her eyes were closed, but she was breathing. Had she fainted?

"Mom, are you okay?" I gently patted her face. "Can you hear me?"

Someone shouted that they were dialing 911, and I called back my thanks. "Does anyone see a girl with pink hair?" I asked. The crowd had enclosed us, blocking my view, and I prayed Dylan had heard the commotion and returned. As I turned back to my mother, I could have sworn her eyes opened a slit, then closed quickly.

Noooo, I thought. *She wouldn't.*

Followed immediately by *Of course she would.*

"Mother," I whispered, leaning in close. "Open your eyes or I'll strangle you."

A woman hovering over us gasped. "What did you say?"

My mother moaned. It was a moan I knew well. On one mid-nineties season of *The Light Within*, Andromeda popped too many pills and drove her car off one of the Swiss Alps. My mother was feuding with the producers at that time, so no one—not even the writers—knew if Andromeda would survive. She did an entire month of episodes lingering on death's door, waiting for the volume of fan mail needed to save her character.

"She's fine," I told the crowd. "My mother's a bit of a drama queen."

"I saw her go down," the hovering woman said. "That didn't look fake to me."

A voice behind me cried, "That's Antigone!"

"Andromeda," I corrected.

The hovering woman whispered to someone, "Looked to me like she was *knocked* down."

The bartender elbowed his way into the circle. An ambulance was on the way.

"I'm not sure we need it," I said. "My mother is fine."

"Someone should call the *police*," muttered the hovering woman.

My mother groaned again, blinking her eyes in a bit of overacting so cringeworthy I couldn't believe everyone in the crowd wasn't embarrassed. A few people videoed her with cell phones.

"Please, no photos," I said.

"Take 'em," said the hovering woman. "It's a crime scene."

"Mom," I lowered my face to her ear. "Please tell these people you're okay. Otherwise, you're headed to the hospital."

She raised a shaky hand. "No hospital," she croaked. Everyone applauded.

"Just relax, ma'am," said the bartender. "Don't move until the EMTs get here."

I twisted to check for Dylan. My mother clutched my arm. "Hope. Don't leave me."

"Of course not, Mom," I said, leaning down, my jaw clenched. "I won't let you out of my sight. Ever. Again."

She closed her eyes and went limp. A ray of light from the chandelier caught her loosened white hair and made it glow, like an angel's.

I had to hand it to her: the woman was good.

BY THE TIME the EMTs arrived, the bartender and I had hoisted my mother into a chair, and the crowd had dispersed, though the hovering woman had staked out a sofa nearby and kept her narrowed eyes on me. My mother basked in the attention of the male EMT, telling him how she'd only gone lightheaded once before, after winning her first Daytime Emmy.

The EMT squatted in front of my mother's chair, raising

her lids and examining her pupils. "Did you see your mother faint?" he asked me.

"Yes." My mouth was tight. "A classic faint. Just like in the *movies*."

"I don't believe you were watching, Hope," my mother sniffed. "You had pushed me aside to get to Dylan."

The EMT felt around the back of my mother's head. "Is it possible you knocked her off balance and she hit her head?"

I counted to five. "I did not knock her down."

"My daughter thinks I'm doing this for attention," my mother interrupted. "Perhaps I had another MI. The doctor mentioned that recently."

His eyes narrowed with concern. "You've had a heart attack recently?"

"What doctor?" My voice had entered the squeaking range. "I've been to all your appointments."

"I saw a doctor on Thursday," my mother said. "I think we can agree you weren't with me then."

I had to give her that one.

The other EMT was chewing a wad of gum. Juicy Fruit, by the smell. She said, "If a doctor evaluated you for a myocardial infarction yesterday, we should take you in."

"Oh," my mother said. "I didn't mean MI. I meant MRI. Too many acronyms."

The gum-chewing EMT looked to me for confirmation. I couldn't speak. The nerve. Had my mother just insinuated she'd suffered a heart attack? I glared at her.

In the end, the EMTs insisted on escorting my mother back to her room, to observe how she managed being on her feet. I trailed behind, fuming silently while she nattered on about her visit to Graceland that morning.

My mother's suite was on the top floor. Her bathroom had a freaking chandelier. As the EMTs gave me final instructions, my mother used a gilded mirror to smooth her mussed hair.

Then I was alone with my mother for the first time since our lunch five days earlier. I fought to keep my voice steady. "Where's Dylan, Mother?"

"How would I know?" she said. "Out exploring, I assume." She removed her Elvis scarf and draped it around her photo, proudly displayed on the entryway table. "I don't expect her back until late."

"For God's sake, have you no shame? You've made me chase you halfway across the country."

She cut me off. "Whose fault was that? I begged you to come, Hope."

"You didn't mention that you planned to kidnap my child."

"Now there's an interesting narrative. Dylan came of her own free will."

"She's sixteen, Mother. She's a teenager. *You're* the adult." I couldn't stop myself from adding, "In theory."

"Dylan is almost an adult, but you don't treat her like one. You were lying to her, Hope. She deserves the truth."

"Oh, and it was your job to provide it?"

"Well *you* certainly weren't." The hotel phone rang, and she moved to the table where it sat. "Exactly when were you planning to tell her?"

Only my mother lifting the receiver stopped me from yelling, "Never!" Because that was the truth. I wouldn't deny it. I'd have never found the right time to tell my daughter I'd lied to her. Whenever I did it, however I did it, I knew she'd be horri-fied, sickened—as repulsed by me as I was by myself. I'd been right.

"Oh, hello, Jon-David," my mother said. So that's how she'd scored this suite! "No, I'm fine. A little dizzy spell. Your staff was all over it." She paused, laughed gaily. "Oh really? Do tell!"

Somehow, I'd imagined all I needed to do was catch up to my mother and explain things. I'd been certain she wouldn't go against my express wishes. But I was wrong. As always, my mother was convinced she knew best.

I needed to find my daughter.

"Hope?" my mother called out as I unlatched the door.

I slammed it behind me.

Chapter 28

Dylan

I pressed a hand to the stitch in my side as I jogged toward the river. Glancing back, I didn't see anyone following. Phew.

Clearly Jordan had ratted me out. Told Mom where Olivia and I were staying. Well, what had I expected after waltzing into the Peabody right in front of her? Why not just hand Jordan a room key? Stupid, stupid girl.

I'd hesitated for just a second back at the Peabody, when Mom called after me in that croaky, pleading voice. Nice try, but I wasn't falling for it. I didn't drive halfway across the country to be stopped now. For better or worse, I planned to meet my father, to size the man up. I'd decide on my next move after that.

Ignoring the "Don't Walk" signal, I trotted across the divided road, toward the river. Olivia insisted this river was the Mississippi, but it didn't seem as mighty as those grade-school books had made it out to be. Or maybe that was just me. I tended to build things up in my mind, and then they disappointed me. Concerts I begged to attend that, in the end, weren't *all that*.

Boys I'd crushed on, hard, until I kissed them, and then, ick. Even things like my beautiful Bug had warts. Next on my list of disappointments? My father.

Until Jordan slipped and told me the truth, I'd never imagined that my father might be a jerk. Why would I? Olivia had made it seem like he was a great guy—that eighteen years ago, when he'd called and left that message, Breckenridge had been heartbroken and desperate to find my mother. She'd made it seem almost romantic. Ha! What if all Breckenridge had wanted, in finding Mom, was to shut her up?

Sweat dripped down the center of my T-shirt and I flapped my elbows to help dry my pits. A long patch of green park ran along the river with a path crawling with runners, bikers, and hand-holding couples. In the distance was the Pyramid and that curvy bridge Olivia said reminded people of Dolly Parton's boobs. Maybe I'd head the other way. Hide out until my appointment with Breckenridge.

"Hey there, little lady!" called out a deep Elvis-like voice.

Whirling around, I saw three college-age guys in Elvis jumpsuits. The guy who'd spoken stepped forward. He had a cheerful, chubby face, and his white jumpsuit was stretched tight around his midsection. He waved a cell phone. "Would you mind taking a photo?"

With a final glance behind me, I trotted over and accepted the phone.

"Thank you, darlin'. Thank you very much," he said. It had to be the worst Elvis impression of all time.

The second Elvis looked more authentic, with dark, wavy hair and a bejeweled jumpsuit that highlighted his broad shoulders. The third was red-haired and freckled. He had a Hawaiian theme going on, with a lei and a flower in his belt. The trio posed sideways, as if balancing on surfboards. I snapped several photos, calling out "Say 'Vegas'" or "Say 'Lisa Marie,'" to show off my Elvis smarts. When the dark-haired one stepped forward to take back the phone, he looked me up and down in my sweat-stained shirt and shorts. I wanted to squirm, in a good way.

"Someone chasin' you, Pink?" he asked. "You runnin' from the law?"

"Just my mother."

The Elvises found this hysterical.

"Come on over to our house," the chubby one said. "It's our Elvis competition tonight. I'm gonna win." When the dark-haired Elvis fake coughed, he added: "It's not the looks, it's the moves." He wiggled his hips.

The Elvises—or was it Elvi?—said they lived in Tupelo House at the University of Memphis. They were taking courses this summer because, well, some of them hadn't done so well in the spring. The dark one's name was Brett, but I didn't catch the others'. One might have been Wayne.

I was meeting Breckenridge at this office at five p.m. and planned to attend his speech at seven thirty, but how often did I get invited to a college party? Like, never. When I mentioned how much my grandmother would enjoy the Elvis contest, though, there was an awkward silence. I quickly explained how Olivia once went on a date with Elvis. That just got a lot of whoops and a few comments about my grandmother that weren't quite appropriate.

"Whaddaya say, Pink?" Brett moved close. He smelled all sweaty. "Wanna be my guest? Come over now for the preparty." He winked. "I'll show you my Jungle Room."

They whooped again like this was a great joke. I didn't mind. I gave them my most adorable shrug. "Sure, why not?" Anything that would make my mom freak the hell out, like partying with college guys, sounded great.

Chubby Elvis threw his arms around Brett's shoulders and jumped up and down chanting, "Pink, Pink, Pink." Hawaiian Elvis joined in, forming a tight circle around me. I begged them to stop without meaning it for a second.

When they broke apart, Brett pointed at three motorcycles tucked away down a little path and leaned in close, his breath hot on my ear. "Take you for a ride?"

Mom despised motorcycles. I was absolutely forbidden to ride one.

"You bet," I said.

Chapter 29

Hope

Back in the Peabody lounge, I ordered another Memphis Blues Martini and kicked at the table leg.

On a cold weekend in early 1998, as I'd been starting my last semester at college and my mother was packing for a quick visit to Memphis, my father had phoned her in LA complaining of stomach pain. Probably indigestion, he said, but it could be the flu. My mother couldn't risk being sick, not with her filming schedule, so she canceled her flight. Two days later, my father's housekeeper found him on the bedroom floor, dead from a massive heart attack.

My mother flew home then, of course, and I endured the usual media-flurry around anything involving Memphis's beloved Soap Queen. She gave phone interviews with the *Commercial Appeal* and *Soap Opera Digest* and sat for a horrifying *People* photo session, gazing at my father's portrait.

What broke me, though, was hearing from my mother's mouth how she'd discouraged my father from calling his doctor. "Oh, for God's sake, Harold," she'd said, "take a Tums." When she relayed this, my jaw dropped.

She'd gotten all huffy at me. "Well I'm not a doctor! Your father never listened to me. How could I know he'd pick that moment to start?"

I barely spoke to my mother after that. For years. No doubt it was unfair to blame her for my father's death, but my grief was bottomless and irrational. Besides, making her the villain kept me from turning the anger on myself. I'd been only ten minutes away at school, after all, and hadn't phoned my father that weekend.

So when my mother fake fainted at the Peabody and had the gall to imply she might be having a heart attack, it didn't sit well with me. Not at all.

I CALLED JORDAN to ask for her help, and twenty minutes later, she breezed into the Peabody lounge, a vision in turquoise. Her matching skirt, jacket, and pumps reminded me of some of the gorgeous church-lady outfits I'd seen years earlier when Shelley had taken me to Al Green's Full Gospel Tabernacle one Sunday morning.

"Reporting for duty," Jordan said, taking a seat beside me. She lifted my drink, examining it curiously.

"Memphis Blues Martini. Help yourself."

Jordan took a sip as I told her about my mother's theatrics. I asked if she'd be willing to take turns watching my mother's suite, in case she tried to leave, or Dylan returned. Whoever wasn't doing that could comb the streets for Dylan.

Jordan volunteered for the first shift of suite-watching. "Honestly, I could use a little quiet time," she said.

BEALE STREET WAS humming in the midafternoon heat, smelling of barbecue and weed. Outside a touristy shop, a bearded man was playing "Fire and Rain" on guitar, and I almost didn't hear my phone ringing. Shoving a finger in one ear, I answered and speed-walked up the street.

"Hope," Gary bellowed without so much as a hello, "the ideas you sent were terrible. Dull. Boring. No student is going to rip apart a textbook for free copies at Staples."

"You said you wanted coupons."

"Yes, coupons! You know! Coffee, donuts, fries. Stuff kids want."

Thank God Gary couldn't see me slap my forehead. "Do we really want to encourage that, Gary? What about something healthier?"

"For Pete's sake, Hope! Students aren't going to destroy a $150 textbook for a fruit-and-nut plate."

I'd arrived at an intersection and pushed the walk button. "Let me play around with some different ideas. I can't talk right now," I said as a truck roared by. "I'm on a street corner."

"You volunteered for this, Hope. You said you could put in the hours. Then you skip town, and every time I hear from you, you're closer to the border. Are you on the lam?"

He was joking, right? "Give me until Monday. It's the weekend."

I stopped midstep as a group of motorcycles crossed the intersection. The riders were in Elvis jumpsuits and the last had a girl clinging to his back. Her helmet didn't completely hide her pink hair.

Noooo!

"Dylan," I shrieked, frantically waving an outstretched arm. "I need to go," I yelled into the phone, and hung up.

The motorcycles stopped at the next intersection. I raced down the sidewalk, dodging pedestrians. There were too many, so I veered into the street, sprinting alongside the parked cars. By the time I saw the car door opening, it was too late. I caught the edge hard with my hip and went sprawling onto the pavement. My phone flew out of my hand and into the middle of the street, where a cab, swerving to avoid me, ran over it.

"Oh my God!" said a woman's voice. From where my cheek rested on the pavement, I saw navy sandals leap from the car. "I didn't see you. I'm so sorry!" A young woman squatted down, grabbing my elbow as I peeled myself from the ground. She looked both ways to be sure no cars were coming and ran out to grab my phone. I limped around her car to the curb.

"I'm okay," I said, though the facts spoke otherwise. I was bent in half, holding my hip with both hands. When I looked down, my skirt was ripped, my hands were raw, and blood was dripping from one knee. My elbow burned like the skin had been scraped off.

The woman handed me my phone and I hobbled a few steps to get a clear view of the street. The motorcycles were nowhere in sight. Several people had paused on the sidewalk, clutching their cells, no doubt wishing they'd captured my dooring to share on Instagram.

"Not your fault," I called back to the woman whose car door I'd tried to remove with my hip. My phone screen was shattered in a spiderweb pattern and vibrated erratically. The term "death rattles" came to mind. Was that a call coming in? Had

Dylan seen me fall? I gently pressed the hint of green at the bottom and held it to my ear.

"Hope, don't ever hang up on me. That's the one thing I won't tolerate."

"I can't talk, Gary." I headed down the sidewalk in a furious limp. "That's why I hung up. Because I can't talk." I could feel my voice breaking and fought to steady it.

"Hope, I'm warning you . . ."

My phone made a noise like a duck being strangled.

"You're breaking up, Gary," I lied, pushing something red.

I shuffled away from the stares of passersby, fighting back tears. Not only did I hurt like hell, but Dylan was gone, no telling where, on the back of a motorcycle with Elvis.

Another pathetic duck sound. By scrolling carefully along the side, I could read most of the message, which appeared below the link to Aaron's condo. He asked if I could meet him in Memphis Park in ten—or was it fifteen?—minutes. No matter how I scrolled, I couldn't be sure of the second number.

I took in my ripped clothes and bloody shins. Not my best look, but it would have to do. The sooner I could get to Aaron and the closer I could stay to him, the more likely I could intercept Dylan.

On the shattered keypad, I pecked out what I hoped was "Okay."

THE TROLLEY DRIVER looked me up and down, taking in my Girl, Doored look.

I plopped down in a front seat for some triage. The gash on one knee was deep, and blood had dried in rivulets down my shin. The cut was no longer bleeding, just . . . gaping. My skirt had torn, and a corner of fabric hung near my hip bone. The front of my white blouse looked like someone had driven over me.

It was only a few blocks to my stop. Waving off the driver's hand, I gripped the rail and tottered down the trolley stairs.

As I approached the park, the smell of fresh-cut grass and crepe myrtle filled the air. Carousel music drifted up from a passing riverboat: "Dixie." When I'd lived here, I'd never realized the park had a name, but last night, Aaron had set me straight. It had been Confederate Park—now temporarily renamed Memphis Park while the city chose a permanent name— and the orator statue was Jefferson Davis. Both the sculpture and Civil War cannons were scheduled for removal.

I cut across the grass and gingerly lowered myself onto a bench beside the oak tree Aaron and I had claimed as ours. My phone shuddered in my bag, and when I checked, I'd missed a call from a Boston number. I poked blindly at a few spots, trying to navigate to voicemail. A flash of blue moved in front of me, and I looked up, letting the phone drop into my lap.

The skin around her eyes was deeply lined, but Carly's strawberry-blond hair was still chin-length, as it had been when she'd surprised me here eighteen years ago.

"You're gonna have to teach me this trick," I said.

Chapter 30

Olivia

I peered out the suite's peephole and cursed my bad luck. The large figure in the turquoise jacket and skirt was clearly Jordan, pacing back and forth in the hallway. No doubt Jordan meant to follow me wherever I went. Well, that wouldn't do. My meeting with the Graceland curator was in forty-five minutes.

On any other day, I'd have invited Jordan in and complimented her stunning outfit. Jordan had such a lovely color sense—far better than Hope, who favored beiges and grays that washed her out. Unfortunately, this wasn't any day. It was *the* day. And Jordan was in my way.

I lifted the room phone and asked for Jon-David. I needed a favor.

Ten minutes later, the elevator dinged, and I heard voices in the hall. Angry voices. Someone rapped on my door, making me flinch.

"Olivia, it's Jordan!" Her voice was muffled through the door. "Tell these people you know me."

The voices grew louder, higher pitched. Yelling unnerved

me. That shrieking boy on set. I went into the bathroom and turned on the shower full blast to drown out the noise. I felt badly for Jordan, but Jon-David could be counted on to handle this appropriately. I couldn't let anything interfere with my plan. Not this day.

JON-DAVID HAD CALLED a cab and escorted me down on the elevator.

"I'm sorry to be so much trouble," I said. "That lady in the hallway—you don't suppose she's waiting outside, do you?" I dreaded an awkward scene with Jordan.

Jon-David's face was solemn. "I don't want to alarm you, Olivia, but that was no lady." He peered over his glasses, giving me a meaningful look.

"Well, I'm sure she's a lovely person. She just wants to follow me, is all."

"No worries," he said, holding open the lobby door. "We've taken care of it."

Once I was in the cab, though, and the driver had rounded the corner onto B.B. King Boulevard, I noticed a huge commotion at the Peabody's side entrance. Two patrol cars had lights flashing. The cabbie zipped past, and I twisted in my seat to watch an officer shove someone into the back of the cruiser. Someone wearing turquoise.

Dear God. No.

"Stop!" I yelled.

The driver glanced in his mirror. "Stop?"

"Go back!" I pointed behind us. "I need to speak to those police officers."

"I'll have to circle the block," the driver explained. "It's one way."

"Fine! Just hurry."

When we arrived back at the Peabody, though, the cruisers were gone.

No, no, no, no.

The driver pulled to the curb. He watched me in his rearview mirror.

I found Jon-David's card in my wallet and called. It went to voicemail. Dear Lord, why today, of all days? "Jon-David, it's Olivia. I'm terribly upset. I did not intend for that woman outside my room to be arrested." I paused, unsure what to say next without admitting I knew Jordan. The mailbox beeped and clicked off. I checked my watch. I'd have to figure this out on the fly.

"Go, please!" I fluttered my fingers.

"To?" The cabbie was confused.

"To Graceland."

The cab took off again, and I dialed 911. I was transferred to the nonemergency number and then to a different precinct. Both dispatchers denied sending anyone to the Peabody. On the third transfer, I was disconnected.

I bent forward and dropped my head into my hands. We were now minutes from Graceland. No time to go through it again. I wrestled with myself, then gave in and dialed Hope. Praise God, it went to voicemail.

"Hope, there's been a terrible misunderstanding. Jordan may have been arrested. Please do your best to straighten it out."

I hung up, closed my eyes, and dropped back against the

seat. I tried to calm myself. Hope would take care of it. The situation shouldn't be that difficult to explain, and in truth, Hope was more capable than even she herself realized. The whole thing would make an amusing story someday. Hope and Jordan would have a good laugh at my expense.

As confident as I felt of this scenario, I wanted to do something to make it up to Jordan. I found a pen in my bag and wrote on the back of Jon-David's card.

Hope,

I would like Jordan to have the antique amethyst necklace in the third drawer of my jewelry case.

I tucked the card back in my purse.

That was better. Not perfect, but . . . something. Once again, I leaned back and tried to assume the feeling of peace I'd hoped for on this particular day. At least the weather was cooperating, the late-afternoon sun peeking out from behind wispy clouds. I took out my credit card to pay for the ride. I liked to estimate the tip in advance to avoid the exorbitant percentages offered on the screen. Next to the credit card gizmo was the cab driver's information card. I blinked, refocused. Really? I studied the driver, then examined his card again.

I leaned forward. "Your name . . . is Harold Waites?"

The man nodded.

Harold. My husband's name. The man who loved to proclaim that there were no coincidences, that everything happened for a reason.

I still believed that idea was bullshit. There was no grand

plan, things were not foreordained. Olivia Grant directed her own life, thank you very much. Oddly, though, in recent weeks, the world had seemed full of signs—signs that had led me to this day, that had come together to form this plan. A screaming boy's cries telling me it was time to move on. A beloved photo proclaiming that some souls are never forgotten. A teenager's pink hair and pink car—Elvis's favorite color—providing an unexpected lift.

No, it wasn't that things happened for a reason, exactly. I didn't believe that. What I did believe was that we could make meaning out of what happened. That, in fact, we must.

I squinted again at the cab driver's name. Harold Waites. Here I was, on my way to Graceland, and my husband had reached out to give his blessing.

I was on the right road.

Chapter 31

Hope

Carly smoothed her skirt and lowered herself onto the park bench beside me. "Oh, it wasn't hard to find you," she said. "You've been texting with Veronica."

I frowned, hating to look as dull-witted as Carly imagined me to be.

"She handles everything for Aaron in Memphis. His phone contacts are her contacts."

"And her contacts are yours, apparently."

Carly had a deep laugh that I had to admit was attractive. She cradled a Starbucks iced cappuccino. "Honestly, when I first hooked up Veronica with Aaron's campaign, I had no idea what a gold mine that girl would be. She can't stay out of anyone's business. And loyal! I've known German Shepherds less devoted."

I recalled Veronica's narrow-eyed looks when she popped into the office after hours to see if Aaron and I needed help. Her annoyance when we grabbed sandwiches to eat in the park, leaving her to manage the phone volunteers. I'd brushed it off as envy. She'd chased after us once, stopping us at the edge of the park and saying she'd forgotten the password on my computer.

Carly seemed to read my thoughts. "Really, Hope, there's a lesson in this for all of us. It's important to invite people to lunch now and again."

I picked up the phone in my lap and dropped it into my bag. Of course. So much made sense. Veronica had guessed why I'd ditched her that night and followed me into the park. She wouldn't have had to hover long in the darkness before seeing Aaron pull me behind the tree, our two figures merging into one. That's how Carly had known I was the other woman. And how Fish had known those words—a park, a shingle oak—I'd believed could only have come from Aaron.

"Veronica called you from the fundraiser, I assume?"

"Hadn't heard from her in years! So good to catch up." Carly took in my ripped clothes, bloody shins. "Are you okay, Hope? You look like you were hit by a bus."

"If not, I'm about to be."

She laughed again and patted my leg. "You're funny. It's too bad we've always been on opposite teams. Wanted different things."

"Once we wanted the same thing."

"True! And I won. So I get it—you're not a fan. But you think I'm a bad person, and really, Hope, I'm not." I snorted and her mouth tightened. "Maybe you're not aware, but I run a charity that provides massage therapy for terminally ill children. I founded another that offers therapeutic horseback riding for kids with autism. I've spent my entire life looking out for other people's best interests. Including yours."

I flicked a glance in her direction. Her jaw was set. She was serious.

Carly continued: "Think about it. How many women would provide for their husband's illegitimate child?"

"You tricked me," I said. "You made me believe Aaron knew."

She laughed. "Seriously, Hope? Is that the hill you want to die on? Because, let's face it, honesty is not your strong suit."

That stung and I lashed out. "This from the woman who faked a pregnancy to get Aaron to marry her?"

Her eyebrows shot up. "Fascinating." She thumbed a drip from the side of her iced cappuccino. "Is that what Aaron believes?"

I'd regretted the words as soon as they'd left my mouth. "No, he didn't say that." I fumbled, trying to get back that feeling of righteous indignation. "But let's be honest, Carly. How much of a coincidence . . ."

"Oh, no coincidence at all." She held up a palm. "I saw you coming a mile away. Two weeks after you started canvassing with Aaron, all I heard was 'Hope this' and 'Hope that.' I knew what I had to do. Circle the wagons. Protect what was mine."

I traced a line in the grass with the toe of my shoe. So Carly *had* been pregnant. She'd gotten pregnant on purpose. And miscarried on her honeymoon. "I'm sorry," I whispered.

Carly wasn't one to waste an advantage. "What other private matters did you and Aaron discuss at his condo last night?" My stomach dropped. "That's right, Detective Fish followed you there. Did you enjoy yourself? Relive old times?"

I inhaled deeply, taking a moment to pull myself back together. "May I ask what your stake is in this, Carly? Aren't you and Aaron divorced?"

"Unfortunately. I wasn't happy about it. I'm not used to failing. Oh, I played nice, went quietly, as they say. If you act sweet when men dump you, often as not they come crawling back, tail between their legs. I knew Aaron would change his mind." She took another pull from the straw in her drink. "I finally had to let go of that idea. Earlier today, I managed to get five minutes of his precious time, and he was an incredible dick to me. He straight up told me we are never, ever, getting back together." Carly shook her head, stared off into the distance. "I wasn't even aware he knew that song."

Something in her oddly detached tone made me shiver. "Look, Carly, I haven't told Aaron anything about his daughter or the agreement. The truth is, I can't afford to break it. I can't pay you back. And I don't want Aaron or my daughter to know about it. I'm ashamed of that choice. It came from a bad place, and it's forced me to live in a bad place, but that's my problem." I turned to her. "All I want to do is collect my mother and daughter and get out of Memphis."

Carly was shaking her head. "Too late," she said, sadly. She stood and hoisted her Burberry handbag onto her shoulder. "I'm tired of being the good guy while you and Aaron sneak around and break things—promises, engagements, agreements. He needs to learn a lesson."

"Wait." Something stuck in my windpipe. "You wouldn't do anything to hurt Aaron. Not right now . . ."

"Me? Oh, no, it won't be me who takes Aaron down. Probably not even you, Hope. I'm thinking it will be your pink-haired felon of a daughter."

"Leave my daughter out of this."

Carly stepped back and shrugged. "Karma's a bitch, Hope."

She picked up her coffee and started to turn, then pivoted back with a smirk. "By the way, you never answered my question about last night. Since you and I are being so honest with each other, did you enjoy your time with Aaron? Did you sleep with him?"

I looked up, giving her my best smile. "Yes," I said. "And it was fabulous."

In one motion, Carly pulled the top off her iced cappuccino and tossed it at me. It splashed on my face and blouse, the cubes falling into my lap. "You know," she said, "all those years ago, I could tell Aaron was buying your bullshit. He thought you were such a good person. What a laugh. When you think about it, Hope, which of us has been more dishonest?"

I rose stiffly, brushing the ice cubes off my skirt. "You want to know what's even funnier, Carly? The whole time I've been sitting here, I've been wondering the same thing."

I STOOD THERE for a long time, until Carly had disappeared into the parking lot on the other side of the park. Then, re-membering the missed call, I checked my phone. There were two missed calls, and one voicemail. I tapped the broken screen gently.

The message was from my mother, in a shaky voice that raised the hair on my arms. Jordan had been arrested.

Chapter 32

Dylan

The half-mowed patch of dead grass in front of Tupelo House swarmed with every kind of Elvis imaginable. A tall, skinny Elvis in army fatigues. An unshaven Elvis sporting a karate black belt. Zombie Elvis with a papier-mâché toilet attached to his ass. As I followed Brett to the porch, a Chihuahua in a curly black wig and aviator sunglasses yipped and circled my ankles. "Don't Be Cruel" blasted through the windows.

My legs wobbled a bit. The way Brett had dipped his motorcycle around corners and gunned it at lights had scared me shitless. I'd clung to his jumpsuit and nearly choked from his pit odor. Somehow my walk on the wild side to piss off Mom hadn't been a great decision. What I wanted, I realized, was some time alone, to figure out what to do about Breckenridge. Everything else seemed . . . immature.

"Now that we're here," Hawaiian Elvis said, slipping a sweaty arm around my back, "you get to pick your King."

Gross.

Brett yanked me away and hissed, "Back off." He turned to Chubby Elvis. "You, too, Wade."

Okay, so not Wayne. Wade. And, again, gross.

Inside Tupelo House, it smelled like they'd mopped the floor with Budweiser. The furniture had been pushed aside, and a tattooed girl perched on the ratty sofa, using a Sharpie to draw sideburns on a pompadoured King. Hawaiian Elvis led the way through a swinging door to the kitchen, where the table was piled high with pizza boxes and topped with a bag of Cheetos, like a flaming volcano. Crap. What were the chances they had anything vegan?

The deafening music had switched to "Burning Love."

"Want some punch?" Brett yelled in my ear.

"Does it have alcohol?" I shouted back.

Brett roared. Looping an arm around my waist, he told me it had grain alcohol. I'd drunk beer before, but whole-grain alcohol sounded kind of healthy, so I said sure. My meeting with Breckenridge wasn't for two hours. I'd need to be stone-cold sober for that.

Using plastic cups, Brett scooped punch from the vat in a way that seemed vaguely unsanitary, but I was thirsty and took a big gulp. It tasted like paint thinner stirred into Kool-Aid. I coughed and Brett thumped me on the back, grinning like I'd passed a test. Without breathing through my nose, I downed the rest.

The three Elvi pummeled me with questions as they showed me the house. Where was I from? What was I doing in Memphis? When I mentioned I was only sixteen, Brett threw his plastic cup on the floor and stomped on it. "Crap! Why does this keep happening to me?"

As the horrid-tasting punch kicked in, the top of my head felt like it was floating out through my hair. I clutched the stair railing and thought I might puke. The music was hurting my ears, the boys smelled, and nobody responded when I asked for water. I needed out.

When we ended back in the living room, Brett said he wanted more punch and pushed through the kitchen door, Hawaiian Elvis in tow. I saw my chance and bolted for the front door. I was halfway down the street when Wade caught up to me, holding out a cold bottle of water.

"I apologize for those two," Wade said. "Care to take a walk?"

I shrugged. The water bottle was plastic, but whatever. I'd recycle it.

WADE AND I walked past some dilapidated frat houses to a shady park, where we sat side by side on saddle swings. Wade was studying journalism. I didn't dare ask if he wrote for the *Daily Helmet*. We chatted about everything—my Bug, his bike, my Graceland tour, his Elvis contest. The punch had made me talkative, and I let slip how I'd come to Memphis to meet my father for the first time. No name, just that I'd see him later that afternoon. "Trying to keep an open mind," I said. "I've heard a few things about him that aren't great."

"Like what?"

"He's a weenie."

Wade laughed. "My father could be an asshole sometimes. He yelled a lot. But he also took me to Redbirds games, and we had a blast there, yelling at the umpires." He twisted his swing around in a circle. "I guess he just liked to yell."

I dug my sneaker in the dirt. "Maybe it's my fault. I had this picture of my dad. I wanted him to be a hero. Like in *Die Hard*. Someone who'd walk across broken glass for me."

"Love Bruce Willis!" Wade said, letting his swing spin back around. "You're right, though. Most dads aren't like that. Mine sure wasn't."

"I'm nothing like my mom, so I thought I must take after my dad. I kind of modeled myself on him. What I imagined he was like. But if he's not who I thought he was . . ." I trailed off, drawing an X in the dirt with my toe.

"Look," Wade said, "all this guy did for you was donate a few genes. You don't have to be like him. Think about Elvis. His dad went to jail for forging checks, and he had this weirdly smothering mom. He didn't let his parents define him."

"Huh." Olivia hadn't told me that.

"I mean, even if there was a yelling gene and I inherited it from my dad, I still could use it however I want. I could yell at the CEO of Exxon for fracking." He glanced skyward, shading his eyes from the sun. "Maybe my father didn't think of that."

"Dude!" A voice shouted from across the park. Hawaiian Elvis bent forward, hands on knees, panting. "Been lookin' for you!" He waved at Wade to come.

"Right back." Wade jumped off his swing and jogged over. I watched them argue, two Elvis impersonators on a street corner. Memphis was bomb.

I stretched back in the swing, let the sun warm my face, and thought about Aaron Breckenridge. For the zillionth time that day, I replayed my conversation with Jordan. In the light of day, I couldn't be absolutely certain what Jordan had been trying to say—or rather, trying not to say—about my dad. Sure, maybe Breckenridge was a jerk—that was one possibility. Or maybe Jordan had it wrong. Jordan didn't know everything.

If this trip had taught me anything, it was that adults in general didn't know as much as they pretended to. Olivia acted like she had everything under control, but she'd screwed up badly with her oxygen. And Mom, geez! Even when she wasn't lying, sometimes she was flat-out wrong. Mom thought Olivia was selfish. And okay, Olivia could be, now and then, but not always, and she made up for it by being fun. Plus, Mom told me Olivia wasn't much for physical affection. Not true. Olivia might not know when to give hugs, or how to ask for them, but that didn't mean she was opposed to them.

No, I couldn't trust anyone on the Breckenridge issue. I'd keep a semi-open mind and go with my gut. In all honesty, I was having trouble letting go of the idea that my dad would be excited to meet me. It felt right. For once, I'd take things slow, not rush to conclusions. I had a decent bullshit meter.

I checked my phone. Three p.m. Would Mom still be hanging out at the Peabody? I wanted to change my outfit before my appointment with Breckenridge. I texted Olivia, asking if the coast was clear.

Wade trotted back and apologized. He needed to get back to the preparty. Brett and Hawaiian Elvis, whose name I finally learned was Donny, wanted to rehearse their act. Did I need a ride back to my hotel?

I explained my dilemma to Wade. My mom was a little— how to put it?—unstable. She'd followed my grandmother and me on this trip and had been stalking me around Memphis.

She might be at the Peabody now, hoping to nab me. I needed to avoid her and get to my room.

Wade thought for a moment, then grinned. He had an idea. Back at Tupelo House, he took Brett and Hawaiian Elvis aside. The Elvi huddled together and burst out laughing.

"A distraction?" Brett cackled, turning to me. "Oh, little lady, you picked the right guys."

THE ELVI ENTERED the Peabody first. I slipped inside the door and hovered in a hallway as I scanned the lobby for my mother. Still no message from Olivia. What if my grandmother couldn't respond? What if Mom was holding her hostage in our suite?

Across the lounge by the duck fountain, the three Elvi took their places. Wade called out something about free entertainment and dropped onto one knee. Rotating his arm like a propeller, he belted out the opening of "Blue Suede Shoes."

Wade wasn't bad! Behind him, Brett and Donny thrust their hips left and right and sang backup. Everyone in the lounge stared, stood, or aimed their phone. Time for me to move. Hugging the wall, I ducked into the elevator, pressing the door-close button until it shut.

Once outside our suite, though, I checked my phone one last time. Thank God, I had a response from Olivia. It said, "At Graceland. Don't worry about your mother. I created a little problem that will keep her busy. 😔 Good luck tonight. Love you. O."

That was the first time Olivia had said she loved me. I screenshotted the text and saved it.

Inside the suite, I changed into my gray camo miniskirt, gray T-shirt, and black hoodie with knee-highs and ankle-high black boots. The outfit was fire if I did say so myself. It honored Breckenridge's military background while showing me as someone who meant business. I dumped out all the bumper stickers in my bag, stuffed in a pad and pen, and raced back to the elevator.

Down in the lobby, the Elvi were surrounded by two security people and Jon-David. Brett pointed to me. "There she is! Pink said your hotel would love our act." Jon-David gave me a pained look.

I said we needed to get going.

"Good," he whispered.

The Elvi walked me to the Peabody garage and begged for a spin in my pink Bug. Wade called shotgun, and the others dove into the back. I circled the block and cruised down this long street with the Elvi hanging out the windows, hooting at passersby. When we stopped for a light, I noticed a woman on the next block, half running, half limping along the sidewalk. Her clothes were a mess.

"Jesus. That's my mom."

In the back seat, Brett nearly climbed on top of Donny to stick his head out and look.

"I didn't believe the crazy mom part," Brett said after we drove past. "I do now."

BRECKENRIDGE'S MEMPHIS OFFICE was in a tall white building, nothing special, but the security inside was like an airport, with a conveyor belt and body scanner. Would these people question me? Demand credentials? Thank God I'd cleaned out my bag. My bumper stickers weren't subversive, exactly, but the ones with f-bombs weren't to everyone's taste.

I placed my bag on the belt and held my breath as I stepped

through the portal. On the other side, the security people ignored me and kept chatting. Phew.

Alone in the elevator, I gripped the handrail and gave myself a pep talk. I had this. I'd ask Breckenridge a few questions, make him feel comfortable, then drill down on the past. Mention Hope Robinson. Watch his face. I imagined Breckenridge squinting at me, like I was someone familiar he couldn't place. Maybe he'd feel pinpricks, or a shiver. If he really was my father, wouldn't he have to feel *something*?

Breckenridge's office door had a blue and gold seal that said "United States Senate." The doorknob wouldn't budge. Shit. I noticed an intercom on the wall and pushed the speaker button. When I said my name, the door clicked open.

A middle-aged woman stood behind a desk, her eyes glued to a computer monitor with the concentration of an air-traffic controller landing a plane. She held up a finger. Without turning to look at me, she said: "Just . . . one . . . teeny sec. If I don't write this down, I'll forget."

The woman wore her hair in a bun, and either it was pulled too tight, or she had a really unfortunate nose. Probably this was the office manager Olivia had spoken to. Behind her was an interior office with cloudy glass you couldn't see through. The shadowy figures inside erupted in laughter.

My father was behind that door. The corner of my mouth wouldn't stop twitching. I bit down on it.

The office manager scribbled something on a Post-it and slapped it on her monitor. When she finally looked up, she did a double take. The hair. I was used to it.

"Thank you for coming, Dylan," she said. "I'm sorry to tell you, the senator won't be able to meet with you."

I gripped my bag tighter and stared at her. "I have an appointment."

The woman gave several exaggerated nods, acknowledging I was right. "He was supposed to appear on the Memphis morning show tomorrow, but some local celebrity has shown up out of the blue, so they're taping his segment this afternoon, over at the university. That fit his schedule better, anyway. He's leaving in five minutes."

I fought to focus. "He can't. I've got to talk to him."

"Well, I know, sweetheart. I left several voicemails at the number your adviser gave me."

Shit. I never listened to voicemail. "There must be some other time." I struggled to control the quiver in my voice. "You can move things around."

"I'm afraid not. He has an event tonight, and tomorrow he's leaving on vacation with his sons."

For some reason, this made me furious. "I need to interview him. It's important."

The woman sighed audibly, turned back to her computer, and hit a few keys. She scanned the screen, shaking her head. I assumed she was searching Breckenridge's schedule, though perhaps she'd returned to work and was ignoring me.

What would Olivia do in this situation? Charm, threats, cash. I had no patience for doing things in order. "I'll give you a hundred dollars."

The woman pivoted, her hand on her heart. "Gracious." She laughed. "That won't help. I'll tell you what. You're coming to the speech on campus tonight, right? Senator Breckenridge will do some Q&A afterward, and if you sit up front, I'll make sure he calls on you."

That wasn't the same at all. I needed to speak to him privately. But how could I explain? "I have a bunch of questions . . ." I tried.

"I'm sure other folks in the audience will have the same questions."

I tended to doubt that. Just then, the door to the inner office opened. Two men and a woman in business suits stepped out. Behind them was Aaron Breckenridge, shaking hands and saying he was glad they stopped by while herding them to the door. I slunk back against the wall, heart banging in my chest. As the suits left, Breckenridge turned and gave me a polite smile.

Don't you recognize me?

The office manager jumped in. "This young lady is from the *Daily Helmsman.* I've explained your schedule conflict and said we'd seat her up front this evening, so you can call on her."

"Perfect," Breckenridge said. "I'm so sorry this didn't work out. I'll try to give you a couple questions tonight."

I searched his face, fixed on his one-sided dimple. Like mine.

Breckenridge stuck out his hand, and I offered mine tentatively, like I wasn't familiar with this strange custom. His grip was firm, damp. "Your name again?"

"Dylan," I whispered. *Look at me. You have to feel our connection.*

"Well that should be easy to remember. I have a son named Dylan."

"I know." *Please. Something.*

"Excellent! You've done your research."

"Senator, the car's waiting." The office manager thrust a briefcase into his hand.

His back to me, Breckenridge touched his forehead and asked the name of the TV interviewer he was meeting. The office manager clicked her mouse and found the name. Breckenridge had the door half-open when he turned. "Oh, Veronica?" She lifted her head from her screen. "Call Tom and reschedule our meeting tonight. I'm going to try to see Hope again, while she's in town."

Hope? My insides turned to ice.

Veronica's face dropped. He couldn't cancel, she said. This was the only time possible. Breckenridge strode over and stood behind her as they reviewed the schedule. Their words were muffled and unintelligible to me. I couldn't hear them over the sound of my heartbreak.

See Hope? Again?

Somehow it was resolved, and Breckenridge pointed his briefcase at me. "I'll see you this evening, Dylan. Bring some good questions." Was he mocking me? Had my mother already gotten to him?

I forced a half smile. *Be careful what you ask for, motherfucker.*

Chapter 33

Hope

As I listened to my mother's message, another voicemail popped up. It was from Jordan and told me where the police had taken her. I'd already guessed. Everyone in Memphis knew 201 Poplar. The downtown facility housed a police station, courts, and a jail. When I was in college, frat boys who drank illegally and got unruly in the downtown bars ended up there. The complex wasn't far from the park, so I limped across Front Street in an awkward hitch-trot, like a child riding an invisible stick pony.

Something buzzed around my hip, and I swatted it. Not an insect—my phone, in my skirt pocket, vibrating even more faintly. I pulled it out and poked at a hint of green to answer.

"Just so you know, Hope, I was ready to fire you."

Shit, shit, shit.

Gary continued. "No one hangs up on me once, never mind twice. Terry had to pour me a drink. It took her half an hour to calm me down, but she convinced me to listen to your explanation."

"I hung up on you, Gary."

Silence. "Sorry?"

"I said I hung up on you. I'm in the middle of a family emergency, and I have to prioritize things."

"Hope, you assured me . . ."

"I know I did. And I was wrong. Wrong to take on an idea I thought was goofy to begin with, wrong to think I could turn it into something that wasn't ethically bankrupt, and certainly wrong in imagining I could make you understand how slimy . . ."

"You're fired, Hope."

"I know, Gary." I laughed like a madwoman. "This is my moment." I hung up.

Shoving my phone back in my pocket, I looked up just in time to see Dylan's pink Bug speed by, Elvises hanging out of every window.

BY THE TIME I reached 201 Poplar, both my heels had blisters. The security woman checking bags stared at my ripped, stained clothes but let me through. Inside, the concrete complex was as cavernous and depressing as I remembered, and I spent twenty minutes being shuffled from one long, dark corridor to another. When I finally reached the right office, I learned Jordan was being held for trespassing and resisting arrest. Bail had been set at $2,000. The woman who took my credit card moved so slowly I was still waiting for my receipt when Jordan, her right eye black and swollen, came flying through the door, landing on her knees.

Later, Jordan would explain that she'd received the black eye not at the jail, but in a scuffle at the Peabody, where she'd also severed the heel of one of her pumps. The broken shoe had caught on the jail doorjamb, causing her to trip. In short, what I witnessed was a police officer grabbing at Jordan's back to keep her from falling. What my brain saw was my friend, beaten by the police, being pushed to the floor.

Simple misunderstanding.

I'm pretty sure I screamed, "Get your hands off of her." Jordan says I f-bombed the officer. In the end, it didn't matter. What did was the way I elbowed the cop out of the way as I dropped to the floor to help Jordan. Apparently, touching police officers is a no-no, and—this part I should have guessed—especially elbowing one in the boob. I was on the floor myself in seconds, my arm twisted behind my back, my bottom lip smashed on the tile, the taste of dirt and blood filling my mouth. Jordan shouted and grabbed the woman's arm, which got her back in Dutch. All in all, if I hadn't had a good working definition of a clusterfuck before, I did now.

ONCE WE'D BEEN interviewed and processed, two officers came to take Jordan and me to separate holding cells. I pleaded that they keep us together. They seemed amused, but it must have been a slow night, because they walked Jordan and me to a cell with four bunks—a snoring, rumpled woman on one of them—and a sink and toilet at one end.

"You sure?" asked the cop who'd tackled me. She had gorgeous violet eyes, which, for some reason, made me feel worse.

I said I was sure, and Jordan shrugged. I prayed neither of us would need to use the toilet.

As the cop closed the cell door, I asked when I could make my phone call. She sighed, like I should have asked earlier. Like I did this every Saturday night. She escorted me into a room with a table, chair, and old telephone with square push buttons, and helped me find the number for the Peabody. The front desk refused to confirm that an Olivia Grant or Dylan Robinson was staying there. They asked for a room number, and my description of a "really nice suite with a chandelier in the bathroom" wasn't enough. I replaced the receiver, terrified that I'd forfeited my one call. The cop said she'd wait until I reached someone or could leave a message. When I told her the number I needed was on my cell phone, she had someone retrieve it. That was kinder than I expected for someone who'd just slammed my face into the floor.

Calling Aaron was a gamble. His speaking event was in two hours. But I didn't know who else to try. Dylan wouldn't answer my call and certainly wouldn't listen to voicemail. I didn't know any lawyers, or how in God's name I'd find one on a Saturday night. And I had to believe that Aaron, if he got the message, would surely be able to help.

"You've reached the office of Senator Aaron Breckenridge. We can't take your call right now . . ."

Shit. That didn't sound right. He'd told me the number was his personal cell. Confused, stressed, unable to imagine what else to do, I left a message.

THE WEATHERED AND bedraggled woman sleeping across the cell reeked of alcohol and BO. I blocked my nose so I wouldn't gag. Sitting next to Jordan on the lower bunk, I let my head fall into my hands. When I glanced sideways, Jordan was staring straight ahead, her jaw clenched.

"Are you okay?" I whispered. I didn't want to wake the sleeping woman.

"No, I am *not* okay." The anger in her voice made me cringe. "Jesus, Hope, what the fuck were you thinking?"

"When?" I wasn't clear which fuckup she meant.

"Wrestling with that police officer."

"She pushed you!"

"I fell!" she nearly shouted, whipping off her right pump. "Could you walk in this?" She told me what had happened, earlier, at the Peabody, and how she'd tripped. "That police officer was *decent* to me. She was kind," Jordan grumbled. "Everything was going to be fine until you took a swing at her."

"I didn't take a swing! I just tried to . . . move her."

"You call it what you want. By the time this gets to court, you took a swing." Jordan put the broken pump back on her foot, which I didn't think was a great idea.

"Jordan, I don't know what to say. I'm so, so sorry." Across the cell, the woman moaned in her sleep.

"Did you call your mother?" Jordan muttered.

"I tried. No one answered." I hesitated to say more but had no choice. "I called Aaron."

"Aaron Breckenridge?"

"I know that sounds crazy, but last night, we . . . reconnected."

I watched the slow shift in her face, from angry to appalled. "Jesus, Mary, and Joseph. Tell me you didn't sleep with that guy."

"No, it's okay! I was wrong about him."

"Oh. My. God." Jordan rose, batting away the fumes from the sleeping woman.

"Jordan, it's not what you think."

"What I *think*? What I *think*?" she repeated. She was pacing the cell, occasionally lurching sideways on the broken heel. "How in hell would I know what to *think* anymore?"

"Aaron didn't know about Dylan. He didn't know she existed."

"Hope." She bent down, putting both arms on my shoulders. "We discussed this. You said, very clearly, he wanted nothing to do with her. Did you lie to me?"

"No, that's what I thought! I was wrong." I dropped my head. "I didn't lie . . . I just didn't tell you everything."

Jordan flung both arms into the air. "Well, *there's* a surprise. How unlike you to tell partial truths. I guess I should feel privileged that I got half the story, right?" I'd never seen Jordan this angry. She was in a white rage. "That's one of the *perks* of being your best friend?"

"I'm sorry. It's not that I enjoy lying. I've had to."

"Well that's interesting, because I keep looking around, and I've yet to see a gun held to your head."

"Sometimes, when people don't tell you the whole truth, it's because the truth is too painful or embarrassing." My forehead throbbed. "Surely, you of all people can understand that."

Her eyes grew wide. "Ex-cuse me? Is that what you think? That I've kept secrets because my truth is painful? Because I'm embarrassed by the truth?"

I tried to play back what I'd said. Had I said that? Had I meant that? "No, of course not."

"Because, for your information—and I didn't imagine I'd ever have to say this to you, Hope—I'm happy with who I am. It's the rest of the world who has problems with it. *That's* why I've had to keep secrets. Whereas you, my friend, you're not happy with who you are."

Jordan walked over to the bars of the cell and called for the police officer.

"Jordan! What—"

She cut me off, her voice cold. "That's the difference between us, Hope. I like who I am, even when I've had to hide it."

I didn't know what to say. I pulled a George. Looked at my shoes.

Jordan wasn't waiting for my response. She was on a roll. "You're afraid to let people get close to you because they might see who you are. You push them away. Or run away—I guess you've done that, too." Jordan leaned into the bars, trying to see around the corner. "You know what I think? You didn't disappear eighteen years ago to give Aaron Breckenridge the freedom to choose you. You disappeared so he *wouldn't* choose you. Because you didn't think you were worth it."

She called through the bars again, and a distant voice yelled back. "Coming, already!"

Jordan returned to me. "Here's something I've learned, Hope. You can't conceal your own truth. If you hold it under water, it'll float to the surface. If you bury it, it'll bust out of the ground like Carrie's freakin' bloody arm. So if that's what you want to do? Keep your truth buried? Then I'm done helping you with that."

The violet-eyed officer appeared. "What's the problem?"

Jordan said, "I made a mistake. I don't want to be in this cell."

"Figured," the officer said, glancing my way.

The sleeping woman struggled to raise her head. Pointing at me, she hissed, "Take that one! She smells!"

"Sorry, Diana," the officer said as she opened the door to let Jordan out. "Just hold your nose."

I CURLED INTO a fetal position on the bunk. My upper arm ached where the cop had yanked it back. My bottom lip, ragged and swollen, felt detached. I longed for a blanket to throw over my head and shut out all light.

What an idiot move to call Aaron! With his speech in an hour, he might not even check his messages. Probably some staff member screened his calls.

I jerked upright, recalling what Carly had said. *Shit. Shit. Shit.* The text message I'd saved as "Aaron" was from Veronica. She, not Aaron, would get the pathetic, sniveling message saying I was in jail. Oh, Lord, what fun she and Carly would have with this one.

Sleeping Diana convulsed and resumed snoring. I gagged, tasting bile, and thought I might be sick, but I couldn't bear the thought of my bruised knees on that rough floor by the toilet. I collapsed back onto the hard mattress, chin pressed to my chest.

Jordan was right. As a twenty-two-year-old, I hadn't believed my luck that Aaron preferred me over someone like Carly. I believed it *was* luck. I'd somehow blinded him to who I was, and my darkest fear was that he'd learn the truth. As I'd driven away from Tennessee, mixed in with gut-wrenching pain was also the tiniest whisper of relief. I wouldn't have to witness his disappointment.

The jail-cell pillow was rough and hurt my ear. I had no idea how much time passed, and it hardly mattered. I'd miss

Aaron's speech. I'd lost my chance to find Dylan beforehand, talk to her, convince her . . . to what? Come home with me? Believe me? Trust me to know what was best for her? It all sounded so ludicrous.

I'd failed as a mother, daughter, friend. My mother and Jordan had both used the same words: I pushed people away. I'd even done it with my daughter. My worst nightmare had always been that she'd discover my secret—not that her father wasn't worthy of her (though at the time, I'd believed that, too), but that I wasn't. To prevent her from finding that out, I'd kept my daughter at arm's length. Now I couldn't reach her.

Graceland

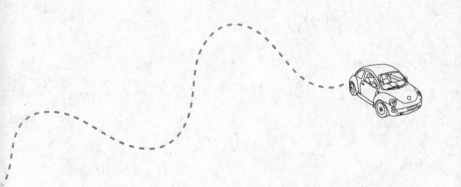

Chapter 34

Olivia

I removed the small cotton throw I'd stuffed in my oxygen cart. Bending down, I spread it across the embossed metal that covered the grave, pulling the blanket higher, so only the name "Elvis" was visible. Like tucking a child into bed. I lowered myself gently until I was seated on the rectangular slab. Elvis's grave, like the others in the Meditation Garden, sat just inches above the surrounding grass. I thanked God for my natural flexibility and years of vinyasa yoga. Not many women my age could still hold a warrior pose, never mind maneuver like this.

Pulling the cart closer, I removed the pill bottle from my bag. Tipping it into in my hand, I took the pills, two at a time, with sips from the Dasani water I'd found in the hotel mini-fridge. I reclined back on the stone and gazed at wisps of clouds overhead. On this day, in the middle of July, there was still some time before sunset.

Two hours earlier, I'd been in the office with Ann Abernathy as the final tourists made their way around the Meditation Garden.

Ann, it turned out, was a rigid, controlling type. She had no interest in my childhood fascination with Graceland, my clandestinely purchased records and hidden magazines, or the letters I'd written Elvis while he was in the army. Instead, she pushed for intimate details on my date with Elvis. After I related how Elvis brought me to his suite, where I partied with him and his entourage, Ann interrupted constantly with questions. "How did Elvis react when you said that?" "What was Elvis doing when you were chatting with Sonny?" "Did Elvis get involved in the argument with Red?" I responded patiently to these inane questions, then resumed where I'd left off. Wresting the interview from Ann Abernathy had been an exhausting tug-of-war.

Indeed, I could tell by the number of times Ann glanced at her phone that the interview was taking longer than expected. No matter. The Elvis biography by Peter Guralnick had required two volumes, *The Godfather* saga three films, and the Bible both an Old and New Testament. Some stories simply can't be rushed.

When I came to the part where the party broke up and Elvis's entourage retreated to their own rooms, I folded my hands.

Ann blinked. "What happened after that? Did Elvis invite you to his bedroom?"

"As I'm sure you'll understand, there are some things I need to keep private, out of respect for the King."

Ann prodded, but I refused to reveal anything more. Oh, I had juicy stuff all right, but how could I share that without hinting at the rest? How Elvis had begun slurring his words, slipping in and out of consciousness. I'd gone into the bathroom for some water and seen the pill bottles, lined up rows deep on the vanity. Even then, seven years before Elvis died, I could tell he'd gone too far down that road. There'd be no turning back. I'd slipped out of his hotel room with the heartbreaking thought that he probably wouldn't remember my being there.

Ann Abernathy was clearly frustrated by my discretion. Still, as we called it quits, I felt emboldened to ask for what I really wanted.

Ann smiled, shaking her head. "I'm so sorry, Olivia. No one but Priscilla, Lisa Marie, and the curator are allowed in Elvis's bedroom. It's been that way since Graceland opened. I'd lose my job if I so much as let you climb the stairs." She glanced down at my oxygen tank, a subtle reminder that getting to the second floor was perhaps more than I was up to, in any case.

"And yet, we've all heard rumors that Nicolas Cage was up there." I sniffed. "Even lying on Elvis's bed."

"Well, if you marry Lisa Marie, you might get an invitation, too. I'm afraid I know of no other way."

As hard as it was to admit defeat, I had a backup plan, and truthfully, some aspects of that plan were preferable. In gratitude for my interview, Ann granted my request for time alone in the Meditation Garden after Graceland closed. Ann would remain in her office, completing paperwork, and come get me at six thirty, before setting the alarms.

I hated to think of Ann's horror when she came for me.

Or maybe I didn't.

THE RAISED LETTERING cut into my shoulder, so I shimmied closer to the edge of the grave. Not exactly what I'd dreamed of as a teenager, when I'd fantasized about being with Elvis at Graceland. Then again, very little ended up being what you expected.

Water burbled in the fountain behind me. Leaves rustled in the breeze. Cars passed outside the gates on Elvis Presley Boulevard. Everything was going as planned. I took a long, slow inhale and closed my eyes. I recited Psalm 23, a prayer my mother had taught me as a child. Though never fond of imagining myself as a sheep, I'd been enchanted by the other images: green pastures, cups running over, the valley of the shadow of death. I wasn't worried about dying. I believed in an afterlife. Oh, nothing like the one my crazy mother had described: choirs of angels, God as an old man with a beard. Something more . . . ineffable. My life energy would merge with that of people who'd gone before me. I'd be with them again: Harold. Beth. Elvis.

I waited for the pills to take effect. As added insurance, at the last possible moment, I planned to remove my cannula. Ideally, I hoped to experience no more than a touch of breathlessness as the pills pulled me under. The timing had to be just right.

Where would Hope and Dylan be, I wondered, when they got the news? They'd be upset, of course, but they'd get over it. It wasn't like I'd been an award-winning mother or grandmother. Still, I was sorry I couldn't share in Dylan's joy at meeting her father. And witness Hope's gratitude for dragging her to Memphis. Maybe not at first. Eventually, though, Hope would realize the journey had been for her, even more than for Dylan. It was my gift to them. I'd embraced my role as mother and grandmother a tad late, but in the end, as always, I'd nailed it.

I had a harder time picturing my fans' reaction to my departure, struggling to put a face to any of them. That windbag waitress in the diner would turn the conversation to herself, how I'd been rude to her and hadn't tipped. The shriveled old gecko in the wheelchair at Subway wouldn't understand, and her son, being a priest, couldn't approve of my exit. Even Frances, my fan-club president, would resent having to find a new hobby. Any tears that woman shed would be for herself. In truth, when I considered the lot of them, all the fans I'd met over the years, I couldn't recall anyone whose opinion I valued.

Dylan had said something similar the night before, as I struggled to supply Frances with the perfect retort for @WhatWouldAndromedaDo? She'd asked why I bothered.

"It's the price of fame, Dylan. You must feed the fans."

"But you don't even *like* those people."

"What do you mean, I don't like them?"

"Everyone we've met you've found annoying."

The child had a point. Ironic, wasn't it? Though I'd never thought of it in this way, fame meant being loved by a lot of people you wouldn't invite over for dinner. Half of them would read the news of my demise over their morning coffee and then turn to the gossip section for more dirt on Kevin Spacey. How odd this hadn't occurred to me before.

Well, Dylan would miss me. We'd had quite the journey together. Sure, the girl's harebrained decisions had created challenges, but wasn't that what made life such a wild ride? Just like Andromeda on *Light Within,* Dylan made things happen, stirred things up. Hope didn't understand that Dylan's recklessness, her impulsive nature, was simply a coping mechanism. By not thinking before she acted, Dylan could pretend she didn't care. I only wished I could have helped the child more. Perhaps the father would step up.

And then there was Hope. I'd brought my daughter this far. Hope could figure out the rest on her own, couldn't she? Face whatever heartache had paralyzed her for so long? Get on with her life? Get unstuck?

A gray fog was seeping into my brain. I heard a sigh and turned toward it. No one there—only that tall statue of Jesus and the little angels beside him, shifting, transforming. The pills were taking effect. I needed to stay alert and remove the cannula, but suddenly here was Dylan, wavy and ethereal. The child was lying down with me, wrapping her arms around me, squeezing me so tight I could hardly breathe.

And now there was a terrible racket, a girl shrieking. Beth. No, not Beth. Hope. As a small child, Hope had hidden in the kitchen and wailed inconsolably each Sunday as I packed my bag for LA. How strange. Perhaps my intolerance for screaming hadn't been from the accident, after all? Had it always been Hope's crying I couldn't bear?

In my mind, I was back on the threshold of our Memphis home, bag in hand, taxi idling in the driveway. I could walk through that door as I always had, or I could return to my daughter.

The sound of the wind in the trees stopped. The wailing quieted. My mother's voice whispered, "You'll be forgotten tomorrow."

Yes, Mother, I will. By almost everyone, and by no one who matters.

I closed the door and put down my bag. I wouldn't leave. Not this time.

My eyes snapped open, and I grabbed at my face, pinching it, trying to jiggle feeling back into it. I struggled to sit up and succeeded only in propping myself on one elbow. Rolling to my side, I clawed in the grass for my cell phone. I had to act fast. The cannula was still in place, but for a woman of my age, in my health, the pills would probably be enough.

The gray fog rolled in again, dragging me under. I was searching . . . but for what? My hand slowed, and I combed my fingers through the grass the way I once had through Harold's hair. A breeze whispered through the trees. The last thing I saw was a little girl—Hope, wrapped in a towel, after a bath. The girl was reaching out, begging me to lift her up.

Chapter 35

Hope

The clanging of the jail door made me heave myself upright. Had I dozed? The violet-eyed cop unlocked the cell door and motioned for me to come out. She seemed intent on not waking Diana, which I appreciated. She locked the door behind us and gestured for me to walk in front of her. "You've been released."

I kept my mouth shut. My father used to joke, "When the judge says not guilty, just say thank you and leave." As I limped down the hallway, my banged-up knee stiffer than before, a wave of excitement washed through me. Aaron must have received my message. He'd be at the university now, about to give his speech, but he'd sent someone.

Then I remembered. The person I'd messaged wasn't Aaron, it was Veronica.

Please God, don't let Veronica be waiting for me.

The officer steered me into a room where a clerk handed me a box with my purse and cell phone. We returned to the dark hallway, and she fumbled with the door lock. I needed a moment for my eyes to adjust to the fluorescent light of the waiting area. I stepped carefully over the doorjamb that had tripped Jordan.

The cop closed the door behind me, and I blinked several times. Across the room, rising from a bench, was Marlin A. Fish.

"Ms. Robinson." He advanced toward me. "You are a very trying woman."

"And you barely know me." I scanned the lobby to see if Carly or Veronica had come for the humiliation party. But no, only Fish, grasping his straw hat. "You bailed me out?"

"I've secured your release, yes."

I shuffled over to speak to the woman behind a bulletproof enclosure, tapping the glass to get her attention. "I need to go back. I can't accept this man's money."

She called to someone through an open door behind her: "Sherise, I ain't never had someone refuse bail before. What do I do?"

Fish touched my arm and motioned for me to step away from the glass. "Please. Let me explain."

"No need," I said, brushing dirt from my clothes. "I get it. You gave me twenty-four hours to leave town. I'm almost out of time, and Carly is giving me a little push. Unfortunately, I can't accept your help."

"I no longer work for that client."

My legs wobbled, no doubt a delayed stress reaction. I limped to the bench and plopped down. "I got you fired, didn't I? You would not believe the streak I'm on."

Fish rotated his hat in his hands. "It was my decision, Ms. Robinson. I terminated the relationship."

I made the face Dylan pulls when she thinks I'm full of shit.

"No, it's true," he went on. "I wasn't kidding when I said I liked you. I thought a lot about our conversation in the park."

Fish noticed my confusion. "What you said about that murky middle. It's true. Not everything is black and white, but that doesn't mean I can't figure out what's right."

"I said that, huh?" I pulled at a loose thread in my ripped skirt. "I should listen to myself."

Fish said after he'd sent Carly packing, he'd received a call from a former associate of hers, a woman he'd spoken with many years ago, named Veronica. "My goodness but she talks fast. I couldn't catch everything she said—something about not recognizing your daughter this afternoon, then getting a call from Mrs. Breckenridge—but the point was, you were in jail, and she needed you out. She wants you to retrieve your daughter."

"Veronica said that?"

"With some urgency! Seems she's quite a loyal employee of the senator," Fish said. "Had more than a few choice words to say about Mrs. Breckenridge. Well, you and your daughter, too."

No doubt. "This is all fascinating, Mr. Fish," I said, "but I'm not comfortable taking your money."

"Oh, no money involved. I served on this police force for thirty years. The chief is an old friend."

"That must be helpful for parking tickets."

"Boy, don't I know it!"

I grinned and thanked Fish for his trouble. "I'd love to accept your offer. There's someplace I desperately need to be right now," I told him. "Unfortunately, I can't leave."

IT TOOK ANOTHER thirty minutes to get Jordan released. By the time we got to Fish's car, parked illegally in front of a fire hydrant, it was seven forty-five. Aaron's speech was underway.

"Where to?" Fish asked.

"The Doubletree, I guess." I twisted toward the back seat. "Jordan, may I use your truck to get to campus? Or should I call a cab?"

Jordan had said barely a word since our release. "Take it," she said to the window.

I had a lot I wanted to say to Jordan, beginning with "I'm sorry," ending with "I'm sorry," and with a lot of "I'm sorrys" in the middle. But from her close examination of the car window, Jordan wasn't ready to hear it yet. I'd schedule some groveling for later that night.

In the meantime, I needed to get to the university. If I hurried, I might make it before Aaron's speech ended. My phone, shattered though it was, showed no enraged texts from Aaron Breckenridge, so at least Dylan hadn't found him before the event. That left me a little time. Not that I had a plan, exactly. Just a better compass.

The parking garage was dark and silent when Fish dropped us by Jordan's truck. "I realize I helped get you into this mess," he offered as we got out. "I hope in some small way I've made up for it." I thanked him and admitted I wasn't sure how things would play out. "Don't worry," he said. "You'll know what to do."

Jordan clicked the key to unlock her truck and handed me the keys.

"Do you want to come?" I asked.

"I'll sit this one out."

I opened the door. "I'm sorry, Jordan," I said, rapidly. "For everything. You've been an incredibly loyal and supportive friend and I've been a shitty one."

"Yes," she said. "You have."

I swung myself up into the driver's seat. "We'll talk later."

"Go do whatever you have to do," she said. I heard the judgment in her words.

Throwing the truck in reverse, I headed out of the garage. I still didn't know what lay in front of me, but I felt a new determination, born in a rank jail cell on a scratchy mattress. I needed my daughter and mother back. To get that, I was prepared to lose everything else.

Chapter 36

Dylan

A Chipotle parking lot may not be the ideal place for a meltdown, but it worked for me. I turned off the Bug and grabbed my throbbing head with both hands.

What in goddamn fucking hell was going on? Had Breckenridge been messing with me? He was "seeing Hope," he said, "while she's in town." How many people could that possibly describe? Not only that—he was seeing her *again*. Clearly Mom had gotten to Breckenridge first, but what did that mean? Had they been plotting together for years to keep me in the dark? To keep their little secret out of the public eye?

And what about the smooth way Breckenridge had pretended not to recognize me? His disarming grin and casual banter. He had to know who I was. Why else would he so pointedly mention Hope? Was he warning me to keep my mouth shut? Well, we'd see about that. There was a special circle in hell for that level of asshole.

The meltdown made me hungry. I bought a Chipotle salad with guacamole and ate in the Bug, then drove to the

University of Memphis campus and parked on a side street. I wandered around campus for the better part of an hour, my fury feeding on itself. Around seven, I headed to the auditorium. Standing out front of the door was that office manager, the one Breckenridge had called Veronica, her nostrils flared and mouth tight. She glared as I walked up to her.

"I know who you are now," Veronica hissed. "And you are not getting in."

I LURKED IN the shadows of the parking garage and pulled my hoodie over my hair, waiting for the right moment.

Veronica hadn't said more, just pointed to two security guards by the auditorium doors and told me they had strict orders not to let me in. I guessed Breckenridge had told her who I was. I backed away, feigning surrender, and circled around the brick building, checking the doors. All were locked, including a steel delivery entrance at the very back, up a small flight of cement stairs. I considered knocking on that door, to see if someone would let me in, but that seemed risky. Who knew where Veronica was? So I waited. One thing I'd learned from Olivia: a little patience and planning could pay off.

Within minutes, a FedEx truck pulled into the alley near the rear entrance. The driver grabbed two boxes from the back and climbed the steps, then knocked on the door. I trotted up behind him.

"Let me help," I said, grabbing the door as someone opened it from the inside.

While the driver entered and handed off the boxes, I slipped behind him into the backstage area. I headed toward the wings and peeked out into the audience. Cameras were set up in the back. Making a beeline for an empty seat in the third row, I scooted in between a whispering couple and a student with his bare feet draped over the seat in front of him.

People poured into the auditorium from two doors in the back. Some were college age, some older. A middle-aged woman with hair like Mom's made my heart flip-flop in my chest. I kept my head down, pretending to read my phone, until the lights dimmed, and some university bigwig took the stage.

The guy gave background on Breckenridge, then introduced him like he was a rock star: "Your senator and—who knows—maybe next vice president of the United States . . ."

Or not.

I ducked down as Veronica slid into the front row.

Breckenridge took the stage to thunderous applause. I listened to his speech without hearing it. He seemed a little stuck on himself and I wondered if he practiced in front of the mirror. I doodled an exploding star on my notepad, then wiped my sweaty palms on my sweatshirt. After about forty minutes, Breckenridge began winding up, using those catchphrases politicians love: hard work, reaching across the aisle, our children's future. When he finished, people applauded, and a few stood. He motioned them to sit down, saying, "We have time for some Q&A. Who has a question?" A thousand tiny needle pricks zipped through my chest, out to my fingertips.

Would Breckenridge even call on me? Without looking in my direction, he pointed to someone halfway up, on the center aisle. A volunteer ran over and thrust the mic so close to the young woman's face, she lurched back. She asked something about #MeToo and sexual harassment.

Breckenridge professed support for the victims of sexual

harassment and spoke about the importance of listening to their stories. I wondered if "listening to" was the same as "believing." I wished the woman would push him for something concrete, like proposed legislation. Instead, he asked for another question. I raised my hand too late. Breckenridge pointed to a far corner of the room. "Yes, in the back?"

The question was about climate change. As I turned to see the questioner, a door opened, and my mom slipped into the rear of the auditorium. I slouched down in my seat.

"He won't see you," the barefoot guy next to me whispered. "Take off the hoodie."

I pushed back the hood and kept my hand into the air. I was barely listening to Breckenridge's answer and didn't realize he'd finished. My barefoot friend stood and pointed at me, and suddenly, Breckenridge looked my way.

"Yes, down front."

The guy with the microphone ran over. I stood up, not looking in my mother's direction. Sweat dripped down my neck.

"Oh, yes, the reporter," Breckenridge seemed oddly pleased to see me. "I promised you a couple questions. It's Dylan, right?"

In the front row, Veronica rose from her seat, shaking her head madly at Breckenridge. He saw her and looked confused. I looked back to see a figure moving slowly down the aisle. My mother. Limping? Breckenridge glanced in that direction as well.

"Yes," I said, taking the mic from the kid. "Dylan Robinson." I flicked a finger toward Mom. "You may remember Hope Robinson, who worked on your first campaign, eighteen years ago? I'm her daughter." I took a deep breath and spoke boldly, channeling my grandmother, the actress, Olivia Grant. "And, as I understand it, your daughter, too."

Silence, then a low buzz rose in the auditorium. Veronica waved at the kid with the mic, hissing "Take it away."

Breckenridge frowned and looked toward my mom. I turned, too. Mom's face looked anguished, as if being my mother were the saddest thing she could imagine.

The kid snatched the mic from me as the crowd's confusion grew louder: "What did she say?" I heard someone ask: "His daughter?" In my peripheral vision, I noticed two guys with shoulder-mounted cameras moving closer, but I kept my eyes fixed on Aaron Breckenridge and wiped my hands on my skirt.

That should do it.

Chapter 37

Hope

A murmur blanketed the auditorium.

"Hope?" Aaron mouthed at me. He wanted to know if what Dylan had said was true. No doubt my appearance—ripped, bloodied, cappuccinoed—added to his confusion. I felt horrible for Aaron. He had the look of a swimmer caught in a riptide, suddenly aware he might not make it back to shore.

I turned to my daughter. Seeing her made my throat tighten, my eyes fill.

I turned back to Aaron and nodded. "Yes," I said. It was true.

Much later, that daughter would dispute the way I'd tell the story. She'd claim the choice to tell the truth wasn't mine. She'd already spilled the beans, after all. Even if I'd denied it, the truth would have come out. Nothing turns the media into rabid sleuths like a good denial.

And if you look at it like that, she was right. For me, though, it *was* a choice: to stop hiding. To stand there in front of my daughter, Aaron, the cameras, the world, with a full understanding of what it would cost. My personal life, including every humiliating mistake of my past twenty years, was about to become tabloid fodder. Worse, my daughter and I had un-pinned a grenade and chucked it at Aaron's career with no idea of the damage it would inflict.

I won't say that none of that mattered. What I will say is that I needed my daughter back, and that had to start with what was true.

I'd never seen Aaron flounder publicly before. He'd lost control of the event, and for a politician, that was disastrous. "Folks, I apologize," he said. "Given the disruption, we're going to call this a wrap. Thank you all for coming." A few nervous claps were drowned out as the murmur in the auditorium be-came a roar.

Aaron crouched down and with one arm on the stage, jumped off, and pushed his way through the crowd toward Dylan. TV crews closed in on her, pointing cameras in her face. She reeled back and shaded her eyes from the lights. Aaron touched her elbow and she turned to look at him. He put a hand on her back and guided her up a short flight of stairs to the right of the stage. He looked back, caught my eye, and motioned for me to follow.

The cameras and cell phones turned on me as I muscled my way through the clogged the aisle. When I reached the stairs, I was face-to-face with two burly security people who didn't seem to understand my pivotal role in this shit show.

Veronica hoofed it back down the stairs and whispered to one of them to let me through. Her mouth drawn tight, she led me backstage at a brisk clip, slapping through a second door and into a hallway where Aaron and Dylan were waiting. Dylan's face was drained of color, though whether from anger or fear, I couldn't say. Aaron, though, was scarlet with rage. When Veronica went to leave, he grabbed her arm, making her stay.

"Hope," he nearly shouted, his eyes wide and wild. "What the fuck?"

I couldn't imagine the right words for such an occasion.

"Who are you working for?" Aaron asked, his voice cold. "And how much did they pay you?"

Veronica raised a hand to her mouth. I shook my head, feeling sick. "It's not like that."

Aaron looked from me to Dylan and back again. "Well, congratulations, Hope. I don't know how long you've been planning this, but you certainly paid me back."

Whatever I started to say, Dylan shouted over it. "Shut up!" She was shaking. "Both of you make me sick." She whirled around and slammed her hands against the middle bar of the door. It was an emergency exit. Alarms sounded.

I pushed past Aaron to follow her. He grabbed my arm, and I wrenched it away. Crashing through the door, I screamed Dylan's name.

A sea of lights blinded me. I was at the top of a short, concrete stairway, and shadowy figures on the stairs jostled one another, trying to shove a mic in my face. Two guys with TV news cameras on their shoulders pressed in. Raising a hand to block their lights, I searched in both directions for my daughter. "Dylan!" I called out again.

"Was that your daughter? With the pink hair?" someone asked.

"Yes! Where did she go?"

A student filming with a cell phone pointed toward the parking garage.

I pushed my way through the crowd. A tall blond woman

shoved a mic in my face. "Your daughter said Aaron Breckenridge was her father." When I didn't respond, she and several
others followed alongside me. They had no trouble keeping up
with my limping. I arrived at Jordan's truck, which, after driving over the grass to avoid the parking lot gate, I'd parked illegally behind a dumpster.

I heaved myself into the truck and found the keys in the
ignition, where, apparently, I'd left them.

"Is it true?" the blonde with the mic shouted over the others.
"Is that girl Senator Breckenridge's daughter?"

I paused to look the woman in the eye. "Yes." How easy this
truth-telling was!

Throwing the truck into reverse, I backed up, slowly but de-
terminedly, forcing reporters to dive in all directions. I rolled
down the window and yelled to the lady with the mic: "Please
don't be too hard on Aaron. He didn't know until ten minutes
ago, either."

I cranked it into drive and sped away.

I KNEW IT was a waste of time to circle the campus, looking for
my daughter. She'd be long gone. I did it anyway.

I'd passed the U of M's giant Ramesses statue for the third
time when my phone gave a couple pathetic shudders. I pulled
into the parking lot to navigate the shattered screen. After some
fiddling, I could see it was a Memphis number, and while not the
one Aaron had given me, I was certain it would be him. It wasn't.

It was the hospital. They had my mother.

THE NURSE BLOCKING my mother's hospital room assured me
she was doing fine. He wouldn't explain what had happened,

only that the doctor was with her. I followed his eyes to my stained blouse and ripped skirt, the dried blood below my knees.

"You should see the other guy," I quipped half-heartedly, then cringed. The other guy was Aaron.

I stationed myself in a plastic chair across the hall to catch the doctor. I started to text Jordan, to ask if she'd keep an eye out for Dylan, then dropped the phone back in my bag. Jordan owed me no favors.

Nice work, Hope. Is there anyone you haven't managed to piss off?

A middle-aged woman with a paper coffee cup rounded the corner and rushed over to ask if I was Hope. She introduced herself as Ann somebody, the curator at Graceland. Apparently, we'd known each other as children, though I had no memory of her. She then launched into a confusing narrative that included my mother, Elvis, and a cotton throw.

"Hold on." I had to raise my hand to eye level before she stopped. "You found my mother where?"

After some back-and-forth, Ann realized I knew nothing about the interview or my mother's request for time alone in the Meditation Garden. "We sometimes grant little favors like that for dignitaries and celebrities. Allow them private tours, after hours. But when I glanced at the surveillance camera, she wasn't standing by the grave, she was lying on top of it! Naturally, I called security."

"She fell?"

"That's what I thought at first. Or maybe she'd passed out."

I recalled my mother on the floor of the Peabody lounge earlier. Could she have pulled that stunt twice in the same day? My mother wasn't shy about reusing her best material, so it was in-character to a point, but she hated hospitals. Mom wouldn't have let anyone bring her here if she'd had any say in it.

My second thought was more frightening: What if she hadn't been faking earlier? What if something really was wrong with her?

Ann continued: "The blanket, though."

"Blan-ket," I repeated phonetically.

"Yes, a little throw. It was draped over the grave. Almost as if she'd placed it there, laid down, and gone to sleep." Responding to my confused expression, she nodded. "I know! But she wasn't sleeping. Neither the security people nor I could wake her, so I dialed 911." She held a hand on her chest. "I nearly had a heart attack myself." I caught the displeasure in her voice. She hadn't appreciated this stunt, whatever it was. "I don't think I did anything wrong."

I was lost again. "I'm sure you didn't . . ."

"As you can imagine, I'd like to keep this between us, if possible. I don't think Graceland has any liability."

I understood then: she was afraid we'd sue. I assured Ann that whatever my mom had intended to do was not her fault.

Clearly eager to hand off responsibility, Ann pressed a business card into my palm and told me to call as soon as I knew anything. After she left, I pulled out my phone and was struggling to type a brief message to Jordan when the doctor emerged and said I could see my mother. He lowered his voice. They'd had to pump her stomach. Apparently, my mother had taken sleeping pills.

"Sleeping pills?" I wasn't aware my mother had any.

He fished around in the pocket of his lab coat then handed me the empty bottle. The prescription was from three months earlier. A doctor at UCLA.

"Your mother claims it was a mistake," he said. "Says she thought they were baby aspirin." The doctor was watching me carefully, trying to read my expression. "Does your mother sometimes get confused?"

"Not really," I said. "Her hobby is confusing me."

He patted my shoulder, gave a once-over to my clothes, and said, "Well, best of luck . . . with everything" before hurrying away.

My mother's bed was cranked nearly upright, but her eyes were closed, her hands folded on the blanket. Her face looked almost as white as her hair. As I gingerly lowered myself into the chair beside her, my arms shook.

Without opening her eyes, my mother said: "Well, that didn't go very well, did it?"

I leaned forward. "No, Mom, it didn't. What in God's name were you thinking?"

"Me?" Her eyes opened. "I meant *you*." She reached beside her on the bed and lifted the remote to click on the TV. It was tuned to one of the local news stations. Across the bottom of the screen: "Breaking News: Breckenridge speech disrupted by paternity allegations." When the image shifted from the anchor, it showed Aaron jumping down from the stage and me climbing into Jordan's truck, surrounded by reporters. "Channel 11 also offered some nice footage," my mother said, clicking off the TV. "You might want to give more thought to your outfit next time."

"Thank you," I said. "I'll certainly consult you going forward. Assuming you don't off yourself in the meantime."

Her head dropped back as her eyes implored the ceiling. "I opened the wrong bottle. My lower back was acting up."

"Stop it, Mom. Just stop. I'm calling a moratorium on bullshit."

"Fine. Your bullshit, too? Or only mine?"

"Everyone's bullshit," I said. "We'll start with yours, though. What were you trying to do?"

She fiddled with her blanket, sighed. "Write my own script."

"Not following," I said. "Use more words."

"I never wanted to be old, Hope. I wasn't designed for it. People like me . . . we should go like Elvis did, in our prime."

I couldn't help myself. "That was his prime?"

She shot me a look. "Close enough." She ran her thumb, almost lovingly, down the side of the TV remote. "I've already lived too long. So few people recognize me anymore. I can go anywhere—grocery shopping, the hair salon! No one looks twice at a woman with a cantaloupe strapped around her face."

"Cannula."

"I know what it's called! You never did get my humor." She reached for her water. "I'm on my way out. I simply wanted to do it with . . . panache." She smiled, pleased with the word.

"You saw nothing worth hanging around for, Mom? Not Dylan? Not . . ." *Why was it so hard to say this?* "Me?"

"You don't need me, Hope. Never have." I started to protest, but she waved me off. "No, let's face it. I've not been much use as a mother." Her voice was growing scratchy, and she coughed to clear her throat. I fished around on the tray, and finally, inscrutably, handed her a napkin. She wiped her mouth before continuing. "I thought in Memphis we could all stop pretending. I'd reconnect with Elvis. I'd help you stop hiding from Dylan, from whatever happened in your past. It was my parting gift."

"I don't recall asking for your help."

"You were pushing Dylan away. You weren't there for her."

That was a bridge too far. "Mother, how can you, of all people, say that to me?"

"How can I say it?" She lifted a shoulder from the bed to turn to me. "How do you think I *recognized* it?" When I didn't respond, she leaned back against the pillows and fiddled with her rings. "I've already admitted I wasn't a good mother to you, Hope. What more do you want? We didn't work well together."

If I was supposed to protest, I wasn't going to. "No, we didn't," I said. "But thank you for your honesty. This is a conversation I've wanted to have for years."

She snorted. "And now, being a Christian woman, you can't?" I frowned, trying to place the familiar words. "*The Wizard of Oz*," she explained. "When Auntie Em tries to tell off Miss Gulch." She brushed some imaginary crumbs off her blanket. "I thought I'd help you by casting myself as the witch."

"Give me a break, Mom. You chose Miss Gulch because she's the most interesting character. Naturally, you'd see me as Auntie Em."

"I didn't make you Auntie Em. You were *born* Auntie Em."

"Plain? Colorless?"

"Reserved. Inscrutable. Kept everything to yourself. Even as a toddler, you gave me no clues, nothing to work with."

"Well, I'm sorry, Mom. If I could do everything over, I'd be more like Beth." I'd never spoken Beth's name in her presence, and I expected some reaction. A surprised look, at least. When she gave me nothing, I pressed on. "I'm sure it was easier to be a good mother to her."

"No." My mother sighed. "I pretty much sucked with her, too."

I studied my mother's face, waiting for her to acknowledge

the joke. Of course she'd loved Beth more. I'd seen the photos. My mother beaming as she pushed Beth on the swings, holding her in the pool, posing with her in a new Easter outfit. I'd been so different from Beth. Hard to love. "You don't have to lie, Mom," I said, finally.

"No, it is true." She coughed again and handed me her empty water cup. "I tried with both of you. Acted the part as best I could. I wanted to do well for Harold's sake. He was so awfully good with children." I filled the cup with water and handed it back to her. She took a long sip. "By the time you were a toddler, studies were starting to show that depressed mothers raised depressed children. I decided it was better for you if I wasn't around."

I wasn't letting her go that far. "Come on, Mom. You wanted to be back on TV. Admit it."

"Well of course I did! I loved acting. That's what you do when you can't stand to be yourself—pretend to be someone else." She put down the cup and smoothed the blankets around her legs. "But it doesn't work forever. And it never works at all for some people."

"Yes, Mom, I know. I'm a terrible actress."

"Dreadful."

A nurse interrupted to check my mother's vitals. I took out my phone. Nothing from Dylan or Aaron, but every news organization in the country somehow had my email. It was going to be a long night.

I asked my mother if she'd heard from Dylan. To my astonishment, she reached over to the nightstand and retrieved a cell phone. When I shouted, "What the hell?" she explained she'd bought it for the trip. "It's a safety issue, Hope. You need a phone to do almost anything these days." I closed my eyes and counted to twenty.

My mother messaged Dylan, and we waited a few minutes with no reply. "Go check the Peabody, and see if Dylan is there," she said. "Just be sure to come back soon. I may need your help getting out of here." Her fleeting look toward the window made me nervous.

"Don't move until I get back," I warned. In my hand, my phone quacked half-heartedly. A text from a Memphis number.

"Can you meet me somewhere?" it read.

The night was warm, and the earthy smell of mud wafted up from the river. Aaron leaned over the wrought iron fence, his back to me, staring out at the Mississippi. I hobbled over and stood beside him. He kept his eyes on the river.

"I'm going to need some genetic testing," he said flatly.

"I understand."

"I've contacted a friend, a doctor, who says he can have the results back in twelve hours. It would go quicker if he could have a sample from you as well as Dylan."

"Of course." If I could find Dylan.

His head was down, his eyes heavy. "It's not that I don't believe you, Hope. The truth is I do. Though God knows why since you've given me every reason on earth to mistrust you." My turn to look at my shoes. "But other people are demanding proof." I could imagine: his campaign advisers, his financial backers, the DNC. "So that's where we are. I've postponed my camping trip so I can make a public statement about this before I go."

"Aaron, just to be clear: no one is paying me. No one is behind this . . ."

He held up a hand and tilted his head to the sky. "If I seemed a little upset back there, you have to imagine my"—he bit down hard on the word—"surprise."

"I didn't want this to happen. I was doing everything I could to prevent it. When I ran into you at the fundraiser, I was trying to find Dylan, to convince her to come home . . ."

"*Home?*" Even in the dwindling light, I could see the set of his jaw. "You mean *Seattle?*"

"Oh God," I whispered.

"Or maybe it's *not* Seattle, but actually as far from Seattle as possible. Perhaps *Boston?*"

I tapped my fingers on the railing. "I've got nothing. Can't even explain that one."

He turned toward me, his face full of rage. "Hope, why didn't you tell me?"

I took a deep breath. The truth. "At first, because I was heartbroken. You'd chosen your path, and your wife, and it wasn't me." I held up a hand. "I know, my disappearing didn't help. We don't need to go there again. But I was devastated and didn't want to speak to you ever again." I turned and rested my back against the rail. "I planned to keep the baby. I assumed you wouldn't want me to. So, better if you didn't know."

He held out a hand again, asking me to stop. "You're going to have to give me a minute here, because honestly, I can't recall when I've been this furious with someone I cared for." His use of the past tense made me cringe. "I mean, we spent last night together. A really nice time, I thought. And you didn't even mention you had a daughter, never mind that it was *my* daughter."

"Aaron, I'm not asking for your forgiveness. Just let me explain."

On the way over, I'd debated whether to tell him about Carly and the money. On one hand, Carly was still the mother of his children. On the other, it was the truth. Whenever possible, I would let that guide me, even when it didn't show me in the best light. So I started from the beginning. How Carly had confronted me in tears almost eighteen years ago. How she'd known about us. Veronica's spying. How I'd lost my pills when I left Memphis in a hurry, and later discovered I was pregnant. I told him about Fish and the money.

I could tell by his white-knuckled grip on the fence that he'd been blindsided by the stuff about Carly and Veronica. When I got to the part about the agreement, he kicked the fence and let out an enraged "Jesus F. Christ."

"I understand this makes things worse for you."

"Worse? No, not worse. A fucking nightmare. Even if Carly comes forward and says I had no part in this contract, no one will believe it. Christ, even I wouldn't believe it." What could I say? He was right. "I'm not trying to blame you, Hope, but when this man offered you money and wouldn't say who was behind it, did you even think of calling me?"

"You *are* trying to blame me, Aaron," I said with some warmth. "And I get it. This sucks for you. But no, I didn't consider contacting you. I thought you'd chosen to marry the rich girl, keep her father's backing, and make your inconvenient child disappear. I believed you'd sold your soul."

"Yeah, well, thanks for your faith in me."

"Put yourself in my shoes. I'd just read how someone leaked that dirt on your opponent, right before that election." I glanced over at Aaron. He looked stricken. "I'm sorry, I know now you wouldn't do that. But at the time . . ." My words trailed off as I watched him close his eyes. It took a moment before I understood. "You *did* do that."

His head dropped. "I lost Shelley over that," he said. "I justified it to myself. I wouldn't have won otherwise." He scuffed the toe of his shoe back and forth in the dirt. "And here it is, back to bite me. We never know what some decisions cost, do we?"

He asked if I'd give him a minute and I nodded. He walked the path to the other end of the park, by the remains of an old wall, where two stone tablets were carved with the Ten Commandments. Surely the irony didn't escape him. He ran his hands through his hair, then squeezed both elbows together, covering his face.

I shuffled over to the bench under the oak and checked my phone. *Dylan, where are you? Please, please, be safe.*

Aaron returned and dropped down beside me. He lifted a fallen twig from the bench and twirled it, as he used to do with pens. "I'm sorry about your run-in with Carly. It took me a long time to accept that her mean streak wasn't going away, no matter how much I tried to love her." He said Carly had called him earlier, after the speech fiasco, to insist he have nothing to do with Dylan. She wasn't his real family. "I hung up on her," Aaron said.

I thought of the financial ruin I faced if Carly chose to enforce our agreement. Could Aaron calm down his ex? Hanging up on her wasn't a good start. I brushed a bug off my ripped skirt. When I lifted my head, he was staring at my clothes.

"You know, I didn't want to ask . . ."

"Yeah, don't." I pulled at my coffee-stained blouse. "Though Carly's iced cappuccino was a nice touch."

The night was growing darker, a few stars visible despite the park lights. A couple wandered down the path holding hands. Aaron's phone beeped and he checked it, said he needed to go. This might surprise me, he said, but he had a public relations disaster to attend to. "Thank you for explaining everything," he added, then did a double take. "That *was* everything, right?"

I nodded.

"Even if I don't agree with it, I'm glad there was a reason you kept my daughter from me. I've been struggling with whether you thought that little of me."

Aaron said he'd walk me to my car, which I had to explain was a truck, and not mine. I also admitted, hesitantly, that I didn't know where Dylan was at the moment but would text him as soon as I found her. *Please God, let me find her.*

As we reached the truck, he said: "I'm going to need time to process this all." He wondered if I could stay in Memphis until they completed the genetic testing, and he issued a press statement. Given I was unemployed, I could. He said he'd be in touch and raised a hand to wave, then hesitated. "I meant to ask. Her name? Dylan?"

"What was the line? Something about staring straight ahead and trying hard to do what's right?"

He nodded. "I thought so."

He waved again and I climbed into the truck. I rolled down the window and closed my eyes, leaning back against the head-rest. At the sound of his voice, I jumped.

"Sorry." Aaron's hand rested on the window. "One more

question. When you disappeared all those years ago and I couldn't find you, I thought maybe I'd made more of our relationship than had really been there."

"No," I assured him.

As Aaron walked away, he threw up both hands and called out, "What is it with me and difficult women?"

Chapter 38

Dylan

The Peabody lounge was full of overdressed people sipping cutesy cocktails. The ducks were gone, though, tucked away in their private rooftop villa. Sounded heavenly. As bone-tired as I felt, I couldn't go back to the suite. Olivia would be there and want to hear about my meeting with Breckenridge. I couldn't talk about it. My father was a douchebag. Both my parents were seriously messed up, but of the two, he was worse. The blowhole wouldn't even cop to being my father.

I spotted an open seat at the bar. Well, almost open. A woman in a dress cut down to her ass had left her clutch on the chair next to her while jabbering to her date. I hovered close by and, when the woman leaned in to whisper to her companion, pushed the bag off the chair and squeezed onto it. I could tell the guy on my right, in a T-shirt and jeans, was staring at me. I refused to look his way.

The bartender lifted his chin. What was I having?

"Michelob," I said with the kind of authority I hoped might keep him for asking for ID.

The guy to my right said, "She'll have a Shirley Temple. On me."

My head jerked around. It was George, his hands cupped around a beer. I turned back. "Jesus. What does a girl have to do to be left alone in this town?"

"Been wondering that myself," George said.

The lady with the low-cut dress spun around, searching for her clutch. I pointed at the floor, then stared her down until she bent to retrieve it. The bartender added a cherry to my drink and passed it to me. How much more humiliating could the night get? I hadn't had a Shirley Temple since I was ten.

I twirled my glass, keeping my eyes on the bartender while speaking to George. "Didn't go well tonight."

"So I heard."

My back went up. "Mom told you?"

"No." He pulled his phone out of his pocket, swiped across the screen, and clicked on a saved video called "WREG Breaking News." It showed Aaron Breckenridge jumping down off the stage, a swarm of reporters enveloping him, glimpses of my pink hair through the crowd. Then it cut to Mom outside the auditorium, squinting and trying to block the lights shining in her face. Across the bottom of the screen: "Teen and mother allege paternity at Breckenridge speech."

"Jesus." I rummaged in my bag and pulled out my earbuds. "Can I listen?"

"Be my guest."

I inserted the earbuds and jacked up the volume. A reporter outside the auditorium said she had no information yet about the girl, who said her name was Dylan Robinson. The studio anchor wondered if this revelation, if true, would affect Breckenridge's chances of being chosen as the presidential running mate? Certainly, the reporter replied. While an illegitimate child wasn't necessarily a career killer, it raised a lot of questions. Had Breckenridge cheated on his wife? Did he know about this child? Had he tried to hush it up? "A circus like this couldn't have come at a worse moment for Breckenridge," she concluded. "No presidential candidate wants this dominating the news cycle."

I removed my earbuds and slid the cell back to George. "Well, Aaron Breckenridge deserves it. He's a jerk. He went apeshit at Mom and me."

"Really! Apeshit, you say?"

I flicked him a look. "Yes! He screamed at us."

"Imagine that."

"Not appreciating the sarcasm." I wouldn't let Mom talk to me this way, but I'd always taken it on the chin from George. "Breckenridge is a weenie. That's the word on the street."

"You're right, not good father material. He's got emotions, opinions. Flaws, even. Almost like a real person."

"Enough. I get the point. You weren't there." I sipped my drink. The damn thing was delicious.

"He's not your fantasy dad anymore, Dylan. While he was in your head, he could be anything you wanted him to be. Not so much now."

"I didn't expect him to be perfect."

"Really?"

"Why are you defending him? This guy who, according to you, didn't want anything to do with me?"

"Did I say that?"

"You looked at your shoes."

George frowned—no doubt wondering about the shoes—but admitted, "Yeah, I guess I believed that. Turns out, I didn't know the whole story."

According to George, Mom never told Breckenridge about me. There'd been some . . . miscommunication. That was all George knew, and he was withholding judgment until he learned more. "No doubt Breckenridge could have handled it better, sweetheart, but maybe cut the guy a little slack. You blindsided him. He had no idea whether you're his daughter or some attention-getting troll. You dropped a public bomb-shell during arguably the most pivotal weekend in his life. I dunno . . . maybe not ideal?"

I drained my Shirley Temple, then tapped the glass on the counter to get the bartender's attention. I'd have another. This new information, that Breckenridge hadn't known about me, was making me feel a little shitty. "Politicians do worse stuff all the time. He'll be fine."

George shrugged. "Probably. What gets politicians in more trouble is the cover-up. He'll have to prove he wasn't hiding you all these years." He picked up my earbuds, wound them around his hand, and slid them back to me. "All I'm trying to say is that you took the man by surprise. Slow down. Give him a chance."

I swiveled my chair to face George fully and forgot what I was going to say. His right eye was bruised and swollen. "Jesus, what happened? Did someone hurt you?"

"I believe the person most directly responsible is your

mother," he said, "but I'm over it." George recounted the mix-up at the police station.

I was almost afraid to ask. "Is that . . . why you're dressed like that?"

"Naw. My clothes needed dry cleaning. Jordan will be back tomorrow."

Chapter 39

Hope

I street-parked near the Doubletree and limped across the intersection toward the Peabody. Inside the lobby, as I waited for the elevator, I scanned the lounge. No sign of Dylan. The elevator dinged, and as I moved aside to let a man using a cane exit, a flash of pink caught my eye. My sixteen-year-old daughter sat at the bar, her head on the shoulder of an older man with his arm around her. I speed-hobbled over, ready to sucker punch the asshole.

George glanced up first, which gave me a moment to register the situation before Dylan pivoted to see what he was looking at. A lump the size of Texas lodged in my throat, and I couldn't get out the right words. "Thank God," I wanted to say. Or "I'm so glad you're safe." Or even "I fucked up." Instead, I lurched forward to hug my daughter, who stopped me with a raised hand.

"*So* not ready for that," she said.

George slid off his bar seat, professing a long-held desire to visit the penthouse home of the Peabody ducks. I mouthed a *thank you*, and he raised his eyebrows. *Good luck*, they said.

I slipped onto the chair George had vacated. The bartender, wiping the counter, asked if I'd like another Memphis Blues Martini.

Dylan scowled. "You two know each other?"

"I'll have whatever she's having," I said, pointing to her Shirley Temple.

As the bartender walked away, Dylan balled up her cocktail napkin in her fist. "I don't want to talk about it."

"Okay." I'd take things slow.

Barely a second later, she blurted, "This is all your fault, you know. Why did you lie to me?" She trained her eyes on the bartender as he shook a cocktail. "You could have just said, 'Your father's a jerk. That's why I don't want you to meet him.' I would have accepted that."

"Would you, now!"

Dylan exhaled in disgust. "You sound like Olivia," she said.

I flinched. Dylan didn't know about her grandmother. I'd have to tackle that next. One dumpster fire at a time. "Look, Dylan, Aaron Breckenridge is not a perfect human being. He can be pretty sure of himself. He sometimes loses his temper. Occasionally, he takes political positions that I find convenient. But for the past eighteen years, I've blamed him for things that weren't his fault. That was my mistake, not his."

Dylan fiddled with the paper straw. "Well he sure acted like a flaming asshat tonight."

"I know it seems that way. You may not have caught him at his best."

She pushed her glass forward and twisted in her seat, planning her escape. "I've already been over this with George. I don't need another lecture."

"Okay." I held up a hand. "What *do* you need?"

"How about the truth? Do you think perhaps I deserve that?"

"Yes," I said.

So I told Dylan the truth. When I got to the part about Fish and the money, she gave a little head jerk of surprise. I braced myself for her judgment, but she simply said "Huh" and sipped her drink. I ended with my meeting with Aaron, barely a half hour earlier. "He's still a bit unhappy about how it all unfolded, but he's angry at me, not you."

Dylan used her crumpled cocktail napkin to wipe at something on the bar. "He's not mad I hurt his chance to be vice president?"

I shrugged. "He probably wishes you'd found some other way—"

"I tried!"

I held up a hand. "But that's not where he'll end up, trust me. Give him some time."

She sat with this for a moment, then flicked her head in my direction. "What happened to your clothes?"

I explained that I'd been doored but got more sympathy when I showed her my shattered phone. For a teenager, a fate worse than death.

"It's been a rough two days," I admitted. "But bottom line— and no, I can't believe I'm saying this—I'm glad you forced me to make this trip."

She put a hand over her mouth to suppress a laugh. "You should tell that to Olivia."

"Never," I swore. "And if you do, I'll deny it."

I took a deep breath before telling Dylan about her grand-mother. I explained that she was in the hospital, and why. I held nothing back. Tears pooled in Dylan's lower lids. She turned her face from me as they spilled over, some landing on the bar.

"Olivia wouldn't do that," she protested. "She loves me."

I longed to hug my daughter, but sensed it was still too soon. Instead, I handed her a napkin. My go-to move lately.

"Your grandmother does love you. She has her own strug-gles, and we'll have to be more attentive to that. *I'll* have to be more attentive to that."

"Not everything is your fault, Mom." Her mouth was still trembling, and she pressed her lips together hard before add-ing, "I mean, *most* things are. But not everything." She sniffled and gave a little smile. My daughter was so beautiful when she smiled.

WHEN I EXPLAINED to the doctor about my mother's PTSD with overnight hospital stays, he agreed to discharge her to my care. Her tests had shown an irregular heart rhythm and though she was in no immediate danger, he suggested she see her cardiologist in Boston about a pacemaker. Naturally, as soon as the doctor left, my mother nixed the idea.

"What would be the point?" she said.

Dylan was having none of it. "Seriously?" she said. "You're going to die and leave me with Mom?" I wasn't sure I appreci-ated that particular tack, but when my mother patted Dylan's hand and clasped it in her own, I sensed she was more affected than she let on. As Dylan pressed her face under my mother's chin, I realized I'd never hugged my mom like that. Not that I recalled, anyway. Which, of course, didn't mean I couldn't try.

We brought my mother back to the Peabody and I helped her into bed. Dylan lay on the sofa, clicking through TV news stations. Video of Aaron's speech debacle had been picked up by the national news organizations, who'd wasted no time in figuring out who Dylan and I were and where we lived. The fact that my mother was a legendary soap star didn't detract from the story's interest. All three of us had been forced to silence our phones.

The Boston TV stations had interviewed one of Dylan's teachers, a woman who looked like she'd been hauled out of bed, and the owner of the restaurant where my daughter waitressed, who spoke affectionately about her table-clearing skills. When the stories started repeating themselves, I turned off the TV and sat in the chair beside Dylan, a glass of water in hand and an ice pack on my knee.

Dylan was still sprawled on the sofa so all I could see was the back of her head. "I don't know if you remember this," she said. "Once when I was little and you were tucking me in bed, I asked you for a photo of my father. You said you didn't have one."

"I remember." I recalled every question she'd ever asked about Aaron, and the gut-wrenching sensation of lying to her.

"Afterward, I heard you crying in the bathroom. I thought you were sad about him."

I stared at the ceiling. "Maybe," I admitted. "I was also angry at myself for the choices I'd made. I've had some trouble forgiving myself."

"For lying to me?"

"Among other things."

"Because I sort of get it now. You were keeping a promise. That's kind of admirable."

Of all the ways I'd imagined Dylan interpreting my actions over the years, it had never occurred to me she might see it like that. She'd made a choice, I understood. She chose to see it that way because she loved me. I started to say thank you, but my voice cracked.

She cut in. "Don't get me wrong. It was a stupid promise to make, lying to everyone about your child's father." This sounded more like my daughter. "But I get why you made it. And once you did, you were stuck." She raised herself to a sitting position and plunked her bare feet on the glass coffee table. I didn't say anything. "So here's my question," she said, still not looking at me. "If you had the chance to do it all over again, would you still sleep with Aaron Breckenridge?"

Okay, we were having this conversation! I took a deep breath. "Honestly? I wouldn't change anything if it meant I wouldn't have you."

She seemed pleased enough with that answer. "So we're only telling the truth from now on, right?"

"Trying."

"Okay . . ." I could hear the grin in her voice. "What do you think of my hair color?"

I took a deep breath. "Hate it. Always have."

"Well," she said, dropping her phone on the coffee table. "That's progress, I guess."

As CEMETERIES GO, this one was lovely: lush, green, with stunning white oak trees and a stream. According to my mother, it was the cemetery where Elvis had been buried before his father moved his body to Graceland. I'd never been there before. My father had chosen to be cremated and my mother—never a hiker—had let me scatter his ashes on a scenic ridge in the Great Smoky Mountains National Park.

I parked Dylan's Bug where my mother directed and walked beside her, pulling her oxygen cart across the uneven grass. Even on the short walk, her breathing was labored. We stopped in front of Beth's headstone, which stood by itself under the shadow of a huge oak, a stone bench close by. My mother lowered herself onto the bench, her spine erect as always. I joined her, reading my sister's stone.

ELIZABETH OLIVIA ROBINSON
August 5, 1971–August 21, 1975
Beloved Daughter

"It's a lovely spot," I said.

"Your father picked it out. I was incapable."

Was it too late to tell her how sorry I was for her loss? Would she brush aside any hint of vulnerability, as she so often did?

My mother broke the silence. "Beth would have hated it here. Too quiet."

"Dad said she was a lively kid."

"Loved music. She was belting out 'Hound Dog' at eighteen months."

I chuckled at the idea that Beth had shared my mother's passion for Elvis. But why not? Beth had been born in 1971, not long after my mother's famous date with the King.

I looked again at the headstone. Not that long at all.

I pulled out my phone and Googled the date of Elvis's Los Angeles Forum concert. November 14, 1970. I did the math.

"Mom." I shifted on the bench to face her. "This is a personal question, so you don't have to answer, but . . . did you sleep with Elvis?"

"Not much sleeping went on with Elvis," she said. "He was quite the insomniac."

"You completely dodged the question."

"I did not."

"You did."

"I said we didn't sleep. I didn't say we didn't have sex."

"Jesus, Mom! You *slept* with Elvis?"

"For heaven's sake, Hope. I wasn't the only woman who did."

"I'm not judging," I said, then added, "Well, maybe a little . . ."

"I know I shouldn't have. I was dating your father at the time. Very seriously. But my God, Hope. It was Elvis. What was I to do?"

I stared at her, shaking my head. "And Beth?" My sister, born—as I could now clearly see—nine months after the LA Forum concert. "Was Elvis her . . ."

She threw her hands into the air. "Oh, who the hell knows? It wasn't like today. You couldn't just spit into a tube."

I was grabbing at my hair again, trying to take in all this information. "What about Dad? Did he know?"

"I confessed everything to your father. Went to him the day after my date with Elvis and spared no details. I said, 'If you don't want anything to do with me, I completely understand.' But he did. Amazingly. It was the early seventies, the time of free love. Nobody really knew what the rules were. His solution was to get married quickly, as people did in those days. Then, if

I was pregnant, we wouldn't know for sure who the father was. Harold never mentioned it again. He loved Beth like he loved you, with his whole being. He had no regrets."

"Yes, but . . ." I hesitated. This was a question I'd wanted to ask for a long time. "Your marriage to Dad . . . wasn't ideal."

"By what measure?" she shot back. "Just because a marriage isn't conventional doesn't mean it's not good. Our marriage was as good as most. Probably a damn sight better." She was playing with her rings again. Was she aware? "I loved your father. He loved me. I know you blamed me when he died—for not being there, for not saying the right thing."

"It was the way you talked about it, Mom. You treated that conversation like a joke."

She waved a hand. "That's the way I talk." She adjusted the cannula around her ears, grew quieter. "Guilt and regret are not emotions that sit well with me. Doesn't mean I don't feel them."

We remained silent for a long time on that bench facing my sister's grave. "So, just to be clear on Beth? Her father?"

"No one knows." She smoothed her skirt. "Not even me."

"But Beth's eyes, Mom," I said, remembering them in the photos my father had showed me. They were haunting, deep-set, icy blue. "Her eyes."

"Yes." She smiled. "Lovely, weren't they?"

THE FIVE OF us wandered around Graceland in groups, sometimes catching up with one another, sometimes hanging back to give people space. Jordan was the only one wearing headphones and listening to the narration. She hung on every word and lagged behind the entire way. I let Aaron and Dylan walk ahead while Mom and I lingered to examine Elvis's ancient microwave, the carved Jungle Room chairs, the photos from his youth.

Aaron had pulled strings to get us this private end-of-day visit. I was frankly amazed that Ann Abernathy would allow my mother back on the property. Perhaps she was still afraid of being sued, or maybe she was eager to use my mother's interview. Since Aaron's speech and its aftermath, Olivia Grant had become quite the media darling again, with more talk-show invitations than she'd had in decades. On Memphis's morning show, she'd seemed a little dismayed that so many of the questions posed were about Dylan and me but answered with more pride than I would have expected. She hadn't committed to any national shows yet, though she'd mentioned twice she was "awfully fond of that Ellen DeGeneres."

Not surprisingly, Aaron wasn't chosen for the VP spot on the Democratic ticket. I'm sure he was devastated, but he told everyone that the senator from Virginia was a great guy. After two days camping and fishing with his sons, Aaron was tanned and more relaxed. He was still a bit abrupt with me at times. I expected he would be for a while. He seemed to have put the gruffness aside that afternoon.

The results of the genetic testing had been no surprise: Dylan was Aaron's daughter. Aaron had held a brief press conference with Dylan and his sons by his side. He wanted to introduce his daughter, Dylan Robinson, a delightful addition to his family and surprise to everyone, including him. The reporters had chuckled, then asked some pointed questions about his relationship with a young staff member given his engagement at the time. He acknowledged his lapse in judgment in falling in love with one person while engaged to another. He said he'd tried to do the right thing by sticking with his original commitment, but that things are often more complicated than any of us can foresee.

Out of all that, it was the phrase "falling in love" that made my stomach twist. The two of us had certainly screwed things up.

Aaron had allowed Dylan to answer a few questions about how she'd come to Memphis and her journey to find her father. I thought she presented herself well, though she seemed a different person because of her hair. While Aaron was away, Dylan had gone to a salon and dyed her hair back to her natural brunette color. She claimed she was tired of being defined by her pink hair, but I suspected she wanted to play up the resemblance to her father. It wasn't only the hair, though. Dylan seemed to move differently, more thoughtfully. She often paused before speaking. Perhaps I was imagining it. Or maybe the seeds of a new maturity had been there before, and I'd failed to notice.

I'd brought Dylan to Aaron's condo before the press conference so he could prep her. The media hadn't caught wind of the money Carly had paid me, so the question was whether to raise the issue ourselves. Aaron voted to get out in front of it. Secrets will bite you in the ass, he said, and given the last several days, I couldn't disagree. Of course, he wasn't happy about the probable fallout for him politically. Even though Aaron had known nothing about Carly's agreement, his complicity would be assumed. We'd both seen it happen before. When the wife of a Massachusetts congressional rep was convicted of tax fraud and her husband denied knowledge of it, no one believed him. The congressman lost the next election to a primary challenger.

Aaron's dilemma was compounded by his desire to avoid a

war with his ex and protect his sons. We finally decided on a strategy that, while not perfect, all of us could live with. Aaron would announce at the press conference that he'd learned, through me, I'd been paid to conceal he was Dylan's father. He'd state categorically that he was neither involved with, nor aware of, that agreement. Any further questions would be directed to me. Aaron didn't hold back in explaining what this would mean. I'd be mobbed by reporters thrusting cameras in my face. I'd be vilified by some people, praised by others. I should stay away from Twitter at all costs.

I dreaded the prospect, but it was the least I could do for Aaron. As expected, reporters swarmed around me after the conference. I didn't duck my head or try to hide. I told them the truth: the only person I'd ever met with, and who'd signed the agreement and checks, was a private detective. And no, I wasn't giving up his name.

The coverage played out just as badly as we feared. Aaron's opponents came right out and accused him of paying me off. "Nothing we can do," he texted back when I messaged him to apologize. "We can't control the media."

Then something surprising happened. Later that evening, a Memphis station aired breaking news. A detective named Marlin A. Fish had come forward and admitted he was the person who'd negotiated my agreement. No, he couldn't say who his client was. The one thing he was willing to say: it was not Aaron Breckenridge. Yes, he was quite sure. His client had gone to great lengths so Breckenridge wouldn't find out.

Most people probably didn't see what I saw. As the reporter badgered Fish, asking, "Was it one of Breckenridge's political backers? Someone in his ex-wife's family?" Fish gave an almost imperceptible smile before turning away.

AFTER THE PRESS conference, Aaron invited Dylan to go out on his boat with him and the boys, and she eagerly accepted. Dylan wanted to grill him on some political issues. Exactly what Aaron was hoping for, no doubt.

When I dropped Dylan off at his condo, Aaron asked to speak to me. He flipped on the TV, told Dylan to make herself at home, and motioned for me to follow him. He opened the door to his bedroom.

"Sorry, it's the only place to talk privately."

I could feel the warmth in my face as I recalled the last time we had been in the room. It didn't help when Dylan called out, "You two behave in there."

Perhaps in response to her comment, Aaron walked to the other side of the room and leaned against the windowsill. "We should discuss financial arrangements."

"I'm sorry?"

"I have a responsibility here."

"I hate to bring this up, but your ex-wife already contributed a fair amount. As long as she doesn't sue me for trashing our agreement."

"No worries," Aaron said. "Carly will never mention that agreement again. And that isn't the point, anyway. This money should come from me."

"I don't want your money," I said.

"Well, it's not for you, Hope." He did an exaggerated eye roll. "I can at least help pay for Dylan's college."

"Fine. You talk to her about college. Good luck with that."

He raised his eyebrows. "Duly noted."

GARY CALLED ME on Wednesday. After seeing the news coverage, he'd felt bad about the way he'd treated me. He didn't apologize, exactly, but if I wanted my job back, he'd listen. He believed in me.

I thanked him and declined.

"No?"

I laughed. "I'm working on a project for a new client."

Gary was appalled. "Who's *that*?"

"Me. And you know what's even funnier? The *project* is me, as well. Turns out, it doesn't matter if you believe in me, Gary. Only matters if I do."

I've made myself sound braver than I was. In the days between the speech debacle and press conference, I'd found career support from an unexpected source: my mother. I shared my desire to join a nonprofit, work for a cause I believe in, as I'd done on Aaron's campaign. When I said I couldn't without a college degree, she puffed dismissively.

"Go back and get it now," she said, as if it were the most obvious thing in the world.

"Easy for you to say, Mom. I have a mortgage. I can't take out loans."

"I'll pay for it."

"Thanks, but I can't let you do that. Not after what happened with Rafe."

"Rafe?" She frowned.

"The guy who took all your money?"

"*All* my money? Did I say that?" she asked. "Oh, dear, no.

The man took everything in that checking account—and it was a sum, I won't deny that—but you didn't think I'd give him access to everything, did you?"

"Oh," I said. Because I *had* thought that. Living as frugally as I had all my life, it never occurred to me someone might have more than one checking account.

"You may not realize this," she continued, "but in the past, I've had trouble parting with money."

"You, Mom?"

She gave me a sidelong glance. "Nothing like lying on Elvis's grave to grant one perspective."

AND NOW WE were back in Graceland's Meditation Garden, my mother and I, reflecting on the graves of Elvis, his parents, and his grandmother, and the memorial to his stillborn twin. As I studied the dates, I realized for the first time that Elvis had been survived by both his father and his grandmother. How sad when a parent outlives a child, at any age.

Dylan and Aaron had finished the tour. She was taking selfies in front of the mansion while Aaron strolled back in my direction. I went to meet him, leaving my mother to commune with Elvis.

"What would you think," he said, pausing to feel out this new coparenting relationship, "about Dylan spending the rest of the summer in DC? She could do intern work for my office. It would look good on her college applications."

I raised my eyebrows. "You've known her for four days and you've talked her into college?"

He grimaced comically. "Well, I'm not sure how you feel about this, but I floated the idea of a gap year between high school and college." He stepped back, unsure whether I might hit him.

I tamped down my inner mama bear. "Keep talking."

"What impresses me is her interest in policy. She and I debated different issues for almost an hour on the boat, until my sons were ready to kill us. It's something she might want to explore." He glanced at me nervously. "Just an idea."

I tried to picture my daughter by herself, in a city ten hours from Boston. Only she wouldn't be by herself. "Let's take this one step at a time," I said. "Pitch me the summer idea first."

Aaron had clearly given it some thought. Dylan could stay with him, or, if he were traveling, with a couple he knew. It would be a great opportunity for them to get to know one another. I tried to focus on the upside but kept imagining my summer without Dylan. I hadn't been prepared to let her go so soon. Maybe I hadn't been prepared at all.

"Be careful what you ask for," I warned. "Dylan can be a challenge."

He gave a little head tilt. "I'd say she comes by that honestly."

"Hope," Jordan called out, emerging from a turn in the path. "Don't leave without me. This place is fascinating."

I waved my reassurance. She was wearing a new tangerine skirt and polka-dot blouse that Dylan had helped her pick out. They'd been shopping.

"By the way," Aaron said. "I like Jordan a lot. But she took a selfie of the two of us in the TV room and it's not flattering. My eyes were closed."

"That's your concern? Your eyes?" I teased. "Not to worry. Jordan would never post a photo without asking."

"Well then, I'm reassured," he deadpanned. "God knows, I can put a lot of trust in you, Hope."

As he jogged back toward Dylan, I thought, Yep, gonna be some time before he forgives me.

My mother untied the red scarf from around her neck and tossed it over the low fence. It caught a breeze and unfurled, dropping on the corner of Elvis's grave. She turned to me. "This is the part where you tell me I was right all along."

"I wouldn't hold your breath on that, Mom."

She adjusted her cannula. "Oh, be honest! A trip to Graceland was exactly what this family needed."

"Apparently it was what you needed. You got to commune with Elvis, unite Dylan with her father, and meddle in a presidential election. Are you satisfied?"

"For now." She looked to where Aaron was taking a photo of Dylan. "But Hope, you need to be honest with that man about your feelings."

I bristled. "And you know my feelings how?"

"You're a terrible actress."

"Trying to hear that as a compliment."

"He cares for you. I see it in his eyes. Take the initiative. Go after what you want." She removed her sunglasses. "I've been thinking . . . ," she said.

"Oh God." I closed my eyes.

"There are some Elvis artifacts at the Smithsonian." She'd lifted her face toward the setting sun, which gave her cheeks a reddish glow. "And before I die, I'd like to visit Washington, DC, again."

"Nice, Mom. We'll discuss later."

"Well, you know," she said, turning toward the exit, "I don't have much time."

I put my arm around her waist in a way that was unfamiliar, but perhaps not as uncomfortable as I might have imagined, and guided her toward the drive. The two of us stared straight ahead, being extra careful of our footing on the path in the waning light.

Acknowledgments

For me, writing a novel didn't just take a village, it took a small country. Plus a bit of Canada.

I'd been writing short, humorous pieces, and I thought all I had to do was string together, like, eighty of them. Ha! Pride cometh before a workshop. Happily, I had a few great mentors and a lot of amazing friends and fellow writers who were both encouraging and—more importantly—honest.

A thousand thanks and vows of eternal devotion to the following people:

My agent, Paige Sisley, for believing in my writing and laughing at my jokes. I'm sorry I made you spit your tea.

My editor, Asanté Simons, for loving *Graceland*, especially the character of Olivia. Olivia loves you right back, Asanté. She's asking about a road trip to New York City.

The extraordinary Michelle Hoover, who leads a year-long course called the Novel Incubator at Boston's GrubStreet and guides writers from shaky first draft to ready-for-prime-time. Michelle helped me take *Graceland* to the next level while chuckling in all the right places and being an unflagging cheerleader.

My nine compatriots in the Novel Incubator program

offered (and some continue to offer) invaluable insights. Thank you, my dear friends: Shalene Gupta, Madeleine Hall, Eson Kim, Meghana Ranganathan, (Lily) Yichen Shi-Naseer, Richard Sullivan, David Schiffer, Reid Sherline, and Kristin Waites Bennett.

Michelle Wildgen, for an amazing developmental edit that that allowed me to see new possibilities in my work and kill some darlings who, quite frankly, were asking for it.

Michael Lowenthal, who writes critique letters so gorgeous and funny that the Pulitzer people need to create a new category. Mike's brilliance and charm are matched only by his devastatingly good looks. (Ha! Didn't think I would take that bet, did you?)

Henriette Lazaridis and the writers in a twelve-week novel intensive course, who workshopped early chapters and kept me from steering my road trip down some odd rabbit holes.

Mary Carroll Moore and the students in her online course, for helping me breathe through the labor and delivery of newborn scenes. Mary once sat with me at a conference breakfast and offered advice that kept me from stabbing my novel with a butter knife.

Christopher Castellani and his workshop group at the Bread Loaf Writers' Conference in Sicily (yes, that's a thing, and it's fabulous), for a memorable week of critique and pasta. Tricia Crisafulli, your enthusiasm for my story was life changing.

Graceland is a work of imagination, though sprinkled with some real people, settings, and events. Some aspects of the novel required a lot of research, like pinpointing a concert date when Elvis might have been free from other entanglements and available to party with Olivia Grant. Others, like what goes on in a jail cell at 201 Poplar in Memphis, are mostly imagined. (Though I thank the unnamed officer there, who guardedly answered my questions, not buying a word of my "I'm writing a book" story.)

Thanks, too, to the following advisers for their assistance with important details. Any errors are my own.

Sensitivity readers Milo Todd, Declan DeWitt Hall, and Suzanne DeWitt Hall provided invaluable guidance with the character of George/Jordan, and Raina Brown offered amazing age- and era-appropriate insights for Dylan.

Dr. Heather Awad and Dr. Jan Richardson generously advised me on medical issues.

Wayne Dowdy at Benjamin L. Hooks Central Library in Memphis provided background on how the city changed over the eighteen years of this story.

The spunky, unforgettable Betty Pike taught me about COPD and life with oxygen tanks back in 2015. Betty always spoke her mind, though she tended to do so more nicely than Olivia.

Many friends read drafts of the entire manuscript, and I am forever in their debt: Elizabeth Atkinson, Heidi Love, John Mercer, Sharon Adams Poore, Pam Richardson, Julia Rold, and Elizabeth Weinstein. Others read early chapters or shared their expertise: Chuck Latovich, Susan Paradis, Holly Robinson, Cyd Raschke, Adair Rowland, Donna Seim, and Bettina Turner. Cynthia Albrecht and Cynthia Ward helped with eleventh-hour editing questions.

The alumni from twelve years (and counting) of the Novel Incubator program have become a huge family, and many offered mentorship, encouragement, query-critiques, and publishing advice. Pam Loring, Louise Miller, and Cameron Dryden come to mind, though I'm sure I'm forgetting others and will beat myself up later. Julie Carrick Dalton has been an invaluable mentor, generously sharing her publishing experiences. My cohort from a post–Novel Incubator class provided pandemic companionship and critique: Lisa Birk, Marc Foster, Carol Gray, David Goldstein, Rick Hendrie, Rose Himber Howse, Sharissa Jones, Eson Kim, James LaRowe, Emily Ross, Mandy Syers, and Leslie Teel.

Thank you to the Unbound Book Festival for choosing the first page of *Graceland* as a winner in their "First-Page Rodeo" back in 2016. It was, indeed, my first rodeo.

Thanks to my sisters, Carol Dunlop and Jeanne Schmitt, for believing I could do this, and to Mary Rider for cheering me on. To my book group, you are too numerous to name but I love you all, and your champagne toast when I got a book deal meant more to me than you know. To my dear friends Clark Baxter, Sharon Adams Poore, Roy Craig, Rhona Robbin, Lisa Pinto, and Susan and Rob Shaw-Meadow, thank you for ceaselessly buoying me up with emails, Zoom check-ins, phone calls, and pomegranate martinis.

Riding shotgun on my trips to Memphis were two BFFs who also read multiple drafts of the manuscript. My partner-in-crime since kindergarten, Tracy Plass, has always played Butch to my Sundance, and someday we'll end up in Bolivia together. Susan Beauchamp, my Tobacco Princess, you are my ride or die. The next one's for you.

Finally, nothing would have been possible without the loving support of my husband, Paul, and two daughters, Danielle Cantor and Rebecca Crochiere, and their spouses and families. Thank you for your patience, belief in me, and nonstop cheerleading. I'm sure you're just happy I'm no longer writing columns about you.